Cakewalk

"Brown has said that the Runnymede novels, starting with *Six of One*, are the ones she was born to write. . . . This is more loving domestic comedy of small-town life when times were simpler. Recommended for fans of Brown and beyond." —*Library Journal*

"Two independent and free-thinking sisters, Louise and Julia Hunsenmeir (called Wheezie and Juts), push against the old-fashioned ways of drinking, dancing, and courting. . . . Characters were inspired by Brown's own mother and sister, adding realism and depth to this uplifting story. Fans of Amy Hill Heath and Mary Kay Andrews will eat up this multigenerational 'slice-of-life' novel." —*Booklist*

"Written with witty humor and endless exuberance, *Cakewalk* is a joy to read." —*Midwest Book Review*

"With each new day, and the way the world is changing all around Runnymede, readers get a full, colorful, vibrant story that encompasses everything good in life. This huge tale that moves along quite quickly delves into everything from love to whiskey to religion, fashion and even baseball, as it explores the small town that had 'one foot in the North and one foot in the South.'" —*Suspense Magazine*

"There seems to be no end to [Rita Mae Brown's] imagination, inventiveness, or storytelling artistry. . . . What is [*Cakewalk*] about?

Life, love, baseball, war, peace, good whiskey, fashion, sex, religion, friendship—all in a rollicking and lively story that just keeps rolling along at a brisk pace. Ms. Brown paints such vivid scenes. . . . [*Cakewalk* is] entertaining, outrageous, thought-provoking, nostalgic, and great fun." —My Merri Way

"[*Cakewalk*] is brimming over with [Rita Mae Brown's] distinctive Southern voice that infuses every page with merriment, which allows her vibrant characters to take over the story and touch readers' hearts. Her depictions of the inhabitants and the era are pitch-perfect as are the many subplots. . . . An utterly delightful story." —*RT Book Reviews*

"*Cakewalk* is both nostalgic and outrageous, a feel-good novel told by an expert storyteller who delights in creating colorful and quirky characters and subverting readers' expectations." —*Shelf Awareness*

Six of One

"Joyous, passionate and funny." —*The Washington Post Book World*

"It's like listening to Virginia Woolf and her pals gossiping and philosophizing." —*Glamour*

"No matter how quirky or devilish, Brown's people cavort in an atmosphere of tenderness. . . . It is refreshing to encounter this celebration of human energy." —*Chicago Sun-Times*

Bingo

"Genuinely funny." —*Los Angeles Times*

"Vividly drawn characters . . . and tart, loving humor." —*Self*

Loose Lips

"Surprises . . . come from Rita Mae Brown's comic timing and her affection for eccentrics." —*The Seattle Times*

"[Brown] does an admirable job of portraying the effects World War II has on one small American town." —*The Arizona Republic*

Cakewalk

Cakewalk

a novel

WITHDRAWN

Rita Mae Brown

Bantam Books
New York

2017 Bantam Books Trade Paperback Edition

Copyright © 2016 by American Artists, Inc.
Reading group guide copyright © 2017 by Penguin Random House LLC

Published in the United States by Bantam Books, an imprint of Random House, a division of Penguin Random House LLC, New York.

BANTAM BOOKS and the HOUSE colophon are registered trademarks of Penguin Random House LLC.
RANDOM HOUSE READER'S CIRCLE & Design is a registered trademark of Penguin Random House LLC.

Frontispiece: John Singer Sargent, American, 1856–1925, *Mrs. George Swinton (Elizabeth Ebsworth)*, 1897, oil on canvas, 231 × 124 cm (90¾ × 48¾ in.), Wirt D. Walker Collection, 1922. 4450, The Art Institute of Chicago. Photography © The Art Institute of Chicago.

Title spread art: (background) ©iStock.com/Spiderplay, ©iStock.com/MKucova

Originally published in hardcover in the United States by Bantam Books, an imprint of Random House, a division of Penguin Random House LLC, in 2016.

LIBRARY OF CONGRESS CATALOGING-IN-PUBLICATION DATA
Names: Brown, Rita Mae, author.
Title: Cakewalk : a novel / Rita Mae Brown.
Description: New York : Bantam Books, [2016]
Identifiers: LCCN 2016009034 | ISBN 9780553392654 (hardcover) |
ISBN 9780553392678 (trade paperback)
ISBN 9780553392661 (ebook)
Subjects: LCSH: City and town life—Mason-Dixon Line—Fiction. |
Interpersonal relations—Fiction. | Sisters—Fiction. | BISAC: FICTION /
Sagas. | FICTION / Historical. | FICTION / Lesbian.
Classification: LCC PS3552.R698 C35 2016 | DDC 813/.54—dc23
LC record available at lccn.loc.gov/2016009034

Printed in the United States of America on acid-free paper

randomhousebooks.com
randomhousereaderscircle.com

2 4 6 8 9 7 5 3 1

Book design by Liz Cosgrove

Dedicated to Bob and Sue Satterfield
on the occasion of their Fiftieth Wedding Anniversary

"Amor vincit omnia." —Ovid

Dear Reader,

Thank you for picking up *Cakewalk*. Please know that you will not be breathlessly turning pages to find out who killed whom, etc. *Cakewalk* is you and I sitting out back watching the sun set behind the Blue Ridge Mountains, horses grazing in emerald fields, hounds asleep at our feet, and far, far too many cats imperiously surveying all.

I'm recalling stories told to me by mother, my aunts, Dad, his brothers, and uncles when I was seven, eight. Stories about people then in their sixties, seventies, eighties, and even a few in their nineties, stories about my people. Given that everyone was an honorary aunt or uncle this included multitudes. Often, the storyteller, bourbon and branch in hand, added flourishes.

Such close connection between the generations doesn't seem to happen much these days. What passes for communication, especially electronic and public communication, is pitched to the lowest common denominator.

I am not pitching to the lowest common denominator. I am pitching to you.

Come, let us sit a spell to chat, ponder, laugh, lots of laughter. Let us bow to the silent power of Time until we, too, walk into the Sweet Bye and Bye.

Ever and always,
Rita Mae Brown

Introduction

Runnymede sits astride the Mason-Dixon Line. The Marylanders declare their side of town was founded in 1659, eighteen years after the king granted Maryland's charter. Those on the Pennsylvania side consider this piffle but did admit that William Penn did not receive his charter from the restored Charles II until 1681. However, they swore a few farms had been established before that.

It's never a good idea to get into an argument with a Marylander. The residents of Baltimore fired on federal troops on April 19, 1861, furious that their repose had been so rudely disturbed. But then, Baltimore has always been peculiar.

Finally Charles Mason and Jeremiah Dixon surveyed the dividing line between the two contentious states, no easy task. They began in 1763 and finished in 1767. As neither state felt satisfied, it can be concluded that the Mason-Dixon Line is accurate.

The Marylanders regarded the residents of York County, Pennsylvania, as vulgar. The Yorkers considered the residents of Carroll County, Maryland, dreadful snobs.

As residents from both sides of Runnymede paraded around the beautiful square in all but the worst weather, they were unfailingly courteous to one another. The minute a pleasant exchange ended between people from opposite sides, each felt the other a hypocrite. But then, hypocrisy has always greased the wheels of society.

Men tipped their hats to ladies. Ladies smiled sweetly. Folks admired one another's dogs and said they admired their children. Business was beginning to crawl out from the doldrums of World War I. York began to boom and, across the Susquehanna River, so did Lancaster.

On the Maryland side it was a hop, skip, and a jump to Baltimore and, thanks to a good harbor, that city was recovering as international trade tried to return to prewar activity.

As the town was named for Runnymede in England where King John signed the Magna Carta under a large oak tree on June 15, 1215, that great day was celebrated by all. Veterans marched in uniform. The ladies' auxiliary societies also marched in their colors, gray and gold or blue and gold. Veterans of the Spanish-American War marched, as well as the younger men recently home from the Great War.

A large bandshell sat at the Baltimore Street entrance to the square, half on the Maryland side and half on the Pennsylvania. While such attention to detail seemed excessive, it had proven prudent over other years, given the liberal and frequent application of libations for all. Fistfights could be broken up by each state's police department. Years back, when the cannon was discharged in an attempt to topple General George Gordon Meade, both police departments worked together to see to the safety of the public and of General Meade.

The two high school bands played together in the bandshell. Chairs were set up for everyone, as well as a wonderful dance floor which circled the bandshell. These were dismantled every autumn and preserved for the next year. The cakewalk, a pageant on the dance floor, proved a high point, various cakes being baked by the ladies of the town. One paid a quarter to participate. The proceeds were divided between the two veteran associations. Since many young men fought overseas, the hope was that enough money could be raised to help those in need. For a lady's cake to be included was a great honor and her name was prominently printed in the Magna Carta Day celebration program. The Maryland newspaper printed the programs on even years, the Pennsylvania newspaper on odd years.

Peculiar as it was, being divided by the Mason-Dixon Line, Runnymede burst with pride and civic participation. Fuss and fight they might, but sooner or later, the residents of Runnymede would pull together.

It was declared that the oak under which King John signed the Magna Carta still stood in England's Runnymede. So the American Runnymedians planted an oak in the mid-1600s, now huge and smack in the middle of the square, a baroque fountain on the western side perhaps twenty-five yards away from the oak tree.

Each June 15, the Magna Carta signing was reenacted followed by speeches predictably bleated by civic worthies that our Declaration of Independence and Constitution, the American documents of life, liberty, and citizenship, had their genesis in the Magna Carta. Each year since the late 1870s, this was challenged from the gathered women, for they did not have the vote. As it was 1920, the Pennsylvanians ratified the Nineteenth Amendment, which granted women that right. Maryland and all the southern states rejected it. One state was left to vote on suffrage: Tennessee. If Tennessee voted yes, the amendment would have the three-fourths majority and become the law of the land. However, most people felt Tennessee would reject it, it being a southern state.

As that state's momentous vote would not come until after Magna Carta Day, all the planners devoutly hoped Runnymede's ladies and those gentlemen who supported their efforts would behave. After all, Pennsylvania and Maryland had already voted.

How lovely it would be to have a calm Magna Carta Day, an event whose planning began in January of each year. However, it was secretly suspected that if calm reigned among the ladies, something else might erupt. You could never tell about Runnymede.

In Runnymede everybody knew everybody. Nobody forgot a thing, not one blessed thing, especially if a whiff of scandal attended it. You could be held accountable for your great-grandfather being roaring drunk in the square and exposing his shortcomings. And, like all close-knit places, the child of that great-grandfather had to hear that he was the spitting image of same, along with the warning that G-pop was a notorious alcoholic who dropped his pants with alarming frequency. A kindly male adult might mention that jewelry shrinks in the cold so as not to make one overly concerned with one's own equipment.

History was wielded as a weapon, or so the young believed. Their elders knew without a doubt that this new generation dancing the Charleston, with women smoking and hemlines shrinking, this generation was going to hell in a handbasket. To hell!

A very large basket would be needed.

Cakewalk

Chapter One

· · · ·

January 31, 1920
Saturday

Excited because *Pollyanna,* staring Mary Pickford, was now showing at the Capitol Theater on the corner of Frederick Road and Runnymede Square, Louise Hunsenmeir, nineteen, and her younger sister, Juts, not quite fifteen, hurried through the light snow.

The elder sister shot out of her job at the Bon Ton department store as though she'd been fired from the cannon on the south side of the town's center square. Julia, called Juts, ran to catch up with her as she flew from the store.

"Wheezie, hey!"

Slowing down a bit, the slender Louise called over her shoulder, "Come on, we'll miss the first few minutes."

The two trotted, slipping a bit, reaching the theater. A line, not long but long enough, curved down Frederick Road.

"Good. They won't start the movie with people still outside." A puff of frosty breath escaped Louise's lips, artfully enhanced with a light shade of lipstick.

"Isn't Orrie going to meet you?" Juts named Louise's best friend.

"You know Orrie, she slides in at the last minute." Louise peered up the line, then whispered, "Get a load of Lottie Rhodes."

Juts stepped a bit out of the line to look at the attractive young woman: too much lipstick, too much of everything.

When the line started moving, Juts then said, voice low, "She's got the same coat you do, only yours looks better on you."

The two fought night and day but were best friends when they weren't fighting. Louise smiled. "You know how she is in summer. At least she's covered up in the snow."

"How do you know? You can't see the front of her and she loves to show it off. Maybe she has snow in her cleavage. And you know who is just as bad? Dimps. She pushes her bosoms on the boys at school, then pretends she has to squeeze by them. *Ugh.*"

Delilah Rhodes Jr., called Dimps Jr., as her mother is Big Dimps, obviously had studied her sister Lottie's ploys for male attention. Both of the Rhodes girls, drilled by their mother, teased but drew the line. Big Dimps ran the cosmetics counter at the Bon Ton. She made certain her girls, cosmetics artfully applied, looked alluring. Given a lackluster marriage, Big Dimps's view of same had narrowed to a man's financial capacity or potential for the future. The purpose of this bosom barrage was to ensnare the richest young man possible. As Big Dimps felt she had married beneath her, she was determined her two daughters wouldn't make the same mistake. Surely they would make other ones.

"I can't see Lottie's date," Louise grumbled.

"Me neither. He's at the window, I think."

Paul Trumbull, new to Runnymede, an army veteran from the Great War, purchased two tickets. He'd been seeing Lottie over the fall, a desultory courtship discouraged by Big Dimps because he was a lowly housepainter. As a small rebellion against her mother, this made him somewhat more attractive to Lottie. Also, Paul was quite handsome. Sooner or later Lottie would cave to her mercenary matrimonial purpose, but for now, why not string along as many young men as possible?

Southerners referred to such fellows as conquests. Lottie hoped to be spoken of as a woman of many conquests, a trail of broken hearts left behind her.

Juts took the ticket her sister had bought for her once they'd reached the ticket booth. "Thank you."

"When you get a job, you can take me."

"Soon," Juts promised.

"You have two more years of school."

"I'm bored. I'll finish tenth grade. That's enough."

The two greatly resembled one another. Louise had attended Immaculata Academy, paid for by Celeste Chalfonte, their mother's employer, since Louise evidenced musical ability. Louise had converted to Catholicism. Juts, on the other hand, attended South Runnymede High School. She dutifully went to the Lutheran church and didn't believe a word of it.

They walked down the right aisle of the clean movie house, finding three seats near the front.

"I'll go in first. You can save a seat for Orrie," Juts suggested.

Louise sat down, did not yet take off her coat.

Still in her coat a few rows behind them, Lottie also sat holding a seat for Paul, who was buying popcorn.

Just as Paul entered the aisle the lights flickered, the house went dark, the organist began to play. The film title appeared, Keith Morgan, the organist, hit a few notes, and a rustle of anticipation filled the theater.

Squinting, popcorn in hand, Paul walked by Lottie, who had turned to talk to one of her girlfriends down the row. The theater, filled with young people, grew quiet.

He came upon the empty seat, noticed the coat, sat down before Louise could protest, put the popcorn box toward her, then kissed her.

Louise hauled off and slapped him. "How dare you! You beast!"

"Hey, don't you touch my sister." Juts leaned over Louise.

Stunned, Paul couldn't find his voice but the usher found him.

Tall Walter Rendell yanked Paul out of his seat. "Come on, bub."

"I didn't do anything. I mean, I thought she was someone else."

"That's what they all say." Walter dragged Paul up the aisle, popcorn falling from the red-and-white box Paul grasped.

Having seen the kiss, Lottie shrieked, "You two-timer. I never want to see you again." She stood up and smacked him with her purse.

"Lottie?"

She smacked him again.

Seeing a furious Lottie, Louise's mood improved considerably.

Walter continued to drag an increasingly resistant Paul.

Proclaiming for all to hear, Louise enunciated quite clearly, "Lottie, if you can't keep your boyfriend happy, it's not my fault."

Juts laughed out loud, as did others.

Orrie finally arrived in the theater. Baffled as to the uproar, Orrie sidestepped the two men just as Paul hauled off and belted the usher.

"Goddammit, I didn't come home from the war to put up with this!"

Walter struck back, hitting the smaller but wiry man in the chest. Ever happy to help a brother veteran, other young men jumped Walter. Walter's friends jumped the vets.

Louise, Juts, and Orrie turned, sitting on the backs of the seats in front of them, as most other people did, to enjoy this show.

Inflamed by the insult, Lottie stomped away, her largesse bouncing with each determined stride, pocketbook in hand. She swung it at Louise, who ducked.

"You hussy. Kissing my date."

Louise ducked another swing. "Lottie, he kissed me."

"If he'd known he was kissing Runnymede's religious nut, he would have gagged."

Louise cocked her fist, landing a good punch right on Lottie's left glory.

"I'll throttle you." Lottie dropped her pocketbook, reaching to choke Louise.

Juts blocked Lottie's hands. "You touch my sister and I'll tear one of those zeppelins right off your body."

Orrie added to the defense, but Lottie's friends in the theater came to her aid.

Yashew Gregorivitch was a big shambling classmate of Louise's. He'd left school to join the navy. He was stuck down front, fighting to get up to his friends, who were all fighting to help Paul. He threw his popcorn box over his shoulder.

"You'll get popcorn in my organ!" yelled Keith.

Yashew began to part people in the aisle like Moses did the Red Sea. "For Christ's sake, the only organ you need to worry about is between your legs." Whistles blew, but that stopped no one. The house lights went up, all the better to see who you were punching. Harper Wheeler, a young cop on the beat for South Runnymede, pushed into the fray. Outnumbered, he yelled for the ticket taker to call for reinforcements. And he asked the fellow also to call the North Runnymede police department.

Within fifteen minutes, police from both sides of the Mason-Dixon Line filled the theater, hauling out pugilists, one by one. The paddy wagons filled up with men.

A confused Harper asked the police chief, now on the scene, "What do we do with the women?"

Chief Archibald Cadwalder, a handsome man now in his mid-sixties, grinned and answered, "Get the hell out of their way."

As the two paddy wagons drove off in their separate directions, the girls finally wore themselves out. They tore posters off the wall, emptied out the popcorn machine, but other than that, most of the damage they did was to one another.

Al Dexter, the theater owner, also called by ticket taker Robbie Anson, flicked the lights then pushed the females out of the theater. He locked the doors, leaning against them.

"My God, Robbie, what in the hell happened?"

"I don't rightly know. I heard Louise Hunsenmeir holler and then all hell broke loose."

Al surveyed the damage. "Could have been worse. Tell you what,

Robbie, let me call my wife so she doesn't have a cow since I'll miss dinner. Then you and I and Walter can clean this up."

"Archie took Walter in the paddy wagon, boss."

"Ah." He thought some more. "Well, let me call her. We can at least sweep up the popcorn."

Leaving open the door, he walked into his small office. The upright phone squatted on his desk. He dialed knowing full well that telephone operator Martha Shortride was listening in.

"Honey pie, I'll miss supper—"

Minta Mae interrupted him. "Why? You know the Creightons are coming."

"There's been a, well, a riot among my customers. I've got a lot of cleaning up to do."

"A what? A what? Alvin, if any one of those rioting miscreants is a Sister of Gettysburg, you tell me, you tell me right now and I will eighty-six her, oh yes, I will."

Minta Mae Dexter presided over the Sisters of Gettysburg, which she considered the pinnacle of acceptance for anyone living in North Runnymede. The Daughters of the Confederacy, South Side, obviously thought differently.

"Honey, these were young people." The minute this escaped Al's mouth he was sorry, adding quickly, "Most of your troops, sugar, lack your youthful good looks."

Smiling, she replied sweetly, "Were there any Daughters there?"

"If there were, I would have had to call an ambulance. Those poor girls need canes now and they can barely see to swat anyone."

That satisfied Minta Mae. "Well, you just get here when you can, darling. If you're late, I'll keep Katie and she can warm up the food, but of course, you know Fannie Jump Creighton will want to know everything, so I hope you make it."

"I'll do my very best."

He would, too, because when Minta Mae called him "darling," a nighttime reward came his way. Al often wondered if other husbands were kept on thin sexual rations. They never discussed it.

Louise, Juts, and Orrie walked along the south corner of the square along with other ladies, to await the Emmitsburg Pike trolley. Lottie and her crew headed toward Baltimore Street to tend to one another's wounds at Lottie's house, a lovely white-painted-brick affair built in the mid–eighteen hundreds.

Juts, the youngest of the group, laughed. "We look like something the cat drug in."

Louise raised her voice. "I tore Lottie's shirt. I nearly exposed her breasts then stopped myself. She'd enjoy it too much. You know, she would cry out, run out into the lobby, and let all the men see both of her assets. I hate her. I truly hate her."

Boots Frothingham, a class ahead of Juts at South Runnymede High, chimed in. "We all do, Louise, and her sister is even worse."

"You can't get any worse." The temperature had dropped into the twenties. Louise hoped the trolley would soon arrive.

"Oh, yes, Dimps Jr. is worse. She rouges her nipples," Boots declared, and this was seconded by others in the group.

Louise was aghast. "What?"

"She does. In gym class when we shower, she turns her back, towels off, then goes to the mirror and dabs on a little rouge." Boots blinked with disgust.

"Whatever for? Who is going to see them?" Dumbfounded, Louise was curious.

"When it's warm, she wears a brassiere and a thin blouse. You can see, and you know what else she does? Oh, this is even worse." Boots took a deep breath as everyone leaned forward toward her. "She will pick up a cold pop bottle and hold it next to her breast so her, you know, stands out."

"She freezes her nipples!" twelfth grader Anselma Constantino shouted.

"Why do boys pay attention to all this?" Juts wondered. "We don't care." Juts considered the difficulties of protuberances. "Why would anyone want to get smacked in the face with a big breast? They get in the way."

"You'd have to ask the boys," Boots sensibly said.

Anselma airily answered this. "My brother says it gets them hard. Just thinking about breasts does it, so anyone pushing them onto a boy can usually get what she wants."

Boots shook her head. "Anselma, that's horrid."

"Maybe, but that's what he said. But he added, much as they like it, they would never marry a girl like that."

"Oh, well, that's a big relief," Juts sarcastically said as the trolley at last pulled up to the corner.

Chapter Two

. . . .

February 1, 1920
Sunday

Winter, long and cold this year, offered no relief. The light snow of yesterday became heavier. The trolleys still ran but people didn't linger after church in the morning. Everyone knew how easy it was to get stranded. You couldn't trust the automobiles either. Even with chains on the tires, a machine could get stuck in a snowdrift.

There were more and more automobiles in Runnymede. Trucks hauled tools and heavy supplies. Once businessmen figured out the cost of maintaining a truck, many switched because in some ways the machines proved easier to repair than horses. Even throwing a shoe could cost half a day's work, because you had to get the animal to the blacksmith, and hope there wasn't a backup and that he hadn't quicked the hoof, which would keep the animal off hard work for some days. However, many folks still swore by their draft horses or their harness horses because they sure were reliable in snow and muck and they loved them to boot. It was harder to love a truck.

Louise and Juts lived at the top of Emmitsburg Pike on a small farm called Bumblebee Hill. The trolley line on Emmitsburg stopped at the bottom of the hill, which made for a strenuous walk down, but with a setting this beautiful, the journey was well worth it.

The young ladies' mother, Cora Hunsenmeir, fed small, precisely cut logs into the wood-burning stove and checked a pork roast, the glorious aroma of which filled the small wooden home, much to the delight of the dog and cat.

A *chug, chug, chug* drew Juts to the window.

"Momma, there's a truck outside," she exclaimed. "It's one of Douglas Anson's paint trucks."

Cora wiped her hands on a dish towel, straightened her apron, hurried to the door, and opened it after a few knocks.

"Mrs. Hunsenmeir?" Cuts on his face, flowers in one hand and a small box in the other, Paul Trumbull raised his hat. "I've come to apologize."

"Well, sweetie, no need to apologize in the cold. You come right on in here."

He stepped in, bashfully looked toward Louise, who stared blankly at him. "Miss Hunsenmeir, I am so sorry."

She set aside the socks she'd been darning in front of the tidy living room's fireplace, and stood up.

Juts, astonished, kept her smart mouth shut.

Paul walked over, handing Louise the bouquet. "You should have flowers every day." His wide grin made him more appealing. "I . . . your coat looked so much like my date's and there was the seat she'd been saving and, well, you know the rest. I meant no harm and I am deeply embarrassed to have troubled you."

Louise, tongue-tied, took the bouquet of perfect pink roses.

"Oh, here." He handed her the box.

Juts wordlessly took the flowers her sister handed to her as Louise opened the box. She stared, then pulled out a roll of tickets.

He grinned again, looking right into her wonderful gray eyes (all the Hunsenmeirs had lustrous light-gray eyes). "Movie tickets for the rest of the year."

Louise looked at Paul, then back at the tickets. She laughed. "I've never been given anything so wonderful. Ever."

Cora stood behind him. "Let me take your coat. You need a hot meal. Bachelors always do."

"Oh, ma'am, I couldn't put you out."

"You aren't putting me out one bit. I haven't cooked a meal for a handsome man in too long." She took his coat then ordered Juts quietly, "Come on in the kitchen and set the table."

"Yes, Momma." Juts reluctantly followed her mother as the two young people stood facing one another in the living room.

Louise motioned to a rocking chair. "Oh, please sit down."

She sat opposite him on a worn old wingback favored by Felicia, the cat, attesting to her clawing prowess.

Resting at Louise's feet, the handsome English setter, General Pershing, was satisfied that this young man passed muster.

"How did you find us?" asked Louise.

"Well, once I was released from jail, I walked back down to the Capitol Theater. I wasn't kept long in jail. I knocked on the door and Mr. Dexter came to the door, I offered to pay damages and he said forget it, wasn't much. I asked if he knew who was the young woman whom I inadvertently kissed and he said, 'Louise Hunsenmeir.' He told me where you lived and you know, what a nice fella, he called his friend Mr. McLaughlin, the florist. He said he'd stay open if I hurried over to the shop. So I did."

"Thank you. You did give me a scare."

"You gave me one."

They both laughed uproariously, the awkwardness evaporating.

"I don't know your name," she said.

"Paul Trumbull. People call me Pearlie."

"Come on, you two," Cora called from the kitchen. "Dinner's on the table."

Paul inhaled spoon bread's odor, the pork roast, wonderful green beans that Cora and the girls put up in August. On the kitchen table covered with a checkered oilcloth, a glass of water sat by his plate

Cora had overheard his name. "Mr. Trumbull," she said.

"Pearlie, please call me Pearlie."

"Would you like something stronger? I have home brew and some beer."

"No, thank you, Mrs. Hunsenmeir. I have to drive the Anson truck back." He smiled.

Once Cora convinced Pearlie to call her Cora, they all chattered away. The cat, Felicia, proved an even bigger pest than General Pershing.

"Lots of Trumbulls Green Spring Valley way," Cora said, referring to a lush part of Maryland a bit east of Runnymede.

"I'm one of them. I came home from the war and couldn't find a job. I might have found one in Baltimore but I can't live in a big city. My mother reminded me that my grandfather was once a constable in Runnymede. I was kind of curious, so I came out here and found a job with Anson's. Mr. Anson has been real good to me."

"They're good people." Cora nodded. "I know there are many of you fellows looking for work. Hard times. I'm so glad you found a job."

"I like it and I like Runnymede."

Paul was reluctant to talk about the war, but he did offer that he'd seen a part of the world that he would have never seen otherwise.

Juts couldn't help herself. "Was it awful?"

Louise quickly corrected her sister. "Juts, that's not a proper question."

"I'm sorry," Juts replied.

"It was awful," said Paul. "I don't know what was worse, when the big guns fired all the time or when they stopped." He paused. "I hope there is never another war again."

"Me, too," the two sisters said in unison.

"Jigs for coke!" Juts happily crowed.

"All right." Louise laughed.

If two people say the same thing at the same time, the first one who says, "Jigs for whatever" has to be awarded the desired item by the other person.

"Juts, let's clear." Cora, after clearing all the dishes, brought out an apple pie while Juts carried a large pot of tea.

Now as warmed up as the tea, Juts giggled. "I bet you won't go out with Lottie Rhodes again."

Put on the spot, Paul took a moment to reply. That moment seemed an age to Louise. If he disparaged Lottie, he wouldn't be a gentleman.

Finally, he replied. "No, I expect I won't, but I am grateful to her for introducing me to people here. If you think about it, Louise, she introduced me to you."

This made them all laugh.

"I go to school with her little sister and she's worse than Lottie," said Juts. "She rouges her nipples."

Shocked, Cora sputtered, "Juts, control yourself."

Too late, Paul's face shone beet-red, as did Louise's. Then Cora rumbled a little, Juts started to laugh, and then all laughed until tears rolled from their eyes.

After the pie, Paul offered his help to Cora. "I can wash dishes with the best of them."

"Pearlie, you will never wash a dish in my house. You go sit by the fire."

He glanced out the window. "Oh, ma'am, the snow's really shaking down and I have to get this truck back. Your hill's pretty steep."

"It is that."

"I thank you for this wonderful meal and for making me laugh, and"—he looked at Louise—"for forgiving me."

"Well, we certainly started a rumpus." She laughed, then abruptly changed the subject. "Pearlie, are you a churchgoer?"

"Not much before the war but I learned to pray there. I was baptized an Episcopalian."

"I'm a Catholic," Louise said with pride.

Juts sighed. "Momma and I are Lutheran. It's a long story."

Cora handed Paul's coat to Louise, which she held for him to put on. "Pearlie, all roads lead to God. We just keep walking." Cora smiled.

As though a weight had been lifted from her shoulders, Louise nodded. "Yes. It's true."

The three women walked him to the door. He put his hand on the old porcelain knob. "Thank you again, and"—he looked at Cora—"I hope you will allow me to call upon Louise." He looked to Louise, whose face glowed.

"Then the house will be filled with laughter." Cora gave him a motherly peck on the cheek and all three watched him start down the hill.

Chapter Three

S tirling Chalfonte's mahogany-paneled office looked down into the ball bearing factory through large, spotless interior windows. Exterior windows afforded a view of downtown Baltimore, with glimpses of the harbor and Fort McHenry.

Celeste put her hand over her heart. "Always makes me want to sing 'The Star Spangled Banner.'"

"Does, doesn't it?" said her elder brother, Stirling, standing next to her.

Every one of the five Chalfonte siblings born of T. Pritchard Chalfonte and Charlotte Spottiswood possessed good looks and good minds. Both parents—now deceased, for T. was born in 1839, died in 1897, and their mother, born in 1849, had passed in 1902—had also been highly intelligent. Both sides of the family could trace their entry into the New World to the mid-1660s and both the Chalfontes and the Spottiswoods seized the main chance, acquiring and controlling thousands of acres of land before 1865. T. Pritchard joined the cavalry, while Armand Spottiswood, Charlotte's father, older, was made a brigadier general of Artillery, and they both lost all their holdings but not their intelligence nor their ability to learn from even a dreadful, wasteful war that both sides now pretended had been inevitable. It was not, and mother and father drummed that into their children's heads.

Stirling soaked up his father's teachings and business acumen. The war veteran said over and over again that one of the reasons the Union won was their rail superiority. Railroads would become the arteries of commerce far superseding our rivers. So T. Pritchard had no problem making alliances, thanks to his wonderful ability to make mergers with men like Thomas Fortune Ryan, a Virginian, and J. P. Morgan. He invested heavily in railroads along with others. Every penny the young Marylander made he poured into railroad stock.

Armand, on the other hand, thanks to his military training and his facility with math that every artillery officer must possess, started a ball bearing factory in Baltimore. He could ship his product anywhere in the United States, thanks to the railroads. And with Baltimore's harbor, he could do business with other countries, something he aggressively pursued. When he died, the company passed to his only child, which meant that T. Pritchard took over. Business boomed under his prudent management and his ability to ship goods out in a timely manner. He still bought stock in western railroads, favoring Union Pacific. He even invested in tinned foodstuffs. In time, T. Pritchard and Charlotte were fabulously wealthy.

Stirling loved his youngest sister and vice versa. They were much alike. Given their age difference, the elder brother lorded it over his sister, who hotly resented it.

"Sit down, Twink." That was her childhood nickname.

"Thank you. You know why I'm here?"

"I believe I do."

"Well?" She raised an eyebrow.

"You look like Mother when you do that."

"I miss her. I miss them all, but especially Spotts."

"I do too. To think I'll never hear his rattling laugh again. Can it be two years since he was killed?" Stirling shook his head. "I often think I should have gone to France with him."

"Stirling, you could not. The government needed you here for the war effort. Don't torture yourself. Plus you were too old."

"I could have found a way around that. After all, Spotts was thirty-six when he shipped over."

"He was a commissioned officer. And a West Pointer. I guess you could say it was his calling. If only, well . . ." She waved her hand slightly as the subject of their brother's death remained ever painful. "No matter. Done is done. Which brings me to the upcoming wedding. Done is done."

Shifting in his seat, Stirling tried to shift the topic. "I hope you haven't engaged in improvident expenditure on this wedding. It is highly peculiar."

"Oh, Stirling, balls. Our entire family is highly peculiar. You just hide it better than the rest of us."

His mouth twitched into a smile that was half grimace, and he truly hoped his sister wasn't going to launch into a critique of his arrangement. "So you say. But you have lived a certain way for thirteen years. We're accustomed to it."

"Margaret is accustomed to it? Stirling, she has come to Runnymede once in the last ten years."

"My wife lacks imagination." Stirling sighed. "She's been a dutiful wife. I really can't complain."

"Well, I can. She's too boring to have been born and you didn't discover that until you were hog-tied. I will never understand why you married her. Yes, she brought a fabulous dowry to the family coffers, but really, you're like Father. You can look at an apple hanging on the tree and it turns to gold."

He smiled. "I wouldn't go that far. See here, Celeste, as a woman you have much more latitude than I do. You flitted off to Paris, Rome, London, and even Istanbul after graduating from Smith. After Yale I went right to work for Father. Getting married was, um, something a man does before he's thirty. You just do it."

"But why Margaret?"

"She paid attention to me."

"Oh, Stirling." Her voice dropped to a near baritone. "You, the handsomest man in your class at Yale. Really now."

He shifted again in his seat. "The only women I really knew were Mother, you, and our dear sister, Carlotta. Who could measure up? And the girls we met at the dances, lovely things, but . . . ?" He shrugged. "Margaret liked the arts, opera, theater, and we could talk. She liked golf and is still quite good at it. The boring arrived with the children. That's all she talked about. She's a good mother, Celeste, you have to admit that, but she's conventional, judgmental, and I now exist to keep everyone in finery, send the children to the best schools, and write handsome checks to whatever charity Margaret is sponsoring this year. She has no interest in me at all. Nor you."

"That's evident." Celeste softened when he recounted his marriage. They could always talk to one another. No evasions. With the exception of Carlotta, the brothers and one sister could be painfully honest with one another, and Celeste and Spotts had been especially close. But even Carlotta could drop the veil of circumvention if she felt it necessary.

He rested his hand on the arm of the leather chair. "Life doesn't turn out as you think, does it?"

"No. We're so fortunate in some ways yet savaged in others. The human condition, I suppose. But see here, Stirling, you've really got to come to the wedding. For one thing, Curtis will be crushed." She named their youngest sibling, who, at thirty-seven, was marrying Celeste's lover. "And Ramelle will be hurt, too. You know how she dotes on you and I truly believe that is one of the reasons Margaret doesn't visit."

He smiled, his perfect silver moustache turning upward. "Ramelle, and that laugh. Like music. I don't know why but I pay attention to the manner of someone's laughter. Ramelle's is utterly adorable."

"Yes."

"Celeste, you're putting a good face on this but it is highly irregular.

Our youngest brother has gotten your longtime partner in a family way. It's"—he thought—"disruptive."

She took a deep breath. "Stirling, that is the first time you've called Ramelle my partner. Usually you say 'friend.'"

"One is never sure of the terms, but if anyone asked I always said that you two were devoted friends. Some perfect ass would push and try to get me to say it was a Boston marriage, but . . ." He shook his head. "I understand why you would want her, I do, but sometimes these arrangements are hard to fathom."

"It's hard for me to fathom."

"Oh, Celeste, you never once tried to do the expected thing. You didn't look twice at all those beaux flinging themselves at you."

She exhaled through her nose. "I did not. Truthfully, I liked the men I rode with in the hunt field best, but Mother did not find riding ability a suitable attribute for my husband." She looked straight into his eyes. "The truth? The raw truth. I love Curtis. I love Ramelle. That doesn't mean I like them sleeping together but I've come to accept it. I can understand it. Some of this gets back to Spotts."

"Was Ramelle also sleeping with Spotts?"

She laughed. "No! But Curtis is the same age as Spotts when he was killed. Yes, he's enjoyed his dalliances in Los Angeles, but Spotts's death changed him. Changed all of us. And Ramelle fell in love with him. How can a woman not fall in love with him? She's wanted to be a mother and so she will have his child—our niece or nephew."

"Has Carlotta responded to the wedding invitation?"

"Not yet but I feel certain a lengthy sermon, either on paper or in person, will accompany the response."

"Better than her erecting a statue of the Blessed Virgin Mother in your front yard." He laughed, a true deep laugh.

She joined him. "Oh, Stirling, how did we come to this pass? You forty-nine and me forty-three? God only knows what will happen next."

"Not just in our lives but the world. It's an unsettled time, Twink. The end of kings, caliphs, and czars. The end of a lot of things but then

I know it's a beginning, too. I try to keep an open mind, but I'm not sure exactly what is beginning."

"You're sure Margaret won't come?"

He nodded. They remained silent for a time.

Celeste then said, "Bring Olivia."

He sat bolt upright. "Celeste, I can't do that. I have to keep to the proprieties."

"Oh, Stirling, all you fellows have mistresses."

"I concede that most of us do and we do, because, in plain words, our wives don't take us to their bed. Or if they do, it seems such a chore. Mistresses we have but we don't parade them. Not if we have any sense."

"A gentleman's agreement?"

"Quite."

"I have a way. If she will agree to it, Olivia can sing in the church."

Olivia Goldoni sang opera, could speak four languages, but lived simply. In contrast to her peers she eschewed most jewelry except for one lovely ring and one necklace, a cross of diamonds. She had sung with the greats of her generation, including Enrico Caruso, who had been born in 1873, the same year as Carlotta. Olivia, twenty-eight, was the child of New York City immigrants and had a wealth of common sense. And she did love Stirling, who treated her with affection and respect.

He considered this. "I will ask her."

"Imagine that angelic voice in St. Paul's? A glorious setting for what we hope will be a successful marriage. And I will tend to Olivia, see that she meets everyone. Appearances will be kept."

"I— Let's try it. She is so good to me." He seemed genuinely relieved and grateful.

"I assume you've taken care of her."

"She asks for nothing. I bought her a brownstone on Federal Hill. She travels to Boston, New York, Philadelphia, wherever there's an opera she's been hired to sing, but she comes back and she asks for nothing. I have given her two hundred fifty thousand dollars in railroad stock and the same in cash. She is a most unusual woman. She throws her arms around me the minute we're alone and tells me she can't live without me."

"Wonderful feeling. You've been generous and more than responsible. I've spent a lot on Ramelle, but I suppose you know that better than anyone, being in charge of the family fortune plus reviewing our personal finances, but she pays it back in her fashion, running the house, planning social events. She keeps me focused, and she is never adverse to sharing a bed."

"Even now?"

"Yes."

Stirling found this surprising and titillating. "Does Curtis know?"

"He doesn't ask but surely he does."

Stirling settled deeper in his chair. "We Chalfontes do things in a big way."

Celeste laughed. "We do. Even Carlotta, who gives me fits, does things in a big way. She's not just a religious nut, she's an incendiary religious nut."

"Praying for you and me and Curtis at this very moment. She's ferreted out that I have a mistress and is suffering deep—Marianas Trench deep—shock."

They laughed as conspirators. "The only thing left for Carlotta is to experience a vision of the Blessed Virgin Mother."

Little did Celeste or Stirling know, their sister was working very hard to get on intimate terms with the Virgin Mary.

Chapter Four

• • • •

February 6, 1920
Friday

Whoosh, clink.

Louise opened the pneumatic tube at the end, pulled out the eight-inch canister, opened it, and gave the change and receipt for the lovely magenta sweater to her customer, Mabel Frost, an attractive woman in her early twenties. "Mrs. Frost, you look wonderful in that color. Just brings out the peaches and cream of your complexion."

"Oh, I hope so, Louise. Winter just washes me out." She leaned forward, taking her wrapped purchase.

Louise lowered her voice conspiratorially. "And so many of the ladies put on too much makeup. You don't make that mistake. It's why you look so fresh even in winter."

Louise had to tread carefully since Big Dimps sold cosmetics.

Beaming, Mabel replied, "Thank you, Louise. Remember me to your mother."

"Yes, ma'am."

Louise liked working at the Bon Ton. In her two years there, her record, quite good, demonstrated her ability to talk to customers. Owner Asa Grumbacher had noticed. He also noticed that Louise got along with the other girls. She even managed to stay on the good side of Sidney Yost, the floorwalker, who lived to find fault.

The same names appeared generation after generation in Runnymede: Yost, Grumbacher, Frost, Anson, Cadwalder, McGrail, Wheeler, Nordness, Rhodes, Rendell, Dexter, Frothingham, Tedia, Constantino, Most, and Wilcox. Though new names also appeared—a Japanese family, the Mojos, had moved in a few years ago—for the most part, the names of the town's wealthy remained firmly English, with a few Scots and plenty of German names. Chalfonte, Creighton, Thatcher, Rife, Spangler, Finster, and Falkenroth were the main ones, but people formerly of what the upper crust called the middling orders were beginning to make good money. Harvey Moon, for one, had developed a fog light for automobiles. His factory was humming. Of course, as in every American town north, south, east, and west, Browns, Smiths, Jones, Martins, and Carters abounded.

Mostly, whomever you met, except for the Mojos, was related to someone else. Fortunately, everyone pretty much knew everyone else, but one had to teach newcomers who was who before they insulted an old Runnymede citizen's beloved but slightly potty aunt.

The other odd thing about this small town perched on the Mason-Dixon Line was that people might leave, but they most always came back. Thrilling as New York City or faraway San Francisco was, eventually one longed for the square, or the special celebrations like Magna Carta Day in June. A person might even begin to miss the mad musings of poor Patience Horney at the train station, who would go on and on about how the space people who lived on Saturn's rings loathed the tiny pink people who lived on Mars. The Saturnians had told her so.

Since the middle of the seventeenth century, generation after generation had built this town, farmed the fields around it, loved the four distinct seasons, the coming of the robins, the honking of the Canada geese flying south in the fall and the sunsets, each one different from ones before and each one spellbinding.

Yes, they bickered over which side of town was founded first, but only a few passionate local historians cared. For the rest, it was an excuse to fuss. Few could resist that.

Those on the Maryland side paid scant homage to Annapolis, an astonishingly beautiful town but the state capital with all that entails. Baltimore exerted greater pull.

For the Pennsylvanians, Philadelphia was the cultural center, the lodestar. Harrisburg, the state capital, was visited only in extremis, and Pittsburgh! Surely you jest. Pittsburgh might as well be in Ohio, and the hell with it.

Celeste would laugh at that. Friends with the Mellons, Mr. Carnegie, and the food fellow, Heinz, she found Pittsburgh rather exciting. After all, Lillian Russell hailed from Pittsburgh, and Celeste knew the beauty and her Diamond Jim Brady quite well. Too well perhaps. They had met in Saratoga in the summers when Celeste was in her twenties. Even though Celeste would bring her adored Ramelle, she found ways to keep her occupied while she disappeared with Lillian or Jim. Or maybe just Lillian, who radiated eroticism to an intense degree.

Now that Ramelle was pregnant and about to marry, Cora, and even the girls, felt the pot was on the stove and sooner or later would come to a boil. Celeste, generous, kind in her fashion, was also a bit spoiled. She was not averse to affection.

A shadow of this crossed over Louise's face when the elegant beauty entered her department.

"Mrs. Chalfonte, how good to see you. I don't believe I've ever seen you in the Bon Ton. Mr. Grumbacher will be happy."

The older woman smiled. "Your mother tells me you're doing very well here."

"I am. All the clothes, the seasons, the buyers going to New York." Her eyes widened. "It's so exciting."

"That it is."

"Can I interest you in something?" Louise was on duty, after all.

"Yes, you can. My sister Carlotta's birthday is in March. I usually get her something from Paris but I ran into Big Dimps yesterday. She wore the most becoming coat which she had bought here. She told me about her employee discount as well."

"I know the coat. That's Georgina's department. I'll walk you over."

"Thank you, don't leave your department. Just discreetly point." She paused. "My sister will be at the wedding. That was like negotiations between France and Germany." Celeste halted that train of thought because Louise was devoted to her sister, the headmistress of Immaculata Academy. "I need your help."

"Me?" Louise was surprised.

"You are one of Carlotta's most successful graduates and you two . . . how to say this? You two seem quite attuned on religious matters."

"Yes."

"She disapproves of my brother and Ramelle getting married. Could you find a way to occupy her, so she doesn't make a scene and spoil a special day? That's a lot to ask, Wheezie, I know, but you are one of the few people who can handle Carlotta. God knows Herbert can't." She named her sister's husband.

"I'll try."

"Good girl." Celeste squeezed her shoulder, then left for the coat department.

Asa, who could look down into the main floor of the store from his office, beheld the exchange. Hurriedly he trotted down the stairs to Louise's department. Every clerk watched, shoulders back. Sidney Yost pasted on a smile and moved closer to Louise's department, hoping to hear a tidbit. As Sidney was a war vet, the girls put up with him but they didn't like him. However, all felt that one should try to get along with any veteran.

Asa noticed his snooping. "Sidney, I have business with Louise. Not you."

"Yes, Mr. Grumbacher."

"Louise."

"Yes, Mr. Grumbacher."

"How did you get Miss Chalfonte into the store? I've been trying for years and she waves me off saying she buys her clothes in Paris or Milan."

Quick on her feet, Louise replied, "She saw Big Dimps Rhodes wearing that polo coat, the winter one in navy-blue cut for a woman. She thought it might make a suitable gift for her sister and be far more reasonable than the cost of something from overseas."

He smiled at her. "Good work. Good work."

Sidney didn't hear the exchange, but it was obvious Asa was pleased. The owner paid attention to young, pretty Louise, but he, Sidney, kept the place running and stopped thievery before it happened.

Noting the odd quiet among the staff, Celeste turned to see Asa talking to Louise. She'd picked out the coat, paid for it, and swept by the stocky man. "Asa Grumbacher, you do know how to run a business."

Floored, he found his voice. "You're too kind."

"I've been foolish thinking only the French and the Italians know fashion. You have some lovely things right here." She leaned toward him, her eyes hypnotizing him. "If you would be so kind as to send fabrics to me with Louise from time to time, I would be most grateful."

"Of course, Miss Chalfonte, of course." He smiled expansively.

Celeste nodded to him then left. Asa looked at Louise, the grin plastered on his face.

Louise, grateful to her mother's boss and to the woman she'd known since her cradle days, said in a low voice, "You do know how to run a business, Mr. Grumbacher."

Beaming, thrilled, blissful, Asa Grumbacher climbed the stairs as though a Roman general celebrating a triumph.

At six that evening, Louise left the store. Standing outside, scarf wrapped around his neck, lad's cap securely on his thick black hair, Paul Trumbull tipped his hat.

"Hello. You could have come inside."

He offered Louise his arm. "I don't mind the cold. People don't like people in stores who aren't buying stuff."

The Bon Ton commanded the corner of Hanover Street on the north side of the square. The two walked to the western corner to Cadwalder's drugstore.

"Wheezie! Wheezie!" Juts shouted as she ran through the cleared path in the Square.

"Oh, no." Louise groaned. "I'll get rid of her."

"How about if I buy her a hot chocolate and then you can send her along? It will put her in a good mood."

She squeezed his elbow. "You must have a little sister."

"Not like that one."

Now even with them, Juts told them, "Momma sent me down to Brown's meat market."

"Looks like a heavy package," Paul remarked, looking at the white paper wrapping.

"A pot roast for Celeste. It's half a cow, I swear it, but you can't believe what happened to me! Dimps Jr. tried to steal Dickie Yost, and he's *my* date for the Saint Patrick's Day dance. She said in front of everybody, why would he bother with me? She called me a smart mouth and then she said I didn't have good clothes, I'd look out of place at the dance. I'm going to kill her."

"Why don't you wait on that?" Paul suggested. "Sounds like she'll do herself in. Come on, I'll buy you hot chocolate then you can go back to Miss Chalfonte."

Juts looked at Louise, who affirmed, "You can come with me. I thought I'd sit and talk with Paul, but come on, Juts, a hot chocolate is a good gift."

Paul brought three hot chocolates, welcome in the cold. They sat in a nice booth while Flavius, the owner, occasionally came over to bring little dishes. He also wanted to keep his eye on Paul. Louise Hunsenmeir had better be properly treated.

Juts chattered, feeling so grown up to be with her sister and Paul, who seemed very mature. Really grown up. Once she'd downed her hot chocolate, Juts left the couple alone.

Paul wanted to take Louise to a nice place to eat but he'd spent most of his money buying her the flowers and all the movie tickets. He asked Knute Nordness at work, a fellow becoming a pal, what should he do? Wait until he had the money again and treat her to something special or walk around the square and go to the drugstore? He didn't want Louise to think he was cheap.

Knute advised not waiting. "Girls hate to be put off. They think you don't like them. If she's any kind of girl, she'll be happy to see you. I know the Hunsenmeirs. They aren't gold diggers."

Knute was right. Once Juts left, with prodding from Louise, the two sat there and talked about everything. He ordered more hot chocolates because he didn't want to make Flavius mad. Flavius just smiled. He was starting to like this guy.

"And the boss was happy." She beamed.

"That's swell."

"I really like fashion. I read everything I can." She thought a moment. "When you came to visit, you said you liked house painting. Boy, did you surprise us."

"Surprised myself." He laughed. "I do like house painting. I want to learn everything. Different paints give you different results, and I tell you, Louise, buying a cheap paint is throwing your money away. Doesn't hold up."

She leaned her elbows on the table even though it wasn't proper. "Ever think about the future?" She rested her chin on her hands.

"I sure did in the trenches. I told myself if I made it home, I'd learn a trade and if I worked hard, saved my money, I'd start my own business. I'm going to do it. I know I don't look like much now but I'm not afraid of hard work."

"Me neither." She looked right into his warm brown eyes. "You'll do it."

Pleased by her confidence, he blushed a bit. "You make me feel like I can."

Louise volunteered, "I don't want to start a department store but I'd like to work as long as I can. Even if I marry."

"Really?" His black eyebrows rose.

"It costs a lot to live and, well, my father ran away in 1907 and left Momma and she didn't have a dime. I want to put some money away."

"No man who's worth anything would leave you."

Now it was Louise's turn to blush. "I hope not. You're sweet to say so."

"I know so. I haven't heard many girls say they want to work."

"I bet Lottie or her harridan of a mother tried to pry out of you what they could. Lottie intends to marry and that's it. Money, money, money."

He waited a long time, then spoke. "I feel sorry for her."

"You weren't—"

He shook his head. "Sure, I noticed her. I didn't know anyone in town. Her mother didn't like me, like you said, because I had no money. I'm just a working fellow. Lottie only went out with me to irritate her mother. That's no way to live."

"But you kissed me thinking it was her."

"I did. Lottie was, uh"—he thought and thought—"somewhat free with her favors. I liked her but not that much."

"I will never understand men."

"It's kind of hard to explain but I didn't take advantage of her, Louise. You gave me the way out without hurting her feelings. I owe you and that box of popcorn." He laughed.

She laughed back. "We'll both work and see where it takes us."

"What if you get married?"

"Unless he's a Rockefeller, I think I should work to help out. It costs so much to establish a household. Celeste tells me these things. I know she's trying to prepare me for the day when I leave Momma. She sure helped me out today at the Bon Ton."

"If you work, won't you feel your husband is letting you down?" Pearlie wondered.

"No. We'll work it out together. We'll save our pennies. I don't want someone to think I'm a deadbeat."

"What if you have children?"

"I can work up until I have them. Then I'll stay home until they're in grade school. Paul, I see some of the girls I went to high school with and they're married, one kid already, and they're bored, they complain. That's, uh, tedious." She used one of Celeste's favorite words when someone or something bored her.

"You're different, you know that?"

"I'm not going to be a burden and I don't ever want to be in the position of my mother."

He nodded. "Your mother is such a sweet woman. Someone should horsewhip your father."

"If we knew where Hansford was, we would."

Flavius came over, and Paul said, "Nothing more, Mr. Cadwalder. We had three hot chocolates and took up this booth."

"I can see you two have a lot to talk about."

"We do," Louise agreed enthusiastically. "We can talk about anything."

Flavius picked up the cups. "Honey, that's a great gift."

Paul walked her down the Emmitsburg Pike to stand at Celeste Chalfonte's imposing door. It was just about time for Cora to finish her work for the day. "I had a wonderful time."

"I did too."

"May I ask you out for next Saturday? I could take you to the movies and a place to eat."

"Pearlie, I'll take you to the movies. I have all the tickets." She laughed.

"Guess you do." He wanted to kiss her so bad it hurt.

Instead he tipped his hat. "Pick you up at your house."

"Okey-dokey."

Louise stepped inside the door as Juts ran up to her in the Chalfontes' grand foyer.

Apron on, Cora called out, "Have a good time?"

"We sure drank a lot of hot chocolate." She laughed. "But we had such a good time. He's not flighty, Momma."

"I suspect he's not," came the alto reply.

Celeste, followed by Ramelle, descended the curving staircase with the big landing, passing the full-length portrait of Celeste painted by John Singer Sargent. "It's getting so cold. Don't take the trolley tonight, Cora. I'll have the chauffeur drive you home."

"That's a treat." Cora stuck her head out of the kitchen.

Seeing a new audience, Juts launched into a blow-by-blow of the dreaded Dimps Jr. and her trying to steal—yes, steal—Dick Yost.

"How dramatic," Celeste replied.

"She's jealous," Ramelle said. "Ignore her."

"And she rouges her nipples."

"Juts, that is enough out of you."

Celeste, amused, countered her employee and dear old friend. "Cora, I think I should hear this."

"Yes, me, too." Ramelle laughed. "Sounds very daring."

Juts could never resist an audience. She told her tale, an embellishment here and there. Dimps Jr.'s protuberances grew in cup size with each telling.

"I'm surprised the poor girl can walk. She must be a triumph over gravity," Celeste replied.

As this was over Juts's head, she tried to come up with another insult for the lewd boyfriend pouncer. "She's always tilting at windbags."

Celeste burst out laughing. "Windmills, dear."

Chapter Five

. . . .

February 11, 1920
Wednesday

Brilliant sunshine reflected off the snow. People shaded their eyes or pulled down their hats to cut the glare. Clear skies often accompany bitter cold and this day was no exception. The mercury refused to budge from 17°F. Celeste waited inside the dark-green-painted doors of the railway station. Patience Horney lurked just inside, ready to take up her position selling pretzels right outside the door. The stationmaster had made her come inside.

"Have you watched Orion lately?" Patience asked Celeste.

"No. Pity, for the February sky is so bright and clear."

"Umm." Patience nodded, a knowing acknowledgment. "They visit from the Belt, you know?"

Celeste, long used to Patience's celestial pronouncements, nodded. "Yes, you've often spoken of them, as well as those on Saturn."

Patience folded her thin arms across her chest. "Orion is different."

Peering out the windowpanes in the door, Celeste murmured, "I'm sure."

"Heroes made into constellations live on Orion. Yes, they do. The gods and goddesses are still here, of course, but they don't show themselves to us anymore."

Far from being irritated, Celeste dropped one dollar into Patience's cup.

"How many pretzels do you want? They're hot."

"Patience, not a one. That's a small contribution for reminding me to pay homage to the gods." She smiled and thought to herself that Patience, like others with mental afflictions, may not be stupid, but may in fact see the world differently and thus offer insight.

Patience looked up into those intense eyes. "You're one of Athena's own. You must never, never marry."

Celeste smiled. "We're secure in that."

"And beware of Hera. She is wary of any woman who doesn't follow her example."

A whistle blew and the people waiting inside the station stood up. Most of them she knew and nodded to. "Patience, I will bear in mind your advice."

For a fleeting moment Celeste felt the crushing discomfort of knowing there was nothing she nor anyone else could do for the Patience Horneys of the world, people lost to themselves and others.

As the train engine glided to a stop, on time, with steam billowing out, Celeste felt its tremendous power, a power that changed the world. She loved trains, she loved travel, and she loved her brother, who stepped off the train, carrying one large leather bag after tipping the porter handsomely.

As Celeste opened the station door to run to her younger brother, she heard the porter call out, "God Bless, Mr. Curtis, you got you a beautiful girl."

Recognizing the man on the regular train from Philadelphia, Celeste smiled at him as Curtis hurried toward her. He dropped his suitcase, embraced his sister, giving her a big kiss.

"Welcome home. You'll give me a rash." She laughed at his bristly chin as they stepped back into the station.

Walking by, Curtis dropped money in Patience's cup. She thanked him, recognizing him, but she couldn't remember his name so she said, "Thank you, Brother."

On the street side, Francis awaited and opened the door of the 1916 Packard Twin Six. Brother and sister stepped in. Celeste threw the heavy plaid car blanket over their legs.

"Sorry about the rash. The train was late last night getting into Philadelphia. The trip across the country was actually pretty good, on time. Anyway, late, I overslept, just made this one and no time to shave.

"Whenever I look at pictures of King Edward's friends, I am astonished at the beards and muttonchops, or the sideburns that made it down to moustaches. I suspect these fellows spent a fortune at the barbershop."

"Bet they did." She squeezed his hand. "I'm so glad you're home. Ramelle is waiting at the house. She wanted to give us a few moments together."

"Do I need to do anything to help with the arrangements?"

"No. Everything is in order and you will be either amazed, happy, annoyed, or all three. La Sermonetta"—their name for Carlotta—"will be there, Herbert in tow and so will Stirling."

"Really? Did Carlotta receive a vision?"

"No. What she received was a compassionate—you would have loved hearing me—a compassionate plea for Christian understanding, forgiveness, and love."

Her voice dropped as he shook his head. "Well, it worked. I did have to promise to attend Carlotta's church with her after your wedding. She extracted a promise that I go to Mass with an open heart and, I expect, an open pocketbook."

He laughed out loud. "We've been keeping popes in jewels and splendor for over fifteen hundred years. Time to do your part."

"And so I shall. Louise Hunsenmeir will attend to her former headmistress, which should relieve us somewhat. I just hope Fannie Jump doesn't drink too much and review the causes of the Reformation."

Fannie Jump Creighton and Fairy Thatcher were Celeste's childhood friends, and the three knew far too much about one another.

"I should have brought along an actor or two. Creighton never notices."

Creighton, Fannie's husband, was too busy making money to notice his middle-aged wife's seductions. She surprised her girlfriends, as they never knew where she found the energy. So many men.

"As you and Ramelle requested, the service will be at St. Paul's. The party after the wedding will be a bit more lively. Thank God you don't have a bachelor's party, although in a way the supper the night before fulfills that function."

"This is a great deal of work and I am grateful."

Celeste leaned up and tapped the window, which Francis slid back. "Yes, Miss Chalfonte."

"Drive around the square one more time."

"Yes, Miss Chalfonte."

"Margaret will not be in attendance but Stirling will."

"I'm rather glad about that. She's such a censorious bitch." Curtis could always tell Celeste the truth.

"Olivia Goldoni will be coming. It's all discreet. She will sing at the service."

"You don't say. Well"—Curtis pulled the rug up higher—"I give Stirling credit."

"What you can give him is a part for Olivia in one of your films. Some small thing."

"Did he ask for that?" Curtis was incredulous.

"No, I am."

"Pity no one will be able to hear her."

She leaned on her brother, as much for support as for warmth, for the car took a corner and slid on the ice. "No reason her recordings can't be for sale in the lobbies."

"That's an idea. I don't know if there will ever be sound in film, the technical difficulties are enormous, but it would be wonderful to hear a beautiful voice." He noticed the snow-covered statues in the square. "Much as I love California, the sunshine, the warmth, I do get homesick. Nothing ever changes here."

"Does and doesn't. On the outside, Runnymede is timeless but in other ways we're changing. It's change or die, I think. The war." She left it at that.

"Yes." He was solemn, then changed the subject. "And how is my bride?"

"Showing a little. The dress has artful folds—not that some people don't know, which is to say by this time everyone."

"The Runnymede human telegraph."

"Well, it is a scandal too good to be true. The elegant and ever-so-rich Chalfontes have transgressed in interesting fashion." She laughed. "Curtis, you gave her what I could not. She'll be here half the year, with you the other half during winter."

He held his sister's hand, drew it from under the blanket, and kissed her hand. "I do so love you, Celeste. I do, and . . ." His voice trailed off and then he said softly, "It just happened, you know. Neither one of us planned it."

"I know. She always wanted to be a mother. I do understand—oh, not the being a mother part. I mean, I understand for her and I certainly understand how you could find yourself in the position in which you now find yourself. I was never meant to be a mother. Even if I could have given her a child, I don't think I would. However, I will be a sensational aunt."

He kissed her hand again. "That you will."

"Ramelle told me you will call the baby Spottiswood regardless of being male or female."

"Yes." He sighed as they turned onto the Emmitsburg Pike. "I hope in succeeding generations there will always be a Spottiswood." Then he added, "I hope you won't be lonely in the winters."

"Certainly not." Her eyebrows rose. "I've never been lonely in my life and"—she drew this out—"I always have Fannie Jump as an example."

He laughed uproariously, thinking of Fannie's many affairs, as the long car pulled into the attached garage, built to match the rest of the house.

As they walked through the connecting arcade, Curtis, with a flash of nervousness, said, "I hear women become peculiar when they're with child. Tell me what to do."

"How would I know?" She laughed. "Ask Cora, she's had two. One of those girls would have been quite enough."

They opened the side door and slipped in. Ramelle ran toward him from the front hallway. "I thought you'd never get here."

"He came and his beard came with him," Celeste remarked.

Ramelle stepped back, running her palm over his cheek. "Oh, just a bit of unmowed lawn."

He kissed her, then promised, "I will be slick as an eel for dinner."

Cora pushed through the door to the kitchen, arms open wide.

Curtis rushed to her, giving her a mighty hug. "Oh, Cora, now I know all is right with the world."

And so it was, for now.

Chapter Six

. . . .

February 13, 1920
Friday

Walking home from school along the south side of the square, Juts and Ev Most chattered about the day's events at South Runnymede High. A brilliant male cardinal swooped to perch onto the Confederate war statue, then, wings spread, glided down onto the snow.

Juts admired the sight. "Red on the snow."

"Mom puts out seed. Not enough to eat in the winter." Ev did try to listen to her mother, imitate her, as her mother was well liked.

"Yeah, mine does too." Juts stared at the bird lifting his topknot. "Ever think about what a battle in snow looks like? All that blood on the snow."

"No, but sometimes I think about the peach blossoms fallen on the dead at Gettysburg. They all changed from peach to red." Ev shivered. "I'm glad we don't have to take another trip to Gettysburg. I don't want to go to battlefields."

Juts slipped her arm through Ev's. "History class is so boring. All the dates of wars, then all the dates of the peace treaties. Why bother? There's just another war."

"Two more years of school." Ev sighed. "Then we're free."

"I'm going to quit after June."

Ev turned to look directly at her best friend. "Your mother will pitch a fit and Louise will be one step ahead of a running fit."

Juts shrugged. "It's a waste of time. Except for algebra and art class, I sit there and think of all the things I want to do, like get a job, make some money, help Momma."

"Don't tell her that," Ev wisely counseled.

"I won't, but Momma works so hard. If we need something big, Celeste helps out, but Momma doesn't want to take anything. I always tell her Celeste has more money than God." Juts kept her lips together but smiled. "She said God doesn't care about money. He cares about our hearts. Good. I care about money and I want to make some."

"Doing what?"

"I don't know yet. If people didn't know me, I could do like that countess who talks to the dead. The one they write about in the paper."

"You don't believe that, do you?"

"I'm not a ninny," Juts replied. "There's money to be made."

"Not that way."

"I know, Ev, I know. Sometimes I feel like the dead are crushing us. We see statues of them. We hear what they did, the kings, the queens, the generals and admirals. Then we hear about our great-grandfathers and grandmothers. Okay, they did a lot, some of them, but all I have is now. I'm not a queen and I want to be happy. And I'm not happy at South Runnymede High. At least if I go, I won't have to look at Dimps Jr. anymore."

"Oh, yes, you will." Ev picked up the pace, as she was feeling the cold.

"Suppose so. Do you ever feel like we're stuck here?"

"Nah. I belong here. You, too."

"I guess," Juts said unconvincingly.

They reached Cadwalder's, pushed open the door, to find many of their classmates already at the drugstore.

"Hey, hey, Juts and Ev, come on over here," Richard Bartholomew called. "Did you see this?" He pointed to an open newspaper on the table.

"Yeah, Celeste read it to us when Momma came in to work today."

Betty Wilcox, a classmate, declared, "Wouldn't you love to visit the countess? To think that she calls down spirits. She said that Teddy Roosevelt walks Rittenhouse Square."

"Betty . . ." Juts thought better of pointing out to her the absurdity of this, so she stopped talking.

"What?"

"I like your sweater."

"Bought it from Wheezie at the Bon Ton."

At the mention of Wheezie's name, Dimps Jr., at the next table, sang out, "Your sister's cracked. First, she clobbers Paul Trumbull with her purse and now she's going out with him."

Juts leapt to Louise's defense. "My sister is not cracked and it was a mix-up."

"Oh, la." Dimps Jr. waved her hand dismissively. "Everyone in Runnymede knows that. He was dating my sister. She was getting ready to dump him, he's such a bore, so Louise made it easy."

Although she didn't know Paul Trumbull well, Juts felt compelled to speak up for him. "Maybe he was bored too, Dimps. Lottie is as dumb as a sack of hammers."

A moment of silence filled the tables then Richard Bartholomew closed the paper and joked, "Yesterday's news."

The others, relieved at his mollifying attempt, soon realized Dimps Jr. was not to be put off.

"Momma says he won't amount to anything. All those men came back from the war and now they don't know what to do." Dimps Jr. lifted her chin. "And Momma says they all paid French women to— you know."

"Dimps, shut up." Betty Wilcox glowered. Her elder brother, Edgar, had survived the war minus his left arm.

It dawned on Dimps Jr., slowly, that a few of her classmates did have brothers who returned with varying degrees of damage and some had damage you couldn't see. They shook uncontrollably sometimes. Spiteful and proud, however, it did not occur to her to apologize.

Quiet until now, Dick Yost spoke, "Betty, maybe our class should do something for the vets. You're such a good organizer."

Dimps Jr. tried to squelch this. "They don't want anything to do with us."

"Why not?" Ev smiled at Dick. "They all graduated from South or North Runnymede High."

"Well, there's a lot of men from the Spanish-American War," Richard chimed in. "They're a lot older but they're here, and there's some, pretty old now, from the Big War." South Runnymede people did not say "Civil War."

Wiping down the counter, Flavius called to the kids, "That's a great idea. We've never done anything like that and if you do it, I promise to bring the drinks. You'll have to work on Reuben Brown for hot dogs and hamburgers if you have a picnic but I think he'll come around. Magna Carta Day would be good. Everyone comes out for that and the veterans march around the square."

Enthusiasm built and Dick said, "I know I can get Dad to put this all in the newspaper. Come on, let's do something."

Ev nodded. She wasn't the leader type but she had good ideas and her classmates liked her.

Juts threw her arm around her best friend. "We will have so much fun."

Dimps Jr., knowing she'd lost favor, finally had the sense to shut up.

A bit later, walking with Juts down Emmitsburg Pike, Ev's house was on the block before Celeste's, Ev and Juts happily chattered.

The iron fence gate outside her house creaked as Ev lifted the latch to open it. "Want to come in?"

"Thanks, but no. There's so much to do to get ready for the wedding. I need to get to Celeste's to help."

"You know the church will be full. People will show up whether they're invited or not." Ev laughed.

"Celeste knows it's been a hard winter and a lot of people don't have work. There will be tons of food at the dinner the night before, and then at the party. And Momma says since it's private, the liquor can be out in the open. Momma says there's always hard times after a war, then things pick up. She says people need a celebration."

"What is it you have to do?"

"Make guest cards," said Juts. "Since we don't know who will be there the night before at the church hall, I sit at the table with invitation cards. It's kind of backward but everyone will feel special, so Momma says."

"So you'll make them out as they walk through the door?"

"No. I have to make one for just about everybody now. But if anyone shows up that night that we forgot or don't know, I'll make them one then."

"So it's a keepsake."

"I guess. Weddings are a lot of work. I don't want one. If I ever get married, I'm going to go to the justice of the peace."

"You say that now." Ev hung over the gate, beginning to feel the iron's coldness through her coat.

"You just wait. You, of course, will have a big wedding. Your mother would kill you if you didn't."

"I think about getting married and then I don't," Ev honestly replied.

Saucily, Juts said, "I don't think about it."

"Oh, Momma wanted to know why Ramelle and Curtis are getting married on Sunday, Washington's birthday, instead of Saturday."

"Because the Battle of Verdun started on February 21, 1916. They don't want to be reminded of the war at the wedding."

Ev pondered this. "I'll tell Momma."

When she did, her mother nodded to show she thought that this was a wise decision.

Neither Ev nor Juts truly understood how the war to end all wars pervaded the lives of those even slightly older. They just knew that it did.

When Ev told her mother about the reunion idea, maybe on Magna Carta Day, a day special to Runnymede, her mother smiled. "We must never forget our veterans."

Later that night, Ramelle in her own room and Curtis in his on another floor, Celeste stopped reading in bed and thought about what Juts had told her concerning some kind of reunion for the veterans. She put her book down and mused, "Out of the mouths of babes."

Some things are right under your nose. You don't see them and when someone does, you wonder how you missed it.

She'd picked up a book by a new historian, Max Weber, finding it provocative. She also found provocative the situation with which she was now encumbered. Ramelle's pregnancy was one thing, the wedding was another. Stirling counseled her against "improvident expenditure," his words, and so typical. Marriage did not come cheap. Nor did raising children. She had not broached this subject with Curtis. Should he pay all the bills or should they split them? He paid those when Ramelle was in California for half the year, she paid the bills in Maryland. As to the best private schools and then college, Smith, it had damn well better be her alma matter if it was a girl, Yale if a boy, she supposed they would split that. Should they discuss this before or after the child was born? There was no guarantee the little thing would live or be healthy. One always prayed for a safe birth and a healthy child, and no one—not Celeste, Cora, Curtis, or the girls—breathed anything but good thoughts. Why worry Ramelle? She probably had those thoughts but kept them to herself. Celeste couldn't imagine that any woman who would give birth wasn't aware of the dangers.

The wind picked up outside, rattling the windows. The baby was due in May. One associates new life with spring.

She pulled the covers up higher. Ramelle slept with her until Curtis showed up. The warmth of another body is comforting but it did make sense that she would return to her room now, he to his. Can't be sleeping with the bride too close to the wedding. She laughed to herself: how odd the rules were and yet they did make sense. Actually, no one was ever to sleep with a bride before the wedding, but like so many ideals, that one proved difficult to achieve.

The planning exhausted her. If she didn't have Fannie Jump Creighton, Fairy Thatcher, and Cora, she didn't think she could get through it. Reliving their own weddings, Fannie and Fairy were godsends. What amazed Celeste was that each childhood friend remembered every detail, most especially their mothers' unwelcome intrusions.

Picking up Weber, she read his thoughts that the very definition of a state is a monopoly on legitimate violence. "Hobbes was onto it first," she whispered, then put the book down, turned out the light, and fell asleep.

Chapter Seven

. . . .

February 18, 1920
Wednesday

The extra minute of daylight each day after the winter solstice just added more time to be cold. February always seemed especially dark and cold.

Weary after another long day of preparation for the upcoming wedding and the barrage of questions about what to her were unimportant matters, Celeste gladly retired to her room by nine o'clock that evening. Curtis slept on the third floor, his room next to Spotts's. Ramelle's room on the second floor rested between Celeste's and what had been the parents' big bedroom. For whatever reason, once they passed, Celeste evidenced no desire to take over that large room. Her room was big enough and kept her warm with its massive fireplace; the surround was a rich mahogany, fashionable when the house was built, shortly after the Revolutionary War. Mahogany stayed fashionable, too.

Sometimes her bath kept her up but not tonight. She slipped between the sheets, pulling up the covers. Picking up her book, she put it down again to watch the shadows from the fire flicker in the room.

As a child she argued that Carlotta's room was bigger, which it was. Her mother informed her that Carlotta was older but that she, Celeste, enjoyed a much better view of the long back lawn, the stables, and the rose garden. Carlotta's room looked out onto Emmitsburg Pike. Weighing these facts at eight, Celeste determined she really did have the better room. On a night like tonight, when the wind rattled the panes on the north side of the house, the Emmitsburg Pike side, she still thought she'd gotten the better room.

A light knock at her door, the door opened a crack. "Are you asleep?"

"No. Tired, though. Come in."

Ramelle slipped through the door. Her silk robe, a swirl of blue, could have been warmer.

She sat on the edge of the bed. "If this is a small wedding, I would never survive a big one."

Celeste sat upright. "Pull the woolen throw around you."

Ramelle took the tightly woven Scottish cloth from the foot of the bed, wrapping it around her shoulders. "Why are some winters so cold and snowy? Well, most are, but every now and then we get a respite. This one is a beast."

"You'll soon be out of it. Orange groves, Pacific breezes. It will be lovely."

"Maybe so, but I don't know if it will ever feel like home."

"Time will tell." Celeste smiled. "And Curtis will do whatever you wish. Remember, he grew up here, too, so he made the leap of faith. I think of moving to California as a leap of faith."

"It is, but you always liked it when you visited your brother."

"I did. I missed getting on a train, stepping off in Philadelphia, New York, or Boston to visit a museum or a great library. For that matter, Baltimore has a beautiful library. Out there, well, perhaps it's all too new and they're all too wrapped up in making money. It was probably like that here in the seventeenth century." She smiled. "Then again, there are those who would say we still live in it."

Ramelle's light laugh filled the room. "Minta Mae Dexter. When I read the guest list I saw you invited all the Sisters of Gettysburg as well as the Daughters of the Confederacy. No one can say mine won't be a balanced wedding."

"As long as they check their swords at the door. Did I tell you that Caesura Frothingham threatens to once again redecorate her house?"

"No." Ramelle's eyes widened. "When did she tell you that?"

"The other day in the hunt field. God, it was brutally cold, but it's mating season so the foxes gave us a run. I told you. Well, no matter. Too much to think about."

"I will miss you." Ramelle paused, then asked about Caesura Frothingham, the new president of the Daughters of the Confederacy. "Did she say how she was going to redecorate?"

"Better. She showed me drawings. Early Reign of Terror."

Ramelle clapped her hands. "Ha. Oh, Celeste, I truly will miss you. There's no one I can talk to or listen to like you."

"All will be well. Surely there will be some women or men out West who delight in folly."

"I hope so. Curtis occasionally lets slip a remark. He's such a good man."

"He is. Father left his imprint on his sons: Duty, Charity, Profit. He believed in vertical hierarchies yet he took people as he found them. Neither Mother nor Father was a snob, but they understood the social order. Mother would tell us, 'Know where you belong.' I was never quite sure about that." Celeste smiled. "I felt I belonged with you."

Ramelle reached for Celeste's hand, lifting it from under the covers. "We will always belong to each other."

"I think so. Perhaps the surface changes but the depth remains."

"You're not angry, are you? You've not said much at all. Not even when I told you I was pregnant."

"What's to say? Part of me hopes love is a hallucinatory abandon and part of me hopes not."

"You've taught me so much. I didn't plan this. When Curtis visited in September, a whirlwind of seeing his old friends, your old friends in

New York, you came back early and . . . I don't know. I looked at him while we were in the Metropolitan Museum and something just happened."

"Hallucinatory abandon. Good. He deserves that kind of love, as do you. I can be distant. I am distant," she corrected herself.

"Celeste, you're generous. When you and I first embarked on our relationship, you were so cautious."

"The world does not smile on two women in love."

"They ignore it as long as you play your part. Don't bring it up. At social occasions, always be escorted by a gentleman. We were. There will always be men around you. We did have a wonderful time, didn't we?"

"We did."

"I love you. I truly do."

"I know. We'll be together in spring and summer. Curtis will come out for part of the seasons. All will be well. It will be different but it will be well. You'll be the mother you always wanted to be."

"Do you love me, really?"

"After thirteen years, Ramelle, you surely should know the answer to that. I accept what is."

The fire popped, sparks flew.

Ramelle squeezed Celeste's hand. "My own mother and father refuse to attend. You'd think they'd be glad. I love you and I love Curtis for making this wedding happen and—to be blunt—paying for everything."

"Your parents, Ramelle, have always been small-minded. You're better off without them. And if you aren't, I am. They worship a fractured bourgeois world, with its deceiving comfort and sameness. Families can lift you up or ruin you. One has to determine how to handle them. For whatever reason, we Chalfontes can usually come to an accord—even Carlotta."

"She takes a great deal of work."

"And prayer." Celeste burst out laughing. "Hers and mine."

"In all the years I've known you, you never discussed marriage other than your parents' sending you to England. Did you ever think of it?"

"I became the man I always wanted to marry."

Chapter Eight

. . . .

T he angelic voice of Olivia Goldoni, dressed in a simple choir robe, filled St. Paul's Episcopal Church.

Rejoice, all ye believers,
And let your lights appear!
The evening is advancing
And darker night is near.
The Bridegroom is arising,
And soon He will draw nigh
Up! Pray and watch, and wrestle.
At midnight comes the cry!

The watchers on the mountain
And proclaim the Bridegroom near;
Go meet Him as He cometh,
With hallelujahs clear.

The marriage-feast is waiting,
The gates wide open stand;
Up, up, ye heirs of glory;
The Bridegroom is at hand!

On cue, as Olivia sang the next two choruses of Laurentius Laurenti's hymn from 1700, Curtis and his best man, Keith Goldschmidt, walked from the side of the church to their places before the altar.

Keith, another movie producer, had gotten in two nights ago. Although Curtis had wanted a small affair, of course he invited his true best friend, to the delight of the ladies, especially Fannie Jump Creighton. Keith was a Yankee with a strident accent to match. He bristled with the energy of a film producer and glowed with his California tan.

Waiting in the back, Cora opened the side door of the vestibule a crack. The two bridesmaids listened. Ramelle's college roommate, who had unknowingly arrived on the same train as Keith, fussed over Ramelle's bouquet of white and pink roses. Lovely and simple, they matched her bridal gown, also white with a diagonal slash of palest pink from her left shoulder down to the hem which touched the floor. Ramelle had decided against a train, beautiful but a royal pain.

Celeste had been happy to concede the slot of maid of honor to Helene Hartsfield. If she had to be the one standing right next to Ramelle as she was wed, Celeste would somewhat feel like her father, giving her away.

At the last minute, over protests from his wife, Carlotta, Herbert finally found his balls and offered to act as Ramelle's father. He walked her down the aisle when the traditional bridal music played. Trailing behind her in perfect step were Helene, then Celeste.

The invitees allowed themselves a shiver of delight at seeing Celeste, stunning as always, even in her lover's bridal train.

Stirling and Carlotta sat next to one another in the front right pew. Juts and Louise sat in the front left pew. The church pews were packed with friends, neighbors, those who worked for Celeste, those who attended grade school with her and beyond as well as those who grew up with Stirling, Carlotta, Spotts, and Curtis.

Olivia Goldoni sat with the rest of the choir.

The Episcopal service, clear, concise, satisfied everyone, but most especially the bride and the groom. They looked very much in love and were.

After the ceremony, they walked down the aisle, arm in arm, Curtis smiling so large it looked like his face might crack. Behind them Keith walked with Helene. Celeste, head high, smiling, walked with Herbert. Outside, those who couldn't fit into the church threw rice and confetti. As it was cold, people hurried to their cars or horse and buggies to go to the Chalfonte home.

Once there, somehow they all crammed in. As the newlyweds greeted everyone and accepted their good wishes, Cora, Louise, and Juts as well as Francis, the chauffeur, hung up coats and guided people to food and drink or to a chair if a bit overwhelmed or elderly.

Louise played the grand piano until Bonnie Chalmers, the St. Paul organist, arrived to take over. The two covered for one another, so each could eat and drink.

Celeste had hired the best caterer from Baltimore, Harbor Lights. People had been working for weeks on the menu. She'd instructed the caterer to make extra food and set it aside for as she put it, "my people," as they wouldn't be able to eat anything at the party.

Finished with the receiving line, Celeste whispered into Ramelle's ear, "Honey, you need to toss your bouquet." Then she told her brother, "Take her up to the balcony. I'll announce the toss. The ballroom will be packed since half of Runnymede wants to be the next bride."

Curtis helped Ramelle up the back stairway. Even without a train, her dress demanded attention. The balcony, small enough for a modest orchestra, looked over the ballroom's gleaming wood floor.

Celeste rang a triangle. "The bride will throw her bouquet."

Squeals among the young followed this, but everyone did go in. Those married women stood along the walls to allow the unmarried the center of the ballroom.

"Is everybody ready?" Ramelle called out.

"Yes," came the enthusiastic reply.

Helene, on her toes, readied to spring and with one graceful motion, Ramelle flung her exquisite bouquet toward her roommate. Had it been a tennis ball, the throw would have hit its target, but the flowers took a different trajectory. As it fell a bit short, a young arm shot up.

Everyone screamed in delight as Louise clasped the bouquet to her breast. "I can't believe it!"

The crowd laughed as they moved to other rooms. Juts, next to her big sister, remarked, "Good that you caught them. I don't want to get married."

"They were too beautiful to let fall on the floor," Louise stated. "Everything is so beautiful. Everyone is so beautiful."

Louise left the ballroom, for she knew one of her tasks was to attend to Celeste's sister, Carlotta Van Dusen. Paul, who had accompanied her to the wedding at her request, grinned. "You should have beautiful flowers every day. You really should."

She tilted her head upward a bit. "I'd be happy to have them once a month and I pressed the pink roses you gave me between the pages of the dictionary. So I do have flowers from you whenever I want them."

He wanted to put his arm around her waist and guide her through the crowd. He knew she had a duty, but for whatever reason Paul was half afraid to touch Louise. He'd held women before. He'd kissed them. She was different.

"Paul, you know some of the people here. Miss Chalfonte wants me to do things for her sister, my headmistress when I was in school. I think I told you I went to Immaculata Academy. I'm going to put these flowers in the big refrigerator in the kitchen. You know, if all else fails, that Knute is here and the Ansons."

"You go on. I can take care of myself."

Louise put away her prize, searched, and found Carlotta in the dining room, hovering over the potent punch.

"Would you care for some, Mrs. Van Dusen? The caterer said it's mostly champagne with a little something extra." Louise held the silver ladle in her right hand. "The new law says people can't sell, make, or transport liquor. Doesn't say you can't drink it. At least, that's what he said."

"A small glass, dear," said Carlotta. "Have you kept up with your reading?" She truly liked Louise.

"I have. I read *Ben-Hur*. I mean, along with my Bible readings," she replied.

"A wonderful book. I wish there were more books like that. So much of what is published today is vulgar. Exceedingly vulgar." Carlotta sighed and looked around. "Ah, a vacant chair. I need to sit down a moment."

Louise walked her to the chair.

Patting the chair beside her, also vacant, Carlotta said, "Sit with me for a moment. Herbert is off talking business with Stirling. How they can find ball bearings and tractors thrilling, I don't know. Herbert bought a truck dealership. I told him, Herbert, horses have been pulling goods for thousands of years. Who is going to spend the money on a truck or tractor? Well, he won't listen. Husbands." She uttered this word with finality then sipped a little of the very pleasing punch. "I wasn't going to come to the wedding and you know the real reason, Louise. You are a good Catholic and we don't go into other churches. Ours is the one true church but as you see, I relented, as did you."

"How could we hurt people's feelings?" Louise kept her voice even.

"Yes. Yes. And truly, Ramelle is a sweet person if dreadfully misguided, misguided by my own younger sister, no less. Now this. I hope my baby brother knows what he's doing."

Nodding, Louise said, "It was a beautiful wedding and Celeste looked so happy as she walked down the aisle with Herbert. He loves you, Mrs. Van Dusen, as do we all."

Carlotta glowed. "Well, thank you and yes, I know he does but Louise, a truck dealership. What goes on in men's minds?"

"I don't know, Mrs. Van Dusen." And she didn't. "You made so many people happy coming today. It was a great sacrifice but you did it."

"I had recourse to Our Lady in my perplexity. She always counsels forgiveness and love. And remember, Louise, it is she who intercedes with her Son. People forget that Christ can be"—she searched for the word—"determined. After all, He threw the moneychangers off the steps of the Temple. But Our Lady softens His heart when needs be, and she softened mine." A radiant look crossed Carlotta's face. "I'm forty-seven now, Louise. I know that doesn't mean much to someone as young as you, but the years fly by, disappear. The one thing I want more than anything in the world is to see the Blessed Virgin Mother. I can endure all things through her and I can do all things through her."

"Yes." Louise didn't know what else to say.

Fannie Jump Creighton, in the parlor, fire blazing, didn't have that problem.

She leaned toward Keith. "All those beautiful women. What a temptation."

He blushed slightly. "Curtis once said to me, 'Beauty is as beauty does.' I've found that to be excellent advice."

"Humor me." She smiled. Though a bit overweight, she was good-looking. "How do you sort through such pulchritude? How do you know who to choose for a part?"

"Ah." He laughed. "If I had a ready answer for that, I'd be the richest man in Hollywood."

Her eyebrows arched upward. "As it is, you aren't poor."

He laughed. "Well, no. The truth is, Mrs. Creighton—"

She interrupted. "Please call me Fannie."

"Fannie. The truth is, the camera loves some people. You can take two women or two men, equally dazzling in the flesh, but the camera adores one and not the other."

"How curious."

"Curious and maddening." He nodded. "What if the camera loves the one without a snippet of talent?"

At this, they both laughed.

Celeste, chatting briefly with the Rhodes family, noticed her old friend chatting with Keith and thought she'd seduce that man before eight tonight. Old, young, rich, poor, Fannie could get the pants off a man with such finesse one could only watch in admiration.

After the pleasantries, Celeste moved on to Flavius Cadwalder and his wife, two people she genuinely liked, sitting in the huge living room with the fire roaring.

Out of earshot, Lottie Rhodes whispered to her mother, "Cool as a cuke."

Delilah—Big Dimps—tilted her head to one side. "Celeste always was, always will be."

Dimps Jr. said, "How about Louise catching the bouquet?"

Lottie grumbled. "Who cares? No one is going to marry her. She started a riot at the Capitol."

"Lottie, don't you start." Big Dimps grabbed her elbow. "Both of you. Smile. Look happy. This house is filled with men with money. Let them see how vivacious and pretty you are. Do you hear me?"

Lottie, sour, shot back. "If you're so smart about money, Momma, why did you marry Dad?"

"That's why I have hopes for you. Why I'm trying to put your feet on the right path. And first of all, I didn't know your father was, shall we say, not a hardworking man. All I ever saw when we were keeping company was the beautiful house, which he did inherit, thank God. Unfortunately, that's all he inherited. Now put a smile on those faces." She stopped a moment. "And pay special attention to Mrs. Thatcher." She called out, "Fairy, oh Fairy, how lovely you look. You could have been one of the bridesmaids."

Fairy smiled. She was a fragile creature, almost porcelain-like. "I had a bit of fun watching Celeste as a bridesmaid. She looked utterly sensational. Can you imagine what it was like to go from grade school to Smith with her? Well, then with Fannie, too, who voices opinions more freely than is expedient."

"You look lovely," Delilah praised her.

"Thank you."

"Might I ask you to introduce my girls if there are any interesting young or even not so young men here?"

Fairy knew exactly what Delilah was asking. She didn't much like the Rhodes girls, nicely built and attractive as they were. But Fairy also knew, if Delilah kept pushing the girls, one or both of them would rebel, and that would be worse than parading them in front of suitable men. Suitable didn't always mean boring.

"Of course, Delilah. Lottie, Dimps Jr., come along."

Watching Fairy trot the girls around, Juts considered putting a plate of tidbits on Dimps Jr.'s bosom, so each time she lifted those glorious appendages to a new set of eyes, one could reach down and pick up something to eat. She looked for Louise to tell her this idea, found her in deep conversation with her former headmistress, and returned to circulating among the guests to see if anyone needed anything.

Celeste sheparded Olivia Goldoni around and found she liked her. The two started discussing music between introductions then moved on to painting, literature, the ballet, and horses. How wonderful that Olivia followed the races, both flat and steeplechase.

She left Olivia with the bridegroom and Keith for a moment.

On her way to the punch bowl, Stirling reached out. "Twinks, thank you." He appreciated her attention to Olivia.

She turned. "She's ravishing, Stirling, utterly lovely and highly intelligent."

He accepted this with a quiet smile, looking down into his glass of straight scotch. "Life's a funny thing, isn't it?"

"Today is proof." She smiled back.

Wrapping his arm around his sister's waist, Stirling bent down (tall though she was, he was taller) and whispered in her ear. "I'm proud of you. I don't know if I could have done the same if it were me."

"You would, Stirling, you would. You always do the right thing." She slipped her arm around his waist, and for a moment they stood tightly together. "The world is changing. I guess we change with it or it passes us by."

"That's a sobering thought." He knocked back his scotch and they both laughed.

In the dining room, Celeste first noticed the enormous silver punch bowl being refilled by the caterer, then spotted her sister sitting with Louise.

Thinking that Louise had done double duty, she sat down without filling a glass for herself. She'd had one glass. That was enough.

"Louise, how good to see you with my sister. Carlotta, it's been such a long time since we had time together." Celeste looked at Louise and winked.

"Mrs. Van Dusen, I'm going to check and see if my mother needs me."

"Of course, dear." Carlotta then turned to Celeste. "Lovely young woman. My best musical talent."

"Runs in the family. They can play anything by ear."

"Remarkable." A long pause followed this. "I do hope that Curtis and Ramelle will bring up the baby in the Church."

"Oh, I'm sure they will," Celeste airily responded. "The question is which church."

Glaring for a moment, Carlotta nodded. "You know to which I refer."

"I do. But it's not your decision nor mine."

Draping one leg over the other, Carlotta, just this side of tiddly, said in a hushed voice, "Did he ever tell you what happened?"

"What do you mean?"

"How he came to, how he is now in the position by which he will become a father."

Celeste stifled a laugh. "I expect the way every man finds himself in that position."

"He knew of your arrangement." She stumbled over *arrangement*.

"Yes, he did."

The elder sister leaned even closer to the younger. "Is it not a form of deception?"

"Carlotta, when I found Ramelle, you declared, 'If only a good man would find her and save her from this life of sin.' Now you have what you wanted."

Flopping back in her chair, Carlotta mumbled, "Perhaps. Perhaps."

"They're happy. He's a Chalfonte. He's doing the right thing."

"Of course he is! He's a Chalfonte." Carlotta repeated Celeste's sentiment.

"You've never said I was doing the right thing," Celeste snapped back.

"That's entirely different, Celeste, and you know it. Now that they are man and wife, now that she will return to California with him, might you find a presentable gentleman? You always had scads of beaux."

"As did you."

Carlotta smiled, thinking of their youth. "We did, didn't we?"

"Would you like another glass?"

Waving her hand, "No, no. I fear I'm becoming indiscreet."

"Well, we are sisters. We should tell the truth to one another."

"I just couldn't. I just couldn't and still do not understand such a relationship, but I concede, yours was one of stability and affection."

"Yes."

"Celeste, we're getting older. I'm forty-seven, Stirling will be fifty next year, and you're forty-three. You're free now. Don't dally."

"Oh, Carlotta, no one is free. And Ramelle will be here half the year."

"But it won't be the same."

"What do you mean?" Celeste was reminded that Carlotta, as much as she irritated her, was far from stupid.

"Bearing a child changes a woman."

"Of course it does."

"Some experience diminished enthusiasm for physical relations." Carlotta held up her hand. "It can cause husbands to wander."

"I'm not a husband."

"Curtis is, but you do like attention. You've thrived on it since childhood."

"That doesn't mean I need physical attention."

"Must you be so blunt? It doesn't matter in the sense that being a mother truly changes a woman. You aren't going to be first with Ramelle, Celeste, and you have to be first."

This statement, true, hit Celeste like a thump to the chest. She felt the sting of truth in it.

"I'd like to think I've outgrown that," Celeste softly replied.

"You can't outgrow that any more than I can stop being your big sister. I know I have faults." She sighed, then smiled. "But being wrong isn't one of them. Come to church with me. We'll be fine."

"I promised you I would."

"And I pray for you every day, and for Stirling and Curtis. For Mother and Father, whom I trust we will see in the sweet bye and bye, and for Spotts. We will all be together again. My nephews and now a new nephew or niece."

"And Herbert?" Celeste couldn't resist. "Do you pray for him?"

"Yes, although I occasionally lack the proper enthusiasm. I ask the Blessed Virgin Mother to help me. You should become acquainted with her."

"I'm acquainted with you. Perhaps that's close enough."

"Do you think so? Do you really think so?"

Herbert came into the room, noticed the unusual flush on his wife's cheeks, and knew spirits had produced this glow. "Mrs. Van Dusen, come and take a walk with me. I have missed your company."

As she walked out on the arm of her husband, Celeste took a deep breath and stood up. She chatted with guests, reached the grand staircase, stepped up halfway to gaze down upon the rooms below, buzzing with people. Attractive as some of these people were, there was not one for whom she felt even the slightest twinge of sexual excitement. What an odd and sad commentary. She had been more or less faithful to Ramelle, but no matter where she was, there was nearly always someone to catch her eye, provide that sweet surge of energy. Celeste realized she was becoming mature when she no longer slept with everyone she was attracted to, but this was different. Her body—alive, strong, vibrant, capable of various pleasures—felt not the slightest urge toward anyone.

Behind her loomed John Singer Sargent's extraordinary full-length painting of Celeste, completed in 1897, when she was twenty. It almost glowed. She looked like a dazzling Artemis then. Now with the first blush of middle age on her high cheekbones, one might hear a whisper of vulnerability, a touch of mortality: Artemis older but Artemis still.

Celeste remembered her Virgil. In *Eclogues* a tomb appears with an inscription to Daphnis and this idyllic setting was later made famous by the painter Nicolas Poussin in the seventeenth century. "Et in Arcadia ego." Death tells us that even in beauty, he is there. It's a line known by most people in the Western world and it came to her now with peculiar force. What Celeste didn't know was what or who was dying. Or was it simply a warning? Best to live while one can.

Chapter Nine

* * * *

February 24, 1920
Tuesday

"It's like a shroud." Celeste stood at the window, watching the mid-afternoon snowfall.

Fannie Jump and Fairy laid down their cards on the table. A good game of Five Hundred failed to alleviate the dismal feelings about a winter that wouldn't end. Even the main fashion magazines from France, Italy, and England didn't entice them now that the card game ended. They liked to study fashions together but not today.

Celeste returned to her seat. "Sherry?"

"Oh, why not?" Fannie played with the edge of her cards, then tried to peek at Fairy's hand.

"Stop that," Fairy commanded.

"I thought we'd finished," Fannie replied.

Cora stuck her head in the warm library where the table had been set up. "Sandwiches?"

"Yes, we're ready." Celeste smiled as Fannie rose to pour herself something stronger than sherry.

Crystal decanters sparkled on a built-in bar. The shelves, jammed with books, reflected Celeste's wide range of interests. Fannie poured a sherry for Fairy, then sat down.

When Cora came in with the tray of sandwiches, she looked to Celeste, who said, "We've finished. We lost heart."

For years, Cora had circled the card table offering sandwiches and condiments. A system had developed so she would move a sandwich to give Celeste a hint as to what the other card players held in their hands. Celeste's old school chums never caught on, but that was the only thing she could slide by them. They knew her too well.

"Is Stirling selling the shoe factory?" Fannie reached for a ham and cheese sandwich cut into a perfect triangle.

"No. Why?"

"Creighton wants to know. Since Stirling is no longer managing the company, he thought perhaps it would be for sale. He's feeling quite competitive with Herbert Van Dusen, who's taking a chance and buying some sort of a motor dealership. Creighton swears the internal combustion machine naysayers will eat their words."

"Stirling keeps his eye on the leather market." Celeste settled back into her chair. "He'll never let it go, because Owings Shoe keeps winning those army contracts. I asked him what about a war's end. Stirling said we'd lose a great deal of business, although he did hope there would be no more huge wars. However, if one should occur, Owings Shoe will be ready. We still have the army business. But he gives all his attention to the ball bearing factory now. Stirling is prudent in selecting people to run companies, no matter what the product. He's found a man who believes he can move production into civilian men's shoes."

Fannie agreed. "I'd perish from boredom, wouldn't you? One ball bearing looks pretty much like another." She held up her cards as she giggled behind them.

"Oh no. Different sizes. Different uses, but those ball bearings are critical for industry. You should hear him."

"But wouldn't you be bored, dear?" Fairy asked in her perfectly modulated voice.

"No. No. I'd want to make deals, to sell more to make even more deals with other companies in other countries." Celeste fanned and folded her cards with a snap.

"Worshipping at Our Lady of the Cash Register, are we?" Fannie prodded.

This reminded Celeste of her discussion with Carlotta at the wedding party, which she relayed.

"How very odd. Carlotta, civil." Fairy inhaled the word *civil*.

"She was tight," Celeste informed them, "but we actually sat in the dining room and did not engage in intense disagreement." She held up her hand. "She did, as you would expect, bring up the Blessed Virgin Mother, but she surprised me."

Fairy thought about this. "She is your big sister. She is brilliant and well educated, as you all are. She just took a turn down an avenue to the Vatican, I suppose. Who is to say why?"

Fannie, enlivened by the thought. "Say, Celeste, you don't think she's suffering some sort of guilt about having a child out of wedlock. Oh, wouldn't that be juicy!"

"No. She never went away for any extended time. Carlotta suffers no guilt, period. Mother never said anything either. Well, she wouldn't, but the strain always showed. Mother couldn't hide anything."

"I adored your mother." Fannie smiled.

"Everybody did," Fairy added.

"I always felt I would never measure up to Mother," Celeste confessed. "Not that she criticized me, but I took such a different path."

"We all feel that way. Can you imagine measuring up to Amelia Schneider?" Fannie named her deceased mother. "She starved herself so she'd fit into those Worth gowns."

Celeste recalled the elegant woman: "Perfection."

"Yes, well, I am not starving myself." Fannie glanced down at her ample bosom.

"Did you enjoy the company of Keith Goldschmidt?" Celeste inquired lightly. "He seemed to think your proportions perfect."

"A sweet man."

That always meant she'd slept with him.

"Just so," Celeste remarked, and Fairy laughed.

"Here we are and I forgot to ask how Ramelle and Curtis fared. I assume they made it to the train. All is well?" Fairy tilted up her chin, a smile poised on her lips.

"A flurry of hugs, kisses, promises to write, and send news the moment the baby is born. Curtis handed her up to the porter as though she was the loveliest, most fragile treasure on earth."

"She is," Fairy said.

"She is," Celeste agreed, then lowered her voice, glanced from friend to friend. "But I had the oddest sensation standing on the steps as the festivities raged on. I thought, 'Et in Arcadia ego.'"

Startled, both women stared at Celeste.

Fannie, trying to put a good face on it, replied, "But of course. In the midst of rejoicing, we must remember that constant shadow. Don't you recall Professor Loomis's lecture about Virgil and then Epicurus our junior year in Latin?"

"God, eight years of Latin. Four in high school and four at Smith." Fairy also wished to lighten the mood. "No one can say we don't tote around the wisdom of ancients."

"That's just it, isn't it?" Celeste, enlivened now, spoke a bit louder. "We deny it. How can death spur us on if there is resurrection? Does not death drive us on and on? The sheer fear of it and we've blunted it. I think the Greeks and the Romans were more honest than we are."

"About everything. Especially sex." Fannie laughed.

"Darling, you would know." Fairy teased her. "But Celeste, Saint Augustine wrote that 'It is only in the face of death that man's self is born,' and who is more Christian than Saint Augustine?"

"I hadn't thought of that." Celeste felt the soft bread between her fingertips, putting the sandwich down on her small plate for a moment. "My conversation with Carlotta must have affected me more than I thought."

Fairy and Fannie again stared at her. In silence.

She looked at them. "Well, it did."

"Celeste," Fannie simply said, her register low.

"Ah." Celeste's shoulders dropped. "Is it true? Does being a mother change a woman?"

"You're asking that? It hasn't changed me and when my younger beloved son leaves for college, I am changing the locks on the doors!" Fannie burst out, followed by peals of laughter, her cheeks rosy.

"You are awful. Truly awful."

"Fairy, you didn't have children and I know you wanted them. I'm sorry that couldn't be, but I had three and I would have strangled all three were it not for the nannies and then the governesses, and thank God, truly, thank God for their grotesquely expensive schools out of state."

"Fannie." Fairy frowned.

"I was not meant to be a mother."

"But you love them."

She wiggled in her seat a moment. "I do love them but that doesn't mean I want to listen to every word, to constantly set their feet on the paths of righteousness."

"We don't worry about that." Now it was Celeste's turn to erupt in laughter.

Fannie squared her shoulders. "Celeste, who knows how Ramelle will act? She may become one of those women who thinks her baby is the alpha and omega and she will constantly be wiping the alpha and omega. You won't know until the blessed event occurs."

"And she'll come home for six months each year." Fairy brightened.

"Um," was all Celeste said.

"Oh, darling." Fannie leaned over to touch her elbow. "If she's lost her desires as Carlotta suggested, you put a good face on it and take a mistress or a divine young man. I assume you haven't lost your eye for a beautiful woman, a handsome man, a good horse. And that's the real problem here. There is no ill that can't be cured by a good canter. No one has been able to ride for three weeks!"

Celeste was relieved to slide out from under the topic she had initiated. "I'm sure that's it."

Fairy finished one of her triangles. "No one can make a sandwich like Cora. You know I thought of our philosophy class. Montaigne wrote, 'Although the physicality of death destroys us, the idea of death saves us.' So you see, we are deepened, enriched. All is well, Celeste."

"It really is." Fannie, for all her joking, loved Celeste, and she knew heartache also attended the joy of seeing her lover get what she always hoped for: motherhood.

The back door slammed. Juts could be heard tromping into the kitchen.

Cora, carrying back the emptied tray, called out, "Did you wipe your feet?"

"I did. I did, and Momma, I am going to kill Dimps Jr. She called me flat-chested in front of all the girls in gym class. I am not flat-chested."

"Pipe down. Celeste is playing cards."

Celeste called from the library, "Juts, come in here."

Crestfallen, fearing a reprimand first from Celeste and then her mother, Juts walked through the open door to the library. "Good afternoon, Miss Chalfonte, Mrs. Creighton, and Mrs. Thatcher. I'm sorry I yelled."

Fannie turned to fully face the fourteen-year-old, soon to be fifteen. "She's spiteful and jealous. Pay her no mind. You look quite nice and you have a few years to go in the development department."

"That's what I tell her." Cora put her hand on her youngest daughter's shoulder. "Your sister has curves. Don't worry, honey, you will, too."

"Your mother is right, Juts." Fairy smiled.

"But Dimps Jr. is my age and she's . . ." Juts made a curving motion with her hands over her own bosoms.

"Dear, Dimps Jr. looks like a cow." Celeste pronounced this with finality. "I suggest you send her to Green's Dairy."

Delighted, Juts laughed as did the others. An idea popped into her head for the St. Patrick's Day dance at school. She wouldn't kill Dimps Jr. This would be worse.

Chapter Ten

. . . .

March 5, 1920
Friday

"They need to be taller." Juts eyed the wooden representation of the fork and spoon that ran away with one another.

The cat, the fiddle, and the moon were finished but not yet painted. Although the approaching dance was a St. Patrick's Day dance, the high school always seized upon a theme. This year it was "The Cat and the Fiddle," done up to be Irish, of course. Large shamrocks, cut out from heavy paper, with green sparkles, were lined up in a vertical bin. The school's art teacher, Mrs. Stiles, worked with each art class to produce the objects.

Arms crossed over her chest, she studied the fork and spoon. "You don't want them too tall."

"How about our height?" Juts motioned to Ev to stand tall.

"Well—"

Dick Yost walked over. "Mrs. Stiles, the fork should be a little taller. My height." He smiled at Juts. "After all, the fork is a man."

"Where are we going to get his shoes?" Ev wondered.

"We'll find something." Juts smiled back at Dick. "But a fork doesn't need shoes."

Ev disagreed. "He has feet."

Juts studied the figure. "You're right. Like I said, we'll think of something."

Dimps Jr. called out, "Mrs. Stiles, I can't find the glue pot."

"All right, make the fork four inches higher, and don't forget, big smiles. They're happy." Mrs. Stiles unfolded her arms to walk to the other side of the room.

Glue pots, while not expensive, would dry out or some student would sit on one. Mrs. Stiles kept careful books, as did most of the teachers at South Runnymede High.

"I'll bring shoes," Dick volunteered.

Juts glanced down at his feet. "I'd better measure your foot if you're bringing an old pair of your shoes."

He bent over, untied the right shoe. Juts slapped down a piece of heavy construction paper. He placed his foot on it. She outlined his foot.

"Okay, the left." He untied his left shoe.

As Juts traced his foot, Dimps Jr. sashayed by. The lost glue pot had been found, and she just happened to toss a dollop onto Juts's hair.

Jaw open, Dick stepped back as Juts shot up, grabbed the glue pot from Dimps Jr.'s hand, whipped the brush out, and smacked her flat across the face with it.

"Oww!" Dimps Jr. screamed, although it didn't hurt.

Not satisfied, Juts jammed the brush into Dimps Jr.'s mouth. Ev, behind Juts, put her hands on Juts's shoulders to back her away.

Dimps Jr. squalled like a baby. Mrs. Stiles, furious at both the girls, charged over, snatched the pot from Juts's hand, gave it to Dick, who still hadn't said a word. "You two. The principal's office right now!"

Head high, Juts marched out of the room, Dimps Jr. following, weeping. Mrs. Stiles, a yard ruler in her hand, walked behind the two, every now and then giving them a good crack across their calves.

Back in the room, the other students talked at once, some laughing. Dimps Jr.'s coterie feigned tremendous shock and disapproval.

"Juts should be thrown out of school!" Maude Ischatta loudly proclaimed.

Betty Wilcox came right back at her. "Dimps started it. She's got it in for Juts because Dick Yost asked Juts to the dance."

As this was news to Dick Yost, he blushed.

Richard Barshinger, carefully oiling his small handsaw, said, "Oil and water." He looked at Dick. "She does have her cap set for you, but Dimps has had it in for Juts since first grade. Really, oil and water."

The others agreed.

Ev wisely changed the subject. Everyone knew she was Juts's best friend. No need to defend her.

"Juts is good with her hands. We need her for these decorations and we need Dimps to sell tickets. She's got a lot of friends in the junior class and some in the senior. We need them both."

"Oh, the seniors aren't going to come. We're beneath them." Betty shrugged.

"They'll come if Maude and her friends tell Dimps that this is a good way to make up for the fight. And"—she pointed at Maude and the little group—"tell Dimps she was right, but also she has to do this for her class, the Class of 1922, and for Mrs. Stiles."

The girls conferred for a moment, then Maude asked, "What's Mrs. Stiles got to do with it?"

"She's our class sponsor." Dick nearly rolled his eyes, he couldn't believe they were that stupid.

Ev then promised, "I'll keep Juts in line, but you have to help me." She wagged her finger at Dick.

"No one can keep Juts in line." He smiled because that's why he liked her.

"Make sure she dances every dance and"—Ev swung round to Louis Negroponti, the football center—"you ask Dimps to the dance."

Louis was an all-round athlete, football, baseball, track and field when possible.

"Me? She doesn't even like me." The huge, sweet fellow threw up his hands.

"She'll like you well enough." Betty Wilcox smirked. "She doesn't have a date."

"That's not true." Maude stepped toward Betty. "Percy Morris asked her."

"Why didn't she say yes? Percy's a good guy," Richard said.

Maude, turning her head up slightly, declared, "She's not going to a dance with a boy who's shorter than she is."

"Well, there!" Ev said triumphantly. "Louie will make her look like a peanut!"

Louis grinned sheepishly.

The sound of steps coming down the hall shut them up. Everyone went back to their tasks as Mrs. Stiles opened the door, shut it firmly, and scanned her students. They ignored her. She walked through the room, checking each piece being made or painted, then she hoisted herself up on a long table, her legs dangling. Mrs. Stiles, young herself, was a popular teacher.

"Class. There's so much to be done before the dance. We've lost Juts for a few days. The principal has sent her and Dimps Jr. home. In disgrace, I might add. Two less pair of hands when we most need them."

Dick, shoes back on, addressed his teacher. "Can they work from home?"

Mrs. Stiles's eyebrows shot up. "How do you propose that?"

"Like you said, Mrs. Stiles, we need them. We need Juts to do the fork and spoon and we need Dimps to sell tickets. A couple of us can take the fork and spoon to Juts and the girls. And they"—he indicated Dimps Jr.'s group—"can take rolls of tickets to Dimps at home, and she can sell tickets after school door-to-door."

Mrs. Stiles abruptly stopped swinging her legs. "Dick, that just might work." She clapped her hands. "All right then. You have my permission."

"What about Mr. Thigpen?" Richard named the principal, a strict person.

"Mr. Thigpen will be fine. In fact, when you all come back to school on Monday, when you see him, do thank him for his latitude." Mrs. Stiles was certain he'd go along with it, for, if nothing else, poor old Mr. Thigpen couldn't take his eyes off Mrs. Stiles.

After school, Maude and the girls raced to Dimps Jr.'s house, where Big Dimps, on her day off, was ironing in the kitchen. They knocked on the door.

"Junior, go see who that is," the harried mother called out.

Opening the door, the tenth grader smiled, then gave a little nod of the head to signify where her mother was. "Mom, it's the gang."

"Ask them in. It's cold out there."

Maude was first through the door and hurried back to the kitchen. "Thank you, Mrs. Rhodes. We won't be long and we're here to tell you that this was all Juts's fault."

Mother knew her daughter well but pretended to believe it. "I'm glad to hear that."

Returning to the front door, Maude informed Dimps Jr. that Mrs. Stiles had agreed to her selling tickets after school, house to house.

"Here." She handed Dimps Jr. two big rolls of tickets.

Staring at this formidable task, the somewhat chastened girl said, "How can I sell all these?"

"We'll all help you. We'll meet after school, and here's the best part," Maude breathlessly said. "We can sell to the kids at North Runnymede High. They don't have a St. Patrick's Day dance."

"All right." Dimps Jr. began to divide up the tickets while the others thought about how to divide up Runnymede.

The large brass lion's head knocker thudded against the door.

Celeste had laid out fabrics that Louise brought her. The dark long table provided a contrasting backdrop for the fabrics.

Back in the kitchen, scolding Juts, Cora didn't hear it. Celeste, having been party to the drama when Juts came to the house early, opened her own front door.

A surprised Ev, Dick, Betty, and Richard looked up at her. She looked at the young people carrying the fork and the spoon.

"And the little dog laughed to see such a sight. Oh, come on in. I've heard all about it, but not the fork and the spoon."

"We're sorry to bother you, Mrs. Chalfonte, but we knew Juts would be here."

"Indeed she is, with a black cloud hanging over her head. You all go sit in the library and I'll bring Juts out to you." Then she lowered her voice. "You know, Sunday is her fifteenth birthday and her mother is furious. Perhaps you can alleviate some of Cora's distress and of course, Juts's too."

Within moments, Juts and her mother traipsed into the library, where the fork and spoon were being held by Dick and Richard.

"Oh, Mrs. Hunsenmeir, this is all Dimps Jr.'s fault. She's jealous about Juts and she goes out of her way to make her cross. Really, Dimps started it," Dick said.

The others all murmured assent. Celeste asked the kids, "Would anyone like a refreshment?"

"No, ma'am, but thank you," Richard replied.

Celeste sat down by the fireplace. "You know, that fork and spoon are well made. All you need is some silver paint."

"Mrs. Stiles said we could give them to Juts to take home because they are her special project. And we need her to make the little dog and the cow. She's gotten the rest done. She drew out all the patterns. No one is as good as she is, and this dance makes money for our class."

Celeste had gone to private schools and didn't know much about the public variety. "And what do you do with your profits?"

"We save them and then in our senior year we decide what to do with them. The Class of 1920 is giving the school a new scoreboard. Really big." Betty was impressed.

"And we, the Class of 1922, want to do even better." Dick smiled.

Celeste looked at them, listened, and realized this was important to them. Though she evidenced no desire to bear a child, she liked young people, and she particularly liked these young people.

"I'm sure you will." Celeste turned to Cora. "What do you say?"

"Momma, I promise I won't shove glue in her face again."

"I'm afraid you'll do worse." Cora sighed deeply then examined the fork and the spoon. "How are you going to get these utensils up our hill and how are you going to build the other things you need?"

"We'll find a way."

Celeste smiled. "Leave them here. Francis has every tool since the building of the Pyramids. Put the fork and spoon into the garage and you all can work there after school if Cora permits Juts to participate."

"All right, but Juts Hunsenmeir, if you don't behave yourself you will find yourself in more trouble than ever. No dances, no movies, no walks around the square even. Do you hear me?"

"Yes, Mother."

Each young person thanked Celeste as they made their way through the side corridor to the garage, carrying the fork and spoon. Ev grabbed the spoon, Richard the fork, and they danced in a little circle, celebrating their good fortune.

Watching them with Cora, Celeste laughed. "Do you remember those days?"

"I do." Cora smiled.

"Let's promise to never stop dancing." Celeste held up Cora's hand, twirled her around the hall.

Celeste dropped her hand, both of them laughing. "You know, Cora, it's your friends who get you through life."

Chapter Eleven

....

March 7, 1920
Sunday

Sitting on a red cushioned pew in Christ Lutheran Church next to her mother, Juts listened to Pastor Wade drone on from the pulpit. Every Sunday, the three Hunsenmeirs trooped down the hill, walking in good weather on Emmitsburg Pike, where the Lutheran Church reposed perhaps two hundred yards behind the South Runnymede City Hall on the corner of the square. Each Sunday, Louise would kiss her mother and continue around the square to the northeast corner, where the more elaborate St. Rose of Lima Catholic church was located.

Juts, not inclined toward dogma, thought her sister silly to make such a show out of leaving them for the Catholic faith. While Juts enjoyed the service, the church calendar, and its reflection in the colors of the surplices and even the choir robes, she loved the rumble of the majestic and celebrated organ originally shipped from Hamburg in the early nineteenth century and considered church a necessary ritual.

Somewhere, an archangel sat at a table with a clipboard checking the times you attended church, paying special attention to additional services in Lent. For Louise, dogma, the path to heaven, assumed prime importance.

The two sisters quarreled over it during the four years that Louise attended Immaculata Academy. As Juts was nine when Louise began, her arguments revolved around Louise's turning into a killjoy. Dogma had nothing to do with it. Now, at the ripe age of just fifteen, it being her birthday, she did grasp some of the differences between Catholic and Lutheran teachings. Still, she couldn't understand why it mattered.

During one of her fulminations concerning Carlotta's influence on Louise, Celeste encouraged Louise to become an Episcopalian, which Celeste called a natural compromise.

Juts would have been as happy in a Shinto temple. The High Georgian architecture of Christ Lutheran made her feel party to a world of beauty, and a Shinto shrine, with its purity, would have produced a similar effect. Once, years ago, Cora visited a much older aunt, who lived in a Shaker village. This too had impressed Juts.

Louise, also, reveled in the colors, the incense, the candles flickering everywhere, the statuary, most especially of the Blessed Virgin Mother, arms lowered but outstretched in blessing. The statue of Jesus, the sacred heart poses, reminded her of the necessity of sacrifice. Granted, best the sacrifice be given by others but Jesus did provide the ultimate example.

And so, the morning of March 7, birthday or not, began as all Sunday mornings for the Hunsenmeirs. You paraded to church. The Grumbachers, Bleichroders, Epsteins, and others attended services in the temple Saturday night, but for all the others, Sunday it was. The Baptist churches tended to be off the square, some out on little country roads. The Methodist church sat near the temple over on Baltimore Street.

As Orrie was Louise's best friend, she prayed for her daily. Orrie stayed firm in the Methodist faith. The two chose not to discuss religion.

The Presbyterian church, white-painted brick, was two blocks off the square on Hanover Road.

But in the main, the churches with social and political pull lined the square: Episcopal, Lutheran, and Catholic. Founded by Catholics, Maryland ensured that this faith had high status, certainly more so than in the other original thirteen colonies. Henry VIII's Dissolution of the Monasteries left its bloody stain throughout the centuries. St. Rose would have been built on the Maryland side but for an unusually devout Pennsylvanian, an Italian officer who had fought for King George. After being captured by the Yanks, he chose to stay when the war was over, and he prospered. He bought the land on the Pennsylvania side. Over time, other places of worship were added.

These three buildings reflected the aesthetics of the place as well as the time in which they were constructed. Christ Lutheran was red-brick with white pediments, white pillars with clean Doric columns, and huge, long, hand-blown-glass windows, a real testament to the wealth of the parishioners, as it was built shortly after the Revolutionary War. So was St. Rose of Lima, but there the embroidered, gilded, lush Italian influence overwhelmed the senses. St. Paul's, the Episcopal Church next to St. Rose, provided a contrast. Its imposing edifice was constructed of light gray stone, two enormous brass doors, scenes from the Bible on them, and so many stained-glass windows that when the sun shone through in one direction, the colors were cast onto the snow through the windows on the other side of the church. The interiors reflected the temperament and times, as well.

Juts, affected by the silent pull of architecture and interiors, as is everyone, dutifully found the hymn, sharing the book with her mother.

Would this service never end? It was her birthday, after all. Surely Jesus didn't mean for services to be so long and so dull.

Finally, with the last hymn still echoing, Pastor Wade proceeded down the wide right aisle to the vestibule doors, Bible in hand. The choir procession followed and then the pews emptied out in orderly fashion, the people closest to the pulpit and the lectern first—Lutherans were nothing if not organized.

As Pastor Wade took Juts's hand, he smiled. "Happy birthday, Juts."

"Thank you, Pastor Wade, and thank you for your sermon." Juts was learning the ways of the world. Just because Pastor Wade's sermon bored her didn't mean she couldn't thank him. As her mother told her, any performance takes a lot of work.

He beamed up at Cora as he next took her hand.

Emerging onto the square, where the snows were packed down, shining like hard vanilla sauce, Louise came toward them, now accompanied by Paul.

"She likes him," Juts said, without much intonation.

"She does." Cora squeezed Juts's gloved hand. "He treats her right."

"But Momma, you told us men always treat you right in the beginning."

"Yes, most do. Sometimes when you're young you aren't as good a judge of character as later, but your sister has always had a way with people. Think of all the boys who've tried to court her. This fellow is different."

"I want you to know, Momma, I am not getting married."

"Yes, dear." Cora didn't even bother to ponder why that popped up. She remembered saying the same thing in the 1880s.

Celeste descended down the long, wide steps of St. Paul's, followed by her two closest friends and their spouses. Every trace of snow and ice had been removed, ensuring a safe passage. The elderly and infirm always had someone to help.

The brisk air caused the three friends to pull their scarves tighter.

"Creighton, dear, I will be home by one," said Fannie to her husband. "But I did promise to go over to Celeste's for Juts's birthday and to see the transformation of the garage."

He'd already heard all about the St. Patrick's Day plans.

Fairy Thatcher also bade her husband adieu, with instructions concerning what to tell the cook.

Arm in arm, the three watched the two Rife brothers—Julius and Pole—climb into their father's 1914 Gräf und Stift.

"I would have thought they'd have sold the car. Cars are much improved now," Celeste remarked.

"Slow. They're taking everything slowly," Fairy remarked. "And the investigation into Brutus's demise is slow."

"Slow, as in slowly the Ice Age ended," Fannie remarked with a smile. "No one really cares, including Brutus's wife or three sisters. Older than dirt, those three. I don't even think his sons care their daddy's dead. You know Julius is twenty-one and Pole not far behind. But Julius will take over the businesses. I heard he walked into the canning factory the day after his father died, sat at the desk, and began giving orders."

"Products of Cassius's first marriage." Fairy mentioned Brutus's father. "Always makes a mess, and Brutus's sisters aren't going to challenge the sons. They can't make money. They only know how to spend it."

"Which is how they earned the title La Squandra Sisters."

Celeste shortened her stride, as Fannie's and Fairy's legs weren't as long. "Whatever is done is done. We're all the better off for it."

"Quite," Fairy said as they reached Christ Church. "Remarkable."

"Hmm." Fairy nodded as the three watched Patience Horney being led down the marble stairs, carefully guided toward the direction of her mother's house.

Once at Celeste's, Cora set the table with both daughters' help. Ev Most, Orrie, and Paul also assisted. A large birthday cake was brought out from the kitchen.

"Devil's food!" Juts exclaimed, her favorite.

Fifteen candles circled the outside, which she quickly blew out.

As they accepted their plates, Fannie pleaded, "Not so big, Cora, remember I must go home to Sunday dinner."

"Me, too," Fairy added, but she could have devoured the whole cake, she was so thin.

A tray with wrapped gifts awaited Juts.

Louise gave her a pale pink sweater. "Spring has to come, Juts."

"It's beautiful," her sister gushed.

Ev gave her a belt, Orrie a small bottle of perfume. Paul, with Louise's guidance, had gotten Juts a box of good pencils, a pencil trimmer, and a tablet. Celeste gave her a lovely pair of pearl earrings.

"Mrs. Chalfonte, they glow!" Juts allowed her friends to inspect the box.

Celeste smiled. "You're old enough for pearls now."

Fannie gave her a box of embroidered handkerchiefs, while Fairy provided a thin spring scarf in pale green that would pair nicely with the sweater.

Obviously, everyone had conferred.

Fannie listened as the clock struck twelve thirty. "This is more fun than Sunday dinner. I hate to leave."

"Me, too," Fairy agreed.

"You create glorious Sunday dinners," Celeste added. "Both of you."

"Yes, well, every shirttail cousin of my esteemed husband appears. Every Sunday, it's the miracle of the loaves and fishes." Fannie stood up, shoulders squared.

Fairy giggled. "Well, it's a good thing you attend services every Sunday. Prayer will help."

"Is there a saint for freeloaders? That's to whom I should address my heartfelt requests." Fannie smiled wryly.

Fairy turned to Louise and Julia. "Girls, if you can possibly marry a man light in the relative department, the marriage will not suffer. You'll endure less strain."

"My God, the Creightons are the most fertile people in the Mid-Atlantic. Therein lies your true genius, Celeste. You avoided all this." Fannie laughed.

Fairy, smiling, reminded them, "She does have three surviving siblings, two nephews, and a third niece or nephew on the way."

"Fortunately, we don't live close, and Margaret"—Celeste named Stirling's wife—"can't stand me. It's mutual."

"Isn't that Olivia Goldoni a prize?" Fannie regretted this the minute it flew out of her mouth and hastily amended it for the young people. "Thinking of Ramelle's child made me think of that beautiful voice at the ceremony."

Juts, Louise, Ev, and Orrie took that at face value. It wouldn't have occurred to them even to think that someone as old as Stirling might have a romantic life.

Fannie and Fairy kissed Juts on the cheek, promising to come back later in the week to see the figures she'd made with her classmates.

As they walked down the steps and out to the graceful gate, Fannie Jump's car awaited them.

"Fairy, dear, I'll drop you home."

They settled in the rear of the cavernous vehicle, her driver at the wheel.

"I told Mr. Thatcher"—as Fairy called her husband—"I'm going to learn how to drive."

"Really?" Fannie registered surprise.

"I want to come and go as I please. Mr. Thatcher swears an automobile is too much for a woman to hold on the road. He tells me they are hard to steer. Well, perhaps, but I can hold a twelve-hundred-pound Thoroughbred in the hunt field. I am going to do it."

"That's so thrilling." Fannie looked out the window as beautiful pre-Revolutionary then post-Revolutionary homes glided by. "I don't know if we'll ever hunt again. What a terrible winter."

"Has been."

They rode in silence then Fannie Jump, burrowing down in a fur throw, voice low, said, "Celeste is lonely. She's always been social and a charming hostess, but now she likes people in the house. My first clue was when she allowed the kids to use her garage."

"They were unusual circumstances."

"Fairy, I would have paid good money to see Juts smash that glue pot onto Dimps Jr.'s bosom. Those two girls are being groomed to be courtesans, I tell you."

"It does give me pause." Fairy turned to her old classmate. "What else can they hope for? They aren't well-born, I mean, the Rhodes are respectable enough but neither of those girls is going to land a rich young man. At least I don't think so. For one thing, where will they meet them? They aren't going to be presented to society."

"Big Dimps will find those demimonde places. Trust me, Fairy, she is relentless."

"All she's doing is making up for her own discomforts. You see that so much with parents, do you not?"

"You do, and I hope I'm not one of them."

"You raised your boys with benign neglect." Fairy smiled.

Ignoring this, Fannie asked, "Now really, truly honestly, are you going to learn to drive?"

"I am. You will be my first passenger."

Fannie Jump wondered if that was a good idea. Nonetheless she returned to her topic. "I thought I would take Celeste into Baltimore with me. The symphony is playing a Russian-themed night. Why I don't know. There is no more Russia. Baltimore has some treasures. Philadelphia is too far away and Washington is dead, just dead. The real reason our government is there is that there's little temptation."

"I expect there's enough without the arts." Fairy smiled. "Thinking on Celeste, she says she receives a letter almost every day from Ramelle and she writes one as well. The baby is due early May. Actually, I think Celeste is doing well."

"But not well enough. She likes sports. I was thinking about getting a few tickets for the Orioles. The season's not far off, she likes baseball."

"You can try it."

"And those boys need jobs. They make so little that if she becomes enthused perhaps she can twist Stirling's arm to find work for them in his various endeavors."

Fairy turned to smile at Fannie Jump. "There, it's settled then."

. . .

What wasn't settled was Juts's announcement as she and Louise were clearing the table.

"Now that I'm fifteen, I'm going to quit school."

"You can't do that." Louise placed the dessert plates in the sink of hot water.

"Yes I can."

"A high school diploma helps you get better jobs." Louise pushed open the kitchen door, which swung behind her as she went out to find Paul in the library.

"Reading?"

He put the book down. "I've never seen such beautiful books. The bindings, the colors, the gold stamping or silver. It must be a fortune in books."

"It is." Louise took his arm. "Come on, let me show you what they're making for the dance." As she propelled Paul toward the side door and out onto the arcade, she said to Juts, "Don't say anything to Momma. Not yet."

"Why not?"

"We have to prepare her."

Juts glowed. "Wheezie, that means you agree."

"Maybe. You need to finish out the year."

"No, I don't."

"A tenth-grade education is better than a ninth-grade and really, Juts, you have to finish out the year to get even with Dimps."

Chapter Twelve

• • • •

March 9, 1920
Tuesday

"Is there any way to hide them?" Juts, neck craned upward, watched as Louis Negroponti shimmied along the heavy rafters, chain in hand.

Richard Barshinger approached him on the rafter from the opposite end.

Ev walked to the side of the cafeteria.

"Ev, what are you doing over there?" Juts asked.

"You go to the opposite side. Louie and Rick have to fix the chains, then backtrack and drop the ends to us."

"Ev, we can't do that. People will see. The dance isn't for eleven days," Juts replied.

"Do like I tell you," Ev commanded. "I'll explain later."

Still looking upward, Juts watched the two boys fix the chains with U-bolts. They then shimmied backward, repeating the U-bolt procedure every ten yards.

Slowly Louis fed out the chain while Richard did the same thing for

Juts. Once the chains were in the girls' hands, they held them still against the wall.

"What do you think?" Ev asked.

"It will work. Okay, let go. I'll pull it up and fix it here."

"Why not just fix up the pulleys now?" Richard asked.

Louis, busy wrapping dark baling twine around the chain, which he carefully flattened out, called over, "Because a pulley is easier to see than this baling twine. Come on, Richard, think. Use your baling twine. We don't want anyone to see this."

"Okay, okay." Richard pulled the dark twine out of his pocket and imitated Louis's procedure.

This task completed, the girls held the respective ladders as the boys climbed down on each side of the cafeteria.

"You can see the twine but you have to look for it," Juts declared. "Who's going to look for it?"

Louis nodded. "That's why we can't put the pulleys up until the night before the dance. All we need is for someone to open their big mouth and some teacher will butt in."

"Yeah," Richard agreed.

Twilight deepened. The four, working after hours, shut off the lights, and pulled on their winter coats, for it was still cold outside. Carefully closing the door, they walked down the hallway and let themselves out of the old, pretty building.

"We'll walk you home," offered Louis.

"Sure." Richard chimed in, mad that he hadn't thought of it first. After all, Ev was to be his dance date.

They came up Frederick Road, reached the square, turned left, then reached Emmitsburg Pike and turned down that tree-lined expanse.

A truck rumbled by, gold lettering on black sides, *Van Dusen Hauling.* Yashew Gregorivitch waved to them from the driver's seat. They waved back. Edgar Wilcox rode with him. He worked in his father's bakery but, like Yashew, was hoping to make extra money. He made every effort to become strong, since he had only one arm.

"I thought Yashew got a job at the Red Bird Silk Mill," Richard remarked.

"He did. He works two jobs now." Louis liked Yashew, a friend of his older brother's. "He said he's got to make a lot of money. His mom can't work anymore."

The truck stopped behind them at Christ Lutheran Church, turning down into the narrow alleyway. They heard the engine cut off.

"What are you all doing out late?" asked Louise, with Paul, when they came upon the high school group.

"Waiting for you," Juts flippantly said.

"Well, here I am." Louise, too, noticed the new truck at the church.

The six young people turned back to look as they could hear the truck doors open.

Yashew, Edgar, and Rob McGrail unloaded barrels which they rolled to a side-door cellar. When they reached the side door, they put a barrel on a ramp and rolled it down. Someone was down there because the barrel stopped at the bottom.

Wheezie, hearing the thud, asked, "What are you all doing? Rob, you're a Catholic."

"I'm working. Wheezie, we've got a lot of calls to make tonight. The trucking business is picking up. We haul lumber, bricks, even Rife's canned food if he gets behind. Mr. Van Dusen was smart to buy four new trucks."

"What's in the barrels?" Juts innocently asked.

"Stored potatoes," Yashew quickly answered. "Now that winter's almost over, everybody's run out of potatoes, red beets, turnips, you name it. Nobody put up enough. Nobody thought winter would be this long or hard."

Edgar smiled shyly. He liked Juts, Louise, and Ev. He felt no girl would look at him now.

Paul, getting the picture, nodded to the workmen, turned, and herded the group back toward Emmitsburg Pike.

Juts, over her shoulder, called out, "Who's in the cellar?"

A deep voice, sounding like that of the sexton, Herschel White, boomed, "The Archangel Michael. You kids go home!"

Back out on the pike, going first to Ev's house, Paul walked on the outside of Louise, which she appreciated.

Richard opened the gate for Ev. "See you tomorrow."

"Hey, Juts, how are we going to get all the stuff to the cafeteria?" Louis asked as they left Ev.

"How much do you have?" Paul inquired.

"We can show you." Juts, as they neared Celeste's, led them to the garage.

She opened the door to reveal painted figures leaning against the wall. Most were three-dimensional papier-mâché stretched over wire. Others, like the fork and the spoon, were made of wood, with braces to keep them upright. The cat and the fiddle remained unpainted. The little dog, however, had been painted brindle, a hard job.

"That's huge." Paul pointed to the black-and-white cow.

"The cow jumped over the moon." Louis recited part of the poem. "I'm afraid we'll bang this stuff up moving it all and we won't have time to repaint."

"Yashew's truck would do the job." Rick wished he had a better answer.

Louise turned to the man who was becoming her steady fellow. "Pearlie, you're thinking about something."

He smiled. "Give me a couple of days. You want the figures protected and if it turns out to rain when you move them, that's a bigger problem than a scratch or a dent."

"Darn, I hadn't thought of that." Richard shoved his hands in his coat pockets.

"And the other thing is, once we hang the cow over the moon, how do we get her to jump over it?" Louis went on to explain to Louise and Paul how they intended to use pulleys to hoist the cow over the moon.

"Yeah, that is a problem," Paul agreed. "Let me think about that, too. Might be something as simple as you have two people on the floor who jump it over, you know, with long sticks controlling or something."

Francis opened the front door. "Are you kids going to work now?"

"No. I wanted to show Louise and Paul how much we've done," Juts replied.

"Hells bells, you kids could put these things in the Mummers' Day parade." Francis whistled, citing the huge annual parade in Philadelphia.

"Well, I have a date." Louis smiled. "Elizabeth Chalmers."

"The senior? You got a date with a senior?" Rick blurted out. "And she's pretty too."

"She's nice. Most all the girls in our class are taken, and Dimps Jr. turned me down flat. She's a real snot. Anyway, Elizabeth came with her father after school to the garage. Old man's Olds broke down again and while they were talking I asked her. She's kind of shy. She said she watched all my games and she could hear the crunch when I hit someone or someone hit me." Louis related this with some pride. "So I asked her to the St. Patrick's Day dance and I promised she wouldn't have to hear a crunch. I didn't think she'd say yes but she did."

"Wow, an older woman." Rick looked at Louis with new eyes.

"Ah, what's two years, especially when you're as big as I am? People come in the garage and they think I work there, you know?"

Juts complimented him. "She has good sense. Don't forget to get her a corsage, Louie."

"Mom's gonna help me." Louis turned to Rick. "What are you getting Ev?"

"Mom said shamrocks and roses, white roses, and she said I had to wear shamrocks in my jacket."

"Hey, that's a good idea." Louis smiled.

As the two boys left, Juts opened the side door into the house where Cora was finishing up.

"You're late."

"I am, Momma. Lots to do, plus I had to make up the days' work I missed."

"Mmm, where's Louise?"

"Outside, making eyes at Pearlie."

Celeste had walked into the kitchen just as Juts said "making eyes."

"This sounds promising."

"Oh, Miss Chalfonte, she perks right up every time she sees him, she hangs on every word. She's worse than, I don't know, she's worse than Genevieve and Dancedelot."

"Lancelot, dear," Celeste said with a smile.

"Right." Juts had strained to come up with two famous lovers.

Just then Louise, looking impossibly happy, entered the kitchen from the side door.

"You kissed him! I know you did." Juts pounced on Louise.

Affecting a superior air, the older sister huffed, "I don't know what you're talking about."

"Ha!" Juts sounded victorious, although why, no one knew.

"Girls, let's go home. Celeste doesn't need your foolishness and neither do I."

Emboldened and wound up, never a good thing, Juts then asked Celeste, "Did you ever make eyes at the boys?"

Cora was aghast. "Juts, what's gotten into you? You apologize right now, you little hoyden."

Laughing, Celeste leaned down toward Juts. "No. I did not make eyes at the boys. They made eyes at me."

"Oh."

"Are you satisfied?" Cora looked at Juts, then at Celeste.

"Well, how am I supposed to learn? I know what I'm supposed not to do but I don't know what I'm supposed to do. The boys like me but I don't want to kiss anyone."

"Maybe they don't want to kiss you," Louise shot back.

Cora stepped toward Louise. "That's enough."

"But Mother, all she does is make fun of me and she even spies on me if Pearlie and I sit by the fire at home. She's like a tick."

"I hate you." Juts doubled her fist.

Celeste, tall, wonderfully fit, stepped between the sisters. "Let's go sit by the fire in the library for a moment, shall we?"

As they had never been asked like grown-ups to sit by the fire with

Celeste in her favorite room, both immediately shut up, meekly following the great beauty into a room that glowed. Cora turned back to the kitchen to take off her apron, get her coat. She moved slowly to give them more time.

"Louise, sit here. Juts, there." Celeste stood between them, fire behind her. "You two are like banty roosters. That's natural among sisters and brothers, but Juts, Wheezie is a young lady now, of marriageable age. Things change. Your sister has been wise in her behavior. Some women are fatally attracted to bad men."

"Like our father?" Juts blurted out.

"Well, yes. Juts, you are still a little young to understand feelings toward boys and men. That changes as you age. You don't have them yet but Wheezie does. Please don't ruin it for her."

Juts had never thought of these things. She wasn't feeling guilty, but she was ill at ease.

"Miss Chalfonte, did you feel like that? When you were Louise's age?"

"Sometimes. I thought the whole thing quite confusing. When I was nineteen, it was 1896, and I was shipped off to England for polishing, you might say. Mother truly wanted me to marry a duke or an earl. Since I could ride, and ride well, I even rode in the hunt field with the empress of Austria, who was most kind to me. I did have suitors. All those titled boys."

Louise, wide eyes, breathed, "A duke?"

"A smattering. Most were poor as church mice and they craved my American money. A few young men, though, I believe truly liked me."

"But you didn't like them?" Juts was now as breathless as her sister.

"One. I liked one fellow very much. He had no title. He was a jockey for the duke of Portsmouth. No hope for either of us really but he kissed me once, and I will remember that kiss for the rest of my life."

The two, spellbound, at that moment could see the nineteen-year-old Celeste.

Louise, tears in her eyes, said, "You have a broken heart."

Celeste smiled, put her hand on Louise's shoulder. "For a time. I deeply disappointed my mother, but I felt like a heifer at auction. I couldn't do it and I discovered the longer I was in England, the more American I felt. I wanted to come home and I did. Now, there, you know everything."

"And no one here kissed you?" Juts was incredulous.

"Well, they tried. It wasn't right. So if the day comes when someone appeals to you and he's kind, especially if he's kind and he's honest and he works up the nerve to kiss you and you never felt anything like that before, that's the right one. Juts, remember all this. In time you will have your turn, but I repeat, don't spoil things for Louise. There's no hurry to do anything, but"—she turned to look Louise full in the up-turned face—"he's a nice young man and a strong one."

Tears spilling now, Louise dabbed her eyes, saying nothing.

Juts asked, "Do you think Ramelle felt that way when Curtis kissed her? Men chased her all the time. They chase you, too."

Louise could have killed Juts right then. The sisters never discussed Celeste and Ramelle's relationship, and probably Juts really was too young to figure it out. Louise knew and the way it was settled for her was when her mother answered her questions by saying, "Love is love."

Celeste, nonplussed, nodded. "I think so, Juts. She wouldn't have married him otherwise. In her own way, Ramelle is a sensible woman."

Cora peered into the library. "You've calmed the wild Indians."

"We were discussing men, love, the important things in life."

Cora noticed Louise's glistening eyes and Juts's unnatural silence. "Must have been good."

"I hope so. I'm sure you have things to say on the subject."

Cora, her coat on, folded her arms across her bosom. "What I've learned in life is that men fall in love with their eyes; women with their ears."

Chapter Thirteen

. . . .

March 14, 1920
Sunday

Apart from a rash of gilt, the chapel at Immaculata Academy felt calming. Its white interior filled the interior with light from tall, arched, clear windows.

Celeste knelt next to her sister, who had given her a rosary. Although Episcopalian, Celeste did know her rosary, finding comfort in feeling the beads, repeating the words. Not a woman inclined to religious fervor, she responded to ritual. Like the family, but especially their mother and father, Celeste was shocked when Carlotta had converted to Catholicism to marry Herbert. He had had ample time to repent of this, as Carlotta became ever and ever more devout over the years.

The whole point of the conversion was that Herbert's late mother had pitched a full-scale hissy fit, an emotional conflagration on a par with the burning of Atlanta, when Herbert announced the intentions to wed the lovely and rich Carlotta. Vivien Van Dusen announced that no grandchild of hers would be anything but Catholic. T. Pritchard and Charlotte Spottiswood Chalfonte took issue with that. For one thing, the Catholic church, not beneath the salt in Maryland, nonetheless seemed too rigorous for Carlotta's parents. One attended church, one listened, one obeyed the Ten Commandments, and one went about the business of life with little concern for excommunication, hellfire, or damnation.

The coolness between the parents of the couple only heightened their determination to wed. Carlotta converted. T. Richard and Charlotte Spottiswood Chalfonte accepted it with good grace. Done is done. Their remaining unmarried brood, Celeste, Spottiswood, and Curtis, accepted it. By that time, Stirling was already married to Margaret, a good Episcopalian.

The worry about grandchildren proved unfounded as Herbert and Carlotta produced one daughter, who, though raised Catholic, merely went through the motions. Now, at her first year of college, away from her mother, she didn't even do that, her mother was unaware.

Carlotta, perhaps inspired by raising a daughter, decided to dedicate her life to improving, educating young women, preparing them for whatever their future might hold. She put up part of her personal inheritance in her own name. Herbert put up the rest. Herbert was proving a good businessman.

Stirling would not reduce the bulk of the Chalfonte fortune no matter how much closer such generosity would ensure him a good berth in heaven. But each of the Chalfontes had been bequeathed a handsome living wage while the bulk of the fortune stayed intact to be skillfully managed by Stirling. Carlotta built a quiet, tree-lined academy. Every walkway was lined with either a deciduous tree good for fall color or an evergreen as a contrast to the snow. All the Chalfontes had a good eye for symmetry, color, proportion. The academy's buildings, Federal-style, surrounded two quads with a huge quad in the middle. The chapel sat smack in the middle of the central quad, all paths leading to it. The buildings, white-painted brick, were all of the same height. All had six-over-six sash windows with maroon shutters sporting gold pinstripes.

Carlotta, like Celeste, believed in women's suffrage, and the colors of the suffragettes were maroon and gold.

After the service, the day cool but promising spring, Carlotta stood outside the chapel doors at the foot of the steps with her very beautiful sister. Carlotta wore her robes as headmistress, which made this good-looking woman even more imposing. She greeted every girl by name, asking a question about the young person's favorite interests or probing about some studies.

After a half hour, the two sisters took a leisurely walk through the campus. Both believed in walking as the perfect exercise, and riding helped too. Both were terrific athletes, but then Chalfontes always were.

Celeste had occasionally visited her sister, but she had never worshipped with her, nor seen her with the girls as she just had. Four years separated them, but what really put distance between them was Celeste's relationship with Ramelle.

"You remember every girl's name," said Celeste.

"I do." Carlotta strode under a massive elm, buds threatening to open.

Stride for stride they moved in concert before turning to walk along Oak Alley, framing the back quad.

"I forget how much I loved school," Celeste remembered.

"Mother and Father gave us the best. Mother always swore the foundation of democracy is the education of women. Remember, she was there in 1878 when the amendment to give us the vote was first introduced into Congress. Mother endured a great deal for this and Father stood by her."

"Didn't he get into a fistfight over it?"

"Cassius Rife insulted Mother in 1887. Said women should never vote, they're too irrational, and I guess that turned into a donnybrook. I was ten. You were in first grade. If the Nineteenth Amendment doesn't pass, I actually believe there will be violence, and I don't think it's going to pass. We need one more state to reach that magic number of thirty-six states. That's Tennessee, and as the entire South, including Maryland, has rejected this, I feel certain Tennessee will also."

Celeste nodded. "And yet the very amendment I thought would have cities erupting into flames became effective in January. Then again, you and I wouldn't be in the company of Carrie Nation and her type, but plenty of others are."

"I think the reason there hasn't been bloodshed is that Carrie Nation, quite brilliantly, cast this as a moral crusade, an uplifting of behavior, to protect women and children. It's nothing of the kind. Moral uplift can only come from the church. And let us remember Jesus and the Apostles drank wine."

"I laid up as much as my cellar could handle." Celeste laughed. "Not for me, for Fannie Jump."

Carlotta smiled. "She's going to need a girdle with iron bands if she doesn't slow down. Alcohol will put the pounds on." She surveyed her younger sister. "Not you."

"I drink so little. And I ride so much." Heading toward the two-story headmistress's house, the Rectory, Celeste said, "You and I keep our distance from one another. At Ramelle's wedding, you asked me to come to Mass. I expect you want money."

Carlotta stiffened, then relaxed. "Of course, I want money. I'm not a fool. You added to your personal finances. I depleted mine, but in a great cause."

"You're right, Carlotta. I didn't start a school. You have, betting on the future really."

This surprised Carlotta. "Well, thank you. So, why are you here? Let's discuss this over tea. It's not cold but it's not warm either. I need a spot of tea."

Within fifteen minutes they faced one another, sitting in a small intimate room off the enormous library. A student served tea, then melted away.

"Some of the girls must work to offset their expenses. Louise did.

You know she was the most talented child musically I have ever taught and she hasn't a bit of interest in it."

"Just because God gives you a gift doesn't mean you have to use it." Celeste picked up the cup and saucer.

"How interesting to hear you discuss God."

While intelligent, Carlotta never could match her sister for dry wit, sharp wit, wit in general. She nestled back in her comfortable chair, drank her tea, looked out the window.

The silence was broken by a student, Betty Ermdorf, standing in the doorway. "Anything else, Headmistress? More tea?"

"No thank you. There's plenty in the pot but if there are any short-bread cookies, do bring them."

"Yes, ma'am."

Carlotta set down her cup on the small table between them. "Why are you here? Why are you here when we have led very different lives, when you call me La Sermonetta behind my back and I call you a Latter-Day Sappho behind yours?"

"Ah, I hadn't heard that. Has a ring to it." Celeste started to quote one of Sappho's poems, in the poet's Greek dialect.

Carlotta held up her hand. "Don't. I hated Greek."

"You were the best at French. Italian, too."

Carlotta smiled. "We really did get a superior education. And that is why you are here."

Celeste held her breath, then lightly exhaled. "Yes."

"My dream is that every girl will be a full citizen, be able to partici-pate in politics. We've worked, Mother worked, fifty-plus years of work, and we are about to be cast into darkness. These girls must con-tinue the fight. The United States is not a democracy if women can't vote. I need more money and I am turning to you because of Mother and Father's beliefs and because of the future. And of course, if Ra-melle is delivered of a girl she will attend here, thanks to your generos-ity, but other girls will attend here thanks to your help."

"Must they all become Catholics?"

"It is a Catholic academy."

"Don't weasel with me, Carlotta. Answer my question."

Betty, transfixed in the doorway, hesitated to enter. Celeste motioned with her hand for Carlotta to look in the youth's direction.

Carlotta beckoned to her. "Betty, this is my younger sister, Celeste Chalfonte. Being sisters, we often disagree. Don't be alarmed, she's not going to throw a cup of tea at me."

"Not until you leave the room, Betty." Celeste laughed.

Betty couldn't help herself. She laughed, too. Celeste had a way of making people feel they were all on the same team. She curtseyed and left.

"You've terrified the girl."

"Good. Then I've scared the devil out of her and you have less work to do." Celeste shrugged.

"I knew this wasn't going to be easy."

"Oh, when has it been easy? You and I can fight over a postage stamp. You want money. I want to know if a student must convert. I agree with your assessment of future political participation for young women. I actually do, but I am not bankrolling the Catholic Church, the largest landowner in the world. Nor do I believe the pontiff is Christ's vicar on earth. You know that."

"And I pray for you."

"And you still haven't answered my question, dammit." Celeste's face flushed.

"Calm down."

"Tell me the truth and I will."

"I will not press conversion but a student must attend chapel, and before you raise your voice again, do remember that almost every private institution for women or men demands chapel attendance. I give you my word, no conversion."

"No pressure?" Celeste's eyebrows shot up.

"No. I might indicate I think our faith is the one true faith, but no personal pressure."

The two stared at one another.

"All right. Now that we are laying our cards on the table, as it were, you have ever been censorious of my relationship with Ramelle. I never shoved it in your face. We were discreet. You were ready to put me in one of the lower circles of Hell."

"I'd put you with Abelard and Heloise in Dante's *Inferno*."

"How very thoughtful of you."

"Celeste, it is an unnatural vice."

"Here's the thing, Sister, all vices are natural. That's why there's so many of them. That's why the absurd Eighteenth Amendment passed. To control vice. Is drunkenness a scourge? Yes, it is. Will passing an amendment stop drinking? Certainly not. We've both stockpiled our cellars, and when the cellars run dry, we will all be buying from the Canadians, enriching them instead of our own."

"I think of the Canadians as our own."

"I don't." Celeste, blood up, barked. "They're smarter. You don't see them passing a Volstead Act."

"You're right there."

"And what makes you think your relationship with Herbert is better than mine with Ramelle? Carlotta, you are bored to tears with your husband. At least I wasn't bored."

This hit home; Carlotta's face reddened. She fired back, "At least I wasn't betrayed."

Celeste threw her teacup into the fireplace, where it smashed to bits.

Betty ran in. Celeste, in an unnaturally calm voice, said, "I broke a teacup, Betty. Don't worry about it. Be grateful I didn't throw it in your headmistress's face."

Carlotta, smiling broadly, said, "My sister has always been prone to temper tantrums."

"Your temper is worse than mine." Celeste then looked at Betty, her eyes like saucers. "Excuse me. No one can make me angry as fast as my sister. Do you have a sister?"

"I do," came the wavering reply.

"Is she older or younger?"

"Younger, ma'am."

"Does she make you angry?"

"Sometimes."

Carlotta interjected. "Do you forgive her?"

"I must. If I don't, my mother will fan me but good."

Celeste started to laugh, then Carlotta did, too, and finally Betty giggled.

"Honey, please don't tell your friends how hateful I've been to my big sister. She knows how to pluck my last nerve." Celeste used Cora's phrase.

As Betty left, Carlotta handed over the plate of shortbread cookies. "Care for one?"

"I ought to shove it up your nose." Celeste did take a cookie.

They laughed some more.

"The cool, graceful, magically beautiful Celeste Chalfonte lost her temper, acted like a brat, and, well, her big sister lost her temper too. Do you ever think Mother and Father sent us to those good schools so we'd learn not to show emotion?"

Cookie in hand, hand pausing in midair, Celeste blinked. "I never thought of it. I thought I was there to get a good education and then go to England and find a duke or let a duke find me."

"Think back on how deportment and manners were drilled into us. Am I glad? Up to a point. But we can seem cold."

"Yes, yes, I think that's why I love Cora so much. She wears her heart on her sleeve." Celeste put down the half-eaten cookie. "So here we are halfway through life. What do we do now?"

Carlotta wistfully looked out the window to see the first robin of the spring in a birch tree branch. "Our best. For me, that's the academy. Training the young."

"For me, I don't know," Celeste responded. "My good works are not as good as yours."

"We were brought up to serve. You do it in your way and I do it in mine. And who is to say with your spirit that you won't be the first woman in South Runnymede to run for public office if we ever do get the vote?"

"Carlotta, don't wish that on me." She paused. "I have a condition apart from no conversions if I am to give money."

"What?"

"That if two girls fall in love, let them be. Don't expel them."

"You don't expect me to condone it?" The older sister's voice sharpened.

"No. I know you don't understand, but this is such a sweet and tender age. Girls fall in love with their friends. For God's sake, Carlotta, they even fall in love with their horses."

Carlotta smiled. "They do. What exactly is it that you want me to do?"

"Look the other way. If an attachment becomes too amorous or too public, speak to them but don't judge them."

"I can't speak to them."

"All right, then. I can. Will you let me know when and if such a relationship reaches that level?"

A long, long silence followed, then Carlotta, with finality in her voice, agreed. "I will."

Then they spoke of the robin, just outside, chirping his heart out. A cat sauntered in and they talked about their childhood pets and their pets now.

"Ah, I see Francis coming down the drive," said Celeste.

No sum had been discussed.

"Betty will tell him to wait."

The two, greatly resembling one another in form if not in personality, waited a moment as though waiting to see the first bud on the birch open.

"Carlotta, we rarely talk and then we rarely say anything."

"I know."

"Do you still love Herbert?"

Carlotta waved her right hand. "Yes. But it's not the same. He's a good man, a steady man. I suppose he puts up with me and I put up with him."

"Do you ever long to feel what you felt in the beginning?"

A silky sigh followed. "It was the time of my life when I felt most alive. I felt the future was a golden haze into which I would walk holding his hand. Oh, it all sounds so silly."

"No, it doesn't. I know exactly what you mean."

They stood up and embraced.

Carlotta walked Celeste to the front hall. "May I have your pledge?"

"You may. I will transfer one hundred thousand dollars into your account tomorrow, plus a small sum to cover Betty's expenses."

Carlotta stood stock-still, her eyes filled with tears. "Celeste."

"You know I love you." Celeste kissed her sister on the cheek and swept out the door. "It's just sometimes I can't stand you."

Chapter Fourteen

. . . .

March 19, 1920
Friday

Twilight lingered. Within two days there would be equal sunshine and darkness. The air carried a chill, but the light promised that spring would arrive. Snowdrops had pushed through the snow, followed by crocuses with even a few unopened daffodils pushing ever upward. The annual miracle was about to begin, as was the St. Patrick's Day dance. Another smaller miracle, perhaps, for everything was completed on time: decorations, refreshments, members of the school band ready to supply dance music.

To Dimps Jr.'s credit, she sold more tickets with her friends' help than anyone sold before. Wearing a green dress designed to enhance her figure, she basked near the door to greet people, which infuriated Juts. But Juts, occupied by last-minute touches, worked behind the makeshift raised dais for the musicians. Louis, Ev, Dick, and Richard checked and double-checked the papier-mâché figures placed around and on the dais. The crowning moment just before the dancing started would be the crescent moon dropping down, then the cow jumping over it. Both were shrouded in sheets. Juts wanted to make sure the sheets would drop, they'd pick them up, and the centerpiece would slowly come down. She'd even arranged for musical accompaniment.

Paul worked for no pay after hours so that Mr. Anson would allow him to move the figures from Celeste's garage. Louise assured him this was unnecessary but he said the kids had worked hard. Why not? He'd also helped Louis create a simple slide on the rafter—Louis would need to be up there, so the cow wouldn't exactly jump but would glide over the moon.

Mrs. Stiles chaperoned, along with three other teachers dragooned into giving up part of their Friday night. Fannie Jump Creighton also chaperoned. Never one to miss a party regardless of age or occasion, she moved about, complimenting the kids. She had even dragged Celeste and Fairy Thatcher along. She told Celeste she had to attend if even for an hour to see all the work Juts and her friends had done. Then she had called Fairy and said the school always needed responsible adults and they needed to get Celeste out and about.

To this, Fairy replied, "Responsible adults?"

She did, however, attend, and was now seated in a chair along one wall with a few other adults, one of them the custodian, another the school nurse. Fights, not uncommon, could break out, and as a large number of students from North Runnymede High, all well-dressed, were there, better to prepare just in case.

Dimps Jr.'s date was Bill Whittier. Having the captain of the North Runnymede football team at her side added to her swagger, but it did not add to her popularity among the North Runnymede girls.

Celeste strolled with Fannie Jump. They ran into Louise and Paul.

"Good evening, Miss Chalfonte, Mrs. Creighton," the younger people said.

"What are you doing here?" Fannie Jump inquired.

"Juts wanted us to see the decorations and Pearlie hauled everything here. It's wonderful."

"Indeed it is," Fannie Jump remarked. "A sea of green. We're all a little Irish tonight. Even Celeste."

Celeste smiled. "Of course I am."

The room hummed. Fannie Jump stepped into the hallway briefly, then returned.

"How about if we leave once the dancing begins? I'm not sure I can watch." Fannie half smiled.

"We weren't any better at that age," Celeste remarked.

"Worse, I should think. That dreadful all-girls' school."

"It wasn't that dreadful."

"Celeste, every girl had a crush on you, except myself and Fairy. I say living with all women is a curse. If I lived in a harem, I'd kill the others."

"They do, don't they?" Celeste's eyebrows raised. "Or maybe they kill one another's sons. And every girl did not have a crush on me, nor did I return same."

Arms across her chest, Fannie pursed her lips. "Do you expect me to believe you?"

"I do. Granted, at Smith I had a few moments." She touched Fannie's elbow. "You, of course, never did a thing."

"Not with the girls. The boys visiting from Yale or Harvard, Dartmouth or Amherst, perhaps."

"Oh, Fannie Jump, you looked at more ceilings than Michelangelo."

Fannie had to laugh at herself. "Are we not here to make a joyful noise unto the Lord?"

"Quite." Celeste grinned. "Shall we rescue Fairy? She's looking mournful."

"That's her bored look, Celeste."

"How can you tell the difference?"

"I can't. I just made it up."

The two joined their friend as Louis walked by with his date, senior Elizabeth Chalmers.

The ladies greeted them. Everybody knew everybody. No need for introductions. As he walked by, the three pair of eyes followed him.

"Well, Louie hit a home run," Fannie enthused. "Which reminds me. Would either of you two come with me to Baltimore? Time to meet this season's team."

"Thank you, Fannie," Fairy replied. "You know I'm not one for sports."

Fannie came back, "Celeste already promised me. I thought you might like a change of scenery. Watching young male bodies peps me right up. You, too, if you'd give yourself a chance."

Fairy demurred, then added, "I've been reading Marx."

To this, her two friends said nothing. Before Fairy could explain her new interest in economics and class divisions, the inevitable drone of thank-yous began from the dais.

"I need a drink," Fannie declared.

"Your flask is in your skirt pocket." Celeste pointed out what she and Fairy knew.

"I can't pull it out in front of all these children."

"Perhaps there will be a diversion, dear, and you can fortify yourself," Fairy innocently predicted.

This happy moment, for Fannie anyway, came after the last of the announcements, thank-yous, and exhortations of school spirit answered in kind by the North Runnymede students.

On the dais, which was maybe four feet off the ground, Juts began, "Hey diddle, diddle—"

The rest chimed in. With each mention of a character in the rhyme, Dick, Richard, or Ev behind their cutout figure, walked forward. Louis was up in the rafters.

"The little dog laughed to see such a sight. And the cow jumped over the moon."

The sheets dropped, which worked smoothly. Juts breathlessly waited for Richard and Dick on the opposite side of the room to work the pulleys.

Down came the moon. Then down came the cow and slid over the crescent moon as the gathered screamed, laughed, and stomped the floor.

The cow, a bovine smile on her face and sweet brown eyes, sported an enormous flesh-colored udder with the teats painted riotous red. Also painted in red, on her sides, in tidy lettering, was *Dimps Jr.*

Aghast, Dimps Jr. charged outside, bumping into people as her date blocked for her.

Celeste's hand—large, emerald-cut diamond gleaming—flew to her breast. "Oh, dear."

Fannie Jump used the mayhem to knock back a big swallow from the flask. "What?"

"I feel somewhat responsible."

"Celeste, how can you be responsible?" Fairy asked, shouting above the uproar.

"Dimps Jr. and Juts have been at one another's throats for some time and I, more or less, told Juts not to worry about it. Dimps is like a cow. I definitely said cow."

Thinking quickly, Mrs. Stiles hurried to the band and told them to play. She then made it over to Richard, thence to Dick.

On a signal from her, they pulled up the cow. Louis, still on the rafters, couldn't hear a thing, but he was smart enough to secure the cow. The moon he left hanging and then he backed down the ladder being held by Elizabeth. Mrs. Stiles held the other side of the ladder.

"Louis?" the teacher asked as his feet touched the floor.

"Yes, ma'am."

"Is who I think behind this Juts?"

Not one to rat, Louis said nothing, but he grimaced slightly. Elizabeth, impressed by this, pressed his hand.

"Oh, all right. I know it was Juts."

"Am I in trouble, Mrs. Stiles?"

"Let's not worry about that now." She paused. She really shouldn't have blurted it out, but she did. "A very well done cow. No one will ever forget this dance!"

They did not. Dimps Jr. found herself on the second floor of the school in the unlocked teacher's lounge being consoled in a new and exciting fashion.

Louise laughed until the tears came to her eyes. Paul, surprised, agreed the revenge was funny and clever.

Juts, surrounded by everyone who thought Dimps Jr. a pill, was riding high—even though she knew come Monday she'd be in hot water. Celeste, Fannie Jump, and Fairy, in tow, approached her.

Juts looked up at all five feet ten inches of Celeste. "Ma'am."

"Well?"

"She'll never make fun of me again," Juts defiantly said.

"Hell, Juts. Wish you'd been at school with us. We had a couple of dreary girls you could have taken care of," Fannie enthused.

"Fannie." Fairy's tone reprimanded her.

"I should have not called Dimps a cow," said Celeste. "I never thought you listened so closely."

"Miss Chalfonte, she is a cow. Even worse, she hurts people's feelings all the time. Don't hand it out if you can't take it." Juts stood her ground. "And the cow was my idea."

"What are you going to tell your mother?" Celeste asked.

"I don't know."

"You'd better think of something. If you don't tell her, Louise will," Celeste sensibly warned her.

The other two ladies nodded in agreement and then left. The dance, just beginning, promised a most exciting St. Patrick's celebration.

Coats on, the trio walked out to Fannie's 1917 Chevy V-8 Tourer. Fannie had been learning to drive simply to be competitive with Fairy. This ebullient lady, however, was in no condition to drive.

Celeste walked toward the driver's door. She could do it if she had to, but Fairy scooted in front of her.

"You'll be surprised."

Celeste then placed Fannie, not terribly drunk but not anyone you'd like behind the wheel, in the backseat and joined Fairy in front.

Fairy pulled out the choke a bit, then pressed the clutch, then the accelerator, listening for that engine purr.

She drove Celeste home first.

Fannie boomed, "Alcohol is the answer. I can't remember the question."

Ignoring her, Celeste complimented the dainty Fairy. "You're doing well."

"I love it. I love driving." She pulled in front of the house and said in parting, "I know young people are less restrained, but I do think Juts was unfair."

Celeste, sticking her head back in the car for a moment, replied, "Fairy, if Americans were motivated by fair play, the Indians would still own Manhattan."

Chapter Fifteen

. . . .

March 20, 1920
Saturday

Competing versions of Juts's cow jumping over the moon created some confusion for Cora. On the one hand, Juts and her friends had humiliated Dimps Jr. On the other hand, her younger daughter, weary of being picked on, had fought back. Louise, never one to withhold a criticism of her Lutheran sister, actually gave an evenhanded report, which impressed Cora. Celeste's report, interspersed with laughter, was also evenhanded.

Louise worked on Saturdays at the Bon Ton. Often Juts would walk Louise to the store, then go on to a friend's house, but this Saturday she stuck close to her mother, volunteering for odd jobs around the house.

Making small dumplings from scratch, Cora felt flour fly in her face. She put her finger under her nose to keep from sneezing.

Celeste walked into the kitchen. "You look like a Japanese geisha, your skin is so white."

Wiping her hands on a dish towel, Cora smiled. "Aren't those the ladies of the evening?"

"Not exactly but close enough. We don't have an equivalent. They must be well read, discreet, graceful, able to pour tea, perform dances, and recite poetry. Having never been entertained by one, I can only go by what Spotts told me."

Her late brother had traveled widely, thanks to his army rank. Young, handsome, intelligent, Spotts was being groomed by a few senior officers to rise. All felt he was born to be a liaison officer.

"Think of him every day." Cora returned to rolling the dough. "Think of my father, think of Aimes." She named her late boyfriend. "So many of the people I knew are gone."

"You didn't name Hansford." Celeste cited Cora's husband.

"Don't think of him. For one thing, I don't know if he's dead or alive. Some men aren't worth a second thought."

"Some women, too." Celeste perched on a kitchen stool, picked up a pastry wheel and cut out thin rectangular sheets 24 x 8 inches. "There. No one can say I lack in the domestic arts."

Cora shook her head. "Yes, madam."

Celeste smiled. "Where is Juts?"

"Last I saw her, she was polishing the stair rail." She checked the big striped bowl, into which she had put cooked beef, pork, veal, bacon, 4 eggs, 1/2 cup fresh chopped parsley, 1/4 cup cream, 1/2 teaspoon salt, 1/4 teaspoon white ground pepper, a pinch of ground nutmeg, and diced potatoes. "I guess Monday I'd better go down to South Runnymede before the principal."

"Yes. Yes, you should. You can be sure that Big Dimps will march in brimming with righteous wrath to defend her chick."

"Mmm."

Juts, rag over her shoulder, walked into the kitchen. "What next, Momma?"

"Take a feather duster and lightly dust the painting of Miss Chalfonte on the landing. Lightly."

"Okey-dokey."

"Juts." Celeste put down the dough cutter. "Ben Jonson thought every man had his element. Yours is hot water."

"Yes, Miss Chalfonte."

"And Juts, for what it's worth, she had it coming."

A big smile crossed Juts's face as her mother ordered her, "The painting."

Cora watched those young shoulders sweep back, the kitchen door was pushed open and Juts marched out vindicated. Vindicated or not, she dreaded Monday.

"Granted, the Rhodes girl baited Juts, but you know, Cora, both those Rhodes girls are pushed on by their mother. She made a bad marriage and she's determined they won't so she makes everyone miserable."

"Even black magic can't change a chicken." Cora began filling the dough rectangles then crimping the ends together so the dumplings would hold.

The front door opened. "It's just me!"

"Kitchen," Celeste called out.

Fannie Jump appeared, none the worse for last night's drinking. "The town is abuzz. Some people believe Juts hung a live cow over the moon. Others that Louis Negroponti worked mechanical marvels. And no one knows what became of Dimps Jr. except that she did go home. Don't you just love gossip?"

Both Celeste and Cora laughed, then all heard the front door open and close again.

"Twink, it's me."

"I wish you wouldn't call me that." Celeste shrugged as Fairy entered the kitchen.

Eyes wide, the proper lady breathed, "You won't believe what people are saying about the dance. I've even heard that Big Dimps will sue."

"If Big Dimps sues, it will be lawyers without briefs." Fannie roared with laughter.

Fairy couldn't help but laugh. "She doesn't have the money really."

"No, but she has what she's always had." Fannie Jump pulled up a stool.

Fairy followed suit. "Cora, even with your recipe, I can't get my cook to make dumplings like you do."

Cora inclined her head, with a small smile. "It's the cook's hand. Helps if your last name is Hunsenmeir."

Fairy smiled back. "True enough. Her last name is Garthwaite."

"But Cora, Hunsenmeir is your married name. You were a Buckingham," Fairy added.

"I'll always be a Buckingham, but Hansford's mother taught me how to make her family dishes. What a cook she was, and as wide as she was tall."

They laughed, remembering the big-hearted woman.

"Pity she couldn't raise a better son," Fannie remarked.

"Well, that can be said of many a woman, I suppose." Celeste inhaled the delicious aroma as Cora dropped the dumplings into the broth in which she had cooked the meats.

"Fifteen minutes," Cora, hands on hips, announced.

"You made this for us?" Fairy was surprised.

"Girls, after last night I knew you'd all be here by noon." Cora laughed and they laughed with her. "Fifteen minutes!" she hollered. "Juts!"

"Yes," came the reply from the majestic stairwell.

"Set the table for three."

The door swung open, and a silent Juts marched to the pantry to collect the plates.

The three friends watched her walk, then rose to gather in the dining room, a few decanters on the eighteenth-century sideboard.

Fannie picked up her favorite. "I heard liquor is already crossing Lake Michigan into Chicago. Also heard boats on the Chesapeake are offloading booze to boats coming down the Susquehanna, the Potomac, you name it. We ladies ought to consider investing in a new business."

In a tiny voice, Fairy, pouring an aged sherry, remarked, "Fannie, love, you'd drink up our profits."

"Not if you put them under lock and key," she swore.

Juts had set the table, so they moved from the sideboard to sit. Fannie asked, "How did your people know to buy this furniture when they did?"

"I don't know. I never asked." Celeste waited until all the food was on the table, the friends served, then she picked up her fork. "In the eighteenth century, this was modern. No one knew if it would last. Funny, isn't it?"

"Have you heard from Ramelle lately?" Fannie bit into a dumpling.

"Not for a few days. Neither rain nor sleet nor snow slows down the mail; it must be something else." Celeste sipped some broth, which couldn't have been better.

"The baby's due in May. Maybe she doesn't feel like writing. The closer I got to the due date, the more I just wanted to be rid of the little hitchhiker. It was awful."

Celeste and Fairy chimed in unison, "We know."

Fairy lowered her already quiet voice, as she didn't want Juts, wherever she was, to hear. "Do you think Big Dimps will really sue Juts?"

"How can she? Juts's a minor," Fannie Jump said.

Fairy pressed her line of thinking. "What if she sues Cora?"

"Then every mother in Runnymede would be sued at one time or another," Fannie sensibly replied. "Big Dimps will huff and puff. She'll bedevil Mr. Thigpen, she'll complain to Pastor Wade. Sooner or later, it will blow over. For one thing, the town hasn't had this much fun over something since before the war."

Paul waited for Louise to get off work and they hurried to the Capitol Theater. Buster Keaton enthralled them. After the movie, the evening air cool, the two listened as the nightbirds emerged on the square. A few bats darted here and there.

"I like bats," Louise announced. "And they don't get in your hair. That's silly."

"They eat bugs." Paul reached for her hand for the first time.

He grasped it firmly but not too firmly. She didn't pull away, so the two walked hand in hand along the square toward Cadwalder's.

"By summer, I hope I have enough for an old car. Then I can take you places. Here we always wind up at the drugstore or Dolley Madison."

Dolley Madison was a restaurant, part of which hung over a creek three blocks down Frederick Road.

"I like Cadwalder's. Best hamburgers ever." Louise told the truth but she was sensitive to his slender paycheck.

Once inside, they slipped into a booth.

Flavius came over. "Spring's here. I can smell it."

"You can." Louise agreed. "My usual."

"I know it well." Flavius looked at Paul. "Sir?"

"Hamburger and a milkshake, chocolate."

Louise leaned back in the booth. "You could eat five milkshakes a day, I don't think you'd put on an ounce."

The grin on his face faded as Lottie and Dimps Jr. barged up to the table. With them were their dates, Lionel Tangerman and Bill Whittier.

"If I'd known you were here, we wouldn't have come in," Lottie huffed.

Paul spoke to Lionel and Bill. "There's room for everybody."

Dimps Jr. was plastered to the handsome Bill. While seemingly not as taken with her as she was with him, he didn't appear to mind. Lionel, the twenty-two-year-old son of the police chief of North Runnymede, had seen Paul around town but didn't know him.

Lottie put her arm around Dimps Jr.'s waist. "Your brat sister humiliated my sister, who, you should know, sold more tickets to the dance than anyone has ever sold before."

"Selling tickets is very important." Louise had no idea what to say and didn't want to lose her temper.

"And furthermore, I don't appreciate your behavior in the Capitol Theater," said Lottie, pointing her finger at Paul. "You were always trying to touch me."

Paul did not raise his voice. "I was not."

Lionel loomed over him. "You calling Lottie a liar?"

Paul stood up. "Would you like to step outside? You've insulted Wheezie and you've accused me of whatever you're accusing me of."

Flavius hurried up. "If you two fight, I will call John Gassner. Lionel, your father may be police chief of North Runnymede, but you're in South Runnymede now. If you can't be civil, get out."

Lionel knew his father would pitch a fit. Lottie, on the other hand, still hoped for a scene.

"Who cares?" Lottie tossed her head back.

"This wouldn't be good for my father." Lionel knew that.

"You care more about your father than me!" Lottie shouted.

Lionel didn't reply. Paul stepped back one step, as did Lionel. Bill Whittier had other things on his mind than a fight. He took Dimps Jr. by the elbow to usher her out.

"What are you doing?" Dimps Jr. protested.

Bill brooked no interference. "You don't need another mess."

Lottie turned on her sister. "Well, I'm standing up for you."

"Lottie, Bill's right." Dimps Jr. had some sense. "Come on."

Livid, Lottie again pointed her finger at Louise. "I will get even with you and with Juts." She turned to Paul. "You aren't worth getting even with. I just went out with you because I felt sorry for you. You didn't know anybody."

She slammed the door on the way out. Paul sat down.

Louise took a big sip of her Co-Cola, the correct southern term for Coca-Cola. "Pearlie, I have to ask you, what did you see in her?"

He threw up his hands. "I sure didn't see this side of her."

"But you liked her?"

"I did. I mean, not so much that I wanted to be around her all the time. Going out once a week was fine and I did meet people. It's funny, Wheezie, but she would agree with whatever I said and I started thinking that I didn't know what she thought."

"Now you do." Louise played with her straw. "You kissed her."

"Wheezie, I did. I'm twenty-four. Would you want to keep company with a man who'd never kissed a woman? Sometimes in the war, I thought I'd never see a woman, much less kiss one."

She considered this. "You held my hand."

"I did and I want to do it again."

"You haven't kissed me." She pouted.

"You're right." Paul got up, sat next to her in the booth, and gave her a convincing kiss. Then he returned to his seat.

Startled, Louise's lower lip jutted out slightly. She touched it to see if her light lipstick had smeared.

"I can kiss you more. I'd like that." He smiled. "Here's the thing, Louise. I like you. I've never been out with anyone that I could talk to like you. We can disagree, we can agree, you listen and you work hard, too. You're not some"—he paused—"I don't know the word. You're important."

Louise realized she'd been holding her breath. She inhaled deeply. "You can kiss me anytime you want."

They reached across the table to touch hands as they laughed.

Chapter Sixteen

••••

March 22, 1920
Monday

M r. Thigpen looked like an anteater as he peeped over his spectacles. "Have you anything to say for yourself?"

"No, sir," Juts answered the principal.

"Were you the organizer of the cow jumping over the moon?"

"Yes, sir."

Pushing his spectacles back up on the bridge of his nose, the principal looked to Cora. "We've known one another a long time. I assume you didn't know, uh, the condition of the cow."

Cora folded her hands on her lap. "I didn't."

"I see." He sighed. "You can imagine what I had to deal with and whom?"

"I know Big Dimps is ass over tits."

"I wouldn't put it that way, Cora. But, yes, she has been exercising her considerable emotions." He rubbed his forehead for a moment, then leaned toward Juts on the other side of his huge desk. "Juts, I have seen the decorations, the fork and the spoon, the cat and the fiddle, the little dog. Almost professional. I don't think any dance has ever had such scenery. Even the cow was charming, except for the obvious." He stopped, picked up a pencil just to have something in his hand. "Are you sure you have nothing to say for yourself?"

"No, Mr. Thigpen, I don't. I'm here to accept my punishment."

"All right, then, but I want you to know that Delilah Jr. has also been punished." He raised his voice. "You've got to learn to walk away from provocation, and Juts, you've got to learn to consider the source."

"Yes, sir."

"Now, here is what I'm going to do. I am not going to suspend you. You need to keep at your studies. Your math grades are excellent, your art class also. English and history, woeful, just woeful. Do you have anything to say about that?"

"Well." She sat up straight. "Why should I care about a colon? Or a semicolon? Just a bunch of dumb rules. I want to get things done. I want to make things. And I'm tired of hearing about the dates of wars—" She abruptly shut up as her mother reached out and quietly touched her hand.

"I see." Mr. Thigpen took a deep breath. "You are a strong-minded young lady. I won't belabor this, but all the subjects you take at South Runnymede High are to provide a foundation for the rest of your life. If you don't get it now, Juts, you never will. You don't have to like English or history, but you do need to know it. Those who do not know the past are doomed to repeat it." He gave her a sharp look. "We've gone through the worst war the world has ever known. One of the ways to ensure this never happens again is to learn, to head off problems before they enlarge. No, you don't want to be a diplomat. But Juts, you will become a citizen. It's important to know these things."

"Yes, sir." She had listened carefully. "No more war. But the kings and leaders who started that war, weren't they well educated?"

This startled the middle-aged man. He'd only known Juts as a pretty youngster dashing through the halls, a very good math student. He'd never given her or most of the students much respect when it came to the deeper questions. He'd been bogged down by administration. He was missing a lot and he now knew it.

"They were." He held up his forefinger. "Which is what makes it all the more terrible, but I hasten to add, Juts, the men who started and fed the flames of the Great War were not Americans. We tried to stay out of it."

Cora uttered one word. "*Lusitania.*"

He nodded. "An act of filthy barbarism." He looked at the unlined face before him. "Juts, please raise your grades in your weak subjects. You aren't going to be allowed to be part of the many groups you belong to. You go to school and you go home. And this correction will last until you begin eleventh grade. Furthermore, keep away from Delilah Jr. She's enduring the same punishment you are and I hope you both learn from it, but I warn you, Juts, if she tries to provoke you, walk away."

Cora, too, had listened carefully, so she said to her daughter, "Did you hear Mr. Thigpen? And you'd better hear me, keep your nose clean."

Looking at Cora, the principal said, "I've rearranged some classes so the girls won't be together. There are a few classes where if I separate them they will need to repeat the class next year, so I didn't separate them. There's nothing I can do about the halls, the stairways, the walking to and from school, chance encounters."

On the trolley back to Bumblebee Hill, neither mother nor daughter spoke. Celeste had given Cora the day off to see if she could straighten out the mess. The two didn't want anyone else on the trolley to hear the discussion, but as they walked up the hill at the end of the trolley line, the words flew.

"Momma, I'm quitting school."

"No, you are not."

"I hate school."

"How can you hate school when you are one of the most popular girls there? This is a fine mess and mind you, I do think you were provoked. You went too far. And that's that."

"Maybe so, but I want to quit school. I want to get a job and make some money."

"You can do that after you graduate."

"Two more years!"

"You'll be surprised at how fast two years can fly by."

"Oh, Momma, that's forever." They reached the front porch, General Pershing asleep by the door, his thick coat keeping him comfortable.

"Woof." The English setter awakened, startled to see Cora and Juts so early in the afternoon.

Cora petted him, swung open the door. "Juts, start the fire. Take the chill off. It will be cold again tonight."

"Yes, ma'am." She did as she was told but when finished, she walked outside, where Cora was inspecting her garden on the south side of the house. "Momma."

"Now what?"

"What if I stay till the end of the year and then quit?"

"No. What if you stay to graduation. Two years. This will all blow over."

"That doesn't mean I'll want to waste my time in school come fall."

"Let's wait until fall. We can talk about it then. In the meantime, do your best."

Having finished her daily ride, Celeste dismounted and untacked her Thoroughbred. Her groom, Henry Minton, stood by, ready to perform this service, but she liked contact with her gelding.

"Miss Chalfonte, let me take that." The groom lifted the saddle from her forearm.

"Thank you, Henry."

Henry, a man of color, had been a fabulous rider in his youth. Falls, injuries took a toll on him. He could still ride, and ride well, but he walked with a limp and he woke up each day with pain. Some walking about took care of that.

Celeste, essentially an open-minded person, was nonetheless a creature of her time and her class. She knew that most of the great grooms and jockeys were black men. Her view of the world was, if you had talent you would come forward. She thought of Booker T. Washington. She felt the same way about factory workers, midwives, people who so often lived hand to mouth. She knew people could be crushed by large forces, by injustice and even bad luck, but she thought little about it. If someone needed her help, she gave it. She thought in terms of the individual, not the group.

"How was your ride?" asked Henry.

"Good. I love that we now gain a minute of daylight for each day until June twenty-first. The nights creep in cold but the sun dispels much of it. Winter is on the run."

"Yes, ma'am."

"Henry, ride with me tomorrow, will you? I'd like to pop some hedges and I promised Ramelle I wouldn't jump alone. She was never nervous before."

Grinning, he now took the bridle while Celeste pulled the good leather halter over Roland's ears. "When my Lily was carrying Tim, she saw a ghost every twilight. That woman was afraid of everything. Something must happen inside. And then when he was born, she worried that a tiny little cough was consumption."

"Yes, I do remember. Both Lily and Tim appear to have flourished." She heard a barn swallow swoop overhead. "They're back."

"Building nests," Henry remarked.

"Tomorrow, let's go about eleven. Dew should be off by then, or the frost. Might freeze tonight."

"Once the sun goes down, my bones will tell me."

"Henry, you're more reliable than the thermometer." She walked outside the stable built to match the house.

When her grandfather built the house, it was at the edge of South Runnymede, surrounded by farms. He bought a few hundred acres but, not being a farmer, kept them as pasture. Others did the same, but everyone had a stable by their house as well as a carriage house. The cobblestone alleyways between the large homes reverberated with horses' hooves. They still did, as few owned automobiles. Those who did often left rubber tire marks on the cobblestones when things went amiss.

Celeste's father and mother enlarged the house and her mother designed the luxurious gardens based on the great English gardens of her youth.

Celeste could mount up, ride south or west, and once at the end of the alleyway, be in open country. She could ride through North Runnymede country, too, but the farms and cottages sat on smaller pieces of land, plus there were more factories on the Pennsylvania side, not so many as to be troublesome but enough that she wanted to circumvent them.

Walking back toward the house, she thought the sky startlingly blue. She'd seen much of the world and much of her own country. Memories of Vienna at night, the Opera House shining, beckoning, of walking into the British Library, or looking toward Constantinople from the Asia side, sailing to England and seeing the White Cliffs of Dover, hiking the Lake District while reading those poets. There was so much beauty on this earth, but her heart always turned toward Maryland. This patch of the Mid-Atlantic was hers. She was born here, nourished here, and she would die here.

She thought when Ramelle left for Los Angeles that she would ache for her as she ached for Maryland when traveling too long. She missed Ramelle, but surprisingly, the advent of spring, a bracing canter, laughter with her friends swept the ache away. Then again, Celeste thought she wasn't prone to heartache. Carlotta had hit a nerve, but still, that wasn't heartache. She would be glad to see Ramelle and the baby when they came home for their six months on the East Coast, assuming the child was healthy. With each passing day, she missed Ramelle less. She loved her. She wanted her happy. If there was more to it, she was unaware of it.

No sooner did she walk through the door than the phone rang.

"Celeste here."

"Fannie."

"What? You rarely call, so it must be good."

"I took two rooms at the Belvedere Hotel. We can go down on Saturday, take the early train to Baltimore. Practice game, weather permitting. I'll bring a blanket just in case. I do so love to watch the boys before the season begins. I'll introduce you at the hotel get-together after practice. I know most everyone." She stopped. "You don't want to stay with Stirling, do you?"

"No. Margaret would put a good face on it but no one would be happy. I'd rather stay with Olivia Goldoni."

"I'm sure you would."

"Fannie, it's not like that. She's sophisticated, talented, and I hope to hear her in performance."

"Oh." Fannie sounded disappointed.

"Oh, what?"

"Nothing. I'm in the mood for a scandal. Except for Juts's cow, winter has been dull."

"I'm sure you can correct that, dear," Celeste purred.

Chapter Seventeen

····

March 26, 1920
Friday

A flash of yellow caught Celeste's eye as the train pulled through Carroll County toward Baltimore. She smiled, chin on her hand, watching out the window. "Next come the redbud."

"My forsythias are open but not quite full." Fannie leaned over Celeste to look. "The closer we get to Baltimore, the further along the spring."

"Long past in Charleston." Celeste mentioned the most beautiful city along the Atlantic seaboard. "I love to watch the land change. Heading east, the roll becomes gentler, then nearly flat. If we instead cross the Potomac, head west, the Blue Ridge Mountains greet us. I never tire of looking at our country."

"Are you going to take the train out to California?"

"Not this year. Let Ramelle and Curtis settle in. You know, Fannie, you disembark in Los Angeles and you can smell oranges, especially in spring. The orange blossoms explode. Curtis swears the groves along the trolley line will eventually give way to homes but I rather hope not."

"It's the automobile. The trolley lines are one thing. Look what's happening to Philadelphia."

"True." She lifted her chin from her hand to face Fannie. "What our grandparents said begins to make sense, doesn't it? How the changes upset them. I suppose every generation looks back and believes all was better when they were young."

"We aren't that old. We're forty-three," Fannie quickly replied. "I don't mind getting old. I just don't want to look old."

They both laughed.

"But I thought you'd solved this problem. You're only as old as who you are sleeping with."

Fannie slapped Celeste's left hand with her right one. "Don't be beastly."

"Simply observant."

"Well, then, have you observed the nest of mice living merrily behind the tapestry of the Ascension?"

St. Paul's Episcopal sheltered not only mice but sparrows in the drain gutters, as well as bats in the belfry, literally.

"Time we confirm some cats," Celeste suggested. "Saint Hubert would bless us."

"I thought Saint Hubert was the patron saint of hounds and hunting?" Fannie replied.

"I'm sure in his goodness he can extend his blessings. How did you find out about the mice?"

"Juts." Fannie folded her arms across her ample bosom for a moment. "She prowls around. The Lutheran youth group can hold her attention only so long, so when they visited our youth group, she went off on her own. I became curious and had to inspect the tapestry and you know, I could hear them."

"Reciting the liturgy, no doubt."

"You are sacrilegious. A lightning bolt might hit me sitting next to you." Fannie grinned. "You know, your sister is telling everyone what you gave to the academy. She believes you are halfway to converting."

"I am not. And I gave the money because she brought up a very good point and one I had never considered. She set aside moral uplift to focus on politics. She says we will lose the vote. Another generation must be trained to fight for it. Carlotta said women must be trained to participate in government when the time comes that we can. She says it better than I do but she was rather passionate about future generations."

"One hundred thousand dollars plus one hundred is a lot of passion. Why the hundred dollars?"

"For Betty Ermdorf, a working student."

"Ah. Do you think I should give money to Smith? I suppose we all should, given what women are facing."

"I think you should do whatever you think right."

"I hate it when you force me to do the right thing."

"Fannie, you came up with it."

"I know, but that doesn't mean you couldn't have shown me a way out of it. I mean, you had to give to your sister, really. She'd bedevil you endlessly. If I give, it will be out of the goodness of my heart, and I'd rather go to Nova Scotia." She paused. "For the summer. I've never been and it's supposed to be beautiful."

They chattered, teased, laughed until the train pulled into the Baltimore station with that distinctive thud. Both women carried light valises and Fannie waved to a man in a chauffeur's uniform.

"Come on."

Celeste fell in behind her friend, stepped into the car, and in a few blocks they stepped out at the imposing hotel.

The two checked in to their separate rooms, meeting downstairs half an hour later.

"Fannie, you can't pay for all this. I'm giving you half."

She waved this off. "It's a tiny payment for all your liquor I've imbibed. If you feel like walking, the distance to the diamond is a bracing walk. We can catch a ride back."

"Love to. I can only sit so long."

Twenty minutes later they sat behind first base. Built in 1914 for the Baltimore Terrapins, the stadium had been bought in 1916 for the minor league Orioles. It filled up. Many wanted to see the practice game. The season was a ways off, but fans wanted an early look, for the sportswriters were predicting a banner year.

The temperature climbing into the low sixties, the sky filled with a few fleecy clouds, promised a comfortable afternoon. It was warmer in Baltimore than in Runnymede.

"I've been trying to get you down here for years." Fannie nestled in her seat.

"I go to the high school games." Celeste smiled. "But Ramelle isn't much for professional sports. I gave up on that years ago. It even takes effort to get her to the Maryland Hunt Cup." Celeste cited the most famous amateur steeplechase in America.

A roar filled the stadium and out trotted the boys. They were all Orioles but playing against one another. Fannie explained who was who. The coaches would study each position.

"A few fellows are getting a step slow," Fannie added.

"But if a player is good at bat, isn't that when you move him to first base?" Celeste knew a bit about baseball, as two of her brothers had played, Stirling at Yale, Spotts at West Point.

"Usually."

"What do you think is the toughest position?"

"Umm." Fannie pondered. "Well, the catcher has to be the smartest, really, has to remember all the batters from the various teams, and Celeste, what thighs, what divine thighs. The shortstop needs to be the quickest, maybe the best athlete, and he has to think fast, too. Then again, if you think about it, sometimes the second baseman is almost like a shortstop between first and second. Baseball is complicated. I don't think a man can be stupid and be a good baseball player."

"True." Celeste nodded. "I always thought the biggest sports test, though, is boxing. A man has to be strong, be able to change his plan if it isn't working, all the while he's taking so much punishment. I don't know, it all hangs on his shoulders."

"Does. Same with tennis and golf. You can't blame anybody but yourself. However, I like team sports."

"You were good at them," Celeste complimented her.

Fannie shrugged. "We did have fun, didn't we? Ah, here we go."

"Do you know all these players?"

"In what manner?" Fannie raised an eyebrow, which made Celeste laugh.

"I meant in a conversational manner."

"I do, and that's why we will meet the owner and the boys at a small gathering early this evening. It's a small ritual for the die-hard fans and most especially for the advertisers." She pointed to the billboard for Old Line Manufacturing, one of the Chalfonte companies. "Stirling is shrewd."

Maryland is called the Old Line State.

"I hadn't even noticed." Celeste was surprised. "But yes, he is shrewd. Farsighted."

The game began with the first batter out, the number two batter hitting a blazing single through the second baseman that rolled half-way out into right field. The run was stopped at first, though, thanks to a hard run and pinpoint pitch by the right fielder.

By the time the game reached the fourth inning, the crowd realized that practice game though it might be, it was riveting.

The shortstop, leaping off the ground, almost parallel to it, caught a ferocious drive, landed on both feet, and twirled with balletic grace to toss the ball underhanded to the third baseman. The runner from second skidded to a stop, dirt flying up in the air, turned to run back to second, and the game of cat-and-mouse began. The shortstop stepped close in on the runner, who was clever. The third baseman taking a catch faked a throw to the second baseman but instead pitched it to the shortstop, who caught it and with one swoop tagged the runner out.

The stands erupted.

On her feet with everyone else, Fannie cheered.

Sitting back down, she informed Celeste, "His second year. He's got everything. So does the center fielder. An incredible arm and, of course, he's the number four batter. I think we're going to have a good year."

Afterward, the two took a taxi back to the Belvedere and relived the game, renewed. Just getting out of their routine had rejuvenated the ladies.

"How long before the party?" Celeste asked.

"Six o'clock. An hour."

Players, the coach, the owner, some advertisers, a reporter from the *Baltimore Sun*, and plenty of other people were jammed into the large elegant room, a bar at one end.

Fannie, who knew most everyone, introduced Celeste. After all these years, Fannie was accustomed to men's reactions to Celeste. Celeste appeared never to notice.

They walked up to a group of three men, the center fielder, back to them, was speaking to the shortstop and the left fielder. At first the men didn't notice the ladies.

"Back when men were men—" The center fielder, Frank Lombard, didn't finish.

Shortstop Ben Battle quipped, "and the sheep were scared shitless." He just noticed Fannie and Celeste out of the corner of his eye, too late. "Beg your pardon."

Fannie laughed. "Probably the truth."

"Frank, Ben, Gene, this is my best friend, Celeste Chalfonte. It's her first Orioles game."

Gene Ischatta, a star, stared at the tall beauty, bowed low and declared, "I throw myself at your feet."

Celeste coolly appraised him. "Higher."

Gene took a step back, swallowed hard. He knew he was out of his depth.

Frank said, "I hope you'll come to our games. We aren't all like Gene."

"That's reassuring." Celeste smiled.

Ben remained quiet. Fannie pushed Celeste along until she'd met everyone there.

"I'm leaving you to your own devices. I need a word with Tony." Then she whispered, "Big team star, Gene thinks he can get in any woman's pants. You took care of him."

Tony Kursinksi, a favorite of Fannie's, was from York, Pennsylvania, almost a local.

Celeste glanced around for a second then heard a deep voice behind her. "Miss." She turned to face Ben Battle. "I do apologize for the rough talk."

Ben Battle, at six feet, stood two inches taller than Celeste.

She stared into his deep brown eyes, set in one of the most beautiful faces she'd ever seen. "You were very funny."

"Do you know baseball?"

"Not pro ball, Mr. Battle, but my brothers played, one at Yale, and the brother we lost in the war played at West Point."

Ben reached out to touch her, then withdrew his hand, for a lady must offer her hand, never the reverse. "I'm sorry for your loss. I lost a brother, too."

She reached for his hand, holding it for a moment. "Life changes in an instant, does it not?"

"It does. I was over there. Because I'm speedy, I was a messenger. I never thought I'd see home again, much less play ball."

"Mr. Battle."

"Ben, please call me Ben."

"Then you must call me Celeste. Do you mind if we sit over there? Fannie has trotted me through Baltimore. We walked to the stadium. A good day for walking."

"Mrs. Creighton's a regular at the home games. She's faithful. Well, you being her best friend would know." He smiled, a kind smile. His teeth were white and even.

"You don't smoke." Celeste noticed.

"No."

"Your teeth are so white."

He laughed. "I don't smoke. I don't chew, and my mother made me brush with baking soda. Your teeth are white, too."

"I don't smoke either. Do you ride?"

"I used to ride the plow horses when I was a kid. Gentle beasts." He smiled, held his arms out. "My feet stuck out like this."

"Mine, too, when I was little."

Celeste set aside conventional chat, leaned toward him. "Do you think animals have souls?"

"I do." His voice dropped. "One of the worst things about the war was the horses, the supply trains, the horses being killed. At least we men knew what we were doing. It haunts me."

She reached for his hand again. "I didn't mean to bring up sorrows."

He held her hand, not wanting to release it. "My mother told me, and I didn't know what she meant, but I do now, 'You don't grow up until you learn to thank God for your sorrows as well as your joys.'"

She squeezed his hand before letting it go. "You have a wise mother."

"Yours?"

"Gone. She was wise, but she expected more of me than I could deliver. I was, it seems, a horse of a different color, to return to horses for a moment."

"I can't imagine you disappointing your mother."

"Well . . ." She thought a moment. "I don't know why I'm telling you this, but when I was at that perfect age for the marriage market, I was sent to England. Mother hoped I would become a duchess or at least the wife of an earl. Ben, it was suffocating! I couldn't possibly." She laughed a silver laugh. "And so here I am with you watching my first pro game."

"Practice."

"Yes. You are speedy and graceful. And I assume you like what you do."

"Ah"—he folded his hands together—"now I don't know why I'm telling you this. Yes, I love it. I love the excitement, pitting myself against rivals, but someday I would like to . . ." He paused. "I would like to make stained-glass windows. I saw windows so impressive in France. Yes, we have beautiful things here, but there, windows from the twelfth century, from the fifteenth—such beauty. I would like to create beauty." His face flushed. "Ah, I don't know where I get these ideas."

"Good ones. And really, Ben, there was no baseball in the twelfth century. Had you lived then I'm sure you would have been working on cathedrals." She then asked, "Did you study art in school?"

"I finished high school. I'm not very well educated. Not like you. I can tell you are. I read a lot. I look at buildings. I especially like churches, but pretty much, I'm ignorant."

"Far, far from it."

They talked. One by one, people left.

Fannie came over. "Celeste, shall I see you in the morning? Train leaves at nine. We can take a later one."

"No, nine is fine. I told Henry I'd ride at two, back out on the old steeplechase course."

Ben's face registered disappointment. "I hope I will see you again, Mrs. Creighton."

"You know you will."

As Fannie left with Tony, Ben's face still registered disappointment. "You must look beautiful on a horse," he remarked shyly. "You look beautiful now."

"You're kind. I try to ride every day, and my groom, once one of the best riders in the Mid-Atlantic, often goes out with me. Old though he may be, I have to work sometimes to keep up with him."

Relief spread over Ben's handsome face as he figured out Henry was her groom, not her beau. They talked and talked.

Celeste finally heard the grandfather clock in the front hall chime two. She looked at her wristwatch. "I am so sorry. I lost track of time and you were too much of a gentleman to leave me here. But Ben, I don't know when I've talked so much or enjoyed myself so much."

"Me, too." He stood up and held out his hand for her to hold as she got up.

She walked to the front desk, asked for paper and a pen. She wrote down her address, the name of the train from Baltimore to South Runnymede, and her phone number.

Handing it to him, she smiled. "It's about an hour on the milk train if all goes well. Please come visit. You can stand with a foot in each state. Runnymede is smack on the Mason-Dixon Line. It's actually quite beautiful. You like churches. We have grand ones, and I can show you something no one else can. I can show you mice living at St. Paul's Episcopal church behind a tapestry of the Ascension."

He laughed, looked down at the fine handwriting. "I would like that."

"And within two weeks, South Runnymede High School will play baseball against North Runnymede High School. They do everything but take the field with rifles. You'll be amazed at what's in this little town."

"I know. You're in it."

Impulsively she took both his hands in hers, drew him close, and kissed him lightly on the lips. She was too shocked to apologize or explain.

"Celeste, I will be there if I have to walk."

As Celeste walked to her room, she heard the roulette wheel of love spin.

Chapter Eighteen

• • • •

March 30, 1920
Tuesday

Red buds on trees threatened to open to spring green at any moment. A warm wind from the west enlivened birds flying from swaying branch to swaying branch.

Juts and Ev walked through the square.

"Want to go to Cadwalder's?" Ev asked.

"No. Dimps Jr. will be there. If she even opens her mouth, I'll shove her teeth down her throat. I promised Momma I'd stay out of trouble."

"You have," Ev noted.

"Momma says I have to finish this year. I'm going to quit then."

Ev motioned for her friend to sit on a park bench with her, the one near the Confederate statue.

"If I go home, Mother will first ask me do I have any homework. Then do it. If I do it, she'll give me chores. You want to quit school. I want to run away from home."

"Ah, Ev, you don't mean that."

"Maybe not, but I sure get tired of being told what to do."

"Me, too. It's not Momma so much as Mr. Thigpen. Wheezie can get on her high horse too, but she's left me alone. All she thinks about is Pearlie. She's taken my side against Dimps. We both have to deal with Rhodes messes. Wheezie can be a good egg when she wants to be."

Ev watched a cardinal perched on a branch, announcing his presence to the world. "Mother says if we all just wait, they'll get their comeuppance."

"How long do we have to wait?" Juts tidied her books on the bench.

"I don't know. But Mother says, 'Leave them to God.'" Ev watched people walking around and through the square.

"I wish God would hurry up, but I suppose He has more important things to take care of than this." Juts swung her legs. "You don't really want to run away from home. Not really?"

"No. Do you really want to quit school?"

"I do. What do we do, Ev? Sit, sit, and more sit. This week we're reading *Julius Caesar*. He's been dead since 44 BC. Why should I read about him? Why can't we learn something we can use right now?"

"I don't know. All this stuff is supposed to help us later in life. That's what Mother says, but I don't see where it's helped her any, and she's old." Mrs. Most was forty-eight.

"Yeah. If I leave school after June, I can get a job. I can learn practical things. Make money. Momma needs things and I'd like to buy stuff, too."

"Mother says Celeste is good to your mother."

"She is. She sent Louise to the academy, remember. I kinda wish she hadn't."

"It did give Wheezie polish."

"Polish?" Juts nearly shouted.

"It did, Juts. She learned, as Mother would say, 'deportment,' and look how good she's doing at the Bon Ton. She even got Celeste to shop there."

Juts crossed her arms over her chest, which was growing, thank God. "Yeah, I guess, but Ev, we aren't learning deportment at South Runnymede High School. We're learning about Julius Caesar."

Lowering her voice even though they were in the middle of the Square, Ev murmured, "Shh."

Juts's eyes followed in the direction of Ev's gaze. Dimps Jr. walked with Bill Whittier, who carried her books.

"He must have run all the way from North Runnymede to be there when she got out of class." Juts, voice also low, noticed, "He's sticking to her like a tick."

"Daddy says he'll be an even bigger football star next year, his senior year. Daddy says he's good enough to play in college," Ev reported. "Why go to college unless you're going to be a doctor or something like that? No college for me. I'll finish high school and you will, too. Juts, you can't pick up and leave. You can't leave me there. We have to go through it together. We're the Class of 1922. Twenty-two sounds good."

Juts soaked this up. "Does, kinda."

"You can't leave me. You're my best friend. By the time we graduate, we'll be remembered. The cow is just the beginning." Ev laughed. "Dimps better stay on the north side of the square. Next time it will be more than a cow."

"Cadwalder's. That's where they'll end up." Juts turned to Ev. "You are my best friend."

"Then don't quit."

"I don't know."

"Kids after us will remember us, Ev and Juts, Juts and Ev. And don't forget, we're the ones who have to organize the reunion, especially for the war vets. You said you'd do it."

"We should do it on Magna Carta Day, 'cause everyone's in town that day anyway."

"True." Ev smiled. "Song and dance."

"Shoes and socks."

"Stars and Stripes." Ev started the togetherness game.

"Piss and vinegar." Juts grimaced.

"Hamburgers and fries."

"Ha. Hot dogs and mustard."

"Too easy, Juts. Pen and paper."

"Mary and Joseph."

"Not fair, can't use religious names."

"Why not?"

"Because I said so," Ev crowed.

"Beer and pretzels."

"High and mighty," Ev fired back.

"Doesn't count. High and mighty aren't things. Got to be things."

"No, it doesn't. It just has to be two things linked."

Juts thought then grinned. "Juts and Ev."

"Ev and Juts." Ev laughed.

They rose, picked up their books, skipped toward Emmitsburg Pike. A big Van Dusen truck stopped where Hanover Street reached the square then turned left toward Baltimore Street. Turning in the opposite direction was another square delivery truck, *Rife Munitions* painted on the side.

"Yashew Gregorivitch must be making good money," Juts remarked.

"Hard worker. His sister works at Immaculata and gets her schooling. She works hard too. They have to care for their mother. Hey, there they go."

Dimps Jr. and Bill reached Cadwalder's drugstore.

"Bet Dick and Rick and everyone are in there." Juts longingly stared at the drugstore.

"Come on, let's keep walking."

"Yeah." Juts trudged along. "I don't care. I kind of miss our clubs, but"—she shrugged—"nothing I can do about it. At least Bazooms"—Juts called Dimps Jr. this for the first time—"can't go either."

"If you can't go, I'm not going and I haven't."

"I don't mind. Go if you want."

"Nah." Ev shook her head. "It's no fun without you."

Juts left Ev at her house. She waved to Mrs. Most, outside inspecting her garden, willing her flowers to come up.

Opening the door to the kitchen at Celeste's, she heard her mother in the pantry as well as laughter in the library.

Cora, on a stool, placed dishes on an upper shelf. The pantry cabinets had paned window doors so you could see what was where.

"I'll hand them up to you." Juts put down her books and began handing up dishes. "Sounds like Celeste is having a good time."

"Fairy Thatcher and Fannie Jump Creighton. They all went out for a ride, came back, and took off their boots. Now they're sitting in there in their socks."

"Fannie and Fairy come by a lot now, don't they?"

"They're best friends, old friends, and they want to cheer up Celeste." Cora dropped her right arm, palm upward. "Ready for another one."

"Okey-dokey. Momma, Celeste doesn't need cheering up."

"A little bit. Not so much as before. Celeste isn't one to show emotions. She missed Ramelle, but things are better."

"Why do people," the fifteen-year-old mused, "want someone else around?"

"Didn't all the animals go onto the Ark two by two?"

"I guess, but that doesn't mean we have to do it."

"Now, where do you get these ideas? People just naturally fall into twos. We dance together, we like to walk together, we like someone to talk to, and—"

"But that doesn't mean everyone wants to go two by two. Maybe Celeste does, and Ev and I saw Bill Whittier walking Dimps Jr. along the square. She liked being together. I don't think I want to do it."

Stepping down, Cora brushed her hands on her apron. "Juts, you've never lived by yourself. You'd die of lonesomeness."

"Less chores." She smiled sideways.

"Less laughter." Cora came right back at her. "Listen to them in there."

The laughter rolled out into the hall. The three, boots aligned in the front hall so they wouldn't track the mud, were splayed out, Celeste on the sofa, the others in chairs, drinks in hand, told stories about their old classmates, about one another, mournfully agreed that the Nine-teenth Amendment probably would not be ratified, thought about the year's presidential election, in which they would not be able to vote, made predictions about horse races, baseball, anything that came to mind.

"Fairy, our Celeste made a conquest."

"Doesn't she always?" Fairy remained unimpressed.

"When I left the party, she was sitting down with the shortstop. When I walked by, she was still there and finally I repaired to my room. I have no idea when they bid adieu and I wouldn't have had any idea if I hadn't asked her on the train ride home. She says they parted and I actually believe her. If he'd had noticeable bosoms maybe they wouldn't have parted."

Celeste coolly responded, "We talked about many things. And Fan-nie, I don't care about breasts. What I care about is brains."

Fairy frowned just a bit. "With a baseball player? What could you possibly talk about? Of course, there's intelligence there but, I mean, wasn't it socially awkward?"

"What exactly do you mean?" Fannie leveled her gaze at Fairy, nar-rowing her eyes. After all, Tony fit into that social category.

"Such a different class," Fairy replied.

"Will you throw out Marx?" Celeste ordered. "You've been impos-sible since you started reading *Das Kapital*. Really, Fairy, it's all bunk."

"There truly are classes." Fairy defended her reading and Marx.

"Of course, but why dwell on it?" Fannie boomed, rising to pour another drink. "This is America. You can better your situation. If the Europeans want to stay in their classes, fine. They're welcome to them."

"But the upper classes repress the lower." Fairy was having none of it.

"Given the horrors in Russia, we know the lower classes can fight back. Brutally. Is there an answer? Is there equality ever?" Celeste flatly asked.

"Never," Fannie answered with conviction.

"It's possible but it takes revolution," Fairy said. "It takes a compre-hensive ideology and people with the will to enact it."

"Darling, those about to be chained often think they are being freed." Celeste swung her legs under her and sat upright on the couch.

"Let's change the subject. We're on the cusp of spring. We need to celebrate. Before Christianity, there were fertility rituals, planting festivals. Something. It's been a long, hard winter."

"Exactly what fertility ritual do you have in mind?" Celeste teased. "And don't count winter out yet."

"I don't know. In the Dark Ages in England, didn't they put antlers on the young king? He could mate with whomever."

Fairy, no longer defending Marx, lightened up. "I can't imagine putting antlers on anyone in Runnymede."

"You've got me there," Fannie agreed.

Juts stuck her head in the room. "Momma wants to know if you all need anything."

"A good idea," Fannie responded. "We need to celebrate spring."

"Yes, Mrs. Creighton."

"Give us some time on this, but girls, I do think a garden party is just the thing," Fannie spoke as Juts returned to the kitchen. "That's easy." Fannie knocked back her drink. "The fountain will spout champagne in the middle of the square."

"Fannie, the cost," Fairy sputtered.

"Who gives a damn? We'll all be dead someday. For God's sake, how many of us are gone now? I say we throw one hell of a party with a champagne fountain, I say we live for all the boys who didn't come home and for everyone we love who's left us. I'll even toast Brutus Rife, the dead, miserable wretch." She mentioned a wealthy, hard man who had been killed on February 2 with few mourners and little activity on the parts of both police chiefs to solve the murder. All were quite happy that Brutus was dead, including his family.

Both Celeste and Fairy stared at Fannie, who'd had only two drinks, easy for her to handle. She replied quietly, "Girls, we knew each other when we knew it all. And now what do we know?" Fannie almost whispered. "Celebrate life. Spring. What is spring but life?"

Chapter Nineteen

· · · ·

April 2, 1920
Friday

"Our solar system will die. Are you prepared?" At the train station, Patience Horney pointed her forefinger at Celeste.

"I'm afraid I'm not, Patience. When is this cataclysm to occur?" Celeste politely inquired.

"Twenty thousand years from now."

"Ah, I think I'll be safe." The elegant beauty smiled, then looked down the track.

"We keep coming back, you know. You'll be here. Maybe I'll be rich and beautiful and you'll be like me." Patience wistfully pushed a pretzel on its low tray.

Celeste put her hand on Patience's shoulder. "If we're lucky, we won't even be human. Wouldn't you like to return as a leopard or eagle?"

"A whale. Everyone would get out of my way." Her breathy little laugh testified to the reduced capacity of her lungs.

Celeste had known Patience all her life and thought, "There but for the grace of God go I." She wondered, was a person like Patience incomplete, damaged? If she was happy in her fashion, who was to say it wasn't a decent life? She didn't know. She'd come to realize there were many things she would never know. Perhaps that was for the best.

The train whistle blew. The engine rounded the distant curve, glided past, then stopped. The porters hurried out while the passengers heading west picked up their books and small luggage, getting ready to board.

Celeste dropped a dollar into Patience's cup. "It's always good to see you." As the hiss and clatter filled the air, she looked down at the old bandana wrapped around now frayed hair. "Have you ever ridden on a train, Patience?"

"No. My work is here," the odd soul said with conviction. "Don't forget your pretzel."

"Not today, but I left some money for a future purchase."

"Wise." Patience nodded as Celeste stepped forward.

Striding toward her, a lilt in his step, a banged-up Gladstone bag in his left hand, came Ben Battle. "Hello."

She took his right hand for a moment. "Hello right back at you."

They walked into the station, past Patience, who, seeing Ben, boomed out, "Twenty thousand years!"

Celeste stopped. "Ben, this is Miss Patience Horney. She works here at the station. Patience, this is Ben Battle from Baltimore."

Squinting, she tilted her head upward. "You'll like Runnymede. You're the handsomest man I've ever laid eyes on."

He laughed. "You say that to all the boys." And he slipped a dollar bill in her cup as he and Celeste left.

Celeste explained who Patience was and how she was cared for as they exited the front of the station. Francis touched his cap, opened the automobile's door.

Inside the car, Celeste tapped the window between the back and the front. "Francis, drive us around the square. And Francis, this is Mr. Battle. Ben, Francis, who can fix anything."

As they drove around the square, Celeste explained where the

Mason-Dixon Line divided it, how the cannon on the south side is occasionally discharged at General George Gordon Meade, the Yankee on horseback, sword drawn.

"Bad shots?" Ben raised his eyebrows. "He's still standing."

"I'm afraid we are." She smiled. "But we can depend on the kids from high school to paint both statues after a big game or graduation. The newspapers, one on the northern side, one on the southern, will decry the decadence of youth, the dolorous lack of responsibility but we all would be disappointed if the kids didn't do it. Well, I'm rattling on. It's a small town with big stories."

He grinned. "It's symmetrical, beautiful. The churches are quite something."

"Well, that is St. Paul's, where we worship in the bosom of Episcopalian abundance, standing next to St. Rose of Lima, the Catholic church, where my sister occasionally worships. Oh yes, you will meet her sometime, glowing with her pentacostal flame. She's Catholic, obviously. I'm Episcopalian. That's a story for another day but we have reached an accord. There's the Medical Arts Building, and why they yoke together medical and arts, I have no idea. Okay, we're crossing Hanover Street and there's the Bon Ton department store; law firm next to it, Falkenroth, Spangler and Finster; the Rife offices; the fire station and city hall, a bit too Victorian perhaps. We're turning onto Emmitsburg Pike on Maryland ground. That's South Runnymede's city hall. Now we're passing Christ Lutheran Church. This place is filled with churches, many on the roads off the square, the Baptists and evangelicals farther out in the country. It appears we have great need of salvation." She smiled. "And you?"

"Salvation?"

"Yes."

"I believe God helps those who help themselves." He smiled. "I was raised Catholic."

"Here we are." She hopped out of the car before Francis could get the door. Sweeping her arm toward the imposing Georgian structure, she announced, "Home."

Francis reached for Ben's Gladstone but the young man waved him off, thanking him, as he stared at the imposing yet restrained structure. "It's— I don't have a word."

"Big. Too big," Celeste responded. "Come on."

As Ben opened the gate, Francis asked, "Shall I wait?"

"Oh, Francis, I'm sorry. Give us an hour. Then we'll go to the game. Of course, you'll stay for the game, too. You of all people."

Francis smiled. "Indeed I will."

Celeste looked up at Ben. "Francis hit the winning home run back in '89."

"A bit of luck at the plate," the older man demurred.

Ben quietly said, "I play a bit myself."

Francis beamed. "Oh, I know who you are, sir. Miss Chalfonte is not like some, who don't like their people talking to others. I know she won't be upset with me when I ask, how will we do this season?"

"We'll beat them all." Ben reached out with his right hand to grasp Francis's. "Wait and see."

Inside the front door, Ben saw the John Singer Sargent portrait of Celeste on the stairway landing and was mesmerized.

"Cora," Celeste called, then noticed Ben's trance. "My father insisted it go there," she said somewhat apologetically.

"Then your father knew that the painter had captured your spirit as much as your likeness."

"You're very kind," she replied as Cora walked into the hall. "Cora, Ben Battle. Ben, Cora Hunsenmeir, without whom I could not live."

Just then Juts skidded into the hallway, focused solely on her problem. "Momma, I can't find my gray-and-gold ribbon bracelet."

"Juts," was all Cora said.

Noticing finally the guest, Juts froze. "Sir?"

"Juts Hunsenmeir, this is Ben Battle," Celeste properly introduced the youthful Juts to the man.

Juts held out her hand, which he shook. "Are you here for the game?"

"I am."

"It's the best, the biggest, the fiercest, and we have to win, but oh, Mr. Battle, they have Bill Whittier and he can hit the ball a country mile."

"We'll hope for good pitching, then," Ben replied, all seriousness.

Cora, hand on her daughter's back, propelled her back down the hall, calling over her shoulder, "She's fifteen," as though that explained everything, which in a way it did.

Celeste climbed the stairs to the second floor, then up to the third. The walls, lined with paintings, bespoke someone having excellent taste and pots of money.

Ben noticed two long rectangular stained-glass windows on either side of the massive front door. Here on the landing of the third floor a large stained-glass window splashed colored light on the carpet.

"Do you know who made this and the ones by the door?"

"I knew you'd ask. When the house was built, my grandfather found Czech workers. Fellows must have just stepped off the boat. They were hired and we're all the better for it. Apart from the carpentry, the Czechs made the stained-glass windows with help from a Spaniard. Where he came from, I don't know. I often wonder about those early people—new land, new language for some, new animals, flowers. How brave they were."

"And smart." He followed her down the hall.

She opened the door to a west-facing room, a large fireplace, large four-poster bed. Obviously a man's room; a dresser with silver brushes rested on a silver tray, a captain's epaulettes from a full dress uniform also rested on the tray.

He placed his bag on the bench at the end of the bed.

A silver-framed photograph of a captain, features strongly resembling Celeste's, gleamed at the corner of the dresser, a massive mirror behind it. "Your brother?"

"Spotts." She nodded. "We've each kept our childhood rooms so if Stirling ever comes home, he goes to his, Curtis to his, and Carlotta to hers, although she rarely stays here. I wound up with the house because, with the exception of Spotts, everyone married and of course made their own home."

"Memories." He smiled.

She stepped out into the hall, framed by the doorway. "You settle in. When you're ready, I'll give you the grand tour of the gardens, the stables. Lunch if you're hungry and then off to the game, which starts at three. You're a good sport to come for the game. It's such silly fun."

"I wouldn't miss it for the world," he truthfully replied.

Within fifteen minutes, Celeste was leading Ben through the gardens. "Once you get to the end of Emmitsburg Pike, you're in Emmitsburg." She noted, "The land on the south side of the Pike is ours. All I have to do is ride down the alleyway and I'm in open fields in a few minutes, but Runnymede is reaching ever outward, all four roads, all the crossroads. Still, it's quiet—well, more or less quiet. Ah, here's Henry." She introduced her groom to Ben, relieved to see how much older Henry was. "If you'd like to ride, easily done."

"I would need lessons," Ben admitted.

"I can take care of that. You're a natural athlete. Wouldn't take you long, so long as you remember he weighs twelve hundred pounds and you don't." Celeste pointed to Roland in his paddock with Raj, a younger Thoroughbred.

"Miss Chalfonte puts a store by her horses," Henry noted.

"I can see that." Ben walked through the clean, airy stable, cats asleep everywhere. "No dogs?"

"Ah, well, Miss Chalfonte will have to explain that," Henry replied.

She walked out through the large double doors, open to the sunshine and breeze. "My wonderful Irish terrier died shortly after the news that Spotts had been killed. I don't know. I haven't gotten around to a puppy, even though I love dogs. Well, Cora has a stunning English setter. Perhaps, if he sires puppies, that will be the answer."

"You need a good dog," Ben told her with conviction.

"Yes, I do. Would you like something to eat before the game? No telling how long it will go and I was rather hoping we could walk back. It's a bit of a bracing walk but this feels like spring, doesn't it?"

"I can always eat." He smiled. "And yes, it does feel like spring."

They sat outside the orangerie on the smooth flagstones where a table and chairs had been set up by Cora and Juts. No one really went to school on the big game day since every student worried about finding the appropriate colors to wear plus no one paid any attention to their lessons. Both principals bowed to reason and let them go.

"I'm starving." Fannie's voice carried through the house.

Celeste looked up at Ben. "We walk in and out of one another's homes." She then called, "Out back."

Within a skinny minute, Fannie burst onto the scene. "I'm sorry. I didn't know you had a guest. Hello, Ben." She remembered him, of course.

"What a fibber you are." Celeste laughed. "Go tell Cora to bring out more food."

"I already did and that looks like her chicken corn soup. I really am starved."

As she sat down, Cora walked out with plates and soup bowls. Juts trailed behind with sweet tea in a large pitcher. Fannie looked disappointed.

"Hold your horses," Cora ordered.

"Yes, dear." Fannie picked up her soup spoon.

Cora returned bearing the scotch and a small bucket of ice with ice tongs, which she sat to the left side of Fannie.

"I will survive. No, I will triumph." Fannie poured herself a bracing shot. "Ben?"

"No, thank you, Mrs. Creighton."

"Do call me Fannie Jump or Fannie, everyone else does. How perfect that you're here for the big day. You know we pretend it's only a big day for the kids but it is for all of us. I can never get Tony out here from Baltimore. I'm glad you came."

"He doesn't know what he's missing." Ben tasted the soup, quickly realizing that Cora was a fabulous cook.

"Yes, he does. My husband." Fannie roared with laughter. "Unlike our enchanting Celeste, I am not unencumbered, but I hasten to add, Creighton is a good man. Unfortunately, excitement is not his middle name."

Celeste reached over, lightly touching Ben's forearm. "Fannie does not believe in circumlocution."

"Well, well, no I don't. Saves so much time to just come out with it. You'll meet so many people today. Some you'll want to meet, others perhaps not, but here we are."

"Mother!" Juts, saying "Mother" instead of "Momma," needed something, and it had to be very important.

Fannie leaned forward, voice a bit lower. "Juts is laboring under a dark cloud at the moment, although it's not her fault—well, most of it isn't her fault." She preceded to inform him, every syllable, of the cow-jumping-over-the-moon episode.

He laughed. "I think I'd better stay on the good side of Juts."

"And her sister. You haven't met her sister yet. Louise is nineteen and she has a steady fellow now. We like him. He's a war veteran. What do you think, Celeste? Twenty-three? Twenty-four at the most?"

"Army." Celeste added that detail. "Like you."

"Well, he's from Green Springs Valley and we don't know him but so much, but I have inquired about his people. We have to watch out for the girls. No father. Well, yes, they have a father but he ran off, the drunken sot."

"Fannie, I don't think Ben needs all the biographical details." Celeste smiled.

"Perhaps, but some of them are divinely fascinating. For instance, Celeste's sister became a religious nut as her marriage sank into a torpor, and started Immaculata Academy, but like all the Chalfontes, Carlotta is bright. She's now preparing her girls for their responsibilities when we get the vote. Ben, are you for women voting?"

"Yes."

"Fannie, what else can he say? Ben, we've all fought for this for years, as had our mothers, but what I now realize is, vote for whom? Vote for what? I'm beginning to see what you men have struggled to do."

"Politics brings out the worst in people," he forthrightly said. "I steer clear of it when someone brings something up in the locker room. Sometimes you think someone's an okay fellow and then he says something awful, and you don't want to be around him anymore."

Celeste nodded. "Human nature is various."

"Did Celeste tell you we have a baseball team? Not the high school, but we have the Runnymede Nine and Rooters. Not the Orioles, of course, but a rousing way to spend an afternoon."

"Lefty Rogers was a Nine," Ben brought up.

"He was. Yes. We were proud of him and just devastated when he didn't come back from the war." Fannie stopped herself. "By the way, a couple of these youngsters playing today are good athletes. You won't be totally bored."

"Fannie Jump, I could never be bored in your presence."

She blinked a moment, then nearly cooed, "What a sweet thing to say."

"I've known you for over forty years and I agree." Celeste held up a glass of sweet tea to toast her friend.

"Why did you have to give out the years?" Fannie groaned.

"Why not?" Celeste shrugged.

"Easy for you. You're beautiful. You've always been beautiful. I, on the other hand, feel like I'm carrying around an anvil."

Cora walked back out. "Apple pie, then you all best be on your way. You want good seats in the bleachers, and Celeste, do you want a parasol?"

"No, thank you. We'll manage."

Fannie swallowed her drink, poured another, and swallowed that. "I'm off. I promised Fairy I'd pick her up, and Mrs. Thigpen, too." To

Ben, she added, "The mother of the principal at South Runnymede High. She's gotten on in years, poor dear."

Celeste added, "Mrs. Thigpen had her moments but at ninety-five perhaps she's had too many of them."

Ben, blinking, laughed at all this chatter. He stood as Fannie left the table then sat back down.

"See what you're getting into?" Celeste smiled.

"I'm ready."

Once seated at the game, songs rang out from the bleachers, the north side filled with North Runnymede, the south side with South Runnymede kids in gray and gold. The game this year was at North Runnymede High, blue and gold. The buildings looked like a Norman fortress. There were yells, cheers, people standing, both high school bands blaring away. By three o'clock, the stands were packed. It promised to be a perfect baseball day.

Leaning to speak into Celeste's ear because of the din, Ben motioned to the rows in both bleachers filled with men of different ages.

"Old boys." She cupped her hands to speak into his ear.

He nodded that he understood.

No score the first two innings, but then North Runnymede hit a double. Two outs later, Bill Whittier drove in the run. Those on the south side watched glumly. The north side erupted.

It proved a tight game and one well played. Of course, the ability of the young men was disparate but all tried mightily, no one was sloppy. By the sixth inning, the score was 1–1 and again Bill Whittier hit a searing grounder just out of reach of the little shortstop for South Runnymede. Ben groaned. The run, thanks to a heads-up throw from the center fielder, who had moved up close, held up at third. The next batter, the fifth, hit another single, this one to right field but not deep. The run crossed home plate, even though the fielder threw it in the second the ball was in his hand. The runner had too much of a head start.

Louis Negroponti caught the ball immediately after the runner crossed home plate. Bill Whittier, thinking he could easily gain second, tore toward that base, and Louis, without rising from his catcher's crouch, threw the ball to second like a great catapult.

Out!

The spectators screamed. Even those on the north side had to admit it was a great throw and Louis just a tenth grader behind the plate.

The 2–1 game evened out again in the eighth inning.

By the ninth inning, everyone's nerves were jangled. No score in the top, which meant South Runnymede had a chance in the bottom of the inning.

Richard Bartholomew blasted a single. Next up, Dick Yost also hit a single. Fans, thrilled, worried, stood. No one sat. A cheering rumble could be heard all the way to Hanover. Then, Louis Negroponti tried a sacrifice bunt as instructed by his coach. Rolled foul. He fanned the next pitch, a high inside strike. While they had no outs, Louis was South Runnymede's best hope at bat. He needed to learn to look them over. Louis had guts, he took a cut at the next ball, connected, and it soared over the stands. Three runs crossed the plate.

Celeste grabbed Ben's hand, leading him out of the stands before the uproar and celebration accelerated. Both of them ran once they hit the ground and she headed them down the road toward the square.

Finally slowing down, she clapped her hands. "Revenge for last year! We were skunked."

He came alongside her, held out his arm, and she slipped her hand over his forearm. "Who is that kid?"

"Louis Negroponti. He's the one who built the jumping contraption for Juts's cow. The story Fannie embellished eternally. His father is a mechanic and Louis can do anything with steel, iron. He can make parts. And now we know he can hit the ball out of the park." She beamed.

Behind them the roar grew even louder. A paddy wagon puttered by. Then another from South Runnymede.

"Are they going to arrest them?" Ben wondered.

"No. Probably just hoping to calm them down. You can usually bet on a couple of good fistfights after the game. As to the paint on the statues, they'll do that in the middle of the night."

Reaching the square, Celeste walked to the Bon Ton. She hurried in, found Louise, told her the score. Those in the store yelled with happiness if Southies. The Northies, quiet. She also introduced Ben. Once outside, she took him to the middle of the square and then they walked past the fountain out of the square and down Emmitsburg Pike to the house.

Once there, she gave Cora the news.

"Shall we sit back outside? A little light left. Getting chilly, though." Celeste pulled a coat off the hall rack.

Ben draped it over her shoulders and they returned to the back to sit on a bench.

"Late-afternoon light," she said.

"It's golden. The slanting rays through stained glass have an extra depth in this light."

"You like color?"

"I do." He looked down at his red tie with the regimental stripes. "Not so much on my person but I do think color reveals things. You ladies have a freer hand in such matters."

A bustle inside drew their attention as Juts, Louise, and Paul came in. Louise brought Paul outside, where the discussion revealed that the two men had been within a mile of one another on the front. Finally everyone left, the sun set; a stillness enhanced even the smallest sound. A few bats darted overhead.

"Cora left us her special dumplings if and when you're hungry."

"She's a good cook."

"She is that."

"I'm not hungry right now, but you must be feeling the chill."

Celeste rose. "I hope they remembered to start the fires in the fireplaces, including your bedroom. It can get cold up there. Well, it can get cold everywhere. I never think we're past a frost until mid-April."

He followed her back inside. She offered him a drink, which he refused, but he asked for a cup of tea and then decided yes, he was hungry.

So they ate the dumplings, which Celeste heated. Cora had shown her exactly what to do yesterday.

The kitchen was intimate, cozy, not at all grand. There they sat and talked and talked until Celeste finally said, "You know we'll sit here all night."

"You and I will never run out of things to say." He nodded. "And I don't mind sitting here all night."

"We could be more comfortable. You're still wearing your tie. My father is the only man I've ever known who didn't want to take his tie off when he came through the door." She looked at him. "Did you ask about me after I left?"

"Some. I knew about Old Line Manufacturing. But you remained mysterious. Everyone knew who you were, a bit of gossip here and there, including the stories about England, your foxhunting, your trips across the Continent, but mostly all anyone wanted to talk about is how rich you Chalfontes are."

"Let's check the fireplaces."

They first looked into the library, going strong. The main room, no fire, but Cora and Francis would have known that if they stayed downstairs they'd sit in the library. She walked up the stairs, Ben behind her, pushed open the door to her room, which had been closed to conserve the heat while a fire crackled.

She turned to him and grabbed his tie, pulling him into the room. Speechless, he could scarcely breathe as she removed his coat then stood in front of him, put her hands inside his shirt, and pulled it apart, ripping it to shreds. Then with his tie again, she yanked him to her, kissing him hard.

He put his hand in the small of her back, pressing her so close he thought he'd melt. She kissed him and kissed him, then stepped away to remove her clothing. He untied his shoes, unbuttoned the cuffs on his ruined shirt, and unbuttoned his trousers, which fell to the floor.

He reached for her again, feeling that smooth flesh against his own. She felt the softness of his chest hair.

The bedclothes were pulled down; they almost jumped onto it, and with the fire, the covers stayed pulled down until both had exhausted themselves.

Eyes closed, he rested a moment. She sat up to pull up the covers, looked over at him.

"You are so beautiful," she said.

He opened his eyes. "I thought I was supposed to say that."

"Please do."

"You are so beautiful."

They fell asleep laughing.

Chapter Twenty

* * * *

April 3, 1920
Saturday

Ben wrapped a towel he found lying across the bed around himself, preparing to sprint to the third floor. The ornate art nouveau clock read 6:30.

A note on the towel, blue-black ink on light blue paper, in Celeste's bold cursive hand, read, "There's a fresh shirt on your bed. See you in the breakfast room. No hurry. Ever and always, Celeste."

He tucked the note in the waist of his wrapped towel, noting that his shoes and pants had been neatly folded onto the wing chair by the fireplace. A small table by the chair held three photographs in silver frames. One was all the Chalfontes in 1885, when Celeste was eight. Another was Celeste in her early twenties in riding habit, with her Irish terrier by her side, the first of a succession of Irish terriers. The third was of a stunning young woman in front of the monument to the USS *Maine* at the southwest corner of Central Park.

After a hot bath, Ben appeared in the breakfast room. Celeste, reading the newspaper, looked up.

"Good morning."

"Best morning ever." He sat down.

"Coffee or tea?"

"Coffee, I think."

Celeste rose to pour him a cup from the large silver samovar on the sideboard. Two reposed there. One for tea and one for coffee.

"Cream, sugar?"

"Just cream."

She placed the cup in front of him, kissed him on the cheek, walked to the kitchen door, opened the swinging door a crack. "Ready."

She sat down as Cora appeared with a large bowl of hot oatmeal. A minute later, Cora came back with a tray of scrambled eggs, bacon, and her perfect biscuits. Butter, jams, even apple butter rested on the table.

"Did you ride?" He noted Celeste's riding habit, clothing made for her body.

"I did. I'm an early riser." She appraised him. "The shirt fits. I can have the sleeves altered, as they are a touch long, but other than that, perfect."

He unbuttoned the cuffs and rolled up the sleeves. "I've never felt fabric like this."

"Jermyn Street. My brothers get all their shirts made in England, and that is one of Spotts's."

Cora returned. "Spotts's shirt is nearly a perfect fit. Yes, it is. Terrible to let such good things sit idle."

Celeste bit into a biscuit. "The drawers are full of shirts and you are welcome to every one. In fact, it is wonderful to see such elegant things not be wasted."

"Celeste, that's too generous," Ben quietly replied.

She smiled, looking directly into his soft brown eyes. "I'm not trying to buy you, Ben. I don't think I could. You aren't that type of person, but knowing that my brother's clothes are put to good use, on strong shoulders, makes me happy." She glanced around the room. "I have so much, but there are times when it means so little."

He understood. "Just wait. I'll get even." He grinned.

"You already have," she teased him.

Cora bustled in and out. Juts helped.

Juts, thrilled to be the first with the news, informed them, "The statues are painted."

"How do you know? Did you run down to the square?"

"No, but Evie did," Juts announced. "She came by this morning. We're going to the Bon Ton, too. I mean, once I'm finished helping Momma. But the best part is we got more paint on General Meade than they did on our statue."

"Quite a game," Ben remarked.

"The best. The best game ever. It is one of the happiest days of my life," Juts enthused.

"Juts, I do hope there are many more." Celeste wanted to add that it had been a happy day for her as well but didn't.

"I'm so happy I'll do a hop, skip, and a jump." Juts performed her tricks, which made Ben laugh.

Cora pushed the door open, spied her daughter's high jinks. "Will you kindly leave Celeste and Mr. Battle alone?" She then winked at the two as she hustled Juts into the kitchen. "Dishes."

"Oh, Momma."

"Dishes," could be heard in a louder register.

Ben, laughing, asked, "Did you ever do the dishes?"

"Actually, I did. Mother wanted all of us to learn what she called the domestic arts. I was terrible, but Carlotta excelled and the boys did all right. Of course, they could saw and hammer and build things. Carlotta and I were doomed to the house, except for the garden. Mother loved gardening. Is your mother still alive?"

"She is. Dad's gone but Mother and my sister, she's married, live in St. Mary's."

St. Mary's is at the tip of southern Maryland, close to where the Chesapeake meets the Potomac. Peaceful, unique, the little town has exerted its magic since being founded in 1634.

"How did you wind up in Baltimore?"

"A scout saw me play high school baseball, just like those fellows yesterday. I played right after school, working my way up in the minors. Joined the army, came back. Tried out for the Orioles, which was a step up, double-A. I fit in there. I like using my body. I like that feeling when I make a good play."

"Perhaps not in the same way, but I have a feeling of flying, power, when I jump. When Roland and I are one."

"You are unusually strong for a woman," he remarked.

"Here's the thing, Ben. How do we know how strong a woman is?"

"What do you mean?"

"Look at how we dress. Corsets, those awful shoes, volumes of fabric, big hats. Now dresses are simpler, but still. The fabrics are fragile. There's not much practical about women's clothing, no matter what century really."

"I never thought about that."

"Men don't. They just like to look at us," she said without rancor. "Then again, women like looking at men, but it is so much easier for you-all to dress."

"And undress." He giggled, which she found irresistible.

She laughed with him. "Well—yes."

"I noticed the three photographs on your table. You and your brothers and sister so strongly resemble your parents."

"Carlotta looks more like Mother, as did Spotts, a little bit. Stirling, Curtis, and I favor Father. When you're young, you never see it. You think no one in the world looks like you and then one day you look in the mirror and there it is. You?"

"My father. My brother looked like Father, too. I don't get to see Mother and Colleen as much as I'd like. Colleen looks so much like Mother. I send money and tickets to some of the games."

"You're a good son."

"I don't know about that, but I try. Dad died of a heart attack. Mother works. She seems to like it. She works at a little restaurant by the wharf. She knows everybody and they know her. Like here. Everybody knows everybody." He paused. "The photo of you and the dog is handsome. He looks like an intelligent fellow."

"He was."

"And the lovely woman in front of the statue to commemorate the *Maine*. Who is she?"

With a deep breath, Celeste answered directly. "That is my lover. We've been together thirteen years. She married my youngest brother, Curtis, on February twenty-second. She'll have his child in early May, I think. You probably wondered why I never married. Well, there's more to it than that. I felt like I was a horse at an auction, but then I met Ramelle and never thought of it again." She leaned toward him. "Are you shocked?"

"Nothing about you could shock me."

"I don't know whether to be relieved or disappointed."

"Will she ever come back here?"

"She says she will after the baby's born. Her idea is to live six months in Los Angeles with Curtis and six months here. I expect Curtis will make many visits both for her and the baby. I love her. I will always love her, and I love my brother, but I know things will never be the same, and Ben, perhaps that's good."

"I guess it depends on the change."

"True. What I know is, this is a lilac day filled with gold dust. Let's fling ourselves into it. We're alive, triumphantly alive."

Buoyed by her energy, he speared a sausage. *"Carpe diem."*

"You know Latin?"

"No," he laughed, "but everyone knows *carpe diem.*"

Saturdays, a big shopping day, brought people to the square, especially to the Bon Ton. A few tongues clucked when seeing the defaced statues but most residents smiled, remembering their high school days.

By eleven that morning, lines to the Bon Ton formed around the block. Inside one could barely move. All because of Louise's flair for style.

She had put together models using items from the milliner's department, the dress department, accessories, shoes, and light spring sweaters, her department. She had made cards with the cost of each item and then at the base of the mannequin, a large card announced the cost if one bought the entire outfit.

Her uncanny eye for color and proportion caused women to jam into the store as word got around about the displays. Ladies were shouting, holding their purses over their heads. Screaming that they wanted model number two, the one in mint-green with the burgundy chiffon bodice.

Sidney Yost couldn't keep order. Louise couldn't handle the crush.

Hearing the noise, Asa Grumbacher looked down onto the floor from his sumptuous office.

"Mildred!" he called for his attractive secretary. Mildred hurried to his side. Juts and Ev fought their way to Louise. Being smaller than most of the charging women, they wiggled through.

"Juts, Ev, help me. Grab an order book, in the desk behind the counter. Start taking orders."

Juts was already behind the counter. "How do we know who's first in line?"

"You don't. Do the best you can." Louise had just sent a lady to the fitting room.

Mildred cast her eyes down on the scene below. "Mr. Grumbacher, let me call the girls who have Saturday off. We need help."

"Good idea. I'm going onto the floor to help. When you're done, you come down. My God, the Bon Ton has never had a day like this."

Soon Asa was in the thick of it, pacifying women, telling them to be patient. He, too, grabbed an order book and began serving the customers.

Sidney pushed his way through. "Mr. Grumbacher, I can't keep order. Things will get stolen."

"Close the other departments, except for cosmetics. Temporarily. Send all the sales clerks here. You come back and try to keep order, and Sidney, grab a sales book."

"Mr. Grumbacher, I've never made a sale in my life."

"You will now."

As Sidney reached their department, his female employees locked their cash registers, putting what items they could under counters, sliding the glass, and locking those display counters.

The crowd grew even larger. Asa Grumbacher jollied the ladies along, telling each one how wise she was to come out on the first true day of spring, to find seasonal items first.

A harried Sidney returned, sales book in hand.

Mildred, a smile frozen on her face as she was jostled, managed to deal with Dimps Sr., who was dragooning some of the crowd to the cosmetics counter. Mildred told Big Dimps not to accost patrons. If they wanted foundation and lipstick, they would find her.

Within two hours, every single item in the ladies' department was sold out. The staff slumped against the counters as they wrote for orders to be shipped in.

A few times, Asa Grumbacher needed to hoist himself up on a counter to avoid the female scrum. "Ladies, ladies, we will fill every order. Please be patient and don't push. The girls are working as fast as they can, and won't you all look like spring itself in these new colors?"

Mildred held up her hand and he took it, steadied himself, and leapt down.

Finally, it was closing time. Customers had to be ushered out with the promise that they would be attended to first thing on Monday or whenever they could make it. No one would sacrifice the items they wanted.

When the doors were locked, the sales force sat down almost all at once.

Louise, on her third sales book, wiped her brow.

Asa, near to her as well as to Juts and Ev, asked, "Where did you get the idea for the display? When you asked me if you could do this I had no idea how complete the ensembles would be or the mixing of colors."

"I was looking through some magazines. Miss Chalfonte has fashion magazines from France and Italy. I got a lot of ideas."

He then spoke to Juts and Ev. "Girls, I'm tired. I'm sure you are, too."

He stood up, fished in his pocket, and pulled out two twenty-dollar bills and handed one to each girl. Eyes big, both Juts and Ev thanked him.

No one on Mr. Grumbacher's staff had ever seen him give such a lavish bonus.

"Juts, Ev, I am grateful. If you two girls want jobs after you graduate, you come see me." He looked toward the front doors. "They're still out there. I think we will have to exit by the alleyway door. Sidney, see to it, will you?"

Bedraggled, Sidney led the way as Asa climbed the stairs, Mildred in front of him. He stopped, calling to his workers in a booming voice, "This is the best day the Bon Ton has ever had. Even the stores in New York haven't had a day like today."

The clerks cheered.

Once outside, Louise hurried to the store's front, where Paul usually waited for her. Given the crowd, he stood across the street on the square.

She ran to him, falling toward him as he opened his arms, confused.

"Pearlie, you won't believe what happened."

As she breathlessly informed him, Juts and Ev caught up with her, adding their juicy details, and the four walked to Celeste's, jabbering the entire way.

When they reached the house, Celeste and Ben were just returning from a tour of some of Carroll County. Everyone ran out to the back of the gardens to tell the whole story again for their benefit and Cora's.

Ben stood up. "Paul, the victors should be paraded." He reached for Juts, swung her up on one shoulder, and said to Ev, "Stand on the chair. You can hop up on the other shoulder."

She did, and Ben swayed a little for balance, while Paul bent over for Louise to climb onto his back. Shouting, laughing, being silly, they ran around.

Cora clapped her hands. Celeste just laughed.

High spirits infected everyone. Ben bent low so the girls could hop off, then he walked over to Celeste, picked her up as though she weighed next to nothing, and looked in her face. "I can carry you around like this or you can get on my shoulders."

Inhibitions vanishing, Celeste said, "Shoulders."

He put her down, got down on all fours, and she climbed up. Then Ben and Paul paraded around as Juts and Ev shouted. Juts stood next to her mother.

"Momma, you're crying."

Wiping away her tears, "It's been a long time since Celeste has been so happy."

The phone rang in the kitchen. Cora walked inside to answer it as the men put down their delightful burdens.

"Yes, sir. Yes, sir. If you'll give me a moment I'll fetch her."

Cora left the earpiece dangling against the wall and rushed out. "Louise, Mr. Grumbacher on the phone."

Louise ran inside. Everyone waited. She came outside.

"Well?" Juts put her fingers together like a steeple.

"Mr. Grumbacher asked if we would come into the store tomorrow after church. Some of the other girls will be there. We need to write up the orders and send them off as soon as possible, and guess what? He will pay us time and a half overtime, and that includes Juts and Ev. He'll pay you the same as us."

Cheers went up again, and into the middle of this tumult bustled Fannie Jump and Fairy.

"What's this about a riot at the Bon Ton?" Fannie demanded.

Fairy, hands clasped, added, "I do hope you-all weren't hurt."

Again the story was told and this time everyone sat down, bringing chairs out from inside.

"This calls for a drink," Fannie declared. "I'll fetch the goods."

"The girls can't drink, Fannie," Celeste said.

"They can learn," said Fannie. With Cora's help, she returned with scotch for herself, champagne for the rest.

Ben poured a bit of champagne for Juts and Ev. "Just a sip. It will tingle."

Celeste held up her glass. "To Wheezie!"

They all toasted Louise. Then they talked and laughed until twilight embraced them, the cool air with it. Back inside, Celeste threw on her coat.

Fairy asked, "Where are you going?"

"To knock on Francis's door. Cora and the girls could use a ride home."

"I'll take them. I brought the car," Fairy reported with pride.

And so, Fairy got to show off her driving skills, and Celeste and Ben, finally alone, climbed the stairs to discover a welcome fire in the hearth. She led him into the room where for a few moments they sat in the wing chairs reliving the day, then gladly shed their clothing to crawl into bed.

"You know one of the marvelous things about being with a man?"

"I do not." He kissed her cheek.

"A woman is never in doubt."

Chapter Twenty-One

. . . .

April 4, 1920
Sunday

At nine that morning, Celeste rode Roland while Ben was on Sweetpea, an old, kind gelding. They walked along a winding farm road, past pastures greening up.

"You could have gone to early service," Ben remarked. "I'm as happy to go to an Episcopal church as a Catholic one."

"I know, but I'm a Christian by training not by nature." She looked up. "This is my true place of worship. I think of it as the Church of the Blue Dome."

He also looked up. "No arguments between Catholics and Protestants under this church. It's always seemed silly to me. At one point during the war, some South African troops marched by us as we moved to the front, real Africans with white officers. Who or what did they worship? I never asked. Didn't matter."

"Do you think of the war much?"

"I try not to. Sometimes a thought or a picture jumps into my head, but I don't want to remember. No one does."

"Let's hope that was the war to end all wars."

He leaned over to pat Sweetpea's neck. "This horse has more brains than we do. Have you ever heard of horses making war on one another? For what, hay? The idea of a horse in the sky? Because he doesn't like another horse's color? There's something inside us, Celeste. I don't know what it is but I've seen it. Death, nothing but death. For what? To stop Kaiser Bill? And why would millions of Germans follow Kaiser Bill? He wasn't in the trenches. I try to forget and then questions wiggle into my mind."

"They're the questions we should all ask. I tell myself if we ever get the vote, this will change. No woman wants to send her husband, her son, her brother to war. Maybe we can change it."

"Celeste, you have to change men first."

"Well, you don't believe in it."

"Only because I saw it. I signed up to fight. I wanted to fight."

"Would you fight again?"

A silence followed this question as they rode by masses of daffodils planted by an unseen hand a century ago, or a gift from the birds, who knew.

"If we were invaded, I would. Imagine that your Runnymede Square has two deep trenches on either side of the Mason-Dixon Line in which thousands upon thousands of men sat, lived, died, all along Maryland and Pennsylvania. And we'd built cannons that could lob shells seventy miles, we had machine guns and barbed wire. Insane. The limeys and the French complained that Americans wouldn't be able to fight, that all we knew were what they called running battles because most of our experiences were against Indians. Obviously they forgot about the Revolutionary War, the War of 1812, and the horrors of 1861 to 1865. They really thought we couldn't endure or understand what they called set battles."

"They were wrong," Celeste quietly said.

"It took us a little bit to adjust. Mostly because we thought it was a misuse of men, and it was. Everyone was a sitting duck. You know what? We saved their sorry asses." He stopped before he truly lost his temper.

"Yes, yes, I think we did. I don't grasp how nations that gave us Beethoven or Shakespeare or even this new writer, Proust, I don't understand how they could be so blind."

"I don't either but back to your question. Yes, I hope that was the war to end all wars, but I think killing is bred into us as well as stupidity." He took a deep breath. "I hope I haven't upset you."

"Just the reverse. I want to know what you think and feel. You've lived through things I have not. I live well because you lived through them, as did my father and my grandfather. What I have is a superb education and not a bad brain, but I have only so many experiences, and many of those have been muffled because I'm a woman. I resent it, you know."

A smile burst across his handsome face. "That you are and we can fuss about that, but I don't want you to know what I know. I don't want Cora or Louise or Juts to know these horrors or my sister or mother. Trust me, Celeste. Trust me on this."

A flood of gratitude, respect, perhaps the first flush of deep understanding swept over her. "I do trust you, Ben. I trusted you the moment I met you and I have no idea why."

"One of the fellows in my unit believed in past lives. Maybe we knew one another before. No matter. I'm glad we know one another now."

"I wonder if now with our advancements, can we reduce suffering? Perhaps we knew one another in even more savage times. But maybe we can end this suffering."

"You'd have to eliminate free will."

Celeste stopped Roland and Sweetpea followed suit. "You fascinate me. I watched you think at speed during the baseball game. Your mind is unusual. Perhaps you know that. I have had one of the best educations money can buy, but that thought never occurred to me."

"Maybe that's why. What you learned was orthodoxy."

"True. I did. I also learned the underpinnings of Western culture. I have a lot to learn from you."

"Flattery will get you everywhere," he teased. "I'm not so smart, but I think for myself. And, to change the subject, can we go a little faster?"

"Do you know how to post?"

"What?"

"I'll show you." She did rise on the horse's diagonal, a proper post. He watched, then tried to imitate her. He flopped back onto the saddle.

"You see why it's imperative for men to learn to trot."

"I do." He took a deep breath, tried again, and trotted beside her.

They trotted a bit, no cantering, then walked back to the stable, where Henry awaited them. His church service didn't begin until noon.

Ben dismounted, swinging his right leg over then pushing his left foot out of the stirrup to gracefully land on the grass. Then he reached up to give her a hand, she dismounted properly but also gracefully.

Face flushed, she put her hand around his neck, bending him to her while she whispered in his ear, "If life made sense, men would ride sidesaddle."

He laughed. She laughed. Neither one could remember a time of such laughter as the last few days. Clouds of laughter, torrents of laughter, feeling light as a feather, floating with joy, feeling the sunlight in even the darkest corners. Carefree. Demons at bay, sadness banished. Blessedly carefree.

Chapter Twenty-Two

....

April 5, 1920
Monday

As the caboose lurched slightly, heading east, Celeste felt her heart lurch away with it. He was gone. Once the train was out of sight, she walked back through the station. Patience sat inside the doors, as the morning air was a cool forty-two degrees.

"No stars last night. Clouds." Patience pronounced clouds like "clauds."

"Maybe it will be clear tonight."

"I hope so. I like the stars. I like to look up at my friends."

"And they like to look down at you." Celeste pleased her with that remark.

"People aren't smart. They think they are but those on the stars know more than we do."

"I'm sure you're right, Patience." She dropped a dollar in the cup, this time taking a pretzel.

"I owe you another one. You didn't take one when that handsome man arrived."

"Save it for me. I'll be back and he'll be back."

"Good. I like looking at handsome men almost as much as looking at the stars."

"See, I like looking at horses, hounds, houses, paintings, people. Symmetry. I like that visual harmony."

Patience nodded, a solemn look on her face. "Sure you don't want the other pretzel?"

"I'll hold you to it." She left.

In front of the station walking toward her was Julius Caesar Rife, the twenty-one-year-old, eldest son of the late Brutus Rife. Wearing a fawn-colored Borsalino, a light polo coat over a dark-blue chalk-pinstripe suit, J.C., as he was known, looked every inch the modern young man. A black armband had been sewn onto his coat, for he remained in mourning for his father; the time for that was usually three months. For a wife the mourning period, determined by black-, purple-, then lilac- or purple-trimmed clothing, lasted longer.

"Miss Chalfonte." He lifted his hat.

"J.C.," she acknowledged him.

While she hated his father, she did not hate J.C. After being sent away to the University of Pennsylvania, he seemed to have acquitted himself just fine. The test would be how he would run his father's business interests. His younger brother, Napoleon, "Pole," would not be ready to join him for four years. J.C., it was assumed, would lean heavily on his father's hired men. They assumed incorrectly.

"May I take this opportunity to assure you I am not my father?" J.C. said. "He kept Pole and myself from anyone who thought differently than he did. We knew that, but there was little we could do about it. I hope in time you will discover I will look after my workers' welfare as well as my own profits."

Startled, Celeste responded, "I hope you do."

"Your brother-in-law now has a fleet of four big trucks. He's moving into new business ventures."

"Yes. Herbert, like Stirling, has a gift for investing. He declares business will be strong. He says it takes time to recover from a war, even when you win. So he wants to branch out. Cars, trucks—if it has a motor in it, Herbert is interested."

As Celeste had never spoken to him at such length, J.C. was pleased and emboldened. "People say Rob McGrail killed my father. Others believe it was you."

Looking straight into his eyes, she said, "If so, I did you a favor."

Now it was J.C.'s turn to be startled, but he honestly replied, "Yes, you did. I hated the son of a bitch." His mouth curved upward.

Casting her eyes downward then up into his, Celeste quietly said, "I applaud your truthfulness. Allow me to be truthful back and prevail upon you in your new position. St. Paul's is in need of roof repairs. I have just given a large amount to my sister's academy. Might you cover St. Paul's?"

He bowed slightly, hat still in his hand. "It will be done."

"Thank you. And I have a question which you may not be able to answer. Years ago your father had Cora's father killed and then later the man with whom she lived, who was trying to start a union at the munitions plant. Obviously, he did not do the dirty work himself. He was a hard man. He wasn't the only factory owner to kill union organizers, but those two good men were known to me. If you ever find out who did this, if they are local, will you fire them? It won't do any good to turn them in, as nothing can be proven."

He thought, then said, "I will. If you like, I will tell you who they are if I find out, although I doubt my father kept records of that. But if I do, do you want them? Revenge is sweet."

"There's been enough of that." She reached out her hand, he took it, she squeezed his hand and then let it drop. "Give my regards to your mother."

"I will."

Celeste walked home, wondering if J.C. would prove as astute a businessman as his father but as reasonable as his mother, Sarah Scott.

She wondered if women would be better at running corporations than men. All this hope for the vote made her think about other areas where, in time, women might rise. She felt about that as she felt about J.C.: time would tell.

The deeper question was, is the game worth the candle? She truly didn't know.

While Celeste walked home, wondering what lay ahead, Juts half listened in English class.

"And what did he mean by 'Yon Cassius has a lean and hungry look'?" Mrs. Kinzer asked.

Richard's hand shot up. "Cassius is dangerous and ambitious."

"Yes. Do you think that's a good description? Are there Cassiuses around us? Juts?"

"There was Cassius Rife." Juts said the first thing that popped into her wandering mind, naming the founder of the Rife dynasty.

The others in the class tittered. Dimps Jr. rolled her eyes so her little coterie laughed sarcastically. As there was only one English teacher for tenth grade, they had to take the class together.

Mrs. Kinzer walked to Juts's desk. "It is interesting that the Rifes for generations are given historical names. However, the play *Julius Caesar* is about power, perhaps about the proper exercise of power."

"Yes, ma'am." Juts spoke in an even tone.

Ev, bailing out her best friend, said, "But Mrs. Kinzer, how can there be a proper way to exercise power if people have different ideas? Some places have kings, and some have presidents, and some don't know what they want. They just kill one another."

Mrs. Kinzer's class plan was slipping away and it worried her. On the other hand, students who had shown little interest in this play were perking up.

Dick Yost raised his hand. "Mrs. Kinzer, would we elect Julius Caesar president today?"

"Very good question," she replied.

"Why would he run for president?" Juts's interest sparked for the first time ever in English class. "If he gave an order, it was followed. He crossed the Rubicon with his army, didn't he?"

Mrs. Kinzer, surprised, remarked, "Juts, you did read this play?"

"Yes, ma'am."

"We can't have a Caesar." Dick spoke in answer to his own question. "We learned from history. That's why we have a constitution. That's what my dad says."

As Dick's father owned the newspaper on the Maryland side, dinner-table discussions were often more instructive than what he sat through in school.

"Still, couldn't a dictator arise here?" asked Richard. "Or we go crazy like they are in Russia?" He also listened to his parents as they discussed world issues.

"We'd kill him like Brutus and the others killed Caesar. We *would*," Juts emphasized, as Dimps Jr. raised her eyebrows in exaggerated disbelief.

Ev supported Juts. "She's right. We had gunfights all the time in the West. We kind of do what we want."

Mrs. Kinzer said, "The rule of law should prevent such excess."

"But it doesn't," Juts, ever forthright, announced. "Didn't Rome have a senate? What good did it do them?"

"Wasn't that the reason Caesar was killed?" Richard asked. "He was going to destroy the republic?"

"Yes, and it was destroyed anyway," Dick replied. "Mrs. Kinzer, are we supposed to believe that the assassins are right?"

Put on the spot and feeling rather excited that her class had finally come to life, she leaned against her desk, facing them. "We think so because we are a republic. Our founding fathers knew their history but Shakespeare thought the assassins were wrong. He wrote this during the time of a great queen, perhaps the greatest in all history. Elizabeth I was the equal of Caesar in many ways. Ourselves and Shakespeare are on opposite sides of this argument."

The discussion aroused all of the students so much that Mrs. Kinzer had to shoo them out of class or they'd be late for their next class and that teacher would fuss at her.

They debated walking down the hall and as they turned into the art classroom.

Dimps Jr. made a point of bumping Juts, who, tiring of her good behavior since the dance, shot out her leg and tripped Dimps, then stepped over her.

Art instructor Mrs. Stiles, wiping clay off her hands, had not seen any of this.

Dimps Jr. jumped to her feet, launching herself at Juts.

"Juts, I hate you!"

"Likewise." Juts slugged her.

The two flailed at one another as Ev grabbed Juts from behind while Betty Wilcox grabbed Dimps. The boys then stepped up to separate the fighters.

As they screamed at one another, Mrs. Stiles grabbed each one by an arm, marching them down to Mr. Thigpen's office. She deposited them there, returning to her class.

Without Mrs. Stiles, they socked one another again. The noise brought the principal out of his office.

"Ladies, ladies, stop this unseemly behavior this instant."

"She's a, she's an assassin." Dimps Jr. found the word.

"You stupid bitch."

Mr. Thigpen was horrified. "Juts, that's enough!"

"Mr. Thigpen, I'm tired of putting up with her. You know what, she can't drop her pants fast enough for Bill Whittier and she thinks we don't know. But we do."

This prompted another attack. With difficulty, Mr. Thigpen separated them.

"Miss Rhodes, you sit right here. Julia Ellen Hunsenmeir, you come with me." He took her by the arm and hustled her back to Mrs. Stiles.

Opening the door, he thrust her inside, telling the art teacher, "Keep her here until I call for her."

· · ·

Big Dimps was at work when Mr. Thigpen called the office. Mildred took the message down to the cosmetics counter.

"You'd better go. I'll cover the counter."

Big Dimps threw on a coat and walked as fast as she could to the school.

Celeste took the call regarding Juts, listened intently, reassured the principal that Cora would be there quickly. Then she walked out to find Francis. Once found, she called Cora down from upstairs where the good woman was instructing the housemaids, only on duty two days a week.

Cora, anxious, said, "I don't know what to do. I know my girl wouldn't deliberately start a fight." Cora wanted to think the best of her youngest.

"Perhaps not, Cora, but she would deliberately finish it. Come on. I'll wait in the car while you meet with Mr. Thigpen."

The two mothers sat side by side on the long bench in Mr. Thigpen's office, listening glumly. Neither woman particularly liked the other woman's daughter but they themselves never had words.

Mr. Thigpen removed his spectacles, his voice filled with the weight of his decision. "Mrs. Rhodes, Mrs. Hunsenmeir, I can either be principal of South Runnymede High School or I can control your daughters. I can't do both. I am sorry to inform you but I must suspend your daughters."

Big Dimps's hand flew to her bosom. "What will she do?"

"Well, she can do her lessons at home but she can't come to school."

Dimps Sr. liked having her younger daughter in school. "What about next year?"

"We will review that when the time comes."

Cora, silent, sat still.

Mr. Thigpen focused on her. "Do you think Juts would do her lessons at home?"

"No," Cora simply replied.

"I am very sorry," and Mr. Thigpen was, for everyone liked Cora.

"May I go now?" she asked.

"Yes, yes, of course. Juts is in art class. Please take her home with you and, again, I am sorry it has come to this."

"I understand, Mr. Thigpen. You are doing the right thing." Cora left.

Big Dimps pressed. "Juts has no future. A high school diploma won't make a difference in her life but for my girl, well, it will. I will see that she does her lessons and I will report to you regularly."

He folded his hands. "Mrs. Rhodes, this is embarrassing. First off, I hope you do see to her lessons, but there has been an indication of"—he thought some time—"an intimate impropriety. You might wish to curtail Delilah's social activities for a time."

"What!" She leapt to her feet.

He held up his hands, palms outward. "I received an observation after the St. Patrick's Day dance. Again, this is hearsay, but it is gaining adherents. That's all I know."

"Who? Did Juts accuse my baby of such things?"

He drew a deep breath. "As I said, Mrs. Rhodes, these stories have a life of their own, but I do know how important your hopes for both of your daughters' futures are. I can't say any more than what I have told you."

Big Dimps vacated the office in a fury, picking up Dimps Jr., whom she mercilessly grilled on the way home.

The daughter denied everything. Her mother remained suspicious.

Neither Cora nor Juts, Celeste nor Francis said a word on the ride home to Celeste's.

Once inside, Cora ordered, "Polish the silver. We'll talk about this tonight."

"Yes, ma'am."

Celeste walked Cora to the library. "Well?"

"Expelled. She's to do her lessons at home but she won't." She threw up her hands. "She's wanted to quit school, and I think seeing Louise's success, earning money, makes her want to do the same."

"Wheezie is nineteen and Juts is fifteen. They are different personalities."

"Celeste, it's the old story. You can lead a horse to water but you can't make him drink."

"Let the dust settle. Perhaps things will be more clear. You can bring her to work, and if she works I will pay her until she finds something."

Later that day, after Cora and Juts left, Fannie Jump dropped by. Celeste told her what had happened.

"If you can think of any work, tell Cora."

"She'd make a good rattlesnake trainer." Fannie smiled. "Juts isn't afraid of much."

Changing the subject, Celeste asked, "How was Sunday dinner?"

"The usual charade." Fannie leaned back in the chair. "I've almost grown fond of it. I can tell you what's going to come out of the mouth of any member of the Creighton family. I'm becoming a prophet." She rose to pour herself a drink. "The theory is that your spouse and your children and by extension everyone else related to you by blood will honor you, care for you, and see to your comforts as you totter toward the grave."

"And?" Celeste raised an eyebrow.

"I don't think I'll totter. I think I'll be pushed." She laughed.

"You'll push back." Celeste laughed with her. "Where's Fairy?"

"I don't know. I expect she'll show up sooner or later." She held her glass up to the light to admire the golden amber of very good scotch. "I can never decide what I like better, the fuel from Scotland or from Ireland. So different but so uplifting."

"You never did drink bourbon."

"No one makes bourbon as good as Kentuckians but I love the taste of scotch. Also it works faster."

"Are you going to attend Orioles games once the season starts?"

"Wouldn't miss it. Shall I assume you will be attending also?"

"Yes. You said you sit behind first base because that's where the action is?"

"I do. Most people want to sit behind home plate but I can't see as well behind the backstop. Why?"

"Might you consider sitting behind third?"

Fannie finished her drink, poured another, and sat down. "I see. Well, why not?" She thought a moment. "What are you going to do?"

"About what?"

"About Ramelle, for one thing."

"She's married to my brother."

"But she'll be here half the year once the baby can travel."

"She has to have it first." Celeste rose to fix herself a drink, a rarity. "Here's hoping she is delivered safely of a healthy child." She lifted her glass.

Fannie lifted hers. "To the baby. To you."

"To you." Taking a sip, Celeste then said, "How do I know until she's here? I know the baby will come first. I know Curtis will travel back and forth as much as possible and they'll stay in our parents' big bedroom. The nursery is right down the hall."

"Balls to juggle," Fannie remarked.

"Quite." Celeste laughed again, which provoked an uproarious burst from Fannie.

"Well, whatever you need, I'll help. You're my best friend. Things will work out."

"It's too early to know much of anything, but I know I am intrigued. Fannie, he has a good mind. He's strong, honest, and thoughtful."

"And one of the best-looking things I've ever seen. Here's to lust, love, and laughter in all their permutations." She held up her glass this time.

Celeste walked over to clink her glass, then sat on the hassock of Fannie's club chair. "I will forever owe you for taking me to Baltimore to watch a practice game."

Fairy knocked on the door, opened it, and joined them in the library, where Celeste informed her of Juts's expulsion. Once that subject was exhausted, a meow attracted their attention.

"Who is this?" Celeste rose to pick up a calico kitten.

"A new friend." Fannie smiled.

"Did you bring this kitten in with you?" Celeste looked at Fairy.

"She met me at the door. She's a bit bedraggled."

The kitten meowed more.

Celeste petted her. "She has many opinions, most of which involve food. All right, little one, come along."

The three trooped into the kitchen, where Celeste poured out water, set the bowl on the floor, and then put down another bowl with chicken bits, leftovers from Cora's cooking. The kitten demolished this.

"Poor little thing. How hungry." Fairy knelt down to listen to the big purrs.

Fannie sat at the kitchen table. "Celeste, our life is changing."

"Change is life, n'est-ce pas?"

Fairy looked from the kitten to Celeste to Fannie. "You two are keeping something from me."

"No, we're not." Fannie loved her longtime friend, even if Fairy did everything just right. "I came by to toast Celeste, my ally against normality."

"Ah, but Fannie, what is normal but the average of deviance?" Celeste knelt down with Fairy to pick up the kitten, who promptly fell asleep in her lap.

Chapter Twenty-Three

. . . .

April 7, 1920
Wednesday

"She's a harpy," Louise said to Paul as the erect figure of Big Dimps walked in front of them, papers and books under her arm.

South Runnymede High School was two blocks down Baltimore Street, convenient for Big Dimps, who lived a bit farther down the same street.

"Some people are that way," Paul noncommittally replied.

Paul could sometimes take a brief lunch, so Louise, on her longer lunch hour, had walked to where he was working, painting the interior of Maude Ischatta's house. She had brought sandwiches and a mug of coffee, for the day had turned cool, a light snow predicted for the night.

Watching Big Dimps recede, Louise shivered a little.

Paul opened the door to the Anson truck. "Let's sit in here. Mr. Anson won't mind, if you don't mind the smell of paint."

"Don't."

They snuggled together on the flat seat as she unwrapped the sandwiches and pulled out two linen napkins which she'd brought from the store.

Devouring the food, Paul asked, "Juts change her mind?"

"No. Momma's upset. Celeste's upset. Even General Pershing's upset, I swear."

At the mention of the English setter, Paul smiled. "Dog's smarter than we are."

"Oh, Celeste found a kitten or the kitten found her. A little calico. The cutest thing. Follows her everywhere. We named the kitten Glue because she sticks to Celeste like glue. She said that name wasn't grand enough for such a pretty kitten but she's given in. Calls her Glue, too. You know, Pearlie, I was surprised, but Celeste tried to talk Juts into doing her lessons."

"I expect Mrs. Rhodes will beat them into Dimps Jr.," Paul drawled. "I've never met any woman so ambitious."

A hurt expression crossed Louise's pretty face. "I'm ambitious. I don't want to sit around."

He put his free arm around her; the other hand was holding the coffee. "I meant for her children. It's good to want the best for your kids, but this is, I don't know, something more. Suffocating, really."

"That doesn't mean I feel sorry for Lottie or Dimps Jr."

"You know, Wheezie, you start out feeling sorry for people like that but over time it wears off. Why can't they stand up for themselves?"

She shrugged, changed the subject. "Do you want children?"

"Do you?" He wasn't surprised at the question.

Times were changing. Most young people assumed they would have children but others did not. The war had jangled many former assumptions about life. There were even people who said why bring children into such a cruel world.

"I asked first." Louise took the mug from him for a moment, sipped, then handed it back.

Placing the mug on the floor of the truck, he smiled. "I don't want them if you don't."

Neither one had ever discussed a future. Louise thought a person should keep company with a fellow for a year and then make big decisions, but hearing this from him made her both happy and thoughtful.

"Pearlie, really?"

"I don't want to spend time with anyone but you. Other girls seem silly to me. If you say you're going to do something, you do it. You give your mother some of your salary. You try to keep Juts in line, and I'm telling you now, that will never work. She is going to do exactly what she wants."

Louise giggled. "She is the worst little sister in the world except when she's being the best." Then she thought a time. "Of course, I want children. I think every woman dreams of it, but you have to be ready. I've watched Momma. How hard she works and all for Juts and me. She was left with nothing, Pearlie, nothing. *Pfttt.*"

He adored Cora. "Your mother has a big heart."

"I've seen my mother, tired to death, on her hands and knees scrubbing floors. She worked at the hardware store cleaning up until someone told Celeste what was going on. No one knew. Momma didn't tell. She was so hurt and so ashamed. She thought people would think she was a bad wife and that's why Poppa left."

His eyebrows shot upward. "She did?"

"Pearlie, a lot of women think that. And a lot of women drink in secret, too, to get them through the day. Momma didn't. Anyway, Celeste tore into the hardware store and cussed old Ted Hendricks for working Momma so hard. Well, the place was full of people and Celeste picked up a brand-new broom, passed it over the floor, then took a match to it and threw it at him. She yelled, 'I've swept out Hell and burnt up the broom.' Then she grabbed Momma by the wrist and took her to her house. Well, that was all over town in two minutes."

"How is it that they are close?"

"Played together as children. Then Celeste's parents sent her to that rich boarding school. I think Momma is one of the few people Celeste trusts. Momma, on the other hand, trusts everybody no matter what." Louise smiled, then leaned on his shoulder. "Down deep I have that fear. I don't want to be left and I don't want to be poor."

"You aren't going to be left and you aren't going to be poor. You will own a nice house and you'll be safe because you'll be with me."

Her mouth dropped open.

With conviction, Paul said, "There, I've said it."

"You mean married?"

"Louise, will you marry me?"

"We haven't known one another very long."

He opened the door of the truck, got down on one knee, reached up to take her hand. "Will you marry me?"

Tears filled her eyes. "Say you love me first."

"Of course I love you. Would I ask you to marry me if I didn't?" Then he realized this was too logical for a woman. "I love you more than springtime. I love you bigger than the ocean. I love you more than good eggshell-white paint. I love you. I want to spend the rest of my life with you."

Summoning her courage, Louise replied, "Yes."

He rose, leaned over the seat to kiss her.

"Aren't you worried? That we haven't known one another that long?"

"Louise, I have been talking to a man and one second later he's hit by a bullet, dead. I don't need a thousand answers to a thousand questions. I'm alive. I'm here. I've met the most beautiful, wonderful woman any man can imagine and I want you for my wife. I'll do my best. I'll make mistakes, but no matter how stupid I may be, Louise, I will always love you. Together, we can do anything."

She drew back her shoulders, stared into his eyes. "We can. I need to tell Momma."

"We'll both tell Momma. I'll walk you to Celeste's after work. We're a team now."

After both finished up work for the day and Louise was bundled up, they hurried around the square and nearly sprinted down Emmitsburg

Pike. Opening the side door, they stepped into the warmth, glad to be there.

Glue walked into the kitchen. Celeste followed.

"Good evening, Miss Chalfonte," said Paul.

"Good evening, Paul. You look flushed. Cold again."

"Yes, ma'am."

"Is Momma here?" Louise stooped to pick up Glue.

"Upstairs. She decided she doesn't like the way the linen closet is organized. I might add, this is the third reorganization in as many months." Celeste took Glue from Louise while she observed the two hurry out of the kitchen.

"Momma!" Louise took the stairs two at a time.

"Linen closet." Cora stepped outside the voluminous closet. "You don't happen to have Juts with you, do you?"

"I think she's at Ev's. But I do have Pearlie."

"Mrs. Hunsenmeir." He took a deep breath.

Cora looked from one to the other. Louise was holding her breath.

"Mrs. Hunsenmeir," he began again, "I am here to ask for your daughter's hand in marriage." As Paul spoke, Louise slowly exhaled.

A big smile played over Cora's worn face. She knew love when she saw it and she was not a woman hag-ridden by rules.

"You have my blessing."

Louise screamed, "You're the best mother in the world!"

Cora hugged her and kissed her, then hugged Paul. "Welcome to the family. She's my treasure."

"Yes, ma'am. I will take care of her."

Celeste, hearing a scream, called up from the foot of the stairs. "Cora, is everything all right?"

Cora reached the landing to stand in front of the John Singer Sargent painting as the two young people stood on the step behind her, both a bit apprehensive.

"Celeste, Paul had proposed to our Louise and he has properly asked me for her hand. I've given them my blessing."

Celeste, surprised and moved, replied, "Paul, you are a lucky man."

"I am." He grinned, relieved.

"Well, come on. This calls for champagne."

Once nestled in the library, Glue on Celeste's lap, they toasted, listened as the fire crackled.

Louise, back to herself, mentioned, "Momma, we want to wait a bit, we want to put aside money so we can rent an apartment."

"You do what you think best. You can stay with me if needs be," Cora offered.

"You're crowded as it is. Juts in the house is like having two people; well, anyway, we talked about this on the way here. We think, subtracting our expenses, we might squeak by in six months."

"I can work weekends." Paul really wanted to make money. "I need to buy a proper engagement ring."

"I don't need a ring." Louise wanted one but she wasn't going to spend his money.

"I have an idea." Celeste rose, opened the rosewood humidor, pulled out a cigar, motioned to Paul to remove the band. He did, then knelt before Louise, slipping the cigar band on her left third finger. "Until I have money."

"I love the colors!" Louise giggled.

The side door opened and closed. Footsteps rattled through the kitchen, then Juts appeared in the library doorway.

"I'm here!" She noticed the champagne. "You-all are having a party. Ben showed me how to take a sip."

Celeste rose, putting Glue on her chair, poured Juts a sip, then returned to the chair and the cat.

"Why is everyone quiet?"

Louise, loving every minute of telling her sister her big news, said, "Paul has asked me for my hand."

"What about your foot?" Juts drained her little bit of champagne.

Chapter Twenty-Four

. . . .

April 9, 1920
Friday

Light snow created the illusion of a see-through veil. Juts met Ev a block away from school as it let out for the day.

"Spring can't make up its mind." Ev burrowed her gloved hands into her coat pockets.

"Where're your books?" Juts asked.

"Left them at home. Didn't really need them. We finished *Julius Caesar*." She wrinkled her nose. "Imagine being stabbed by people you thought were your friends? So today we took a test and then in art class we had to draw little vases with daffodils or pussy willows. I fell asleep in history so I don't know much. Mr. Lundquist didn't wake me up. Hey, want to go to Cadwalder's? Dimps Jr. isn't going to be there. Bill picked her up and they went off somewhere."

"Sure. Let's go to Cadwalder's."

Once inside, many of her friends there, Juts chatted with everyone. The Polish countess bringing messages from the dead was in the paper again. This time she was in Baltimore announcing that influenza would not appear again for seventy-five years but when it did, there would be more mass death.

"She doesn't believe in good news." Ev leaned over Rick's shoulder as he read the paper.

Dick Yost squeezed next to Juts at the full table, and declared, "Juts, school's no fun without you. You're the one with ideas."

"True," Betty Wilcox chimed in. "However, it is more fun without Dimps."

"Ev said Bill Whittier picked her up, so she's back in school." Juts's eyebrows furrowed. "Not that I care. If her mother got her back in, fine with me."

"No, she's not back. She met him outside of school," Betty informed her.

"So her mother won't know," said Richard. "Big Dimps doesn't want him calling at the house." He thought the whole thing silly.

"And, you'll love this, Lottie is seeing Yashew Gregorivitch," Betty added with glee.

"What!" Both Juts and Ev responded.

"He bought a used truck from Mr. Van Dusen, is making money hauling stuff for Mr. Van Dusen and others. Who would have thought Yashew would get ahead?" Ev said what others were thinking. "He's not but so smart."

"Hard worker." Dick folded the paper, handing it back to Betty. "My dad says he'd rather hire a hard worker than a smart guy who's lazy."

They nattered, teased one another, and then filed out for home, Flavius calling good-bye to each student. They said good night in return.

Juts had forgotten the new whisk broom she'd picked up at Smitman's Hardware. She ran back, and as she opened the door, there was Flavius, whisk broom in hand.

"Oh, thanks. Momma would have been one step ahead of a running fit."

"Give your mother my regards." He handed her the hand-tied little broom.

"Whew." Juts exhaled as she came out of the store.

Ev felt the tiny snowflakes on her face. "Feels good even if they are cold."

"The best part about snow is it covers the yard," Juts said. "Then when it melts I see everything I have to pick up. General Pershing is always stealing stuff which he drops outside."

"Dad says you should go bird hunting with him."

"Nah. I don't want to hunt anything and besides, I don't have a gun," Juts replied, then looked around. "We're in the clear."

"In the clear for what?"

"Louise is engaged."

Ev stopped for a moment. "You waited until now to tell me!"

"I was afraid you'd leak it out at Cadwalder's."

"People will find out sooner or later but I would have kept my mouth shut."

"I'm surprised I did." Juts laughed at herself. "She's silly. It's all she talks about."

"Girls get like that, but it did just happen, right?"

Juts nodded. "They want to wait until he can see his mother and father and then they'll announce it in the newspaper. Ev, can you imagine getting married?"

Ev slowed a bit. "What else is there?"

"What do you mean?" Juts noticed some of the ladies belonging to the St. Anne Circle going into Christ Lutheran Church.

Christ Lutheran Church had many groups divided by age, interest, men or women's, as did all the rest of the churches. If you belonged to a church in Runnymede, you were never lonely.

"You get married, have kids, that's it. Everyone does it."

"Celeste didn't."

"My mother says Celeste was always a rebel. Gave her mother fits. Carlotta did everything right and Celeste did not, and Mom also said they spent a fortune sending her to England. Can't go by Celeste."

"Okay, but really Ev, can you imagine cleaning house, raising kids, ironing your husband's shirts, making food for potluck suppers at church? There's got to be more than that."

Ev thought out loud. "Mrs. Wilcox works. Your mother works. Mrs. Negroponti works. A lot of the ladies work in their husbands' businesses. They aren't just ironing shirts."

"No, they're doing all that work, and then ironing shirts." Juts sounded miserable. "I don't want to do it."

"Marry a rich man. He'll hire servants. You can travel when he takes off in the summers. Most of those rich guys in Baltimore take off August. That's what Dad says and Mom, too. They go to the Chesapeake or the Adirondacks. It can't be that bad, Juts, everyone does it."

Mournfully, Juts mumbled, "And now Wheezie. I'll be all alone."

"Oh, you will not. I'm here. Your pals are here and she'll be around besides; she isn't leaving Bumblebee Hill for a while. And what do you care if Wheezie gets married? You fight all the time."

"Since the popcorn fight at the Capitol Theater, we've hardly fought at all. Louise is changing."

Ev smiled. "Maybe you are, too."

"Ah, Evie, changing to what? Mr. Thigpen threw me out of school. Momma's quiet about it but she's upset and she's really upset that I let Dimps Jr. get under my skin. Louise says it's hard to find a job when you're only fifteen and she says that business is getting better than last year but it's still hard to find a job. And what can I do? I'm not as musical as Louise but I could play the piano at parties. You get paid for that. I'll work hard. I'm not afraid of work but someone has to teach me what they want."

"That's why you stay away from Dimps Jr., the big cootie." Ev used a word the boys who'd come back from the war used. "Just steer clear. Come back next year. But you need to keep up. I'll help. I have to study anyway, Juts, so I might as well do it with you. You didn't turn your books back in, did you?"

"No."

"Then meet me after school at my house and we'll go over things. I can bring you tests home or, I bet if you ask Mr. Thigpen, he'd let you come after school to take the tests. That way no one can accuse you of cheating."

A deep, ragged sigh escaped Juts. "Ev, you're my best friend."

"You're mine. All for one and one for all." She wrapped her arm around Juts's waist.

"I see Wheezie with Pearlie and they laugh all the time, they talk all the time. She's so happy. I guess he is too, and I guess that's why people get married, but how many stay happy?"

Ev had no answer to that. "Maybe people just get tired. Mom and Dad seem pretty happy. They don't fight. Well, sometimes, but I look around and I see people who don't speak to one another. I mean, look at Big Dimps and her husband. If you pick the wrong person, that's it."

"How do you know you've picked the right one? I mean, everyone gets all cow-eyed and they paw all over one another. I'm not doing that. You should see the way Wheezie and Pearlie look at one another. Oh, it's too awful."

"But they're happy, and Mom said even though they've not been going out a long time, they're made for each other."

"Your mother doesn't know, does she?"

"Of course not, but you can't hide but so much. He walks her to Celeste's after she gets off work. They go to the movies every Saturday. He takes her to dinner and Mom said she doesn't spend his money. Louise is careful and she said that's as good a sign as him being so careful with her. She told Dad they're made for each other."

"I have no idea what that means," Juts despondently muttered.

"I kind of do and I kind of don't. I do think it would be nice to be able to talk to someone, to just tell him everything and listen too. You know, the two of you against the world."

Juts pulled Ev closer. "That's us."

"Yeah, but I think it's different with a man, Juts. Something else. Has to be something else or people wouldn't do the crazy things they do, and I don't just mean the bedroom stuff. Like we aren't supposed to know." She giggled.

"I used to wonder about that with Celeste and Ramelle. You know what I mean?" When Ev nodded, Juts added, "I love you, Ev. I do, but I don't want to kiss you."

Ev roared, "Good, because I don't want to kiss you either."

Juts looked ahead as they'd stopped in front of Ev's lovely Federal home. "Fannie Jump's car. She's all the time at Celeste's. I mean, more than usual."

"Mom says she needs Celeste, and Fairy, too. She says that Fannie Jump is in a dead marriage, she and Creighton just keep up appearances."

"See, that's what scares me. How do you know? You're standing up there in front of the altar, swearing all kinds of stuff. I don't want to end up like Fannie, even if she is rich." Juts liked Fannie but still thought it a sad way to live.

"Me neither. Juts, I don't know. I guess if you think it's right, if you love him, you take a chance. What about the women who married and lost their husbands in the war? You take the chance and it's real far away for us but I'll be there when it happens to you and you'll be there when it happens to me."

Brightening, Juts nodded. "Right."

"So, Monday, bring your books. Nothing's really that hard and you're a whiz at math. You can help me. I don't get algebra. Why use letters?"

Juts smiled. "I'll bring my books." She hugged her friend, then started down the street.

Once inside the house, she heard Fannie.

"This kitten's already bigger."

In the library, Celeste responded, "Good."

"Fairy said she'd stop by and I wanted to see you for a minute before she arrived. She said she's bringing scones. Mrs. McAllister outdid herself in the scone department and she has clotted crème, regular butter, and a basketful of jams. She's embarrassed at eating all your food."

"When did you receive all this information?"

"Oh, we were at St. Paul's. Vestry meeting. And you're right. There are mice behind the tapestry just like Mrs. Creighton told you. I walked into the vestibule to listen."

"Ah." Celeste allowed Glue on her shoulders as they sat together in the big chair.

"Will you consider something?"

"Yes, of course."

"As you know, I love my trips to Baltimore." She held up her hands. "I know, I know, I've worked my way through the baseball team in years past, but lately Tony and I have become quite close. I'd like to attend some of Olivia Goldoni's concerts, the symphony as well as the ball games. Baltimore has a long way to go but there is some culture there. I was rather wondering how you felt about Baltimore."

"As I've always felt about Baltimore, I'm glad it's there and I'm glad I don't have to live there. Stirling does that for all of us. Well, Curtis is making his own money, I should be fair."

"I see." Fannie clasped and unclasped her hands, leaned forward. "I pay off the help at the Belvedere Hotel. I don't want stories to creep back here to Creighton. What he doesn't know won't hurt him. I do not inquire too closely into his doings, but knowing Creighton, his passion isn't women, it's business."

"I would agree. Fannie, you usually get to the point, so do it."

"Well . . ." A long, long pause followed. "I was rather hoping we could together buy a small house so that we could come and go as we wish. We won't lose money and if one wants to buy the other out, fine."

Surprised, Celeste replied, "Give me some time. I've never considered anything like this."

Feeling hopeful, Fannie offered, "Tony says he could find a housekeeper. You and I can't do that. I can barely keep up with what I have here."

"True." Celeste's ear, filled with a mighty purr, tingled.

"When Ramelle returns, you might need some privacy, a day away now and then."

"I hadn't thought about that," Celeste honestly replied.

"Celeste, I've never seen you so happy. I'm happy. How many chances do we have? And who is to say how long anything can last, but I feel alive. I'm not turning back."

"You aren't going to get a divorce? Oh, Fannie, don't do that."

"Of course not. I will never embarrass Creighton. I've tried to keep my little escapades from him, but when I've had too much to drink, I fear my indiscretion. This way, if I am indiscreet, I'm in Baltimore but then again, I will be in Tony's company, so I have good reason to be discreet."

"As I said, let me think about it."

"Ben's dazzling. But then so are you. Always have been. Celeste, the clock is ticking. Everything is changing. I want to be happy, young again, even if it's fool's gold." Fannie didn't mince words.

"I understand. I do understand. Let me think about this and I won't belabor it. I promise."

The front door opened and closed.

Fairy popped into the library, a big hamper basket under her arm. "To the kitchen."

They repaired to the kitchen, Glue still asleep on Celeste's shoulder. Fairy unpacked her scones, the crème, the butter, too many jams.

Cora and Juts found them eating away.

"Please, have some. Mrs. McAllister's special."

Glue woke up. Celeste put her down to treats.

"Well, girls, it is April ninth," Fairy announced. "Appomattox."

"So it is. My father, all of twenty-four, began the walk home to Maryland." Fannie reached for another scone.

"And here we are." Fairy, ready to quote Marx, thought the better of it. "And what have we learned?"

Celeste laughed. "I've learned never show a southerner a lost cause."

Chapter Twenty-Five

....

April 10, 1920
Saturday

Snow interspersed with sleet battered the station window looking out to the train track. At times, Celeste could see only gray and white. The weather prevented Patience Horney's church-lady keepers from walking her to the station. Celeste missed the odd soul as she waited for the Baltimore train. Surely Patience's intergalactic friends wouldn't be inconvenienced by an early spring storm. Humans certainly were.

Few people waited inside the station, but those who did perked up hearing the whistle blow. Through the snow, the big engine appeared. Celeste pushed open the door, umbrella unfurled, which in the wind turned inside out. Stepping down, Ben didn't see her until very close. He reached for the pathetic umbrella, took her arm with his other hand, to propel her into the station.

She raised her voice to be heard above the gusts. "You can't carry the umbrella and your bag at the same time."

The door slapped behind them.

"You're right." He took her umbrella, depositing it in a large disposal can. "You needn't have stepped out. Makes your bones hurt."

"It is a storm of biblical intensity. Well, we have to brave a bit of it to get to the car."

Pushing open the door at the other end of the station, the two dashed for the car. Francis ran toward them and his umbrella also turned inside out.

"Blast," he cursed.

"Mine did, too." She ducked into the backseat as Francis held the door open, squinting, for the snow now blew sideways.

Ben vaulted in after her, setting his Gladstone bag at his feet.

"I can take that, sir."

"Francis, please get in the car. His bag can take a beating better than you can."

Touching his cap, Francis nodded, hurrying to slip into the driver's seat. All three sighed with relief when the Packard started.

Teeth chattering slightly, Celeste leaned into Ben, who put his arm around her. "I don't know why I'm so cold. I was barely out in this."

"The wind cuts." Ben rubbed her shoulder. "Sleeting when I left Baltimore but with each mile moving west the weather worsened. The newspaper predicts it will go on throughout the day and night."

"There's coal in the furnace in the basement and the fireplaces will be roaring," Celeste said. "Cora will never get home today. She thinks ahead, so she brought her cat and dog with her. They're in the kitchen, aware of their good fortunes."

Once at home, they both repaired to her room to strip out of their wet clothing.

"I bet I can get out of my clothes before you do." He untied his shoes, peeling off his socks.

"No fair. Any man can undress faster than any woman. My fingers aren't working as they should."

"Here. I'll do it." He unbuttoned her silk blouse, while his shirt, sticking to his skin, remained half unbuttoned. Once finished, he wriggled out of his shirt, then his undershirt.

She hurried to the bathroom, pulled on her robe, and brought him a heavy towel. He wrapped the towel around his waist as she picked up his shoes.

"We need to stuff these with newspapers. They are soaked." Looking around, she found nothing. "I'll go downstairs. I think I left the paper on the breakfast table. Hang up your coat."

"It's dripping."

"Give it to me, then. I'll take it down and Cora can hang it in the kitchen. We look like two drowned ragamuffins." She laughed, putting the coat over her arm, carrying the shoes.

Once in the kitchen, she handed Cora the coat then snatched the paper from the breakfast room.

Stuffing the shoes, Celeste noticed that Glue, curled up with General Pershing, was sound asleep. "I bet all that fur feels wonderful."

"Felicity would have nothing to do with the kitten." Cora smoothed out Ben's coat. "Let me hang this in the coatroom. If it drips on the floor it won't hurt anything. What did you two do? Walk around the square?"

"No. Cora, all I did was go out to meet him. My umbrella blew inside out. Then we made a run for the car and Francis's umbrella blew inside out. That was it."

The windows rattled ominously. Both women looked up.

"I'll put the shoes in the pantry. That's close enough to the heat but not close enough to shrink them. Well"—she held up one of Ben's shoes—"they might anyway." She held them sideways and Celeste could see the holes under the toes.

"We'll hope for the best."

"Best foot forward." Cora smiled.

"What size are those?"

"The size is worn off." Cora checked the interiors of both shoes.

"Maybe he can wear Spotts's. My brother's shirts fit him. Shoes would be a blessing. They're expensive."

Cora disappeared into the pantry, then returned, agreeing, "Anything leather is expensive."

Celeste rifled through other newspaper sections. "Sports page. I'll take this up. I'm sure our version of sports will be a counterpoint to the *Sun*'s. North Runnymede's paper is even better for that. Everything is about the Philadelphia teams."

"Before the girls left today, Louise read me the article about Prohibition."

"The one about the government hiring more men to enforce it?" Celeste felt a bit of warmth returning to her body.

"That's it."

"Will you make a pot of tea? I'll take it up. We are both chilled to the bone and he's only wrapped in a towel. I can't remember if Spotts's robe is still here. I thought he took it with him. Funny, what you remember and you don't."

"You go to your guest. I'll check Spotts's room and then Curtis's. He always leaves things behind when he visits."

"Good idea." Celeste looked down at the sleeping pets. "Before I forget—I can send Francis to pick up Louise."

"She told me this morning that Pearlie was picking her up after work. On foot or in a borrowed paint truck, I don't know. Juts is staying with Ev. Ev's helping her with her lessons."

"Really?" Celeste was surprised.

"Juts is being sensible."

"Calling Juts sensible may be premature." Celeste laughed, and Cora laughed with her.

A few moments later, Celeste stood outside her bedroom door. "Open sesame."

He opened the door and smiled to see the tray with tea. Before they closed the door, Cora's footsteps could be heard coming down from the third floor.

"Here you go." She appeared at the open door, robe over her arm.

"Wonderful." Celeste took the robe from her.

Ben, holding fast to his towel, reached for the offered robe, apologizing, "Cora, forgive me—"

"It's a big towel." Cora smiled as the wind shook the house again. "If you two sit here by the fire or down in the library, you'll eventually warm up. Once you take a chill, it takes time to thaw out."

"That it will." Celeste turned to him. "Ben, do you like shepherd's pie?"

He nodded and Cora promised, "You'll have it for lunch. Noon."

Alone now, wrapped in their robes, the two sat before the fire, feet on footstools.

"There's no feeling like being inside a house in front of a fire during a storm"—he sighed contentedly—"with a beautiful woman."

"Flatterer." She handed him the paper.

He placed it on his lap, leaned back in the chair. "What do you do with the horses on a day like today?"

"They're in their stalls, with heavy woolen blankets and lots of hay, and Henry checks on the water to make sure it hasn't frozen. Usually, we turn them out in the day then bring them in at night during the winter, but this storm is so bad they stayed in. I expect everything is tucked up, all the foxes, the owls, the deer. Isn't it something how they know a storm is coming before we do?"

"It is." He opened the paper, the North Runnymede paper. "Did you read this?"

"I read both papers every morning and both evening papers, too, although the evening papers aren't from Runnymede. One's from York, the other from Baltimore, although I doubt we'll get our evening papers today."

"I'm glad I pulled in when I did." He looked at the headline. "According to this report, Baltimore hasn't seen so much smuggling since the War of 1812." He checked the banner again. "Isn't this the North Runnymede paper?"

"It is."

"Why an article on Baltimore?"

"Because Philadelphia probably had more smugglers than Baltimore. Best to take the offense while not reporting anything on Pennsylvania's precious mother city."

"I really am going to have to learn about Runnymede."

"We'll be at our most flagrant for the Magna Carta ceremony held each June fifteenth in the square. I'm asking you now to be my escort. And we get to do the cakewalk. You never know. We might win. The music might stop exactly when we reach the little podium. Never hurts to win a cake."

He turned to her. "So long as it isn't a weekend."

"Tuesday, this year." She informed him. "The whole town turns out. You'll see. I assume you play on Saturdays."

"And some weekdays. The big crowds are Saturdays." He wiggled his toes. Feeling was returning to his feet.

"This may be rude, but is playing baseball lucrative?"

"If you're in the majors. We're a minor league team. This will be one of our best years, I know it. Not much money, though." He turned to face her. "I make twenty-five hundred a year. Ty Cobb, majors obviously, used to make twenty thousand. We had to buy our uniforms and clean them ourselves. Finally, our manager got the boss to pick up those expenses. But I buy my glove. I will never get rich." He smiled at her.

"What happens if you get hurt?"

"I'm out until I can play."

"But do the Orioles pay for your expenses?"

He shook his head. "No. That's why I'm careful. I set money aside so I can at least pay my rent."

"You know, I don't even know where you live."

"Not far from Greenmount Avenue." He cited the avenue the stadium was on, a nice stadium. "It's not a flophouse but it's not much. When I step outside and look down the street, I see all the marble stairs from all the houses lined up in a neat row."

"Can you see the Bromo-Seltzer blue bottle?" She named the rotating, fifty-one-foot bottle atop the Emerson Tower. Garish though it was, it had become a Baltimore landmark when built in 1911.

"I can't see it from my window, but when I go out and walk I can see it. I can walk to the stadium, which is good. Saves money and loosens me up a little. I try to clear my mind. I play better when I'm clear."

"I can imagine. Do you want to go to the majors?"

"Well, I'm twenty-eight. My best years really were my war years. But would I go? Sure. Will I be asked? No."

"People say you're a wonderful shortstop."

He smiled. "I'm not bad, but you don't have long in this game, Celeste. I love it and I might as well enjoy it while I can."

She folded her hands. "I was so focused on my brother's death I never thought about the other ways the war could affect a man."

"You play the hand you're dealt," he replied without rancor.

"If you're smart. Others just sink into a morass of complaint or self-pity." She paused. "Then again, who knows what they suffered? No one was prepared for the war."

"No. The carnage was incomprehensible."

"Spotts would write. He wrote about the funny characters in his unit, about how sometimes they could even hear the Germans speaking." She stopped. "I don't want to bring back terrible memories for you."

He reached over with his left hand as she reached out with her right. They held hands in front of the fire.

"Celeste, the best any of us can do is go on. Sometimes a picture will flash in front of me and sometimes it's not horrible." He turned. "You'd be surprised, but we found ways to have fun. When we'd be sent behind the lines, we'd play baseball. The Brits would play cricket and taunt us, saying our game came from their game, so we'd try each other's games. They could be good fellows, the regular fellows." He brightened. "We'd even dance."

"Really?" She was intrigued.

"Somebody would sing, somebody would play a trumpet or instrument they'd dragged with them. And we'd dance. The tall fellows would ask the shorter."

"And you?"

"Well, I'm six feet but I could both lead and follow. There was a tall British sergeant with red hair and he would ask me. He taught me a lot for I wasn't much of a dancer. My buddies would tease me about Patrick. I hope he survived the war. He really was a good fellow with a wonderful sense of humor, especially when we began dancing and I mashed his feet."

"Sounds wonderful. Do you think the men ever fell in love with one another?"

He paused. "We tried not to get too close. Too many of us were killed, we died like flies. But you still draw close to others. Can't help it, I guess. But love, physical relations? I don't know." He sat up straighter. "I wouldn't fault anyone for seeking whatever they needed in that hell."

"Yes."

They sat in silence, then she asked, "I would imagine if you did get leave, you all found girls."

"We did. Some were in dance halls. The places were smoky, the wine was water, some of the girls had seen better days, and some were so young; they were the most sought after, obviously. Poor creatures. Many had lost everything and everybody. They had to get by as best they could." He held her hand more tightly. "We paid them, of course. It probably sounds strange to a woman, but to feel a woman's arms around your neck, to hear her voice, brief though it was, you felt alive. She would smile at you and you knew you'd never see her again. I hoped she would overcome what she had to do to survive. I was careful and I only had three leaves behind the lines. The others were more of a rotation to give us a breather, the baseball leaves." He smiled. "I don't know why I tell you this. I don't think I could lie to you about anything. I don't understand why I talk to you like I do."

"Fate. We're fated to know one another. And for what it's worth, in similar circumstances, I would do the same."

"Fortunately, women don't go to war."

"No, we just die in them."

He dropped her hand, rose to lean down to kiss her. "Not you. Let's hope it will never happen again."

A bell tinkled.

She stood up, kissed him, and said, "Lunch." She called down, "Cora, we'll be there in a few moments. I have to find clothes for Ben."

"Why can't he come down in his robe?"

"Well, what if Fannie comes over or Fairy?"

"Celeste, in this weather?"

The two ate in the dining room but not before Celeste showed Ben Glue and General Pershing still asleep. Felicity was grandly curled up on a cabinet ledge, opening one eye when they came in.

The storm continued. Branches scraped against windowpanes.

When Cora came in to pick up the plates, Celeste said, "You and Wheezie can stay on the third floor and Paul can stay in Curtis's bedroom. There's no point in him walking or driving her here and then having to go out into this himself. I can't imagine anyone is even in the Bon Ton."

"I'll tell him but you will have to tell him too."

After lunch, Celeste led Ben to Spotts's room, where he put on socks, tried on shoes. They fit if he wore two pairs of socks. Then he pulled on a beautiful pair of light wool pants.

"Ah, finally Spotts's wardrobe can be put to good use, not just his shirts."

He unbuttoned the front of the pants, shifted contents in Spotts's boxers, which also fit him.

"You dress on the left," she said matter-of-factly.

"Beg pardon."

She indicated his genitals. "Men dress on the left or the right. When your clothes are bespoke, made exactly for you, the tailor takes that into account. Details are everything and I've always thought it's women that should design men's clothes, as no man will ever look at a man the way a woman will."

"How do you know all this?"

"I grew up with three brothers. Stirling was too old. Spotts was four years younger, Curtis six. Stirling was already on his way and not inclined to waste time on his little sister. But Spotts and Curtis and I talked about everything. Children, as you know, are fascinated with the basics. I would look at their parts and say, 'You'll catch that in something.' How we'd laugh."

He looked down, pulled open the boxer waistband a little. "Made me worry there for a moment."

"Ben, you never need to worry." She teased him. "Okay, now try on his pinstriped flannel pants, his summer pants. I just want to see how you look."

He did and the fit was close to perfect.

"Why don't you put on his charcoal winter pants, just wear an undershirt, and pull over his red sweater? That was his favorite sweater," she continued. "We can go up and ransack Curtis's room, too."

"But he'll be back."

"Oh, Curtis is careless with clothes. He won't even miss anything."

"No, I don't feel right about that, but I appreciate you allowing me to wear Spotts's clothing."

"They're yours." She sat down for a moment, wrapping her hands around her right knee. "I can't stand to waste things. Besides, you need a new pair of shoes. Now you have a closetful."

He smiled. "I was going to get mine resoled." He picked up a folded undershirt from the top of the bed, where the sweaters were lined up along with the underclothes. "Celeste, do you miss your friend?"

"Ramelle? Yes. I do. We had different interests, but when you spend thirteen years with someone you become accustomed to them. Am I sad? No."

He waited a little, then finally said, "I'm not much of a lady."

She looked up at him. "I don't know. Maybe your British friend with the red hair could imagine you as one in his arms but I can't." She stood up, put her arms around his neck. "Nor do I want to." She kissed him.

He savored that kiss, hesitated, then asked, "Did you sleep with other women? Other than Ramelle?"

"Too many. What about you?" Her left eyebrow rose.

"Too many."

They both laughed as they hugged one another.

They heard voices downstairs. She kissed him again then opened the door to go downstairs. "Come on down when you're dressed."

Louise and Paul arrived. Celeste repeated her offer to Paul, which Cora had told him when he first walked into the house.

The front door opened and closed. "My God!"

Celeste stepped toward her friend. "Fairy, whatever are you doing out in this?"

"I wanted to see if I could drive in bad weather."

"You're out of your mind and you're not driving back! This is a big house and there's room for more."

On that note, Ben bounded down the stairs, stopping upon seeing Fairy, and her jaw dropped when she saw him. Celeste made the introductions. As she finished, a furious pounding at the front door startled them all.

Cora opened it to behold a distressed Yashew Gregorivitch.

"Yashew, get in here," she commanded.

He stepped in, looked at Celeste. "Miss Chalfonte—Miss Chalfonte, your sister sent me. The chapel's caught fire. She needs help."

Without missing a beat, Celeste ordered, "Cora, rouse Francis. Paul, will you ride back with Yashew, I want someone in the truck with him. The weather is filthy. Ben, come with me."

"Do you have tools, axes, buckets?" Ben asked.

"In the garage."

Ben took over. "We may need them. Men, before you go, let's grab what we can."

"Dear God," Celeste said under her breath. "Fairy, stay here. Please don't drive home."

"I am following you. I'm going to help."

"Me, too," Louise stoutly declared.

"And me." Cora rushed for her coat.

"Are you all crazy?" Celeste decried.

Cora, back in the hall, said, "No crazier than you are. Carlotta is going to need all of us."

"All right then. Louise and Cora, you go with Fairy. Fairy, Francis will follow you. If there's any trouble, you all will get into my car. Do you hear me?"

"We do."

"Let's go."

Chapter Twenty-Six

. . . .

April 10-11, 1920
Saturday and Sunday

Although they were going only four miles west of town, the trip proved agonizingly slow. When the small caravan pulled in to Immaculata Academy, the lowering sky reflected back the scarlet, gold, and swirling soot from the chapel fire.

No fire trucks or horse-drawn fire wagons had made it. Francis pulled as close to the chapel as he dared; the other vehicles followed, with Yashew in the truck getting out first, the others behind him.

Herbert and Carlotta, along with lines of girls, handed buckets of water to one another in a hopeless attempt to quell the flames.

Ben shouted something to Yashew, who led him and Paul to the side of the chapel in the rear. The three men pulled open the doors, disappearing inside.

Upon seeing her sister, Carlotta rushed over, sweat streaming down her face from being close to the heat.

"Celeste, thank God you're here."

Cora, Louise, and Fairy surrounded Celeste now.

"Carlotta, tell the girls to go back to their dormitories. This won't stop the fire. We've got to find another way."

"How?"

Instead of answering, Celeste ordered Cora and Louise, "Get those girls back inside. Make sure no one has frostbite. Fairy, come here. You-all divide up into the dorms, go into the kitchens, and cook anything that will warm them. Surely some of the girls will know what's in the kitchens. Carlotta, some of them have kitchen duties, do they not?"

"They do."

"Carlotta, you come with me. Francis, you, too. The men went to the other side of the chapel."

Following in the footsteps already being covered by snow, they found the opened doors.

Going into the basement—Herbert with Ben, Paul, and Yashew— the men viewed row upon row of barrels, barrels filled with good liquor.

Joining them and seeing the neatly stacked barrels, Celeste realized what was at stake.

Ben started rolling one out, followed by Paul then Yashew.

"I'm with you, boys." Francis hurried to the nearest barrel.

Celeste walked alongside Ben. "What's the chance of the forward barrels exploding?"

"Chances are the wood will burn, then the liquor. It's not combustible the way gunpowder is. I think we can save what's back here."

Yashew, behind him, called out, "Can't touch what's in front."

Carlotta shouted to her husband, "Where to?"

"Stables."

"No. You can't do that, Herbert. Think of the straw should any of these be hotter than we realize. Where else?" Carlotta thought, then called to Yashew, "Roll them to the base of the Infirmary. It's far enough away. We can divide things up once we've saved what we can."

Carlotta entered deeper into the basement to start rolling a barrel. Celeste came up next to her.

"It will take two of us for one of them. These are heavy." Celeste put her shoulder next to her big sister's and they worked in tandem.

Overhead they heard a smash, a tinkle.

"The floor. If the floor goes, the chapel goes." Carlotta did not cry, she rolled with all her might.

"We'll worry about that later. We can be thankful for this weather. It may yet put out the fire."

Into the night the little band worked. Feet wet, cold; hands swelled even with gloves on. They'd sweat in the basement and then the cold would hit them about halfway to the Infirmary. But the constant work kept them warm except for their feet, while the sleet stung their faces.

Herbert also rolled barrels. Not the strongest of men, he slipped and slid until finally Francis rolled with him.

By one in the morning they'd saved the last barrel they could touch. Two rows of stacked barrels burned below in the basement but the fire was abating.

Celeste, Carlotta, Ben, Paul, Yashew, and Francis returned to the chapel. They opened the side door and slipped in to examine the damage under the pulpit and lectern.

The heat had caused the glass to crack; the floorboards, while not burning, were buckling.

"Can we throw snow on this?" Carlotta, exhausted, asked.

"We can try." Ben motioned for the men to follow and they went outside to pick up the buckets the girls had abandoned in the snow.

Francis stayed in the chapel to touch walls, check what he could.

Yashew ran, finding those reserves of energy he'd found in the war, as did Ben and Paul. They covered the floor with snow, then the pulpit and lectern with snow, which were farthest away from what had been in flames.

Carlotta, Celeste, and Francis moved the flags, took off altar clothes, anything that would burn fast.

By two thirty the little group was done.

Carlotta and Celeste, leaning on one another, reached out and Ben and Yashew came to them, each man helping to hold up a lady.

"Let's go to the Rectory. Yashew, you take them. I'll get Cora, Louise, and Fairy from the dormitories."

"If they're asleep, let them be," Celeste advised.

Pushing open the door to her sister's house, the Rectory, Celeste was surprised to find Herbert, face streaked with soot.

"Men," Herbert said in a quivering voice, "the baths are drawn. I'll show you where to clean up. You'll have to make do with my clothing." He looked at Ben and Paul. "Two of you can fit into one shirt. Francis, come on."

Carlotta came in. "Asleep," she said to Celeste, who filled her in on Herbert's orders.

"Come on. We can take a bath in my room. We're slender enough to both fit into a tub. I can't stand feeling like this for another minute and my eyes burn."

Once clean, Ben, Paul, and Yashew fell asleep on the guest bedroom bed. Yashew took up half the bed but the men were so tired, they didn't really notice until they woke up the next morning, covers and pillows in disarray. Francis fell asleep in a chair.

After Celeste lay across her sister's bed to stretch after her bath, Carlotta couldn't rouse her so she instead pulled a blanket over her, put a pillow under her head, then retired to her husband's bedroom. He sat, head in hands, at his small desk.

Eyes bloodshot, he looked up at her. "Angel, I estimate we've lost fifteen thousand dollars. I have no idea of the damages to the chapel."

"Go to sleep, Herbert. We'll figure this out tomorrow. There's nothing more to be done."

"I have to pay these people. I—"

"My sister won't take a penny. Don't belittle them by offering cash, Herbert. We will find ways to show our gratitude. Now let's go to bed.

I've never been so tired in my life. No matter what happens, this is God's will and we must submit."

Herbert didn't know about God's will but he knew about Carlotta's.

Sunday 10:00 A.M.

Ben, dwarfed by Herbert's shirt, sat up rubbing his stubble. He rocked Paul awake. Yashew snored like a freight train.

"Pearlie, listen."

Eyes now open, the wiry painter sat up. "Are we dead?"

"No."

"Sometimes in the trenches I thought I was dead. But those are angels."

"Put your clothes on. And we'd better get Yashew in something."

"We can wrap a blanket around him." Paul put his hand on the big man's shoulders. "Yashew. Yashew. Come on, Brother, the angels are singing."

"Huh." Hearing the voices, Yashew sat bolt upright.

"Come on now," Paul gently urged, handed him a shirt, which fit although he couldn't button it.

Grabbing a towel, the big fellow headed for the hall, as did the other two, tripping over the pants; too big for them, too small for Yashew.

Standing on the stairway were Celeste, Carlotta, Francis, and Herbert. Below, squeezed into every corner, all the girls of the Academy were singing, with Louise at the piano. Cora and Fairy had found tambourines.

They sang "Amazing Grace," then they hopped to "All God's Children Got Shoes." The spirituals, sweet, strong, promised victory over adversity. They clapped, they sang, a solo would rise up from time to time. Carlotta joined in.

Ben edged down to Celeste, putting his hands on her shoulders. She turned, lifted up her head, and tears flooded down her face. He started to cry and he turned around to see Paul, Yashew, and Francis wiping their eyes. Within minutes, everyone was crying, laughing.

The concert stopped. Louise played a dramatic chord on the piano which asked for attention, then she spoke. "Mrs. Van Dusen, we are all safe and sound. The good Lord has protected us."

Lifting her chin, Carlotta spoke, her voice lyrical. "Jubilate Deo. Psalm One Hundred. Make a joyful noise unto the Lord, all ye lands; Serve the Lord with gladness, come before His presence with singing." She paused, smiling at the girls. "Know ye that the Lord He is God: it is He that hath made us, and not we ourselves, we are His people, and the sheep of His pasture.

"Enter into His gates with thanksgiving, and into his courts with praise: be thankful unto Him, and bless His name.

"For the Lord is good. His mercy is everlasting: and His truth endureth to all generations."

She stepped down to the first floor, walked among the girls, hugged them, kissed them. She especially thanked Cora, Louise, and Fairy. Then she went to the front door, opened it, and called out, "Off with you now. And thank you for the loveliest choir I have ever heard."

As each girl filed out, Carlotta took her hand, thanking her by name. The cold air slipped in like a wedge, a few desultory flakes lazing down. As the last girl stepped outside, Cora called out from the kitchen, "Come on!"

Cora, Fairy, and Louise had hurried in and thrown together whatever they could find. A large pot of coffee filled the air with fragrance, a pot of tea whistled.

Yashew needed no encouragement. Herbert guided him to the big dining room, where unbidden he actually set the table.

Carlotta sat at one end of the table, Herbert at another. All formality tossed aside, they pulled out chairs and passed the food left to right.

"Mr. Trumbull, Mr. Battle, what a dramatic way to become acquainted." Carlotta, never adverse to admiring a handsome man, was quite pleased to have one on each side of her.

Herbert smiled at Ben. "This will surprise you as you swim in my shirt, but once I was as fit as you are."

"Ah, time works its will," mused Carlotta, a bit overweight but not much. "Cora, this is the best spoon bread I have ever eaten and each time I have the pleasure of eating your cooking I forget to ask for the recipe."

"The cook's hand." Fairy tipped her hand and they laughed.

Noticing how Carlotta beamed at Paul, Louise thought this the time. "Mrs. Van Dusen. Paul and I are engaged."

A moment's silence followed this, as even Fairy didn't know.

"A toast. Herbert." Carlotta tilted her head slightly.

He rose, disappeared to the pantry, and returned with a bottle of prewar champagne.

Celeste, seeing the year, raised her eyebrows.

Carlotta, noticing, opened her hands as if in benediction. "We should celebrate. Make a joyful noise unto the Lord."

Driving the four miles back to Runnymede even in the light proved arduous but the little band finally made it to Celeste's. Yashew had stayed at Immaculata. The Van Dusens kept a small apartment there which he could use coming back after late deliveries; the rest of the time he lived with his mother. Once his sister, a scholarship student, graduated, she'd return to Runnymede to be with Mrs. Gregorivitch, whose eyesight was failing.

"I knew it!" Cora announced when she opened the kitchen door.

General Pershing wagged his tail. Hungry, he had opened the cabinets and pulled out whatever might be edible. The General, Felicity, and Glue celebrated their own breakfasts.

Laughing, Cora opened the door so the dog could go outside and relieve himself.

Francis stepped inside. "Miss Chalfonte, will you be needing me?"

"No, but allow me to give you a little something for your pains." She winked to Cora, who went to the pantry, returning with another bottle of champagne.

"You and the missus can sit by the fire and toast one another's good health."

The chauffeur left quite happy and Celeste made a mental note to call Asa Grumbacher to give Francis's wife a spring outfit. She'd send a blank check with Louise. That would mean more to the good fellow than anything for himself. He doted on his wife. Named Prissy, she was anything but.

Still tired and sore, Celeste, Ben, Fairy, Louise, Paul, and Cora slumped in the library, all still dressed in clothing that didn't fit, colors that clashed.

Celeste pulled at her blouse. "I had no idea there was so much of Carlotta." She giggled.

"Oh, now, Celeste, she has a shelf, and a touch of fat hides the wrinkles." Fairy smiled.

"There is that," Celeste ruefully agreed.

"Miss Chalfonte, what do you think happened?" Louise asked.

"The fire?" Celeste swung her feet onto the hassock, she really was bone tired. "I have no idea."

Paul quietly opined, "If someone left a lantern and it turned over, that could have started it. The other choice is that the fire was deliberate."

"Deliberate?" Cora was aghast. "Why burn a chapel?"

"To remove the competition," Ben said.

"What competition?" Fairy and Cora echoed one another.

Louise, silent, was as baffled as they were.

"You-all didn't go down into the basement." Paul held out his fingers, which hurt a bit. "Did you see us rolling the barrels?"

"The weather was so filthy we couldn't see much once we left the kitchen," Fairy replied. "What is going on?"

"Underneath the chapel, hundreds of barrels of liquor were stacked," Paul replied. "Good scotch, I think."

"Christ Lutheran." Louise put it together. "That's why you told me not to ask too many questions when Yashew was over there, isn't it?"

"Yes." He smiled at her. "Again, the fire could have been an accident, but if not, those who intend to sell alcohol are playing rough."

"This early in the game?" Celeste wondered.

"I believe so, Miss Chalfonte. If they establish dominance, they'll have at least the rural western Maryland and southern Pennsylvania market to themselves, for hard liquor anyway. No one will ever stop the Pennsylvanians from making beer."

"Pabst closed down. So did Natty Boh." Ben named two breweries in Baltimore—National Bohemian by its nickname.

"A fortune," Celeste whispered. "Corner the market and you've made millions."

"Upon millions," Ben added.

Fairy waved her hand. "Oh, it will all blow over."

"Fairy, when a politician takes a stand always based on his constituency, he doesn't back down, no matter how wrong he is," stated Celeste. "Carrie Nation and her troops built a convincing case about ending the production and sale of liquor."

"This isn't going to stop anyone." Cora stated the obvious. "But she does have something, I mean, men drinking up their paychecks, leaving the wives and children destitute. It happens."

"But this won't stop it. It will just drive it all underground," Paul said. "I don't know Mr. Van Dusen, but it seems to me when a man of that stature, with that much money, salts away all those barrels, he believes the profits will be huge."

"I wonder if my sister knew?" Celeste thought a moment. "No matter. There's still plenty left."

"Well, he has to hide those barrels, because eventually old man Tangerman and John Gassner will be out there," Cora noted, then added for Ben and Paul's benefit, "As well as the two fire chiefs—both younger brothers of our two mayors, obviously more Tangerman and Gassners. Plus Herbert has to get rid of the burned barrels."

"Why do both fire chiefs have to go? Isn't Immaculata just this side of the Line?" Ben asked.

"Oh, it's just the way we do things. If one mayor, fire chief, or police chief goes, the other side has to go too. Everybody's afraid they'll miss something. Last night, they certainly did." Celeste smiled when Glue came in, clawed up the side of the chair to sit in her lap.

Fairy, working this over in her mind, raised her voice slightly. "If this is about competition—I mean, if someone set that fire, how will anyone know? I suppose if there's a second one . . ."

Louise surprised everyone by speaking out. "Herbert will hide what's left and there's a lot left. Yashew can help. The trick is to keep this away from the girls."

"You'll know if someone goes to whoever has been buying liquor to see if they want to order more." Paul, of a practical mind, had part of the answer.

Ben added to Paul's sentiments. "Whoever did this, if anyone did, probably knows Herbert's customers. First they might try to hire Yashew."

Louise defended her classmate. "He'll never do it. He's loyal. Even if he is dating Lottie."

"Oh, no!" Fairy exclaimed. "Celeste, why didn't you tell me?"

"I didn't know." She turned toward Ben. "You don't think Yashew's in danger, do you?"

"Not if he plays dumb," Ben forthrightly answered. "How tough is Herbert?"

No one said a word until Cora did. "He has a gift for making money."

"And he's discreet," Celeste added. "If he engages in sharp business practices, he keeps it to himself."

"People talk. You'd know," Fairy said. "Herbert might not be a match for someone who would burn a chapel."

"I suppose we'll find out over time." Celeste rubbed Glue's little ears.

The front door opened and closed. Two pairs of feet stamped. They could hear two coats being removed and hung up.

Fannie Jump trailed by Juts, who had spent the night at Ev's, books under her arm, entered the library, studied the motley attire.

"What in God's name have you-all been doing?"

Chapter Twenty-Seven

. . . .

April 12, 1920
Monday

The sun melted most of the snow and sleet bits, although strips of white shone in the western crevices of pastures and woods.

Celeste and Ben drove out to Immaculata. He didn't need to be in Baltimore until Tuesday, which pleased them both.

One mile east of Immaculata, Francis pointed out the side of a tree. "Look at that. Had to be lightning."

Blackened and scorched, one side of the tree bore witness to a strike. Sometimes lightning would hit, burn part of a tree, then lashing rains would save it. Buildings burned faster if they got hit, although they, too, were sometimes saved by rain.

"I never thought of a lightning strike at Immaculata," Celeste remarked. "Well, I didn't see any lightning on the way there. Odd, we've had thunder and lightning during two snows this year—although the weekend wasn't much of a snow."

"It was enough." Ben smiled. "Took half the night and the next day to warm up."

"Got that right." Francis nodded. "Here we are and there she is."

Thanks to Celeste's call, Carlotta awaited them on the steps of the chapel.

The four entered the chapel through the main doors to stand quietly in the wide center aisle. Shards of glass from the windows near the pulpit and the lectern glittered everywhere, on pews, on the floor, on the altar, the pulpit, the lectern. Some glass had even blown back near to where they stood.

Holding out her arm, Carlotta simply stated, "It could have been far worse. Charlie Ischatta is coming out tomorrow with his men to inspect the support beams under the front. If they're firm, this won't be as expensive as I fear."

There was an abundance of Ischattas in the neighborhood and Gene managed the Orioles.

"You'll need to replace the floor near the front doors, what's left of them," Celeste noticed.

"If I'm going to do it then I'll do the entire floor. This was a beautiful chapel and will be so again."

Ben nodded in agreement. "Do you mind if I go up to the pulpit?"

"No, of course not. We should all go."

Standing under the pulpit, Francis knelt down and knocked the hollow raised floor. "Has anyone crawled under here?"

"Yashew did. He said it was charred but not terribly damaged. The sleet and snow saved us. If you-all hadn't carried buckets of snow to cover the floor, it would be far worse." Carlotta walked to the door beside the raised floor. Steps led up to the lectern on one side, same on the other. There was a door by the pulpit, steps behind that led to the cellar.

Descending the stairs with no light, they held the rail, pitted but also intact. Once down in the cellar, the small windows, also blown out, admitted light.

"What'd you do with the burning kegs?" Francis was curious as they had been too hot to even touch.

"They finally burned down, the contents also, most of which leaked out," said Carlotta. "The wind blew sleet and snow in here, which helped. Sunday afternoon, both fire departments showed up with hoses. Increase Martin brought the Old Dixie fire engine, so he used that water, Lawrence Villcher brought huge long hoses with pumps, broke the ice, and dropped them into our pond. That did the trick. Both men brought their sons and those boys worked as good as any men, I can tell you."

"Did they say anything about the kegs?" Francis asked.

Carlotta folded her hands as they walked outside from the basement, a walk they would always remember, since that had been the only way to roll out the barrels. "Herbert took care of all that."

Celeste started to say something then didn't.

Noticing, Carlotta continued, "We all felt it imperative to keep both police chiefs out of this. Increase and Lawrence promised to report it as a spontaneous fire started by lightning." She paused, smiling slightly. "Herbert gave each man two barrels from the Infirmary. He also offered to help in any way if new equipment was needed."

Sighing with relief, Francis murmured, "They'll keep the secret."

"Where are the burned barrels?" Celeste asked.

"Yashew and a few friends chopped them up, stacked them by the tool shed. Did you know his mother will be getting a cataract operation? He's doing everything he can to make extra money and so is his sister. Personally, I think this type of procedure they're talking about is too new, but then again, I'm not going blind." She walked toward the Rectory. "I owe you all a great deal, as well as Cora, Louise, Paul, and Fairy. Celeste, help me think of suitable rewards."

Francis boomed out, "I don't want any money. The girls don't either."

Carlotta patted him on the forearm. "Francis, I do know that, but often in life there is something special someone needs, like Ms. Gregorivitch's operation. Perhaps you-all will know of something."

Celeste, slyly, remarked, "The Good Lord or the Blessed Virgin Mother will tell you when it's time."

Carlotta added to the comment, "Our Lady."

"I think you need Our Lady of the Cash Register." Celeste couldn't help it.

"You are insufferable." Carlotta's frown turned into a half-smile. "My penance is having to deal with you."

"Mine as well." Celeste's comment was just ambiguous enough to make them all wonder.

As Celeste had promised Ben she'd show him St. Paul's and the mice behind the Ascension tapestry some weeks ago she had Francis park at St. Paul's, after they'd returned from Immaculata.

"We won't be long," Celeste told Francis, then turned to Ben. "We need to climb up the long front steps for the full effect."

Once inside the vestibule they paused to admire the anteroom's proportions.

The rows of pews, two wide aisles, and balcony asserted that this was a house of worship with a large congregation. The soaring ceiling, the story-and-a-half stained-glass windows, the impressive altar cross and candles testified that this was also a rich congregation.

Ben took it all in. "Beautiful."

"Late-eighteenth-century. Not Chartres, but we were new as a country. In some ways this church, those early churches, reveal our dreams for the future."

He studied the stained glass. "You know, over the centuries, subject matter changed but not technique. There are only so many ways to create a stained-glass window."

"Saint Jerome." She mentioned the figure in the window as they walked by.

"I remember one church, roof gone, but the windows remained and the light shone, coloring the rubble. Bombardments could be peculiar. I felt something when I stepped inside, something I've never felt in an intact church. It was holy."

"Something elaborate yet stark at the same time perhaps."

"Yes."

She touched his elbow leading him to the enormous Ascension tapestry.

She whispered, "Listen."

Ben leaned toward the heavy woven cloth and heard a tiny squeak, then another.

"Episcopalian mice." Celeste folded her hands together.

"And very Christian mice. They picked the Ascension, so they must believe in the resurrection of the body."

She scooped a handful of cracked corn from her pocket and placed it on the long gleaming Hepplewhite table under the tapestry. "For the body."

"I'm sure they are holy mice." Ben smiled.

"Better than a holy cow."

Once back home, Celeste reported the state of the chapel to Cora and to Juts, who was actually sitting at the kitchen table doing lessons.

Juts glanced up at Ben. "Do you like history?"

"Yes."

"Will you look at this test?"

"Juts, he is not taking your test for you and you are not to bother Celeste's guest," Cora reprimanded her.

"I took the test. I just want him to look at it." She slid the paper toward him.

Standing at the edge of the table, he picked it up, reading it. "'The War of the Roses.'" Scanning the numbered questions, he pointed to one. "Richard the Third was Edward the Fourth's *younger* brother."

She took the page back, erased her incorrect answer. "Gee, thanks."

Later, once they were alone, Ben started the gramophone, bowed to Celeste, took her in his arms, and they danced to Edith Day singing "Alice Blue Gown."

Celeste smiled. "We're going to have to practice. I'm accustomed to leading, not that Ramelle and I ever danced in public."

Looking through her records, he pulled out a waltz. "I can follow."

She cocked her head, then with vigor took him in her arms as the music started and they danced, laughing when the song ended.

He kissed her hand.

She kissed his. "Your British partner taught you well."

"He did. I do hope he's alive. I know I'll never see him again, but I think of him, and after dancing with you, I owe him a debt of gratitude."

"As do I."

He knelt down to scoop up Glue, who had just wandered in. "What do you think a pussycat would like to hear?"

Celeste put on Jolson's "Sewanee." He wrapped his arms around her waist as she held Glue between them. The kitty climbed onto Ben's broad shoulders. He slowed the steps and the three of them finished in good order, Glue thrilled with the attention from two humans. Celeste carried her back into the kitchen, put down food as Ben searched for something for the two of them.

Later, covers up, for the night was cool, fire keeping the chill off, they talked.

"You really are a good dancer." Her head rested against his chest. He was propped up by pillows.

"Did you like me better leading or following?" He kissed the top of her head.

"Leading. I was always the tallest in school, in college, so I would have to lead. It's relaxing not to, but then you're easy to follow." She listened to a log crackle. "Cherrywood."

"Smells good."

"Ben, I will never be able to thank you, nor will Carlotta, for your help in that cold, miserable, inflamed mess."

"No one was hurt. That's all that matters." He left it at that.

"What do you think of my sister?"

"Forceful."

"Always has been. We're like chalk and cheese but I can appreciate her good qualities. Carlotta wants an arcana—a universal remedy." She explained the term in case he wasn't familiar with it.

"I think most people do, don't you?"

"Yes, I suppose they do. You don't seem to need one," she commented.

"I don't. You don't seem to need one either."

"No. I like to understand history, ideas, but the dream of universal illumination, of worldwide understanding, even of agreement in our own country, I don't believe it can ever happen."

"You're way ahead of me. I'm happy to smell your hair, to listen to the birds now that they've returned. I'm simple."

"I wouldn't put it that way. If anything, you're happier than most. What do we have, really, other than the day we are in?"

"Some days you'd rather not be in." He inhaled. "But they pass. You can always find something to see, laugh about. Even in the trenches, we could laugh. I remember one fellow from Georgia. The bombardment started at dawn. We were both waiting for our orders, both messengers, and he said, 'This is torching the barn to kill the rats.' Made me laugh."

She smiled. "Good description. I suspect the rats lived."

"Well, Glue has a big job when she grows up."

This made Celeste smile again as she asked, "Do you think about tomorrow? The future?"

"Not so much. You?"

"I used to, but not so much anymore. When I was young I wanted to run one of the family businesses when I grew up. My father, a wonderful man, really, I'm sorry you couldn't have known him and vice versa, but he thought that just a horrid idea. He'd tell me how cutthroat business was, how a man is never free of it. His phrase was, 'You take the store home with you.' And of course, he made it clear that Stirling would take the store home. When we were all young, naturally we didn't know what we'd be doing, but as the eldest, Stirling did. I resented him for that."

"And now?"

"In many ways, Ben, my father was right. Stirling is bound and burdened in a way I am not but I would have liked to try, you know, to see if I could make things hum."

"You make me hum." He hummed Al Jolson's "Tell Me."

This made her sit up straight and laugh at him. "Broadway lost a star when you decided to play baseball."

"Ha!"

She confessed, "I have to give it to Carlotta, she wasn't allowed to run any of the businesses either but she started a school. Oh, I can't stand the religious part of it. You're Catholic, but people can find their own way on religion. Here are these young women being taught papal infallibility, you name it, along with even worse. Carlotta and I have fought since we were children, but she has done something useful. I have not. I'm not interested in education. I have no artistic ability. Worse, I never wanted to fulfill my place in society. I've lived an exciting life but not such a useful one. You, on the other hand, have been dutiful, useful."

"Depends on how you define useful. Yes, I did my duty but I don't see that you've been useless. You help the people you know. You give."

"I don't know why I'm even talking about this. I blame it on you."

"Me?"

"Yes. You make me think of things in a new way." She kissed him on the cheek. "Now I must ask a favor."

"Anything."

"I want to see where you live in Baltimore."

He chuckled lightly. "It's nothing like this. You'll walk in and walk out."

"No, I won't. I really want to see where and how you live."

"All right, but my landlady doesn't allow lady visitors. If you visit, we have to leave the door to my rooms open."

"Very proper. What surprises me is that you would rent rooms with such a restriction. One, you are terribly handsome. Two, you have a good sense of humor and are kind. Three, all those women ogling you out on the baseball diamond. You could have your pick of the litter."

"Flatterer." He put his arm around her shoulders. "I rented the rooms because I can walk to the stadium. Saves money. There's a little kitchen, so I can cook, which also saves money. I'm not like Cora but I can manage the basics."

"What about women?"

He shrugged. "Before the war I chased the girls, but when I came home, I didn't want to be close to anyone. Just didn't."

"Then why did you hop on that train to come out here?"

"When we talked, a door opened. That's the only way I can put it. You didn't act like other women. Women can be false. A man doesn't find out until it's too late. You're different."

"For what it's worth, men can be false, too, but I know what you mean. I felt the same way just then about you. And here we are."

A long silence followed, then he said in a low deep voice, "Life. I didn't want to die but I wasn't living. I can't explain it. I can't explain much."

"No need. We are both triumphantly alive."

At three in the morning, Celeste was awakened by a deep moan from Ben. He was shaking and sweating, his teeth chattering. She touched him but he didn't awaken, he shook more. She pushed at him harder, his eyes opened but he didn't see.

"It's gas! It's gas. Neddie, get your mask."

"Ben. Ben." She wrapped her arms around him and he grabbed her, his power almost knocking the wind out of her.

"Gas, Neddie, gas." Then he howled.

"Ben, oh Ben, for God's sake, wake up."

Slowly he did, but still sweating, teeth still chattering. He stared at her, eyes wide. Then he buried his head in her neck, stifling sobs.

"You're home. You're safe and you're home." She smoothed his hair, kissing him.

Slowly he stopped shaking, murmured, "I'm sorry," and fell to sleep.

She lay there, holding him, the embers glowing in the fireplace. What did her poor brother Spotts see before he died? Did he know? What did any of them see or feel or know? And she prayed to God to give them peace. She prayed to the Blessed Virgin Mother, even though she would tease Carlotta about Mother Mary, now she prayed to the Blessed Virgin Mother that those who came home, wherever home might be, would find peace.

The next morning, she was already at the breakfast table, reading both newspapers, when she heard Ben pounding down the stairs.

He bounced into the breakfast room, leaned over, kissed her, then sat down.

"Forgive me, Angel. I should have told you sometimes I have a nightmare."

"Nothing to forgive," she replied.

"I never want to frighten you." He looked steadily into her eyes. "I want to protect you."

She put down the paper. "You do. Simply having you in the room makes me feel safe, happy, young."

She did not ask him who Neddie was. She wondered if the smell of the chapel fire, the working through the dreadful weather, did that bring back some horror? Then again, no veteran needed a reminder. It occurred to her that her father had seen hell. She was too young, too self-centered, as only the young can be, to even imagine that her elegant, powerful father had ever shaken in terror, was ever splattered with the blood of other men. Did he see the men he killed or did he just shoot in the direction of the enemy? Surely he heard the screams, saw the carnage. She never asked and he never said.

Spotts, in his voluminous letters or his short notes scribbled on the backs of envelopes, rarely described his experiences. He would be funny or ask about the horses and how was hunting this year?

She knew nothing. She had been and continued to be protected, as was every other woman she knew who had a husband, brother, son, friend who had served. Her women. What of the French? What of the German women? Were those women allies or enemies simply because of the country in which they lived, the men they, too, loved? What did it all mean and why had she never even thought about it?

"Ben."

He looked up from his paper expectantly.

"I am going to be quite forward." She took a deep breath, smiled. "I would like you to know that I love you."

Chapter Twenty-Eight

· · · ·

April 15, 1920
Thursday

F riday and Saturday brought the most shoppers to the Bon Ton. In preparation, Louise worked on a mannequin wearing a lilac chiffon chemise, a bit of lace border around a scoop neck. A white hat, white shoes, and a white parasol with a thin dark green ribbon stripe completed the outfit. Simple jewelry—a slender silver bracelet, large silver squared earrings, and a deep aquamarine set in silver—looked wonderful on the mannequin's finger; Louise had even painted her nails.

Finishing her last mannequin of the day, she stepped back to admire her creation.

Mrs. Rhodes left her counter for a moment to come stand behind her. Louise turned to ask if Delilah needed help.

Delilah looked Louise from head to toe, lifted her head, flounced off in indignation.

Louise watched her, raised her eyebrows, then moved the mannequin to the edge of her area. Back at her counter, she wrote out in fine script the prices of each item.

Sidney Yost came over. Realizing Louise's retail gifts and how she pleased Mr. Grumbacher, Sidney aimed to be on the winning team.

He touched Louise's elbow and cut his eyes to Delilah hovering over at the cosmetics counter, whispering something to Regina Eutaw, another employee, who looked at Louise then quickly averted her eyes.

Sidney, back at the cosmetics counter, missed the moment but he hadn't missed much else. "Wheezie, Delilah is spreading malicious gossip about you. She's blabbing to anyone she thinks will listen."

"She's making it up."

Sidney smirked. "I'm sure. But she's telling people that you spent the night with Paul at Immaculata Academy over the weekend, right under your benefactor's nose. She told Dorcas, who told me."

Dorcas ran the lingerie department.

"What!" Louise's voice rose.

Sidney frowned. "She says that Yashew told Lottie."

Mind working fast, Louise knew that Yashew would not do anything to harm her. She also knew that he probably told Lottie about the fire, the general exhaustion, and Lottie took it from there, embellishing the story of everyone sleeping at the academy to suit herself.

Both newspapers carried reports of the fire identifying the source of the fire as a probable lightning strike. Sunday morning, as the chapel still smoldered up front, Herbert had conducted both reporters through the damage, then handed each reporter an envelope for the advertising director, containing a six months' advertising contract—a half page for Van Dusen Hauling. Naturally, he told the two men that, while the lightning strike could not be verified, nothing else indicated a source of conflagration. He also told them that if they drove back to Runnymede on the direct road they would probably find damaged trees, maybe even old buildings where the wind had flattened them or lightning had struck. The storm was dreadful.

If either reporter thought alcohol had been stored there or shipped from there, it did not appear in the final version of the report.

Louise watched as Delilah, head held high, briefly visited other clerks whom she felt might enjoy the implications of a night at Immaculata. Most all the clerks got along, but since Louise's smash sales day, a current of envy ran through some of the ladies, especially those like Dorcas. She had worked behind the counter for decades, doing a decent job but devoid of all imagination, without a clue as to how to subtly push a product. Quite possibly, some might give Delilah an interested hearing.

"Sidney, people believe what they want to believe. We did all sleep there. The men in one room and we ladies scattered in others."

Sidney always wanted to control the situation. "You can't let her get away with it."

"I can hardly bring Carlotta, Celeste, my mother down here to testify on my behalf." She held out her finger with the cigar band on it. "And I am engaged."

"Honey, that band will disintegrate in no time. No one will believe you're engaged until you have a diamond engagement ring and it's announced in the papers."

"What?"

"People will take you for a fool being seduced by a smooth-talking, good-looking fellow."

At that moment, Louise didn't know whom she hated more, Sidney or Delilah.

Controlling herself, she smiled tightly at Sidney. "I appreciate your warning. This isn't a warning, merely a notice: I think we'll have another crowd on Saturday. If you ask Mr. Grumbacher if you might carry a sales book, just in case you are needed, he'll be impressed."

Sidney blinked. "Yes, yes, of course."

Off he went to climb the stairs to ask permission to carry his own sales book. She observed, knowing full well he would present this as his own idea. Fine by her. She had bigger fish to fry, but first she had to catch them.

· · ·

The late afternoon warmed as the sun shone without a cloud in the sky. Celeste, Fannie Jump, and Fairy sat outside, listening to the birds sing.

Fannie Jump launched into the tea cakes and sandwiches, proclaiming, "You know, Celeste, Fairy and I really must do more at our homes. You are always the hostess."

"No husband to convince, less uproar." Celeste leaned back in her chair. "If you count out Juts; she's been alarmingly docile."

"Really?" Fairy's tone rose.

"She's doing her lessons, helps around here, and spends time with Ev because Ev brings her lessons home from school. I hope she's given up the idea of quitting." Celeste poured herself more tea, the others stuck to cold drinks. "I've heard the Daughters of the Confederacy and the Sisters of Gettysburg are planning a special celebration at our Magna Carta Day. Something about the fifty-fifth anniversary of the end of the war."

Fannie Jump, more relaxed now, boomed out, "They should have done that on April ninth."

"Too cold, plus everyone shows on June fifteenth," Fairy said.

"If they'd done anything last week, they'd have to realize the young don't care," Fannie growled.

"You're right, but Minta Mae versus Caesura will make us care," Celeste noted. "They'll hijack our best day." She paused. "I already have a date."

"Do you?" Fairy remarked.

"Ben," came the answer.

"More fun if you're next to a handsome man on Magna Carta Day." Fannie reached for another tea sandwich.

"I hope so." Celeste held up her teacup as if in salute. "Touché." Fannie held up her drink.

Fairy was on her high horse. "You two. Celeste, I don't recall you engaging in innuendo even when we were at Smith."

"Oh, Fairy. You were worried about Celeste when Ramelle so inconveniently found herself on the path to motherhood. She's happy now."

"Were you worried?" Celeste addressed Fairy.

"Worried is too strong a word but you did endure a jolt, Celeste. You keep things to yourself, but if Archie had become pregnant"—she used a strong word—"I would have either fainted or cast him into darkness."

"No, you wouldn't have, Precious." Fannie Jump glowed. "You would have exhibited him with the traveling circus and further enriched yourself." She drained her scotch. "I'd be thrilled if men could bear children. Knock some sense into them."

"Has it knocked sense into us?" Celeste remarked. "No. All it's done is create an unnatural state, chastity for the marriage market. Then, once married, you throw that to the winds and enjoy physical congress. Should you submit to powerful eroticism before marriage and find yourself in Ramelle's state, you're ruined."

"Unless your parents have enough money to send you on a European tour." Fannie poured another drink.

"What tour?" Fairy was puzzled.

"That's just the point, Fairy. It's a lie so the poor girl can go have her baby, give it up, and come home an intact virgin for the marriage market," Fannie Jump said sarcastically.

"And given that a European tour is something most young women of means embark upon after college, it's a good cover."

"Ramelle, fortunately, was older and found a rich, good man. Plus she married him." Celeste shrugged. "Fairy, thank you for thinking about me. Maybe on one level, I was relieved." They both stared at her so she continued, "She wanted to be a mother. Now she will. I don't want to be the source of anyone's disappointment. I disappointed Mother enough."

"Celeste, your mother loved you," Fairy insisted. "When you returned from England, she was happy. She didn't really want you to live in England. Yes, she did think you would marry well here, but she still loved you and you kept up appearances."

"That she did. Let's go back to this men getting pregnant thing." Fannie warmed up. "Remember when we all read Pliny the Elder's *Natural History*?"

"Yes." Fairy finished her sweet tea, reached for the pitcher, poured more. "I thought it great fun."

"Remember the people he described who live at the far reaches of the earth? There were the people with one big foot. On a hot day they'd flop down and use their foot for an umbrella." Fannie Jump smiled. "Then there were the Blemmyae, whose faces were in their chests but in every other way they were perfectly human."

Fairy nodded. "Of course, I remember."

"And what about the Machlyes?" Fannie Jump leaned toward Fairy.

"Yes, yes, the people who can assume either sex at will." Fairy enjoyed remembering college sophomore Latin, at which she had excelled.

"Well, maybe men could get pregnant. Who knows if there's truth in those stories but some of them have proven true when an archaeologist digs up something." Fannie Jump folded her arms across her chest.

"Wouldn't it be wonderful?" Celeste thought. "No human being could hide behind being male or female to excuse stupid or brutal or selfish behavior. We'd really have to own up to our sins."

"Or enjoy them," Fannie Jump roared.

"Oh, Fannie, I love Archie, but really, *enjoy* is too strong a word." Fairy exhaled loudly through her nose.

"Listen, Fairy, if he knew what he was doing in bed, you'd be thrilled. Our husbands, decent men and good providers, do not have excitement for a middle name. I have this one life and by God, I am going to have excitement." Fannie Jump slapped the table.

"Fannie, dear, don't take another drink," Fairy reprimanded her.

"She has a point." Celeste smiled. "But so do you. We have this one life, this sliver between eternities. Perhaps rules are meant to be broken."

Fairy folded her hands together. "I'd hate to be a man."

"No one said you had to like it. I don't think I'd care one way or the other so long as I could change into a woman whenever I felt like it.

Which I would because I wouldn't want to sleep with women," Fannie declared.

"But if you were a man, perhaps you would." Celeste stated the obvious, although not obvious to Fannie Jump.

Fairy entertained the thought. "Maybe."

"Celeste, I never could understand why you put up with it. The time it takes to arouse a woman, convincing her you truly care, listening to the questions or just listening, period. I couldn't do it. I haven't the patience," Fannie grumbled.

Celeste smiled. "You learn to have it. You and I can't be the only women who can be direct. But it doesn't matter. We are who we are. We are stuck with what we are and we might as well make the best of it."

"Would you like to be a Machyle?" Fairy was honestly curious.

"I'd give it a try. Maybe we're seeing the world with just one eye. Switch sexes at will and you apprehend all reality."

"Maybe that's the point of loving a man." Fairy spoke with firmness. "You do have your other eye opened through his experiences and vice versa. Perhaps that truly is the point of dimorphism."

Both Fannie and Celeste looked at her.

Before either could respond, the back door opened and closed.

"Mother!" Louise's voice carried. "You won't believe this!"

The three walked back into the house and, along with Cora, heard of Delilah's gossip.

Fannie Jump curled her upper lip. "That woman lives in a state of perpetual inconsequence."

"True." Celeste smiled at Louise, then looked at her friends. "We need time to consider this, but it does appear that Big Dimps needs to come to Jesus."

Celeste used the southern term that meant one will be severely corrected.

Chapter Twenty-Nine

....

April 17, 1920
Saturday

The marble steps shone, a receding line of daily washed entrances and exits. A fourteenth-century painter, coming to grips with perspective, would have delighted in the steps, for which Baltimore is famous.

Celeste and Ben reached his rooming house, where Mrs. McCleary, bucket and brush, suds overflowing, vigorously scrubbed her steps.

"Mrs. McCleary, I'm sorry to dirty your steps, which are always whiter than anyone else's." Ben had his hand under Celeste's arm. "This is my friend, Miss Celeste Chalfonte, I'm going to show her my quarters and I will leave the door open. We won't be long, but I'd like her to see how bright everything is, even the stairway."

Mrs. McCleary didn't rise but looked Celeste up and down. She knew a rich woman when she saw one.

"I'm pleased to meet you, Mrs. McCleary."

"Likewise." The stout middle-aged woman forced a tight smile. "Ben. Did you win?"

"We did, ma'am, we did. Eleven to four."

"Saints be praised." She smiled at last. "Monza owes me one dollar."

Monza, a neighbor, had been named for the popular stage star of an earlier day, Monza Alverta Algood, a celebrated beauty. The current Monza missed that boat, but she was tidy, knew what colors looked good on her, and was a stalwart friend to Mrs. McCleary.

"I'll do my best to enrich you." Ben smiled as he led Celeste up the steps.

Mrs. McCleary heard their footfalls recede. Puzzled by something she put down her brush, hurried next door. "Monza, the Orioles won."

Monza, thin, appeared at the door, reached into her skirt pocket, and pulled out a dollar. "I will win it back."

"Monza, help me. Why does the name Chalfonte sound so familiar?"

"Old Line Manufacturing, the B & O Railroad, and God knows what else."

Mrs. McCleary's eyes popped open wide. "There's a Chalfonte in my house. Her necklace and earrings could buy the block!"

"In your house." Monza thought, then genuflected.

Mrs. McCleary gave her a playful slap. "Monza, you'll have to confess that and if you don't, I will."

They both laughed.

Ben opened the door to his rooms: a small kitchen, small living room under a skylight, a bedroom and tiny bathroom. "Here we are."

Celeste stepped inside, looked around. "You are such a clean fellow."

A flat, polished drawing board rested on the porcelain-topped kitchen table, two chairs shoved underneath. Papers on top drew Celeste's attention.

"May I?" She picked up the top paper, good drawing paper, a box of colored pencils resting on the table as well. "Ben, these are beautiful."

He stood beside her. "I thought to do windows of the great ladies of the Bible. Queen Esther, Sarah, Judith." He paused as she pulled out the last one. "I really did this for you. Ruth and Naomi."

A mist colored Celeste's eyes. Who would have thought of Ruth and Naomi, most especially the man you hold in your arms? "Ben—" She took a deep breath, repeating herself. "These are beautiful."

"Well, I thought"—a boyish enthusiasm shone from his face, vibrated in his voice—"Carlotta has lost all her windows and it is a school for girls and, well, shouldn't they look at the heroines of the Bible? I haven't gotten to Anne yet, nor her daughter, the Blessed Virgin Mother, but I'm thinking about it. For the Blessed Virgin Mother, I must use a lot of light blue and—" He stopped himself. "I'm blathering."

"No, no, I'm actually overcome."

"Well." He pulled out a chair for her. "She may not like them but I'm going to try. If she knows about us, she may not like them at all."

"She'll ignore it. Actually, she will take comfort in the fact that you are a man."

"Good." He smiled at her. "I don't know what I'd do if I weren't."

Celeste replied, with a wry smile, "I'd know what to do. Fear not."

He burst out laughing and then with encouragement talked a blue streak.

Outside Mrs. McCleary looked knowingly at Monza. "I'd better check."

"If you toss them out, do it slowly, I want to see Miss Chalfonte." Monza was now glued to her clean front marble steps.

Ben had scribbled in a notebook some rough drawings for Celeste. Hearing Mrs. McCleary's footsteps, he met her at the open door.

She stood there, stuck her head in, but the rest of her considerable body remained on the other side of the doorjamb.

"Mrs. McCleary, please come in. I can offer you coffee, milk, tea, or a Co-Cola."

"No, thank you." She stared at Celeste, notebook in hand.

Radiant smile at full wattage, Celeste said, "You must have help. One woman can't keep a building pin tidy like this."

"I do it all." Mrs. McCleary puffed up like a broody hen. "I have a system, you see. Unless it's pouring rain or blinding snow, I scrub the steps every afternoon. Mondays are wash days, naturally, I take down the curtains and wash them. Tuesdays I iron. I always sweep the stairway before going to bed. Every day I have my list of chores. Of course, I pick my tenants with care. No slovenly people. No loose people either. I prefer churchgoers and Mr. Battle attends when he is in town. Makes all the difference in the world, the caliber of your people."

"Yes, it does, and you are a good judge of character." The wattage remained at full power.

"Mrs. McCleary, we are on our way out. Do you need anything? I can run to the store and come back," Ben offered.

"No, thank you." She turned and thumped down the stairs, each step ringing.

Ben squared up his papers, put his pencil back in the wooden box with the colored pencils.

"Take your notebook. Or, if you like, we can go to an art supply store and get more."

"You really think . . ." He paused, began again. "You think these are good?"

She stood up, walked over, leaned down and kissed his cheek, then kissed him on the mouth. "I thought I'd seen everything when I saw that backhanded catch you made today. Ben, you really are talented."

"I don't know about that, but I'm happy when I draw. Well, I'm happy when I play baseball, too." He stood up, put his arms around her waist, and kissed her.

Going out, he carried his pencil box while Celeste carried his notebook. Kissing her gave him an erection. As Ben was well built, trying to hide the evidence proved difficult with only the pencil box. Fortunately, when he and Celeste reached the sidewalk, Mrs. McCleary and Monza, focusing intently on Celeste's jewelry, missed his.

As they walked along he regained his composure.

Monza bleated to Mrs. McCleary, "That is one of the most beautiful women I have ever seen. Ever."

Arms crossed across her chest, Mrs. McCleary nodded.

. . .

The pleasant late afternoon encouraged walking.

"Your apartment has good light."

"That's why I took it. That, and it's not too far from the park. You'd be surprised at how much difference light makes."

"May I make a suggestion?"

"Of course." He was eager to hear.

"Carlotta responds to what she sees. Imagination is not her strong point, or I don't think it is. If you make large drawings of your stained-glass windows, can you use watercolors to intensify the color—or what about canvas where you can paint deep colors?"

Ben didn't want to remark on how much paint and canvas cost, not to mention the frames for stretching the canvas and the cost of brushes. Good sable brushes ran high.

"How about I do one?"

"A test?" She slipped her arm through his.

"Yes. You can see how you like the true colors. We can go from there."

She was beginning to understand that the issue was money. Celeste had never had to think about it. She'd gone to school with other girls who never had to think about money and in fact were discouraged from doing so. Celeste would never, ever have to worry about money. Those worries belonged to men.

"Yes." She squeezed his arm while thinking about finding a loft for him with wonderful light or living quarters where he could paint, work.

She knew she'd have to find it, show him, then try to convince him. Ben truly did not want to take her money and she respected him for that.

Blue jays squawked in trees.

Ben laughed. "Bet Mrs. McCleary and Monza are jabbering like that blue jay."

"Mrs. McCleary is a censorious character."

"That she is." He patted her hand on his arm.

"How did you make that backhanded catch? It was as though you knew exactly where the batter would hit the ball. I love watching you out there." She grinned.

"Ah, well, even a blind pig finds an acorn sometimes."

"Now, Ben, don't be falsely modest. Tell me, if you can, how you do what you do and in the blink of an eye?"

"First, I study the players. I try to remember who pulls the ball, who pops up, who can thread the needle. Some hitters can see the ball better than others. They can often select where they're going to hit. Between first and second base is always a sure single if you're not powerful, or if the pitch isn't one you can blast out of the park. Most hitters hit toward me because they're right-handed. I know I have to be alert and sometimes a grounder takes a bizarre bounce. All I can do in that case is hope my reactions are fast enough."

"Is that what happened with the backhanded catch?"

"No. That was a line drive just out of my reach. All I could do was fling myself toward second base, glove open. Got it and he was out. Dennis, on first, the guy on the other team, stuck tight."

"What happens when you're at the plate? Do you know the pitchers?"

"Usually. You can always be fooled by a new guy but eventually you memorize his delivery, what he can do well, what he can't. The other thing is to pay attention when your teammate bats."

"Where they hit it?"

"Yes, because I watch how the defense moves about on the field. Who covers what. Who is a step slow and who is a little slow upstairs." He pointed to his head.

"So you know what to do when you hit or where you hit and what to do on base? When you have a chance to steal?"

"Right. In a way, Celeste, baseball kept me alive in France. I listened for firing patterns, I listened for the sound of the shells. I was always alone on the bike and oftentimes the Germans missed our lines. They overshot or they aimed for the roads if they thought a convoy was coming. Paying attention to everything like the sound of the ball off the bat, well, I did that over there. Sometimes I could hear the boom and I hauled my bike into a ditch. Saved me."

"For which I am grateful."

Ben hailed a cab. They'd walked a bit but the Belvedere Hotel would be a long, long walk. Once in Celeste's room, neither wasted any time.

Unbuttoning his shirt, he said, "I'll race you to the bed."

Knowing she'd lose, Celeste accepted. "If you win, you have to draw something for me. A consolation prize."

Lying there afterward, Celeste told him about the conversation she'd had with the girls about Pliny the Elder's *Natural History* and the Machyles who could change sex at will.

"I thought of that because I teased you about Carlotta taking comfort in you being a man."

"You said you'd know what to do if I weren't." He kissed her cheek. "Well, what would you do?"

"I'd beat you to the bed."

"And?"

"Once there I would assault your person." She laughed. "If the electricity is there, the details take care of themselves."

"I believe you, but I don't know what I would do without my details."

"You'd enjoy yourself." She turned to face him, propped up on one elbow. "If you could change sex at will, would you?"

"I never thought about it. Then again, I've never read . . . what's his name?"

"Pliny the Elder."

"I'm thinking about it." He propped himself up on his elbow to face her. "I would have to learn a lot. And the clothes. How much money would two wardrobes cost, especially women's clothing? But, I'd try so long as I'd be in bed with you."

Chapter Thirty

....

April 19, 1920
Monday

Returning to work pleased Paul. Making money was a good thing, but seeing a room enlivened by fresh paint delighted him. He remembered France, sides of buildings torn away, each room a different color. The buildings were like patchwork quilts and it made him sad that their owners would never be living in those rooms again. Now he had a good job, and he liked making rooms, as well as the outsides of houses, pretty. Anson Paint transformed interiors and exteriors.

The day—low sixties, bright sun—promised spring's glory, or so he hoped. Sitting on the front doorstep of the house, lunch pail open, he saw Yashew turn the corner in his truck. He walked out to the road, waving Yashew down.

The large fellow pulled the black truck to the curb.

"Hey."

"Hey back at you." Paul opened the passenger door to chat. "I need to tell you, Lottie's been flapping her big flannel mouth about all of us sleeping over at Immaculata Academy. She says you told her."

Confused, Yashew cut the motor. "I did."

"You didn't do wrong but she's making it out that I slept with Louise."

Turning red, Yashew spat, "She what?"

"I know you didn't say that and I'm not trying to make trouble with your girlfriend but Louise's upset."

Yashew flopped back in his seat, dropped his hands from the steering wheel. "Why would she twist what I said?"

Paul shrugged. "She doesn't like Louise. Dimps Jr. doesn't like Juts."

"I'm sorry for this. I'll straighten it out."

"I know you're not behind it even if you are a navy man," Paul teased him.

Yashew chuckled. "Damn. If I never see the deck of a ship again, I'll be a happy man. Every morning, every damned morning, unless the weather was bad, I scrubbed that deck."

"Funny what you remember."

"Sometimes," Yashew quietly replied, then raised his voice slightly. "Do you understand women?"

"That's a big question. I sort of understand my mother. I think I understand Louise but I wouldn't want to bet my life on it. Why?"

"Lottie telling a story like that. Well, if you don't like someone, avoid them or call them out and knock the tar out of them. Seems pretty simple to me."

"Me, too, but I don't think Louise and Lottie will go into the ring."

"It's the behind-the-back stuff. I hate it, and the mother has it, too. My mother and sister aren't like that."

"Your mother and sister are happy. I don't think any of the Rhodeses would be happy if you blew a fan on them in Hell." He held up his hand. "Sorry. I shouldn't have said that."

"Aw, Pearlie, it's the truth. The other thing I don't understand is, Lottie lets me touch her, she'll rub her hand on my crotch, then she pulls away. If you don't want it, then don't play around, know what I mean?"

"She didn't do that to me. I guess she likes you more. Lottie and I aren't suited for one another. We didn't go out very long." Paul noticed the other painters going back into the house. "The teasing stuff. I think women like to have power over you. That's a sure way. For the record, my Wheezie doesn't do that. Hey, I gotta go back to work. Let me buy you a beer sometime."

Yashew nodded. "I'll come knocking on your door."

"Hey, what are you hauling?"

"What do you think?"

"After the fire, Mr. Van Dusen's back in business?"

Yashew lowered his voice. "He's got a business partner. I don't know who it is, and he's not saying he has a business partner, but I'm delivering to old and new accounts. He rented a warehouse. Has crates of vegetables in the front. The hooch is in the back."

"I'll be." Paul started to close the door.

Yashew leaned over, his arms so long he easily reached the door. "Do you kiss Louise? Does she let you do that?"

A big grin crossed Paul's face. "She does and I do. I could kiss that woman all day."

Yashew shook his head—"Lucky devil"—and closed the door.

Paul whistled back to the house.

Celeste, reading a letter from Ramelle, put it down as Fannie blew through the back door.

"Hello, Cora. Where's herself?"

"Out back." Cora tilted her head toward the back door, opened a crack for the fresh air.

Fannie Jump walked out to behold Celeste. Glue and the letter on her lap. "Madam."

"You usually arrive via the front door. Is this a moment of espionage?"

"No. I'm trying not to be predictable."

"Fannie, honey, don't try too hard." Celeste laughed.

"Have you thought about my proposal?"

Celeste paused. "Would you like a refreshment before we get into this?"

"I'll get it."

"Then tell Cora to bring me sweet tea and"—she glanced down at the sleeping kitten—"milk for when Glue awakens. She's twice as big. I hope you noticed."

"A most impressive kitten." Fannie's mouth twitched upward as she left for the scotch.

Cora came out before Fannie did. "Here you go."

"Thank you. Did I tell you I stopped to talk to Increase Martin?" She mentioned the South Runnymede vice fire chief. "We raked over the fire at Immaculata. He said without gasoline odor or something obvious, he could not determine whether the fire was deliberately set or not. The terrible weather also added to his confusion." She paused. "What is taking Fannie so long?"

"Additional fortification before she joins you."

Just then she walked out. "Girls."

"I was telling Cora about my talk with Increase Martin about Carlotta's fire."

"Have you noticed his beard is even longer?"

Cora, hands on hips, said, "Some people see a long beard and think wisdom. I think fleas."

They all laughed. Cora went back inside.

Fannie Jump, glass in hand, sat down. "Did Increase find anything? There's no way to tell." She took a big sip. "Oh, you ran into Increase Martin and I ran into Father Crofts, who said that Julius Rife gave a handsome amount to St. Paul's to fix the roof and that you suggested it. Thrilled as only Father Crofts can be." She put her glass down. "This may be the first time a Rife ever cooperated with a Chalfonte."

"I have a funny feeling it won't be the last." Celeste then asked, "Are you sure you don't want something to eat?"

"No. I'm going to lose twenty pounds. I know I've said that before but I am. I'm tired of looking at myself." She held up her hand. "No, no one has said anything." By that, she meant Tony.

"Good for you. I have thought about the two of us purchasing a place. Thought a lot about it this weekend. I would need a place with a huge attic that can be heated and has good north light. Even if I have to put in the skylights."

"Are you taking up painting? I don't recall you exhibiting a shred of interest during our school days."

Celeste laughed. "I remain as untalented as ever. There is comfort in consistency. It's not for me, it's for Ben. First, I have to bring him around to the idea. I thought of a warehouse or something down around Camden Station, but that's not the safest place."

"Rough down in the warehouse district," Fannie acknowledged. "The good thing about that is we'd never run into anyone we know."

"Or so we think."

"Celeste, I never thought of that. I assumed, if you got on board, we'd buy a discreet house in a good district, you know, like Federal Hill."

"Lovely. Sooner or later someone that we know would see us there. I expect we will be found out, although there is nothing wrong with two friends sharing a house in the city."

"It's who will be watching the gentlemen go in and out."

"Well, it's not a bawdy house, Fannie. Or is it?"

Fannie finished her scotch. "Ha. We'd make a fortune."

"Fortunately, we both have one. You begin searching. Much as I like being in the west, it's too far away from the stadium. He won't want a car. He doesn't want to take things. I suppose he could ride the trolley. This is going to take time. I'll bring him around. It will be easier, I think, once the house is found, once he sees the light."

"I had no idea he's an artist."

"He made drawings for stained-glass windows for Carlotta's chapel. He fell in love with stained glass during the war. He can tell you better than I can, but Fannie, the windows he has drawn are all of female

Bible heroines. And"—she paused, collected herself, for she felt more emotion than she wished to show—"he did one of Ruth and Naomi. He thought I would like it."

Staring at her childhood friend, Fannie quietly remarked, "How very kind."

"He is. I've never met any man like him."

"He's divinely handsome, the body of a Greek god, I should think. You can't always tell with baseball uniforms, although you can always see the pot gut."

"He's beautiful," Celeste simply replied.

"You attract beauty and are attracted by it. Always were."

They chatted about where to start looking, possible costs, and the necessity of a housekeeper.

Both heard the back door open. Louise came in, followed by Juts. Celeste filled in Fannie about Lottie's nasty gossip.

"The day will come when those Rhodes girls get their comeuppance," Fannie growled. "Ramelle?" She pointed to the letter.

"She says she's going to explode if she doesn't have the baby soon. Curtis will have to build an additional room to the house, she's so big."

Fannie sighed. "A miserable feeling, perfectly horrid. Giving birth is also a loathsome process, then the nurse plops the little thing in your arms and you fall in love." She waved her hand. "I was and remain an adequate mother, not an outstanding one, but I do love my boys and I love them even more as they have made their way in the world. I expect Ramelle will have a nurse, then a governess."

"Curtis will give her whatever she wants."

"And you?"

Celeste exhaled through her nose. "I, too, will give her whatever she wants, within reason. I'm not her husband."

"If you could be, would you?"

A long, long silence followed that.

"No," Celeste finally answered. "I love her, I always will, but I'm not a husband."

"Umm." Fannie understood her old friend. "Well, what are you going to do when she comes here, baby in tow? You wouldn't be taking them to Baltimore."

"I'm going to tell her. Not the minute she walks through the door, but I won't wait overlong. She will forever have my love. I mean that. She's a wonderful woman and she's made her choice. I never thought I'd make a choice. I never thought I'd fall in love. I assumed I'd coast along."

"Love?" Fannie's eyebrows raised.

"He makes me laugh. He makes me feel. He's a tender soul—more so than I am. The day may come when he leaves. I don't know, but I do know only a fool refuses love."

"Have you told him?"

"In my own way. Yes."

Fannie smiled. "Celeste, I walked in here saying I didn't want to be predictable. You've beaten me to it."

Glue woke up, meowed loudly for such a little twerp. Celeste put her by the milk.

"That cat will wind up being bigger than a cannonball," Fannie mused, then added, "I envy you. I don't think I will ever fall in love again. I don't know, Celeste." She looked at her empty scotch glass. "I have got to stop drinking. It makes me tell the truth."

Celeste laughed. "You always tell me the truth."

Before they could argue this point, Louise, trailed by Juts, came outside. Cora followed close behind.

"Mrs. Chalfonte, Mrs. Creighton, you won't believe what just happened," Louise breathlessly intoned.

"We're all ears." Fannie smiled.

"I was leaving work today and Mr. Grumbacher set a date for Mildred and me to go to Philadelphia. Philadelphia, I can't believe it!"

"We don't care about Philadelphia," Juts prodded. "Tell them what happened at Cadwalder's."

"Don't be pushy." Louise glared at her little sister then resumed her story with an air of additional gravity. "Pearlie was waiting for me, as he usually does if he can. We walked to Cadwalder's. The square is just beautiful." Juts pinched Louise, who smacked her hand away but did speed up her story. "Well, everyone was in there, all the kids from both high schools and people off work. Yashew was there with Lottie and Dimps Jr. was there with Bill Whittier." Louise made a face. "I don't know what started it but Lottie threw a malted at Yashew. He ducked and it splatted, right against the wall. Boy, did Mr. Cadwalder come out from behind the counter fast. Lottie was screaming, screaming that Yashew was a big nothing and everyone knew he was running booze because it's the only way a dumb bunny like him could make money. Pearlie got really mad and walked over to stand by Yashew." She took a deep breath. "So Lottie picks up Dimps's glass and throws it at Pearlie. At Pearlie! Then she hollers that Pearlie and I stayed together at Immaculata Academy. I ran up and I smacked her face so hard I think people could hear it out on the square. I called her a liar and a bunch of other names."

Juts, happy to add something, reeled them off. "A tit slinger, a user of men, a gold digger, a dumb broad! Oh, there were more!"

"That's smooth, Juts." Louise then continued. "She tried to hit me but I was too fast. Dimps Jr. grabbed me from behind. Ev grabbed her and threw her on the ground. Yashew stepped toward Lottie, I thought he was going to hit her. He called her a liar, said she was stirring the pot, that all the men slept in a room after the fire and we girls did likewise. Then, oh, then he called her a cock tease."

This created a momentous silence.

"A conspicuous absence of chivalry but the truth." Celeste felt Glue trying to crawl up her leg so she bent over and picked her up.

"Lottie burst into tears, threw some more dishes and glasses, then ran out. Dimps Jr. followed. Bill Whittier, almost as big as Yashew, tried to push his way over to Yashew and Paul. He was yelling that he'd take him down, let's go to the alleyway, it went on, and Mr. Cadwalder is trying to get people out of the store. He said he didn't want anyone to step on the glass and Bill pushed by him to swing at Yashew. Yashew just grabbed his arm, then with his other hand grabbed his throat."

Juts had to garnish the story again. "He did and Bill's face turned red and his eyes bugged out and Yashew said—"

Louise put her hand over her sister's mouth. " 'I fought Germans. I'm not fighting kids, and Bill Whittier, you're sticking your dick in Dimps. You'll be sorry. You play, you pay.' Then he dropped him and you won't believe this! Bill started to cry! Mr. Cadwalder walked him out of the store."

"I'm sorry I missed it." Fannie genuinely was sorry.

"Pearlie stayed back. He and Yashew are helping Mr. Cadwalder clean up the store." Louise said this with admiration.

"I need another drink." Fannie Jump headed for the library.

Celeste looked to Cora then Louise then Juts. "I believe Fannie has the right idea."

Chapter Thirty-One

* * * *

April 20, 1920
Tuesday

Felicity and General Pershing rested by the fireplace, a fire blaz-ing, for the evening temperature had dropped to 42°F. Cora and Juts sat before the warmth, mending socks and two torn pillow-cases, the handiwork of the mischievous cat.

"Momma."

"Mmm."

"Everyone's talking about Wheezie smacking Lottie."

"I expect so." Cora squinted. Her eyes weren't quite what they used to be.

"Some people wish she'd hit her harder. Others are taking Lottie's side and believing what she says about Wheezie. Makes me bullshit mad."

"Juts, don't swear."

"You do."

Cora looked up. "Rarely, but I have not always been the best ex-ample. Forget Lottie and Dimps Jr., too."

"Momma, I can't let them say the things they say, and more—Lottie says Pearlie's too cheap to buy Wheezie a real ring. He's getting the milk for free. That's exactly what she's saying. 'Why buy the cow when you can get the milk for free?'"

"Juts, people can say whatever they want to say. Anyone with a grain of sense will know that Pearlie is a young man starting out in life and he doesn't have the money. As far as your sister is concerned, that cigar band is made of solid gold."

"She's taped it together twice." Juts darned the sock, put the needle through the sock, pausing. "Momma, how come people are saying what they're saying? Wheezie wouldn't do anything out of the way."

"No, she wouldn't, but loose talk tells you more about who's saying it than what they're saying."

"Like they're doing it."

"Mmm," was all Cora offered, but she nodded her head. "Truth is, those are powerful feelings."

"Well, I don't have them and I never will. I'm not making a fool out of myself over some man, letting them kiss me and crawl all over me. Ugh."

"Mm-hmm." Cora smiled.

Juts grimaced. "Mother! It's awful."

"How do you think you got here?"

"Yeah, but you only did it twice."

Cora put down the pillowcase, laughed so hard she shook. "Oh, honey, don't fret over this. In good time, you'll understand."

"I understand now, Momma. People have no sense."

"You've got a point there."

Darning again, Juts listened to the logs crackle and pop. "Bet some flowers die tonight."

"Only if there's a frost."

"Feels like it. Bet by the middle of the night it will be freezing!"

"I hope not. My tulips won't like it." Without looking up, she said, "Forget the Rhodes girls." Juts didn't respond. Cora continued to sew, then remarked, "I hope Ramelle's baby comes soon."

With conviction, Juts announced, "I am not going to be a mother. One more reason not to let boys crawl all over you."

"Uh-huh."

"I mean it, Momma. I'm not walking about like a hippopotamus."

"When have you seen a hippopotamus?"

"In picture books." She blew out her cheeks to look fat, making her mother laugh.

The wall clock chimed nine times.

"Your sister should be getting out of the movies about now. She's determined to use all the tickets Pearlie gave her. She took Orrie tonight."

"She should take me."

"Well, you know she did. Most Saturdays she and Pearlie go. He works late a lot. He's trying to put money away."

"I put away what Mrs. Chalfonte gives me for chores."

As money burnt a hole in Juts's pocket, whatever she put away would be spent soon enough.

"You can shine the mirrors in Mrs. Chalfonte's bedroom, in Spotts's bedroom, and downstairs. That will earn you some more money."

"Good."

They worked in silence, General Pershing's deep breathing and the fire being the only sounds.

Finishing her sewing, Cora folded the pillowcases as Juts finished the socks. Cora took the pillowcases to the chest of drawers in her small bedroom.

Returning, she stirred the fire as she spoke. "Juts, you and Ev are doing your lessons?"

"Yes. I still haven't made up my mind though."

"Be that as it may, you have made up your mind to get even with Lottie."

"I didn't say that."

"You didn't have to."

Chapter Thirty-Two

. . . .

May 2, 1920
Sunday

Pink dogwoods next to white dogwoods bloomed along Emmitsburg Pike. Azaleas were open, although not quite to their fullest. The daffodils had come and gone. Now late-blooming tulips dotted flower beds with red, white, yellow, pink. The early blooming tulips were already done.

Swallows darted in and out of the barn, a warning chirp as they swooped low. Henry put up Roland. Celeste gave the handsome horse a lump of sugar before returning to the house.

Cora, newspaper spread over the kitchen table, placed loving cups on it to polish.

"Silver tarnishes quickly, doesn't it?" Celeste noted as she entered the kitchen.

"I try to keep up with it. Juts promises to do the silverware, but I like to shine up the trophies."

A loud knock on the door caused Cora to rise.

"I'll get it." Celeste left.

"Mrs. Chalfonte." Outside, the Western Union young man lifted his cap.

"Ah, Johnny, what have you here?" She opened the door and took the envelope from him. "Wait a minute."

Returning, she gave him a good tip, fifty cents, then walked into the library and tore open the small yellow envelope and read the message inside.

May 2, 1920
3:45 P.M.

Spottiswood Bowman Chalfonte born 6 1/2 pounds. Female
Mother, child fine.
Love, Curtis

"Cora!"

Celeste hurried into the kitchen and she read the telegram to Cora.

"Thank the good Lord for everyone's health." Cora smiled.

"Yes." Celeste sat down opposite Cora. "I suppose I should go down to the Western Union office and send a telegram in return." She put the envelope and opened message on the table. "How did you feel after giving birth?"

"Tired." She was still smiling, though. "It will be good to have the baby here. No doubt she'll be beautiful."

"I'm sure she will. She won't be here for months, but . . ." Celeste paused. "Where am I going to put her?"

"If Ramelle and Curtis come with a nurse, third floor."

"I'm sure they'll come with a nurse." Celeste picked up the message again. "I'll do my best."

"Of course you will," Cora reassuringly said.

"Cora, I know nothing about babies."

"I do." Cora smiled. "Everything will be fine."

"Yes. I'll buy her a pony."

Cora reached over to touch Celeste's hand. "Wait a few years."

"You're right." Celeste laughed. "It's the only thing I know to do. Well, let me go down to Western Union."

The office was on the northern side of Runnymede. Once there, Celeste sent congratulations, then, she didn't know why, sent a telegram to Ben announcing the birth. She also sent one to Carlotta and Stirling. She wasn't really sure why she did that either.

Then she walked through the square, exceptionally beautiful on this May day. Stopping at the Confederate statue, she heard a car horn's beep.

Fairy slowed down. She was driving a lot these days.

Waving, Celeste trotted across the square. Fairy had pulled to the side of the road.

"Ramelle had a girl," Celeste announced.

"Get in." Fairy motioned to the door. "We'll take a celebratory ride."

"Just think, Fairy, you can always be a lady chauffeur if life changes dramatically."

Fairy laughed. "It would have to be quite dramatic. Well, congratulations to all concerned. You must be relieved and excited."

"I guess. Fairy, what I feel is trapped."

Heading west, Fairy soothingly said, "It's a big day, although none of it was your decision. But trapped? No. You'll be a wonderful aunt and you won't have to be a wonderful aunt every single day."

"Everything has changed."

"It has," Fairy honestly replied. "But you will change with it and in time, you'll love watching—"

"Spotts."

"Ah, of course. How good of Ramelle. Well, you'll love watching Spotts grow."

"She's growing up in a different world than we did."

"I guess every generation does. One glorious thing is she will never know war, 1918 took care of that. Although with my reading I'm starting to wonder if we won't experience violence in different ways."

"I expect we will always have violence, but this morning I walked into the library, turned on the radio for a moment, then turned it off. I don't want to hear about Mary Pickford. If I have to hear about something or someone I don't know, it should be important, not entertainment. I think, Fairy, that Spotts's world will be vastly different than our own. Superficial, or perhaps I might say more superficial."

"Oh, I don't know. You're a little lost right now, Celeste. Don't make judgments," Fairy said, as only an old and true friend can say.

Watching the emerald-green fields slide by, Celeste sighed. "You're right. I don't know why I'm confused. It's not my baby. I'm not the one who has my whole life turned upside down."

"Strange, isn't it? I would have done anything to be a mother. You never wanted to be one but Ramelle did. I suspect it's something one is born with and most of us are meant to be mothers and fathers but some of us aren't."

"Well, one can't say that publicly."

"No, of course not, but you can say it to your dearest friends." Fairy glanced at Celeste for a moment, then returned her eyes to the road. "You should put an announcement in both papers."

"Yes."

"And Cora should put in an announcement about Louise's engagement to stop the silly gossip."

"I'll do it. I should have suggested that when he asked Louise, but he couldn't give her a ring. If the poor fellow had to wait until he could afford even a diamond chip, that would be a year. The proposal was spontaneous." Celeste smiled. "And all the better for it. What she has is the cigar band off one of Spotts's cigars."

"You put both announcements in the papers. As for a ring, maybe you, Fannie, and I can come up with something."

"A ring?" Celeste was surprised.

"The three of us can go through our jewelry. There's got to be something we can lend or even give Paul."

"That's a good idea. He has to agree to it. I am learning about getting men on board, so to speak. It's not anything I've ever mastered," Celeste confessed.

"Oh, don't worry. I can help you there." Fairy laughed lightly. "If there's one thing marriage teaches you, it's how to manage men. Both Fannie and I have gotten quite good at it. The key is to make them think whatever it is, is their idea."

Celeste inhaled. "Seems like a lot of work."

"It can be. You grew up with three brothers. Consider that a head start. With men who aren't your brothers, though, you can't haul off and hit them, something at which you excelled."

Celeste, spirits climbing, nodded. "Guess I did."

"But you encountered the male need to be in charge, to dominate, and to compete with other men."

"I don't know. I never thought of it that way."

"Essentially you listen to every word out of their mouth as though it is of supreme importance and they are terribly smart and you tell them they are. You also point out every mistake every man around them makes. And if you're married, you tell them how physically competent they are. Simple."

"Good God, Fairy, have you been doing this for the last twenty years?"

"Twenty-one. I married at twenty-two, remember?"

"I'm deeply impressed, but it's so much work."

"Oh, now, dealing with Ramelle was work, too. You just say different things and you spend more money. Archie spends money on me. You had to spend money on Ramelle. You did. Let's drive to Fannie's. You can tell her your good news."

As Fairy turned toward Runnymede, it occurred to Celeste that Fairy was also managing her, just as she managed her husband. It also occurred to her that her friends knew her intimately and had been managing her since college. All this time she'd thought she was in charge. She burst out laughing.

Fairy laughed, too. "See, you're your old self again."

"What would I do without you?"

"Suffer." Fairy laughed louder, joined by Celeste.

Chapter Thirty-Three

. . . .

May 5, 1920
Wednesday

Three important ladies sat before Archibald Cadwalder, brother to Flavius and chief of the South Runnymede Police Department.

"Yashew was set up," Carlotta Van Dusen forcefully said. "You know it, Archibald."

"Now, now, Carlotta, I may suspect but I don't know." His tone was even.

"We've come to post bail." Celeste figured releasing the young man was more important at this moment than the circumstances of his arrest.

"Of course." Archibald called loudly, "Mark. Bail."

A young officer came in, touched his forehead briefly to the ladies, opened the big book he was carrying.

"How much, Mark?" Fairy inquired.

"Two hundred dollars."

"What? That's outrageous. He's not a criminal. He's not dangerous." Carlotta fumed.

Archibald had to clarify the law as he saw it. "He is accused of carrying contraband. And if convicted, he is a criminal. But you are right, he's not dangerous."

"Archie, you know all this is drivel." Carlotta's face reddened. "You can't possibly believe it."

"Mrs. Van Dusen, Miss Chalfonte, Mrs. Thatcher, I do not have to believe in the law, but I have to enforce it."

The three sat silent for a moment, then Celeste filled out a blank check she had brought, handing it to Mark.

"Thank you, Miss Chalfonte." Like most men, he simply wanted to look at her.

"Chief, I know you, too, are doing your duty and we aren't insensible to that." Celeste found the right approach at last. "And given the wild unpopularity of the Volstead Act, to say nothing of the impossibility of enforcing it, you are at a disadvantage and must face the emotions this act will stir in Runnymede."

"She's right." Carlotta had calmed down. "You're a good police chief, Archibald, and we all sleep safer in our beds because of you. I'm afraid I've let my emotions get the better of me because Yashew has been such a good worker for us, as is his sister, a scholarship girl. We all are close and, of course, quite concerned about Mrs. Gregorivitch. The family can't afford to lose what Yashew brings in."

"Yes, I know that." He cleared his throat. "Perhaps you all can tell me what's at stake here? All I responded to was a phone call, a woman's voice I thought I somewhat recognized, telling me that Yashew was carrying a truckload of scotch and if we wanted to catch him we should post men at the square. I did and sure enough, a truckload of barrels."

"You've impounded the truck?" Celeste sounded innocent.

"Of course."

She continued. "You've been good to listen to us. We all know how busy you are." She paused. "This may have its genesis in a ferocious argument at your brother's drugstore a few days ago. Flavius can give you the details. From any of us, it would be hearsay and a great deal of vulgarity appears to have been spoken."

His eyebrows rose. "I will ask him. He must not have thought it would lead to trouble or he would have informed me."

"Archie, none of us considered this kind of outcome," Carlotta reassured him, quite calm now.

"Flavius works as hard as you do," Fairy complimented both brothers. "And we are sorry to trouble you. This comes down to petty revenge. At any rate, let us take Yashew to his mother since you have his truck. May we do so?"

Fairy, sweetness herself, provoked a smile from the chief. "Of course, Mrs. Thatcher. Mark, bring the prisoner out, will you?"

Celeste inquired after the police chief's garden—he was a good gardener—then slipped in, "We aren't mentioning any of this to Tangerman. First off, it's not his jurisdiction. Secondly, he will butt in."

Indeed, Lionel Tangerman Sr., the aging police chief of North Runnymede, would butt in.

"I appreciate that," said Archibald. "You know, they will need to elect a new police chief soon, as Lionel is losing his memory."

"Yes, he is," Fairy agreed. "But how can this be done without hurting his feelings? You know all the ins and outs of law enforcement protocol. There must be a way."

Flattered, he made a steeple out of his fingers. "You know we have all been thinking about this. Now I don't mean to imply that the men on the north force are talking behind the chief's back but his condition is now so obvious. In a sense, we have to find a way to kick him upstairs."

"Excellent idea," Carlotta chimed in.

"Maybe we can think of something in time for Magna Carta Day," Fairy said almost idly.

Mark arrived with Yashew, who was incredibly grateful to see his liberators.

"Come on. We'll take you home," Carlotta said.

"I'm driving," Fairy bragged.

Packed in the car, Carlotta pressed Yashew. "We know it was a woman who called and ratted on you. Who knew apart from myself, your sister?"

"Lottie Rhodes."

"I knew it!" Fairy triumphantly blared.

Celeste rested her head on her hand. "That is petty revenge."

"I called her—well, I called her something," Yashew almost whispered.

"Wheezie and Juts gave a full report." Celeste half smiled. "You merely told the truth."

"Well, the Bible says, 'Know ye the truth and the truth shall set ye free,'" Carlotta added.

"Be that as it may, you may wind up free to starve, free to be beat up, et cetera, et cetera," Celeste replied.

"Celeste, is there nothing about our faith that has reached you?" Carlotta griped.

"That's a subject for another day. Yashew, lie low. Carlotta, can you and Herbert find things for him to do to keep making money? As it is, there might be a trial."

The poor man's face just fell. "Oh, how can I take the time and I can't afford it?"

"I may have a way. Sister?"

"Of course, we'll find work."

After dropping off Yashew, visiting for a brief spell with his mother, the three climbed back into the car.

"Where to?"

"Home." Carlotta flopped back in her seat.

"No. Rife Munitions," Celeste ordered.

"What!" Carlotta and Fairy shouted at once.

"Rife Munitions."

Once at the imposing factory on the North Runnymede side, the three were swiftly ushered into Julius Caesar's office, for everyone knew this was a day to remember: two Chalfontes and one Thatcher calling on a Rife.

He stood when the ladies entered, motioned for the door to be closed. "May I offer something to drink, a sandwich perhaps?"

"No. We've barged in on you and we thank you for seeing us directly." Celeste smiled, which produced the usual effect.

"Well, ladies, apart from enjoying your pulchritude, I am curious."

They told him everything they knew about Yashew's arrest, his being set up and by whom.

Carlotta, knowing full well that this was the man whom her husband had taken as a secret partner, breathed not a syllable about it. Of course, Celeste figured it out but said nothing to her sister. The Chalfontes were disciplined that way. To do so she would betray both men. J.C. paid careful attention to this.

"A trial would be inconvenient." He sat on the edge of his desk to be closer to the ladies.

"Indeed," Carlotta replied. "He hasn't much in this world and you know Mrs. Gregorivitch needs medical attention." She held up her hand. "Herbert and I will see to that, if you see to something else."

Surprised, J.C. became still. "If I can."

Carlotta had thought this through. "The canning factory. You procure goods from many places, some of it—that which can be preserved—traveling great distances."

"Yes."

"Yashew's truck is impounded. If you can remove the barrels, the evidence of contraband, replace it with, say, barrels of molasses which you have not yet canned, who will know? No one."

He crossed his arms across his vest. "Mrs. Van Dusen, what an ingenious idea."

Next to Carlotta, Celeste said, "I can get into the garage. Archie wouldn't waste a guard on it. He doesn't have the men, nor would he think it necessary. But I can get in if you and your men can meet me there, remove the scotch, and substitute the molasses. That will be the end of it and I believe after this incident, Archie will not be looking for tip-offs."

"When?" J.C. asked.

"The sooner the better. Tomorrow night?" Celeste's voice rose.

"Tomorrow night at midnight. Good citizens will be asleep." A smile played on his lips.

Back in the car, they all talked at once.

Finally, Carlotta said, "I'll be there."

"No," said Celeste. "You have more to risk than I do."

"I suppose," Carlotta agreed.

"I can drive the getaway car," Fairy offered.

"Fairy, seeing your car down at the police station would arouse curiosity. I have to walk."

"Then I will walk too." Fairy was adamant.

"Well, you can be a lookout. Carlotta, stay home. Fairy, we need a replacement lock and a bolt cutter."

"How can you get a replacement lock keyed to the same key as the one at the police station?" Carlotta shrewdly asked.

"I can't. All we can do is replace the lock and leave the key in it. As nothing will be missing, we might be able to get away with it. As it is, Archie doesn't really want this to go to trial. It's bad enough it has to appear in the police record. What saves us, if it does, is that if the barrels are replaced, who can prove the original barrels were alcohol? Fairy, you slip back there, study the lock, and buy a replacement from the hardware store."

"Bolt cutters," Fairy simply said. "I have them."

Carlotta, listening intently, remarked, "What about Lottie?"

"She can't prove anything," Fairy replied.

"Don't you think she'll try something else? Those Rhodes girls seem intent on revenge," Carlotta observed.

Celeste smiled. "Revenge is a dish best eaten cold."

Chapter Thirty-Four

. . . .

Night's chill at 52°F barely touched Celeste, Ben, or the two men J. C. Rife sent to the South Runnymede garage where Yashew's truck was impounded. Dressed in black like the others, Fairy stood against the building side along the entrance to the alleyway, a small bird whistle on the lanyard around her neck.

First, the four would-be bootleggers rolled all the barrels off Yashew's truck, then moved the ramp back to the Rife truck, where they rolled off the molasses barrels, then rolled on the scotch. As the rumble of the barrels couldn't be muffled, they worked as fast as they could, with the rears of the two trucks facing one another.

"Go on!" Ben told the Rife men. "We'll lock up."

The two needed little encouragement since a good bonus awaited their efforts, plus the scotch would certainly be more profitable than molasses.

Ben closed the truck doors. Celeste put the old lock on the back of the truck, leaving the key in the new lock. Then they hurried out to Fairy.

Using back alleys, they walked Fairy to her home.

Celeste kissed her cheek. "You're a brick."

"It's all so exciting," Fairy replied, turning to slip into her back door.

Keeping to the cobbled alleyways, Celeste and Ben reached her long lawn and gardens in twenty minutes.

Once inside, Celeste removed the lad's cap, shaking out her hair. "Luckily for me I could wear Spotts's black pants and sweater. We can both wear his pants, although I have to roll them up."

Ben heard a meow. "We aren't undetected."

Glue, blinking from sleep, padded out to the hallway.

"Come on, squirt." She picked her up, carried her upstairs to the bedroom, and placed the kitten on a plush chair by the fireplace, where Glue fell back to sleep.

Ben sat on the edge of the bed to untie his shoes. "I do think Fairy had a wonderful time."

"Beats being an upper-class housewife." Celeste smiled. "And thank you for coming out tonight. You're strong, the work flew along, and you already knew about the scotch. The fewer that know, the better."

"How long do you think it will take before the police find out it's not scotch back there?"

"Well, I don't know that they do know. Chief Cadwalder didn't mention the contents, only that yes, there were barrels. It's going to be an interesting moment. Lottie can't prove Yashew was hauling liquor."

"Guess not." He stepped out of his trousers then pulled his sweater over his head.

"And Lottie can't press charges."

"Why not?"

"She's nineteen. Still not a legal adult." Feeling the chill, Celeste slid into bed, pulling the covers up. "I expect if she hasn't considered that, her mother has."

Crawling in next to her, Ben touched her feet with his. "Cold." Then he touched her shoulder. "You are cold."

"I wasn't when we were rolling out those barrels but the walk home let the night air reach my bones. It's funny how sometimes night air, even when the temperature is warm, can chill you."

"Lie on top of me. I'll rub your back. I'm actually pretty warm."

She did and he rubbed her back to create a little friction.

"Feels good."

"Celeste, since I've met you I've had"—he thought—"unusual adventures."

She laughed. "So have I. It's hard to believe how petty people can be, isn't it? Especially women. I should amend that—especially the Rhodes women."

Warmer now, she moved off him to prop herself up on her elbow.

"There were some petty fellows in my unit, always the ones looking for a promotion. I used to think, 'Why want a promotion in Hell?'" He ran his forefinger over her lips.

Touching his hand, kissing his fingertips, she answered, "To feel important. To think you're one up on the next guy. But you're right, who cares in Hell? I sometimes understand people and sometimes I don't, but I do know most are weak, abysmally weak."

"I think that's how we wound up in France." He continued, "The kaiser couldn't stand having the English look down on him, or I guess he thought they did, Victoria being his grandmother and all. I used to think when I was over there that none of this had to happen. No one needed to die other than the archduke. That all could have been negotiated but I believe the kaiser really wanted a war. Wouldn't back down. Stood by his ally. That kind of stuff. He didn't want to look weak so he wound up being weak. Maybe we all are."

"I don't think so. Hannibal wasn't weak. Edward the Third wasn't weak. Before him, Eleanor of Aquitaine wasn't weak. Maybe the problem is when a weak person winds up as a king or queen or czar."

"Here we elect them. They aren't born to it." Ben smiled.

"It's all rather frightening. No matter how awful a man is once he's president, we're stuck for four years."

"We can assassinate him."

"Ben." She was surprised.

"Well, we can, and we can shoot the vice president, wipe out the Senate, bomb the House of Representatives, and just mow down the Supreme Court. We don't have to put up with anyone if we're willing to kill." He added, "The war taught me that. You kill and kill and kill and it doesn't matter. Human life doesn't matter at all. I think your life matters and I think my life matters but when you see thousands and thousands killed, learn at war's end that it was millions, how can I pretend anyone truly thinks human life is valuable unless they personally know that human life?"

She thought a long time, glad for his warmth. "Put that way, I can understand. I've known brutal people. The man who sent the truck tonight, J. C. Rife, his father was brutal and so was his grandfather. It's how they built their business empire." She kissed him on the cheek. "Did you ever look at a dead German and think someone loved him? A mother is weeping somewhere, a wife?"

"You bet I did."

"Well, we can't go back, can we?"

"No. And I don't know the way forward."

"Ben—" She kissed him again. "No one does. No one walks into the future. We back into it."

Chapter Thirty-Five

· · · ·

May 7, 1920
Friday

Delilah took her lunch hour to go with her elder daughter, Lottie, to Chief Cadwalder to press charges.

Archibald dutifully listened as Wilfred Frothingham, Caesura's son, wrote everything down. Once done he said to the two, "Mrs. Rhodes, I'll try to have the hearing on your lunch hour. I can't give you a date right now, but it won't be too long."

"What about jury selection?" Big Dimps readied herself for courtroom drama.

"Oh, this doesn't qualify for that. That's one of the reasons we have a hearing first, to correctly assess the situation and proceed. This may or may not be a felony. For one thing, Mrs. Rhodes, the law is new and this is our first case. We want to be correct."

Leaving the police headquarters, Lottie remarked to her mother, "I thought this would be simple."

"Me, too."

"That will teach Yashew to call me the things he called me." Lottie smiled triumphantly.

Big Dimps didn't reply. Already, she was harboring doubts.

As Big Dimps walked out of the imposing South Runnymede police headquarters, Celeste and Ben walked into the once imposing chapel of Immaculata Academy.

"You've done so much work," Ben admiringly said to Carlotta. Next to her stood Herbert.

The blown-out one-story windows had been covered with heavy tarps which could be rolled up, rolled down. Carlotta didn't want them boarded up. She thought it too depressing.

Ben had a rolled-up canvas under his arm, a painting, while Celeste carried his large drawing notebook.

Ben looked around. "The light is beautiful in here."

"I waited a full year before I sited the chapel, just to make sure I could take advantage of the light. In the middle of the large quad, the sunlight floods in."

Celeste walked up to the raised floor, where the altar, scorched, stood, the pulpit on her right, the lectern on her left, as in most every Christian church. She put the large notebook down on the raised floor and Ben unrolled his painting. He held one end and Celeste reached out to hold the other.

"Oh, my." Carlotta's hands flew to her face. "That blue. I've only seen that blue in Europe."

"Yes, ma'am." Ben smiled.

Herbert looked from his wife to Ben to Celeste. He, too, was impressed.

"Of course, Mrs. Van Dusen, only you can select those women you wish to celebrate, who you wish the girls to view, but I've always been fascinated with Judith in the Old Testament. I thought one side of the chapel might be Old Testament heroines while the opposite side would focus on the New Testament."

"May I see the drawings?" Carlotta pointed to the big pad.

"Yes, of course. I tried to think of stories that would appeal to a young woman. You will know better than I." He flipped open to the first page, Queen Esther looking regal.

Excited, Carlotta studied this drawing, then they moved through the Old Testament. "Ah, Ruth and Naomi. Such a lovely story of friendship and finding truth."

Wisely, Celeste said nothing.

"Mary Magdalene. Yes, yes, I see where you're heading. I, myself, find the stories of her occupation vulgar. Even if true, I think we should present her as a faithful follower of our dear Lord, a woman redeemed."

"As we all hope to be." Ben simply nodded.

Carlotta stared at him. "You were raised in the One Truth Faith, weren't you?"

"Yes, Mrs. Van Dusen, I was. I wouldn't say that I am a good Catholic, but I am a Catholic."

Celeste kept silent.

"Celeste, where did you find this artist?"

"Carlotta, you will be surprised. Fannie Jump Creighton. Baseball. She took me to a practice game."

"Really?"

Herbert stepped in. "My wife noted the blue in your painting. Can you find glass like that here?"

"Yes, but I have to go to Italian glassmakers."

"Can you bring me samples?" Carlotta touched her immense pearls.

"I can. The deep colors we both love that we've seen in Europe can be reproduced here. There are people that good, but they are expensive."

"How expensive?" Carlotta asked.

"Off the top of my head, I would guess one large, tall window would be perhaps as much as five thousand dollars, depending on the glass. You can always do this for less if you will accept less vibrant colors. A big savings could be had if you used figures in plain glass, just outlined."

"It has to be stained glass. I want people to make pilgrimages to see our reborn chapel. I want them awash in God's beauty and glory."

"Ben, tell Carlotta your idea for the Blessed Virgin Mother."

He flipped to the last page, where a drawing of the Virgin Mary, arms extended, halo diffuse and soft, beckoned. "Celeste said she is special to you."

"Yes." Overcome, Carlotta stared rapturously at the drawing.

"So I thought, one can't put her on the side of the chapel. She has to be the focus. You could create a huge stained-glass window behind the altar and backlight it or you could have this inside as one enters the chapel. That is, if you like it."

Taking Herbert's hand, Carlotta, voice low, said to her husband, "Herbert, this is the sign I have been waiting for. This is what I must do for the Blessed Virgin Mother."

"Carlotta, it is stunning, but the expense," he sensibly demurred.

She cast her eyes back on Ben. "How much do you want?"

"I hadn't thought about it."

"I have. Ten percent of the project." Celeste spoke clearly.

"Celeste, that's a great deal of money," Ben blurted out.

Celeste was firm. "It's a great deal of work, and you will have to hire help for the simpler tasks. You can't do all this yourself."

He looked from his lover to her sister. "Mrs. Van Dusen, I really hadn't considered any of this. I didn't even know if you would like the drawings."

"I must have it." Carlotta's jaw set. "I must."

Herbert knew he was lost.

"What if we do this?" Ben suggested. "Let me do one window. We'll see what it truly costs. I worry about transporting the glass. There can be unexpected costs and then again, we might get lucky." He smiled, which just melted Carlotta. "If you like what I do, if it truly brings the Bible stories to life for the girls, then pay me. If not, pay me only for my time."

Herbert, dumbfounded, said, "Why would you do this?"

Very quietly, Ben replied, "For my comrades who didn't come home. These girls are the future, you see?" He couldn't express himself as he wished, but they understood.

Tears filled Carlotta's eyes. She reached over, taking Ben's right hand in both of hers. "Yes." Then she turned to Celeste. "Buy a building in Runnymede where trucks can get in and out, where the materials will be safe and where"—she looked at Ben—"there's good light."

"Ma'am, I have to play baseball."

"Of course you do, but when you aren't playing you will be working, and the season lasts but so long. Start the minute you can." Again, turning to Celeste, "Can I count on you?"

"You can. And I might add that Yashew's truck is now filled with molasses barrels."

Herbert burst out laughing. "Oh, that's good!"

Driving back to Runnymede, Ben driving, for he wanted to, the two of them said little, watched the pastures and woods go by, the dogwoods fully opened, a few grandiflora magnolias displaying filling tan buds. Yellow buttercups covered fields, others showed the lavender glow of veronica.

Back at the house, Celeste opened a package filled with photographs of Ramelle, Spotts, and Curtis.

"Ben, here's my niece." She showed him and Glue, too, who was nosy.

"Such a tiny little thing."

"It's hard to believe we all start life so helpless, isn't it?"

"It is." He leaned over her shoulder. "Ramelle is such a beautiful woman. And the baby has a full head of dark hair like her mother."

"Well, the hair will probably fall out." Celeste called Cora in to look at the photographs, then asked her about infant hair.

In the background, Louise could be heard playing the piano. Juts was arguing with someone about something. The late-afternoon sun shone through the windows. Celeste and Ben had been gone longer than they anticipated.

"Celeste, if the baby's hair falls out, it will grow back."

"But doesn't it grow back curly if it was straight, or blond if it was dark?"

"I don't rightly know. Are you worried about having a bald niece?" Cora laughed.

"No." Celeste looked at Ben's dark hair. "Do the men go bald in your family?"

"They do not."

"Good."

"Supper in an hour?" Cora inquired.

"That will be fine. It's entirely possible that Fannie will show up, dying to know what happened at Immaculata. I'll tell Wheezie first, she's an alumna." Celeste smiled.

Juts tromped into the kitchen. "She is such a snob."

"That's enough."

"I can play the piano. I sat down next to Wheezie and she told me to move. She said I'm not good enough."

"Did you do your lessons?" Celeste asked. "The ones Ev brought today?"

"I did."

The playing stopped. Louise entered the kitchen.

Juts pouted. "You're hateful not to let me play."

"Chopin is too much for you," Louise defended herself.

"Oh, pooh, I can play 'Nocturnal Emissions' as good as you can!"

Celeste and Ben laughed. As Celeste recovered she said, "Juts, I certainly hope not."

Chapter Thirty-Six

....

May 8, 1920
Saturday

Leaning over the cosmetics counter, Minta Mae examined a tortoiseshell compact of pressed powder, a youthful shade of peach. Delilah lined up three other shades for the president of the Sisters of Gettysburg. While Minta Mae had expanded a bit over the years, she maintained a lovely complexion, of which she was justifiably proud.

Crowded with shoppers on this perfect May Saturday, the Bon Ton left no time for its clerks to dawdle, which was how Louise liked it. The busier she was, the happier she was, and she'd just sold Caesura Frothingham, the president of the Daughters of the Confederacy, a gorgeous sheer dress, with diaphanous layers of gray.

Caesura waited for the pneumatic tube to bring back her change. "I'm so glad you called me."

"When you move, the layers will sway with you, and I remembered your stunning gray-and-gold sash, which will really set this off," Louise said.

"I'm just glad you thought of me before Georgina saw it." She named her second-in-command, a dedicated woman who wanted Caesura's job.

"Mrs. Frothingham, you are the leader, and furthermore, you have kept your hourglass figure. Every woman in this town would love to know how you do it."

Trying to hide her pride, Caesura lifted her chin slightly. "I walk two miles a day, weather permitting, and I watch what I eat." She smiled at Louise. "Really, it's common sense."

"And discipline." The cylinder clanked in the tube. Wheezie opened it, returning Caesura's change. "Our Magna Carta Day isn't far off. Mrs. Frothingham, if you have any ladies who might need"—she paused conspiratorially—"a bit of help, send them to me. It's so important that the Daughters of the Confederacy outshine you know who." She cut her eyes to the cosmetics department.

"My God, I wonder she doesn't stuff her girls into old Union uniforms." Caesura couldn't resist the jibe, and Louise couldn't help but laugh.

Competitive and silly as the organizations might be, they did maintain the graves of the deceased combatants, they did their best to study history and preserve what they could. The Sisters of Gettysburg maintained three graves said to hold three former slaves who fought for the Union. The Sisters weren't small-minded unless it was about the Daughters of the Confederacy. Both groups worked with the Daughters of the American Revolution and the Colonial Dames, often together. Louise didn't much think about it, but there were few civic outlets for ladies of means. Many of them were well educated, bright, harboring ambition to do something more permanent than throw the best dinner party in Runnymede. Louise had no choice but to work. She liked it. She saw so many people. She'd returned from Philadelphia, the bustling city a revelation concerning marketing and fashion.

Tapping the counter lightly, Caesura leaned toward the young woman. "Wilfred told me that Celeste paid Yashew's bail."

"She did, Mrs. Frothingham. You know how generous she is."

Of course, Caesura knew, as Celeste sent the Daughters large yearly checks. After all, her father had survived the war.

"Mmm." She looked over at the cosmetics counter again. "It's peculiar, Wheezie. Highly peculiar."

Knowing she couldn't truly reply, Louise raised her eyebrows while both women peered at the cosmetics counter. Minta Mae was dabbing at her cheeks before a handheld mirror, when Lottie, face flushed, hurried in.

She had the sense to wait until her mother completed the sale, then leaned over and cupped her hand over her mother's ear. Delilah's face turned pale. She gripped the edge of the counter. Lottie placed her hand over her mother's. A customer walked up. Delilah smiled and went to work. Face grim, Lottie left the store.

Louise and Caesura looked at one another, then Caesura left, her purchase protected by a heavy bag.

Minta Mae trooped over. "Louise, I need something light for Magna Carta Day. *The Farmer's Almanac* predicts the temperature will climb to the mid-eighties."

Anticipating this, Louise, seeing some of the summer dresses at Wanamaker's when in Philadelphia, had ordered a few for the Bon Ton, with Mildred's blessing, of course. All the ladies wanted to be at their best for Runnymede's special day, but the ladies of the two historical organizations really cared, plus they could and did spend. Minta Mae, while not as easy to fit as Caesura, did have a lovely peaches-and-cream complexion.

"Mrs. Dexter, when I was in Philadelphia I saw a dark blue crepe dress, quite a simple line, but I ordered it for you to examine. You can dress it up or dress it down, although your spectacular hat—you always wear the best hat—will set your ensemble in everyone's mind."

"Oh, I must see it."

Louise returned with the dress that would somewhat conceal Minta Mae's extra twenty pounds, which were proportionate, thankfully. Louise draped the dress over her arm while holding out the hem with her other hand.

Minta Mae felt the fabric. "Crepe will breathe a bit."

"It will. I suspect you won't truly be coolish until you sit from the marching."

"Well, there is that. Might I try this on?"

As Minta Mae disappeared into the fitting room, Louise gave her sister clerk in Coats the high sign.

Minta Mae reappeared and Georgina from the coat department slipped over for one second, as though bringing something to Louise.

"Minta Mae, how slimming that dress is, and it accentuates all the right curves," Georgina complimented the older lady.

Minta Mae examined herself in the large three-way mirror. "I'm so glad you noticed."

As Georgina returned to her department, Louise walked around Minta Mae, critically examining the look. "If you'll consider raising the hemline two inches or even one inch, your stride will be easier. You do have to cover distance and you look just wonderful."

"I quite like the cut, Louise. Two inches, I don't know. That's rather daring."

"Yes, it is, Mrs. Dexter, but not quite as daring as your father's charge up Willis Hill." Louise named the action at Fredericksburg in which nine thousand Union soldiers perished, proving the futility of a frontal assault given weapons improvement. Minta Mae's father had distinguished himself; wounded three times, he did not abandon the assault nor his men.

"Why, Louise, I had no idea you were a student of history."

"I'm not, but everyone knows your father was a hero." She paused. "Might I make another suggestion?"

"Of course, dear?"

"Tip up the brim of your hat a bit more. You've just got to show that gorgeous complexion."

Not only did Louise sell her the dress but also another tea dress, and Minta Mae walked out of the Bon Ton with a bearing not dissimilar to her late father's.

At the end of the day, with sales tallied, everything back in its place, the clerks finished up as Sidney Yost moved from counter to counter. Above, Asa Grumbacher and Mildred looked down on another very successful day.

Delilah scooped out cosmetics wrappings from under the counter shelf, placed them in a large wastebasket, checked her counter, which was teeming with many small items. She locked the displays, locked the storage units behind the counter, gave the key to Sidney Yost, brushed the front of her dress, and left as Louise walked to the front door along with other girls.

In her hurry to go, Delilah bumped into Louise. "Get out of my way, Louise."

The younger woman stepped aside, said nothing.

"What's wrong with her?" Georgina complained.

"Oh, I bet she just heard that Yashew's truck had barrels of molasses, not booze," said Paxton Shortride, laughing.

Paxton's mother, the telephone operator for the Maryland telephone company, knew far too much but she couldn't say she heard it from her mother. Everyone knew, of course.

"We heard poor Yashew was in jail for a night," Amy Rendell chimed in.

News traveled fast in Runnymede. Sooner or later, most secrets leaked out, unless they were in the best interest of many to keep locked up tight.

"Lottie calling Chief Cadwalder was a cheap shot." Paxton sniffed.

"I heard that too." Louise wanted to be part of the discussion but not too big a part.

"Oh, we all did, Louise." Amy pushed open the door. "And we all heard about the uproar at the drugstore. I'd have given anything to be there."

"Me, too." Paxton laughed. "You were there, Louise, how come you never said anything?"

Louise demurred. "Oh, I couldn't repeat those words. Awful things."

"Yeah, but true." Paxton held the door open after Amy moved out.

On the sidewalk, Amy shrugged. "Big Dimps has troubles."

Barrels of molasses were the least of Big Dimps's troubles.

That same day in Baltimore, Celeste and Fannie cheered at the Orioles victory. Once back at the Belvedere, Celeste sat with Fannie in the lobby while her friend enjoyed a restorative cocktail. Celeste drank sweet tea.

"Fannie, I have a compromise concerning buying a house."

"Hmm." Fannie swallowed. "What?"

"Rather than commit such a large amount of our resources, let's rent a place. We'll see how much we use it, the men use it. If we all spend a great deal of time here, we'll buy and we'll know the city better. If not, what have we lost? Not much, and it will somewhat temper our desire to decorate overmuch."

Knocking back her drink, Fannie caught a waiter's eye, handed him the glass, ordered another. "That's a good idea." Leaning forward, she remained silent as the waiter brought her another drink, then inquired, "Second thoughts about Ben?"

"No, Fannie, quite the reverse. But I don't think he will live in whatever we rent. He has his small, spare apartment. It's close to the stadium. And Carlotta wants me to buy a building, something commercial possibly near the railroad tracks downtown."

"In Runnymede? Whatever's gotten into her?"

"Ben." Celeste slyly smiled.

Fannie laughed uproariously. "That's good, Celeste. That's good, but what has happened? Really?"

"She's fallen in love with him and his drawings for stained-glass windows for Immaculata's chapel."

Fannie's eyes popped, she held her glass midair. "Good God."

"Precisely."

A silence followed this. "Will he work and live in the commercial building? When he can, naturally?"

"I think he will. He desperately wants to create these windows, and Fannie, his designs are so beautiful. This way it's not like he's eating out of my hand. He's proud. He doesn't want to live off a woman. This way he has a job."

"I see. You aren't going to buy the building all by yourself, are you? If Carlotta is so hot for this, she can come up with some of the money."

"Well, she can, but I'll do it. For one thing, I don't want to be in a partnership with my sister." Fannie nodded on that. "For another thing, she and Herbert will have considerable expense for the chapel and new windows. The insurance will pay, probably, for some fire damages, especially since the fire department declared this could be the result of a lightning strike and not arson. Well, the word *arson* isn't even spoken."

"Mmm." Fannie, wise, knew better to forget that might even be a possibility.

An investigation would slow the insurance payment. A potential trial would hurt future business and Fannie, thanks to Fairy's judicious hints and her own prudence, figured out that the profit from contraband had to be deliciously high. If Herbert had taken on an unusual business partner from a hated family, who was the wiser?

"You see?"

"Yes."

"Well, I have to find something with wonderful light, something where the glass can be shipped in, easily unloaded along with the lead and whatever else is needed. And I have to fix it so he can live there without feeling kept or coddled. Well, he isn't being kept. He will be working."

"True. And he will be out of sight when Ramelle is back."

"I don't care about that but I don't think it the best idea to have them both under the same roof. When Curtis is home it might not be so bad, but still."

Fannie peered at the inviting amber of her Old-Fashioned drink. "Who'd have thunk it?"

Laughing, Celeste lifted one hand, palm outward, flared her fingers outward, smiled. "Never. I never would have thunk it as you say but

Fannie, I am so glad, so very glad my life has taken this turn. I'm going to write Ramelle. It's best to prepare her, even though she won't be here for months. I decided against waiting until she's here. I'd hate to have her hear it as gossip. You know how difficult it is to keep things quiet. I don't think this will be all that upsetting for her. New. Yes, she will have to make her adjustments, but she's already adjusting to being a mother. And I will stay at the glazier place, that's how I think of it, at least once or twice a week when it's not baseball season."

"You will introduce them?"

"Of course. I expect she'll fall in love with him. If Carlotta falls in love, who can resist the man?" Celeste laughed lightly.

"That's a fact. Are you now glad, though, that Ramelle made the first move, falling in love with Curtis, having his baby?"

Celeste thought about this. "If she hadn't fallen in love with Curtis, I think we would have gone on as we always had. I can't say I was dissatisfied. Then again, she might have been a little dissatisfied, you know, feeling time was running out on motherhood."

"Yes." Fannie then, voice lower, repeated, "Yes."

"Fannie, it occurs to me that I know nothing about love. I've felt it but I don't know as I understand it." She put both hands on the cool tall glass. "But I know that you and Fairy love me. I know that through my friends God has loved me. I don't know how to thank you."

"It's your friends who get you through life. You and I and Fairy, I can't imagine life without you. It's funny, isn't it, how hard it is to tell someone you truly love them?"

"It is, and I truly love you."

Fannie beamed, leaned forward. "And I truly love you."

That night, with Ben asleep in bed after playing a long, hard game in hot sun and then making love with her, Celeste rose to sit at the well-stocked Belvedere desk.

Pulling out a sheet of paper, high rag content, expensive, a drawing of the Belvedere at the top, she began:

Dear Ramelle,

It's almost midnight on May 8th, a glorious day for all English-speaking people as Charles II takes the throne, 1660 ushering in many wonderful things, not the least Restoration drama. But as we learn of what is happening in Russia, it does bring back the original insanity, namely Puritanism and Cromwell, of those who believe they can remake the human race, always in their image.

I can't imagine life without *School for Scandal, The Way of the World, She Stoops to Conquer.* Then again, I can't imagine life without you.

Every day I know you fall ever more in love with Spotts and I assume Curtis, as well. How happy I will be to see all three of you once the baby can make the train journey here and I do understand you not wishing to expose her to a deep Maryland winter. And this year's winter took so long to release its grasp.

Now, however, it is May, the merry month of May. The red-buds have come and gone, dogwoods just at the end. But the iris are opening. Stately locust trees are blooming, the fragrance intense as it was for the wisteria which just yesterday finally all turned to green leaf.

I write to tell you so that you have time to sort things out, put all in place, that there is a person whom I have come to love, quite unexpectedly. Artistic, athletic, he is a minor league short-stop for our Orioles and a veteran of the war, army. I can no more imagine life without him than I can without you, although it would seem we are all in separate spheres. He is twenty-eight and, as you might suspect, handsome. Beautiful, actually.

No matter how we found each other. Enough to say he makes me think, makes me laugh. He has little by way of money in this world but is happy with what he does possess and doesn't want my money. It may seem strange for me to put that in writing, but one cannot have what a Chalfonte has and not be wary.

What will amuse you, I think, is that Carlotta is dazzled by him and wants him to create stained-glass windows for her chapel. I've written to you of the fire, how we all worked to save the chapel and I must say, Carlotta bore it wonderfully well. Perhaps the Blessed Virgin Mother does watch over her. In so many ways, she reminds me of Mother. She's forty-seven now and looks so much like Mother, who died when she was fifty-three. It's hard to believe how long both Mother and Father have been gone and it's still painful to think of Spotts being gone.

I know I wrote you about Louise's young man, also an army veteran. Getting to know Paul as well as Ben, my gentleman, I comprehend Spotts in new ways. I do not think, dearest, we will ever truly understand what that war has done to those who fought it, as well as to all of us. It was one of those great pivotal moments in history, as the French Revolution was. I often think we all see through the shadow of the guillotine. Such horror ushered in modern times.

I've been rereading my Lucretius and Seneca. Needed to clean my mind, brace myself up.

On a more gossiping note, Juts threatens to leave school. Cora isn't fighting her but hoping to keep her going until graduation two years hence. The really helpful person has been Ev Most, Juts's friend who brings lessons, does them with her, etc. I've seen these two girls grow up and much of the time under my own roof but I really didn't pay attention. I rather accepted everyone's station in life.

But, you know, both Louise and Juts are intelligent. Vastly different personalities but quite intelligent. I told you about Wheezie going to Philadelphia, which she loved. The girl has such a flair for fashion.

At any rate, thanks to your new situation and mine, I am rethinking many things. All to the good.

One thing I have realized since you left is how much Fannie Jump and Fairy love me. I never gave it a thought but they do love me and have watched out for me. And I know how much I love them. I fear I have taken a great deal for granted in life and I have been given many advantages.

Long day, much of it spent in the heat. Before I forget, the Hanover Electric Company is expanding. I will buy more shares, as I think electrification will continue. I hope the streetlamps on the square are never electrified and, of course, many homes use gas. It's a softer light and gas is more reliable but Stirling declares the ability to generate electric power will magnify as well as simplify over these next years. I don't see that it's any more convenient than gas but he differs with me on that. Nonetheless, I have bought more shares.

You know how I like to very quietly follow the market. I would imagine there are many opportunities out there and we know Curtis will find them.

May this find you well. I love you. I will always love you. This will all work out.

Love, Celeste

Chapter Thirty-Seven

. . . .

May 9, 1920
Sunday

Peony buds swelled to the size of golf balls. Another week and they would open, the colors creamy white, pink, deep pink, pulsating magenta.

Celeste and Fannie walked through Celeste's gardens.

"I do so love peonies." She shaded her eyes from the morning sun. "Ben will get here on the noon train. I thought we might take a ride. You're welcome to join us. He's such a natural athlete, but natural or not, equitation takes time."

"That it does. Thank you, but it's another Sunday dinner, perhaps not as formal as a coronation dinner but, ah, you know. And now, with this new Mother's Day business, we have to attend to that."

"The aunts and great-aunts and your most ancient mother-in-law." Celeste smiled. "Well, did you receive some token of everyone's esteem?"

"No. I expect that will come at dinner. I don't much like these made-up holidays. For God's sake, Christmas and Easter are bad enough. And then we have June fifteenth, which I do enjoy. Fourth of July isn't so bad either, if you can stand all the screaming fireworks, all of them in my backyard, I swear."

"Look at it this way. The made-up holidays are good for business."

"Whose business?" Fannie stopped to touch a small tea rose just opening.

Celeste inhaled the sweetness of a May morning. "Not ours."

"Did you send something to Ramelle?"

"I did not. That's Curtis's job. I did, however, write her a letter which I will post tomorrow, telling her that I love her, of course, but also telling her about Ben."

"You didn't."

"I did. As I told you at the Belvedere, I thought it best to prepare her."

"What about Ben?"

"He'll be fine," Celeste confidently predicted. "Did you find the setting, the one your mother gave you that you thought might suit Louise?"

"I did. I'll bring it by tomorrow. It will suit that diamond of your mother's. Personally, I like the cigar band, but I do understand Louise's upset about such gossip. Not that she's said a word. I mean, she likes the cigar band, what's left of it."

"The Rhodeses redefine petty, do they not?"

"Indeed. You know what would delight me? A cigar band made of enamel. Now wouldn't that just be unique? I suppose one might have encrusted diamonds on it, but so colorful. I'm tiring of major stones."

"No, you aren't." Celeste laughed at her.

"Yes, I am. The bigger the stones, the older the woman. One doesn't wear major stones as a girl or even a young woman. Major pearls, perhaps, but what is the expression, a diamond big as the Ritz—one has a few years there."

"I suppose by then, a lady has worked to acquire them."

Fannie Jump laughed. "God knows that's the truth."

"Neither of us thinks much of this Mother's Day thing, but do you think it disturbs Fairy?"

"No. What disturbs Fairy is all this drivel she's reading. Whatever has possessed her to delve into economics? The truth is, some people know how to make money and most don't. There's no science to it."

"I really don't know. I like it. I mean, I like following the money, reading about banks and stocks, but reading some sort of theory, you know, Adam Smith, leads nowhere."

"Perhaps if one is an academic it leads somewhere. Do you remember when we were at Smith and Professor Fearneyhough made us trace the metaphors for mirrors in *Richard the Second*? How he kept pestering us with Shakespeare, using mirrors to show us how the king was deteriorating, falling away from reality into fantasy?"

"I do remember. I don't think Richard needed mirrors. His lovers were doing him in."

"Greed."

"It will ever be with us." Celeste paused before her English boxwoods, tight and trimmed.

"We aren't greedy."

"Fannie, there are many types of greed. Money. Power. Dissipation. Strange thrills. I can't say as I think about it but I do think about the war, greed, horror, death . . . But I think it started with greed for power."

They walked, the grass cushiony underfoot.

Finally, Fannie said, "I do too. The Wilcox boy without his arm. The ones who came home blind, and not just from this last war. What about old Reggie Anson, blinded at Sharpsburg as a fourteen-year-old? Still with us. He found something useful to do weaving cane chairs. But I think about it."

"It looks as though we will lose the vote but I wonder, if we do get it, if women can vote, will we end war? Carlotta and I talked about it."

"Celeste, this last war really must be the war to end all wars. How can anyone, any nation even think of war after Verdun? Perhaps men have learned at last."

"I don't know. I keep coming back to Ramelle's wedding, standing on the steps, everyone so flushed and happy and thinking 'Et in Arcadia ego.'"

"Darling, you'd just lost your lover. I would have thought worse than that."

"Oh, Fannie." Celeste slipped her arm through Fannie's as they continued to walk.

Blocks away, Mother's Day deeply affected the three Rhodes women. Lottie and Dimps Jr. had bought their mother a bright turquoise necklace and bracelet. They'd saved for months to afford it.

Slipping it on, she said, "Thank you."

However, her mood was dark.

"We could walk around the square," Lottie offered.

"No." Big Dimps gripped the arms of the chair. "There has to be a way to bring Bill to bear."

Dimps Jr. started to cry.

"Shove it, Dimps," Lottie commanded. "Don't be a ninny."

Sniffling, the younger sister wailed, "He says, how does he know the baby is his?"

"We will have to go to his parents."

"Oh, Mother, don't. He'll never speak to me again."

"He isn't speaking to you now," her mother corrected her.

"But I love him."

"Shut up." Lottie's upper lip curled.

"I do. I love him. I only want to be with him."

Big Dimps rose, paced the room. "You aren't going to be with him. He's dumped you. That's that. I've got to bring his parents around."

"Mother," Lottie spoke with clear logic, "they aren't going to budge. They aren't stupid. They know he's gotten Dimps pregnant. But they believe he has a great football career in front of him." She pointed to her sister. "You will only drag him down."

Big Dimps lit a cigarette. "We can go to Pastor Wade. He can talk to the Whittiers."

Lottie said, "Mother, the Whittiers are Presbyterians. They aren't going to listen to Pastor Wade. We have to find another way."

"Aren't there doctors who can, you know . . . ?" Dimps Jr. whispered.

Her mother stubbed out the cigarette after one puff. "Oh, they can kill the baby but they can kill you, too. You're going to have this baby."

Dimps Jr. cried all the harder.

"Mother"—Lottie ignored her sister's hysterics—"we have two choices. We can send her away."

Big Dimps shouted, "With what money? Your father doesn't have a pot to piss in and if he finds out, it will be far worse than it is. He's an idiot."

Lottie let that pass, then began anew. "Or we can find someone for her to marry."

"Never!" Dimps Jr. wailed.

"Shut up. You're an even bigger idiot than your father."

"You married him," Dimps Jr. snarled and Big Dimps smacked her so hard the outline of her hand remained on her daughter's cheek.

Big Dimps sat on the arm of Lottie's chair. "Who do you have in mind?"

"Edgar Wilcox."

"He doesn't have an arm!" Dimps Jr. squealed. "And I love Bill."

Lottie glanced up at her mother. "Mom, the Wilcoxes aren't rich but they're well off. Edgar is okay. He works at the bakery and someday he will take it over."

Big Dimps considered this. "A good living. I heard the war affected his mind. He's withdrawn, rarely smiles."

"He seems all right. He'll recover. He's quiet but I see him at the Capitol. Dimps, does Betty ever talk about her brother?"

The little sister shrugged. "Not much. She likes him."

"Mmm. Stand up," Big Dimps ordered her daughter. "Lift up your dress."

"Mother!"

"Do as I tell you."

Both mother and sister walked around Dimps Jr.

At last Big Dimps pronounced judgment. "We have some time before she shows. Not a lot but perhaps just enough. Dimps, you find a way to get Edgar into bed."

"No!" Dimps Jr. screamed.

"Listen, you little slut." Her mother grabbed her lower jaw. "You haven't much time. If you don't marry, you never will. No man in this town will have you. Do you understand?"

Dimps Jr. nodded that she did, then whispered, "I can't be the only girl in Runnymede who's ever been in this condition."

"You are not, but they were sent away to an aunt or someone in another state, had the baby, came home, and have lied about it ever since. The others married the men. You have to marry. I am not supporting you for the rest of your life. I am not listening to your father whine about money."

"I'll get a job."

"With whom? No one is going to hire an unwed mother. What world are you living in? And why didn't you come to me or your sister? We could have told you how not to get pregnant."

"I was afraid."

"I would have slapped you silly, but I would have told you what to do. Well"—she threw up her hands—"it's too late now." Big Dimps looked at Lottie. "How do we proceed?"

"We start with Dimps buying fresh bread." Lottie stood in front of her sister. "You make eyes at him. Talk. Then a week passes and you have an extra ticket to the Capitol. You ask him will he escort you. It's a start." Then Lottie looked at her mother. "Let's hope it works."

"There's one other thing. You give him whatever he wants. When he marries you, no matter what, you never, ever tell him the truth. You remember that because of him, you have a position. And when you're married you still give him whatever he wants. Dote on him. Keep him happy. Learn from my mistake."

"But Momma, I love Bill," she cried anew.

"He doesn't love you. Put him out of your mind."

A flash of reality hit Dimps Jr. "You're asking me to live a lie."

"Daughter, millions of women do."

Chapter Thirty-Eight

. . . .

June 15, 1920
Tuesday

The boom of the big drums, the rattle of the snares filled the square as the servicemen approached, preceded by the high school marching bands.

The Union men came down Hanover Street. Once they reached the square, they would turn right, make the corner, then when they reached City Hall on the corner of the Emmitsburg Pike, they would turn left into the square, going through the center until reaching the bandshell.

The Confederate men arrived from the opposite direction, filing down Frederick Road, where they would turn right at the square, make the corner, then turn left at Baltimore Street, thence onto the square and to the bandshell.

Unless you were at death's door, you were among the crowd that lined the streets. No one walked onto the square until the veterans were seated. Those few men currently in service stood on the roads and saluted the veterans of 1861–65, followed by the veterans of the

Spanish-American War, who in turn were followed by the young veterans of the Great War. Every man marched in uniform. Granted, some had to alter garments or purchase new ones due to the ravages of time and too much food. But a surprising amount of men could still fit into their uniforms, a testimony to their physical labors.

Many southern men, now in their seventies, had enlisted as children. About twenty men in their eighties marched and two in their nineties. One of the younger fellows, missing a leg courtesy of the skirmish at Hanover the day before Gettysburg, was in a wicker wheelchair.

The young veterans bore witness to their war. Edgar Wilcox was missing an arm. Sidney Yost's brother, Harold, an army man, was blind and being led by Sidney, a navy man. Paul Trumbull and Ben Battle marched together. Paul winked when he passed Louise. Couldn't help it.

The oldest men took or were helped to their seats, then came the other veterans and the crowd respectfully followed them. The high school band continued to play as down the roads came the fire departments, then the police departments. The day gleamed and so did the fire trucks, the horses. The one big engine for North Runnymede had their old fire horses led behind as they were such a big part of the parade. All the horses were braided, ribbons streaming from mane and tails; large, calm beasts who happily accepted the treats of those children who ran out to slip them a bit of apple or sugar cube. Good as the new fire truck was, the horses thrilled everyone, especially those who remembered their service. South Runnymede still used horses, all big grays.

Once settled, each mayor gave a thankfully short speech. Lionel Tangerman was given a heavy pocket watch and a chain and applauded for years of service as North Runnymede police chief. He would be heading a commission to study vandalism, so he wasn't completely retired. Then all were invited to observe King John, this year portrayed by Walter Rendell, sign the Magna Carta. This he did surrounded by men dressed as barons from the thirteenth century.

Once all that passed, everyone could finally talk and listen to the bands playing together, no mean achievement as they had practiced only for the last two months.

Juts, Ev Most, Dick Yost, Betty Wilcox, Richard Barshinger, Elizabeth Chalmers, Louise Negroponti, even Dimps Jr.'s gang—now headed by Maude Ischatta—visited each veteran, handing them a rosette which they'd made, designed by Juts. She used Celeste's ribbons that she'd won at horse shows as her model and duplicated the rosettes, only smaller, in red, white, and blue. As the colors of both North and South were red, white, and blue, this turned out fine.

When Juts pinned a rosette on old Reggie Anson, the blind man lifted up his fingers to feel her face. "She's pretty, I can tell," he jovially remarked.

The other men loudly agreed.

Spontaneously, Juts kissed Reggie on the cheek.

Dimps Jr. rushed to Edgar once people could intermingle, bringing him a cold drink. Her attentions did not go unnoticed.

Returning to the rosette basket with Betty Wilcox, Juts remarked, "She's all over your brother."

"Has been."

Juts grimaced.

Betty, hand again filled with rosettes, shrugged. "He's coming out of his shell. I keep my mouth shut."

"Guess you have to," Juts replied. "But I don't trust her."

"I don't either but there's nothing I can do about it. She makes him happy." Matching Juts stride for stride as they returned to the veterans, Betty added, "This was a good idea, Juts. You're coming back to school next year, aren't you?"

"Yeah," Juts responded without enthusiasm. "And I will kill Dimps Jr. I just know it. So I'll spend my life in jail."

Betty predicted, "I don't think she's coming back."

Before this train of thought could be continued, they were among the men again.

Increase Martin, South Runnymede's fire chief, moved among the men, slapping their backs. He carried a stone jug, which he gave to the old vets for a pull. He was followed by Lawrence Villcher, North Runnymede vice fire chief, who bent down to each older man, whispering something in his ear. A huge smile and a nodding head followed whatever he said.

Ben, who made sergeant by the end of the war, talked with the other fellows. They all moved through the older men.

Herbert Van Dusen, next to Julius Caesar Rife, led some veterans back to the two fire engines, the one having the motor turned off; at the other, horses were being unhitched from the big hand-pumped water tank.

Lawrence spoke to Henry Minton, himself not a veteran but his younger brother was. Lawrence slipped him some money.

Henry began to lead the horses back to the South Runnymede stables, his brother in uniform helping. "Better do this before everyone's roaring drunk, including you and me," Henry said with a laugh.

Increase also moved his horses back to the stables. Veterans crowded around the fire engine and the South Runnymede water tank, in gorgeous red and gold, high up on the wheels. The ladies did not frequent this area.

"Time for another barrel," J.C. observed in disbelief.

Herbert laughed. "Son, you were too young at Magna Carta pasts to keep track of our men's capacity."

The fire companies always kept booze, but it was discreet, as many a lady believed as Carrie Nation did. Now, with Prohibition, it was even more covert. The barrels, one for each department, rested on their sides, a spigot driven into same. The barrels were covered with resplendent blankets in fire department colors. On display were two large lemonade barrels. The men lined up at that barrel while being handed a glass from the scotch barrel. A few men proved two-fisted.

Eventually, all the men made their way in, veterans or not, one of the highlights of Magna Carta Day. King John had recourse to alcohol to overcome his humiliation at the hands of the barons, themselves in need of reinforcement.

Celeste, Fannie Jump, Fairy, and Cora sat under a walnut tree, cooler in the shade. Carlotta, like someone running for office, walked among the crowd chatting, shaking hands, diverting attention from the fire departments. No point in some well-meaning lady blowing the whistle. Most knew perfectly well what was afoot but a few needed serious distraction.

"Ah, Minta Mae, what a beautiful dress, and set off, as always, by your hat." Carlotta meant it. "Well, here we are again and seemingly no closer to the vote."

"I don't know, Carlotta, I just don't know. I was glad though that Otto and John"—she named the two mayors—"kept the speeches short and that no one from the audience was compelled to complain."

"Quite." Carlotta nodded.

As they caught up with one another, Lottie Rhodes just had to bait Yashew by brushing up against him as though pressed by the crowd.

His shoulders stiffened as he stood with Ben and Paul.

"Oh, I didn't know it was you," Lottie cooed venomously.

"Bag it, Lottie," Yashew growled.

Paul, putting his hand under Yashew's elbow, tried to move him away.

"Well, you two stick together. And to think I was blind enough to actually go out with both of you."

"Lottie, I know you called Archie Cadwalder." Yashew pressed his lips together. "If you weren't a woman, I'd bust you right in the mouth."

Paul pulled him toward the fire department gathering. "Come on. She's not worth it."

Lottie glared after them, then turned to Ben, pleased as she was by his good looks. "I recognize that you men who were over there kind of stick together, but I don't recommend the company."

He half bowed. "Which is why I'm leaving."

Her mouth dropped open as he turned on his heel and left her.

A refreshing light breeze picked up from the west. Dancing began and the young women from both high schools, as they had worked on the rosettes, asked veterans to dance. Those men who were able had the attentions of a pretty young student for that dance. For some of the men, widowers, this enlivened them, made them feel young again. For those damaged by combat, the attentions and conversation with a comely girl delighted them. Yes, their wives, sisters, and even daughters tended to them but no man, no matter what he has endured, wants to feel like a burden. It wasn't as though Juts, Ev, and the others discussed this, but somehow they knew and the men laughed louder, sat up straighter, and a few reached out to hold the girl's hand. No matter what, life could still be sweet.

Ben, a lemonade in each hand, walked up to Celeste and her friends. He handed a lemonade to Celeste, another to Cora. "Ladies, I will be right back."

"Ben, honey, will you bring me what is really at the fire engine?" Fannie asked.

He inclined his head. "My pleasure."

He returned with a big, stiff scotch for Fannie and a lemonade for Fairy, then he sat on the grass with the ladies on their blanket.

Paul was dancing with Louise, diamond on her finger. It had taken four women to talk Paul into the loan, they had to keep emphasizing loan, of the diamond reset in size 7 for Louise. Now it caught the sunlight, starting a new round of gossip, all of it praising Paul.

"Love," Fairy simply remarked as she watched them.

"On that note"—Ben stood, offering his hand to Celeste—"may I have this dance with the woman I love?"

Paralyzed, Celeste looked up at him. He took her hand, gently pulling her to her feet. Flushed, she placed her hand on his forearm as he led her to the dance floor.

Fannie Jump watched. "I have never seen Celeste speechless."

Ever sensitive, Fairy said, "Perhaps it is the first time she can honor love openly."

"Good God, I never thought of that," Fairy gasped.

"Why would you? I hadn't until now." Fannie smiled, watching the two begin to dance, and dance well.

"She was always protecting us," Cora said.

"From what? She's our oldest friend and it's not as though we didn't know," Fannie blurted.

"She didn't want people to think poorly of you." Cora folded her hands together. "You know how it is, birds of a feather. If you don't say anything, it doesn't exist. Ignorance is bliss."

"If ignorance is bliss, why aren't more people happy?" Fannie sharply remarked.

"Cora, why did you never say anything?" Fairy ignored Fannie.

"What was there to say? I love her. You love her. All we want is for her to be happy and all she ever wanted was for us to be happy. She saved me when Hansford walked out but she never acted as though anything was different. I would have starved without Celeste. She sent Wheezie to Immaculata as though that was the most natural thing to do. And when Ramelle took up with Curtis, what did we do?"

"Nothing," Fannie replied. "There was nothing we could do except stand near."

"Which you did. Which we all did." Fairy finished her lemonade. "It's fair to say that none of us suffers from emotional hemophilia."

Fannie laughed, then translated for Cora. "Means bleeding."

"Ah." Cora smiled, watching Celeste and Ben.

Glass held in both hands, Fannie ruminated. "All those years of cotillion, college, seeing Europe, knowing what to say and when to say it, manners."

"Protocol." Fairy smiled. "We know exactly what to do and say and when to say and do it. For which our parents spent a great deal of money."

"And I still don't know what life means." Fannie laughed, a rumbling laugh.

"No one does." Cora joined the laughter.

Just then Patience Horney, being walked by two ladies from the Lutheran Dorcas Circle, stopped a moment. "Beautiful day. Comes from the creatures in the Crab Nebula. Good weather always comes with them." Then she moved on, a backward glance and smile from one of her walkers.

"Maybe we don't know any more than Patience," Fairy mused. "And maybe it doesn't matter, although I keep trying, reading, thinking. But maybe it doesn't matter."

Celeste and Ben returned, laughing. He held her hand as she settled back down.

"Mrs. Thatcher, may I have the honor?"

"You may indeed." Fairy brightened, reaching up for Ben's hand.

As they walked to the dance floor, Celeste, breathing a bit hard, said, "He's a divine dancer."

"Celeste, he's just altogether divine," Fannie roared.

Cora laughed too. "Well, if you're going to look at a man for a long time, better he be handsome."

They talked, drank more as Paul delivered libations and Louise sat down with her mother. Ben danced with every lady, including Cora, and Paul also asked each woman.

The music stopped, the breeze grew a bit stronger. John Gassner held up a bullhorn, which Mayor Otto Tangerman playfully grabbed from him.

The assembled, including the veterans and men at the fire engines, watched, a ripple of laughter spreading through the people. John, his arm around Otto's shoulders, tried to speak into the bullhorn together with Otto.

A garbled "Cakewalk" did come out.

"Quarters." Paul reached into his uniform pocket.

Ben stood up, brushing himself off. "Quarters, ladies. Someone will be a winner."

"How many cakes have we?" Fannie Jump perused the program.

"Twelve," Fairy said. "Oh, Cora, you have number seven."

Cora waved her hand. "Caesura said I had to do one for the Daughters."

"Indeed, and it all goes to the vets who need it." Louise stood up, taking Paul's hand. "Let's go."

At the dance floor, Paul handed quarters to Juts and her friends. One does the cakewalk with a partner, so the kids scrambled.

Louise whispered something to Juts, who passed it on. The girls ran off the dance floor, each grabbing a veteran.

Their high school boyfriends watched.

Blind, Harold Yost was being led by Louise, teased as he passed the kids. He could hear the boys, so he baited them, "You're going to have to fight for these girls!"

Each cake brought a new group of partners. By cake six, everyone was crowding the floor. The high school boys asked their girlfriends. Now the older ladies took veteran partners.

Celeste walked with Yashew, their number, 11, was pinned on Yashew's back. This walk seemed to go on forever.

The music stopped as they reached the conductor's podium, his back to them.

"Number eleven!" Otto yelled.

Celeste clapped her hands, then kissed Yashew on the cheek. "You take it. Your mother will enjoy it."

Mrs. Gregorivitch, sitting in a folding chair, wore dark glasses, as she was recovering from her operation.

By cake eight, the walk was jammed. Ben escorted Celeste; Paul had Louise; Fannie actually walked with her husband, who had been talking business throughout the whole day with other men. Archibald Thatcher walked his wife. Everyone was paired up. Dimps Jr. walked with Edgar Wilcox. Dimps Sr. had snagged Sidney Yost, who didn't seem to mind. Even Mr. and Mrs. Grumbacher walked. Lottie walked with King John, a bit unsteady on his feet. Dick Yost squired Juts.

As this walk was overfull, it moved slowly. Some couples crossed arms in front of them, others held hands, others just walked, but who was going to win this wonderful cake: a double devil's food?

The music played. Played some more.

Arms crossed with Celeste, Ben looked over and slightly down at her. "Have I told you you are the most exciting, independent, beautiful woman I have ever known?"

"You have now." She threw back her head, exposing her long graceful neck, and laughed.

On and on they walked and then the music finally stopped.

"Number eighty-one," Otto boomed into the bullhorn.

"That's me!" Dimps Jr. squealed as Edgar grinned.

Thrilled with her cake, Dimps Jr. walked through the crowd, stopped in front of Juts.

"Don't you wish you'd won?" she sneered.

"No, because then I'd have to be you," Juts fired back, "and I'd have to rouge my nipples."

Dimps Jr. smashed the cake right into Juts's face. Juts, eyes visible through the chocolate, hauled off and slugged her with all her might.

Edgar tried to pull Dimps Jr. off.

Neither girl gave up.

The situation allowed old scores to be settled. Yashew socked Walter, who had tried to throttle Paul back during the movie popcorn fight. Ben hurriedly removed Celeste from the battle, then hopped back on the dance floor to flail away with his comrades.

Reggie yelled out at old Donald Simpson, "You always were a son of a bitch."

"If you weren't blind, I'd let you have it, asshole," came the ready reply.

The two old men went at it, Reggie not at a disadvantage by being blind, or so it appeared.

Harold, younger and blind, made his way over to help Reggie; two against one seemed fair odds, considering.

Lawrence Villcher, who had been sampling the contents of another cask, hooked up the fire hose to it.

"Give 'em hell!" he hollered and opened the hose.

Seeing this method to calm the riot, Increase Martin also hooked up his fire hose to his cask—he just opened the top, dumped in the hose, and told the boys to pump.

Scotch poured over everyone. Some of the men fell down flat on their backs, mouths wide open. The women, hands on hats, dresses beginning to cling, hollered, fleeing the dance floor.

Harold, grinning from ear to ear, gulping down the healing waters, as he thought of it, bellowed, "Heaven!"

Celeste, Fannie, Fairy, flounced their clothing, which was wet and smelled of good scotch.

Louise was trying to clean off Juts. "Look at them. They have no more sense than a goose."

"I'll kill her!"

"Juts, stay put," Cora commanded as she helped Louise.

Fannie surveyed the scene. "To think, girls, that fifty-five years ago some of those men were trying to kill one another."

Fairy shook with laughter. "I think a few still are, dear."

"I'll kill her!" Juts persisted.

"Unless I kill you first. Sit still!" Louise commanded.

The fire engines clanged, a lone snare drummer hit a roll.

Slightly bloodied, arms around one another, Ben, Paul, and Yashew extricated themselves from the melee. Soaked, they squished toward the ladies. It appeared some of the sprayed scotch had run down their gullets as well as their uniforms.

Staring at the three young men, Fannie Jump exclaimed, "To think they've faced death. Look at them now."

The ladies did just that.

Celeste remembered Ramelle's wedding, when she stood on the landing looking at the people below and thought, "*Et in Arcadia ego.*"

Laughing, she clapped her hands once and said, "*Vita in Arcadia est!*"

True, Death is everywhere but so is Life!

Dear Reader,

Tendrils of gold flare out from behind the Blue Ridge Mountains. The sun has just set. The cumulus clouds will shortly turn to molten copper, scarlet, then deep pink, finally lavender—perfect timing for I have now finished *Cakewalk*.

It took a trip to Runnymede, my heart's home, to Celeste Chalfonte to show me the price one pays for institutionalized oppression, the subtle price; the political price is obvious. Once the bill is no longer due you can see easily.

Sex is interesting. Sexuality is not. Or as Celeste says to Fannie, "Only a fool refuses love."

May you always be open to love. I add to this the love that comes to your door on four feet.

As to sex, I leave that to you. Should you find it perhaps love will attend it.

The sky is blood red now. Even if one is burdened with sorrow, heavy responsibilities, it is impossible not to be uplifted by such majesty.

Maybe love is an interior sunset?

Onward,
Rita Mae Brown

Cakewalk

a novel

Rita Mae Brown

A READER'S GUIDE

Cakewalk Discussion Questions

1. What are the main themes of the novel? Which do you find most thought-provoking?

2. The introduction says, "It's never a good idea to get into an argument with a Marylander." Did this statement affect your interpretation of the novel? If so, how? How does it play out in the rest of the story?

3. The town of Runnymede is practically a character in the novel. What does it mean to Wheezie and Juts? Celeste and Curtis? How would the story be different if it were set somewhere else? How does Runnymede's position straddling the Mason-Dixon line amplify the novel's themes?

4. Discuss the significance of the title as it pertains to each character.

5. In chapter 6, Celeste reflects, "Some things are right under your nose. You don't see them and when someone does, you wonder how you missed it." How does this prove true for Celeste by the end of the novel? For Ramelle?

6. How would you describe the relationship between the Hunsenmeir sisters? How does their wisecracking reveal their affection for each other?

7. Discuss Celeste's evolution throughout the story. What lessons does she learn about love? About life?

8. At the end of chapter 13, Celeste says to her sister, "You know I love you. . . . It's just sometimes I can't stand you." What do you think she means by that? What other characters in Runnymede have this kind of relationship?

9. Who would you cast to play each character in a movie adaptation of *Cakewalk*? Why?

10. What elements of *Cakewalk* are specific to the 1920s time period? What elements are timeless?

11. Paul and Louise share a second kiss at the end of chapter 15. How does their relationship change after that? How does it stay the same? How is this kiss different from their first?

12. Some of the characters in *Cakewalk* are based on Rita Mae Brown's own family. Which characters, if any, remind you of your family or friends? What other books have themes of family centricity and small-town life intertwining?

About the Author

RITA MAE BROWN is the bestselling author of the Sneaky Pie Brown series; the Sister Jane series; the Runnymede novels, including *Six of One* and *Cakewalk*; *A Nose for Justice* and *Murder Unleashed*; *Rubyfruit Jungle*; and *In Her Day,* as well as many other books. An Emmy-nominated screenwriter and a poet, Brown lives in Afton, Virginia.

ritamaebrownbooks.com

To inquire about booking Rita Mae Brown for a speaking engagement, please contact the Penguin Random House Speakers Bureau at speakers@penguinrandomhouse.com.

About the Type

This book was set in Minion, a 1990 Adobe Originals typeface by Robert Slimbach (b. 1956). Minion is inspired by classical, old-style typefaces of the late Renaissance, a period of elegant, beautiful, and highly readable type designs. Created primarily for text setting, Minion combines the aesthetic and functional qualities that make text type highly readable with the versatility of digital technology.